There ... ... lo
with ... ... n-
haire ... ... e
said ... ... ir
future together.

"Kiss me," he said.

It appeared to be a prophecy that had immediate results. Eden drew closer, took his face between her hands, and pressed her lips against his with a kiss that would have swelled his immortal soul if he'd actually been in possession of one.

Praise for the paranormal romances of

MICHELLE ROWEN

"Let us welcome this fresh voice to the genre."　　—*Booklist*

"I've been bitten and smitten by Michelle Rowen."
　　—Sherrilyn Kenyon, #1 *New York Times* bestselling author

"What a charming, hilarious book! Frankly, I'm insanely jealous I didn't write it."
　　—MaryJanice Davidson, *New York Times* bestselling author

"I have never read a Michelle Rowen book that I did not adore."　　　　　　　　　　—*Enchanted by Books*

"Michelle Rowen's books never fail to thrill."
　　　　　　　　　　　　　　　　—*Bitten by Books*

"Should leave readers breathless."　　　—*Kirkus Reviews*

"I stop everything to read a Michelle Rowen book!"
　　—Larissa Ione, *New York Times* bestselling author

Berkley Sensation Titles by Michelle Rowen

THE DEMON IN ME
SOMETHING WICKED
THAT OLD BLACK MAGIC

NIGHTSHADE
BLOODLUST

Anthologies

PRIMAL
(with Lora Leigh, Jory Strong, and Ava Gray)

THAT OLD BLACK MAGIC

≫ Michelle Rowen ≪

BERKLEY SENSATION, NEW YORK

THE BERKLEY PUBLISHING GROUP
Published by the Penguin Group
Penguin Group (USA) Inc.
375 Hudson Street, New York, New York 10014, USA
Penguin Group (Canada), 90 Eglinton Avenue East, Suite 700, Toronto, Ontario M4P 2Y3, Canada
(a division of Pearson Penguin Canada Inc.)
Penguin Books Ltd., 80 Strand, London WC2R 0RL, England
Penguin Group Ireland, 25 St. Stephen's Green, Dublin 2, Ireland (a division of Penguin Books Ltd.)
Penguin Group (Australia), 250 Camberwell Road, Camberwell, Victoria 3124, Australia
(a division of Pearson Australia Group Pty. Ltd.)
Penguin Books India Pvt. Ltd., 11 Community Centre, Panchsheel Park, New Delhi—110 017, India
Penguin Group (NZ), 67 Apollo Drive, Rosedale, Auckland 0632, New Zealand
(a division of Pearson New Zealand Ltd.)
Penguin Books (South Africa) (Pty.) Ltd., 24 Sturdee Avenue, Rosebank, Johannesburg 2196,
South Africa

Penguin Books Ltd., Registered Offices: 80 Strand, London WC2R 0RL, England

This is a work of fiction. Names, characters, places, and incidents either are the product of the author's imagination or are used fictitiously, and any resemblance to actual persons, living or dead, business establishments, events, or locales is entirely coincidental. The publisher does not have any control over and does not assume any responsibility for author or third-party websites or their content.

THAT OLD BLACK MAGIC

A Berkley Sensation Book / published by arrangement with the author

PRINTING HISTORY
Berkley Sensation mass-market edition / December 2011

Copyright © 2011 by Michelle Rouillard.
Excerpt from *Blood Bath & Beyond* by Michelle Rowen copyright © by Michelle Rouillard.
Cover art by Craig White.
Cover design by Lesley Worrell.
Interior text design by Laura K. Corless.

ISBN: 978-0-425-24493-7

BERKLEY SENSATION®
Berkley Sensation Books are published by The Berkley Publishing Group,
a division of Penguin Group (USA) Inc.,
375 Hudson Street, New York, New York 10014.
BERKLEY SENSATION® is a registered trademark of Penguin Group (USA) Inc.
The "B" design is a trademark of Penguin Group (USA) Inc.

PRINTED IN THE UNITED STATES OF AMERICA

10 9 8 7 6 5 4 3 2 1

ONE

"Ready to hear your ultimate fate?"

Eden glanced warily at the shirtless demon sitting at the tiny dinette table in her tiny apartment with the daily newspaper's Horoscope section in front of him. Seemed harmless enough, and yet a chill ran down her spine. Something about Darrak's statement felt like an omen. A bad one.

Maybe she was just being paranoid. Nothing new there.

She pushed back against the unpleasant vibe. "Sure."

Darrak absently raked his messy dark hair back from his forehead. "You're a Gemini, right?"

"Present and accounted for."

"Be prepared for a blast from the past as an old acquaintance, one whose destiny is irreversibly intertwined with yours, wants to reconnect. Also, buy more crunchy peanut butter as soon as possible."

She nodded. "Let me take a wild guess here . . . you added the last bit yourself."

"Doesn't make it any less true. We're out. And I love it."

"I'll put it on my grocery list."

"Life is good." He studied her for a moment longer before his grin began to fade at the edges. "What's wrong?"

"Wrong?" Eden crossed her arms. "Nothing's wrong. Nothing at all. Everything's wonderful. Fabulous, in fact."

"Overcompensating in your reply only leads me to believe that something's seriously wrong." When he stood the Horoscope page fluttered to the carpeted floor at his feet. His brows drew together. "What is it?"

It was surprising how quickly Darrak could switch from amusement over a horoscope and a craving for crunchy peanut butter to deep concern for her well-being.

He wanted to know what was bothering her. That was a very dangerous question these days.

Ever since Eden woke this morning, she'd felt the unrequested tingle of magic moving down her arms and sparking off her fingertips. She didn't allow herself to tap into her recently acquired powers despite it being a constant itch for her. Magic—at least *her* magic—came with nasty consequences.

She could control it, she kept telling herself. She *could*.

Sometimes she even believed it.

"You need to get dressed," she said instead of answering his question. Her gaze moved over his very bare and very distracting chest. "We have to leave for the office in five minutes."

Black jersey material immediately flowed over Darrak's skin. Since he'd come into Eden's life a month ago, she'd wanted to take him shopping at a mall, but other than a leather coat he occasionally wore—short sleeves in Toronto in chilly mid-November might be a tip-off that he wasn't exactly human—he magically conjured his own clothing, which seemed to solely consist of black jeans and black T-shirts.

She slid her hands into the pockets of her navy blue pants and turned away from him.

Darrak caught her arm. "It's your magic, isn't it?"

The peanut-butter-loving demon could be very insightful. "My magic?"

"I can feel it, you know. Right now. It's coming off you in waves."

"I'm fine. Don't worry about it."

She grabbed her purse, which was hanging off the back of one of the dinette chairs, to fish in it for her new Black-Berry. Andy McCoy, her partner at the investigation agency they co-owned, insisted they become more technically savvy now that their caseload had increased, so he'd bought them both brand-new phones. Triple-A Investigations had been on the brink of bankruptcy only a month ago, but now they were busy with new cases.

The sudden surge in business was directly related to Darrak coming into Eden's life. While working as an occasional psychic consultant for the police, she'd been possessed by the cursed demon after the death of his previous host, a serial killer gunned down right in front of her.

Darrak was able to take solid human form during daylight hours, but when the sun set, he became incorporeal and had to possess her body. She'd recently had the chance to end the possession once and for all, but that would have destroyed him completely. Her privacy was a great motivator to find a solution to their problem, but not at such a high price.

After all . . . she'd come to care a great deal for the demon since they'd first met.

Unfortunately, all roads in their search for mutually beneficial separation had led to dead ends. Some deader than others.

She finally tore her gaze away from the screen of her phone to look at him and cringed when she noticed the searching look in his ice blue eyes. "I said nothing's wrong. Please, Darrak, don't worry."

"Your phone is on fire."

He was right. A spark from her magic had ignited her BlackBerry. She shrieked and threw it before it burned her. It skittered across the breakfast bar and landed with a *sizzle* in the kitchen sink. "Well, damn."

Before she had a chance to move Darrak was right in

front of her. He pulled out the chain she wore around her neck so her amulet lay flat against her freshly ironed white shirt.

"It's even darker than it was yesterday."

She clamped her hand over the visible state of her soul. The more she used her magic, the more damage it did. A black witch, even an extremely reluctant one like her, started with a pure white soul, but it grew darker and darker every time she accessed her very accessible black magic. Eden's amulet was still pale gray, but it had darker veins branching through it, making it look like a piece of marble.

She shook her head. "I haven't done anything."

"Then what are these?" He pushed her hand away and slid his index finger over the veins.

She grimaced. "A glitch."

"A glitch," Darrak repeated skeptically. "Not sure it works like that."

"Then I don't know what to tell you."

"Eden—" All amusement was gone from his voice now. "I'm worried about you."

A demon from Hell was worried about her immortal soul. It sounded like a joke. But Darrak wasn't any normal demon. And she wasn't any normal black witch.

Once upon a time, Darrak had been just as bad as any demon who'd ever existed—as immortal as he was immoral, sadistic, powerful, selfish, manipulative, and deadly. He'd even conspired with a demonic pal to overthrow Lucifer himself in an attempt to take his power as Prince of Hell. However, they'd failed. Rather spectacularly, in fact.

Darrak had been summoned into the human world over three hundred years ago and a curse put on him that destroyed his original body and his ability to manifest a new one. He'd been forced to possess humans ever since. A side effect of this was that he'd absorbed humanity slowly but surely, and it infused his being. The demon had developed a conscience. Morals. A sense of right and wrong.

But that wasn't the whole story.

To add to Eden's growing paranormal resume, she'd recently been shocked to learn in addition to being a black witch she was also a nephilim.

A human mother plus an angel father equaled one very confused twenty-nine-year-old woman—black witch plus half-angel in the same body. It wasn't exactly a combination that was working out perfectly, kind of like oil and water.

And the bonus prize—she was possessed by a demon.

It had been an interesting year to say the least.

Her angel side infused her with celestial energy, something she'd never even sensed before apart from a smidgeon of unreliable psychic insight. But it was what Darrak had absorbed over the last month due to their situation. And he'd absorbed a lot of it.

Bottom line, a human conscience was the least of Darrak's troubles. A demon who'd been neck-deep in celestial energy as he had been in the last month . . .

Well, it was changing him on a core level. Only he didn't exactly know it yet.

Eden knew it would shake his already shaky confidence, not to mention his entire identity, to find out he was becoming a little more . . . *angelic*. Whether he liked it or not.

The news could wait a little longer.

"Eden," Darrak prompted when she didn't speak for a while. "Are you going to talk to me or what?"

"You mean I have a choice?"

"No. No choices. This is not a choose-your-own-adventure novel. Your amulet is darkening and you say you're doing nothing to cause this. Is that right?"

Eden didn't want to deal with this, but sometimes fate didn't give you a chance to catch your breath before it threw another bucket of water in your face.

She looked up at him. "I can feel it this morning stronger than ever. I'm honestly not sure how much longer I can control it."

Darrak took her face between his hands. "But you want to control it."

She touched one of his hands but didn't pull away from him. "Of course I do."

"I wish to hell I could protect you from all of this." His jaw tensed. "Looks like it's time to get some outside help."

He walked over to the kitchen counter and grabbed the phone.

"Who are you calling?" she asked.

Darrak held a finger up to her. She flopped down on a chair at the table, already exhausted from talking about something she would much prefer to continue trying to ignore—magically melted BlackBerry or not.

She really hoped Andy had taken out a warranty on the device.

"Stanley?" Darrak said after a moment. "Do you know who this is?" A pause. "No, it's okay. Don't be scared. I'm not going to do that to you." Another pause. "Seriously, I'm not. Evisceration is extremely messy and the cleanup is a—Come on. Stop crying. Be a man."

That Darrak's "outside help" required contacting Stanley didn't fill Eden with a great deal of confidence. Stanley worked as a minion for just about any supernatural creature who paid or threatened him. Not exactly her favorite guy in the city.

"Is he back?" Darrak asked. "He is? Why didn't you let me know this already? Oh, come on. Stop crying."

Eden's hands tingled. It was so tempting to throw out a spell right here, right now. It still seemed like just a dream that all of this had happened to her. Demons were real. Angels were real. Witches were real, and they came in a few different varieties.

White witches—the good and beneficial nature lovers. Among other things, Eden had heard they could make flowers grow and dying trees come back to life. How nice for them.

Gray witches—able to blend both white magic and black magic with the ability to do this successfully without damaging their souls provided they maintained a perfect balance.

And then there were black witches—able to destroy or

kill things with a mere thought if they were so inclined. Not exactly the life of the party.

"We need to see him as soon as possible." Darrak paced back and forth between her kitchenette and the dinette area. "That sounds fine. Why are you still crying? Suck it up, dude. Seriously."

He hung up.

"You upset Stanley," Eden said. "Actually . . . I'm fine with that."

Darrak shrugged. "He's still intimidated by my fearsome archdemon reputation. Nice to know somebody is."

"Are you going to share what that was all about?"

"We're seeing Maksim. Today."

She stared at him blankly for a moment. "The wizard."

"The one and only. Sounds like he's finally back from his vacation."

Maksim the wizard had gone on vacation after surviving a torture session by Theo—Darrak's former demon friend—a couple of weeks ago. Before he went AWOL, the wizard was supposed to help them find a way to break his curse, even though rumor had it only the witch who'd originally cursed him could do something about that. Since she was now dead it was a moot point.

"You really think he can help me?" She didn't want to hope for too much from a simple phone call. Disappointment was a heartless bitch.

"I don't think he can hurt. Wizards and witches go hand in hand, after all. Didn't you read *Harry Potter*?"

Eden stared at him. "Well, yeah."

"I didn't read the books," he continued. "But I did get to see the movies. A previous host was a fan. He even wore dress robes and pretended he'd been sorted into a house. Hufflepuff, if you can believe it. Who liked Hufflepuff best? I mean, seriously."

"Not sure that's really helpful in this situation."

"A wizard, especially one at Maksim's level, will know how to control black magic, even yours. I'm sure of it."

It was worth a shot. "Okay, so when do we see him?"

"Now."

"Now?" She glanced at the clock that read eight thirty. "But Andy's going to want us in the office."

"He can wait a couple of hours. He can wait a whole day if necessary. Figuring out how to control your magic is much more important."

She took a deep breath. "Maybe you're right."

"Of course I'm right." Darrak's smile had returned, although this time it didn't completely reach his eyes. He still looked worried.

Which was worrying.

"Fine." Eden nodded and clenched her magically tingling hands into fists at her sides. "Then I guess we're off to see the wizard."

"Don't make me start singing." He snatched the fallen newspaper from the floor and put it back on the table. "You know, he just might be the person from your past whose destiny is intertwined with yours, according to your horoscope."

"I think I'd remember meeting a wizard named Maksim."

Darrak crossed his arms. "Then who do you think it was referring to?"

She waved her hand flippantly. "It was just a horoscope. It's fiction. Totally meaningless."

"If you say so."

Out of all the drama in Eden's life lately, an entertaining but silly horoscope was the least of her problems.

Caroline Riley watched from the shadows as her daughter left the apartment building and headed toward her rusty Toyota. She was about to run up and give Eden a big hug, but held back when the demon came into view.

He was tall with unruly dark hair almost long enough to brush his broad shoulders. He casually pulled on a black leather jacket as he trailed closely after Eden. He was very handsome, of course. Most demons had a highly attractive human visage they wore when not in their demonic form. It made it that much easier to prey upon humans.

He was going to be a problem.

She wondered why Eden would spend time with this evil creature and allow him into her home. Maybe he was threatening her. Blackmailing her.

Or . . . sleeping with her.

Was her daughter having an affair with a demon?

Eden had always been a rules follower, a perfect student, a hard worker, although one who'd always lacked any specific career direction. A smart girl like that wasn't one who'd have her head easily turned by one of Lucifer's minions.

Then again, despite Eden's natural beauty—that she'd inherited from her mother, of course—she'd never had much confidence in herself when it came to men, poor thing. This must have been what the demon had preyed upon.

Caroline had arrived just in time. Sure, she had other pressing matters to attend to, but rescuing her only child from the clutches of a demon had now risen to the very top of her to-do list.

It would be so nice to talk to Eden again. It had been much too long since they'd last spent time together.

Then again, Caroline *had* been dead for the last three months.

⇒ TWO ⇐

Maksim Zadravec, the most powerful wizard in Toronto, didn't look like someone from Hufflepuff at all.

Slytherin was more like it.

Darrak eyed him with distaste as the wizard leisurely moved his gaze over Eden's body from head to toe. From the gleam in his eye it seemed as if he liked what he saw.

The wizard had dark good looks, tanned skin, broad shoulders, and wore an expensive-looking tailor-made suit. He lived in a large mansion at the outskirts of the city that looked more like a castle than anything else. If it didn't have a feel of true history Darrak would assume the wizard had it custom-built to give himself more of a magical mystique.

Maksim lived alone . . . if you didn't count the butler and two maids that silently slunk around the ten-thousand-square-foot, non-cozy home.

Darrak disliked him immediately. Knowing an attractive man was taking an active interest in Eden, for whatever reason, bothered him.

He knew it was jealousy, pure and simple. And maybe

he was dealing with a small—or not so small—feeling of possession. No pun intended.

After all, Eden was *his*.

She, however, would likely argue this.

"So you want my help, do you?" Maksim said in a smooth, deep voice.

Darrak and Eden shared a glance.

"We do," she confirmed. "It's just that my black magic is—"

"Difficult for you to control," Maksim finished. "And you are worried for the state of your soul."

Her brows went up. "Well, yes. That's exactly it. How do you—?"

"Know what's wrong with you without first being told?" Maksim smiled. "One of my many talents, Eden."

Darrak wasn't sure how he felt about the wizard's special insight. A lot of magic, even with the more notable wizards, was no more genuine than rabbits shoved up shirt-sleeves. A whole lot of smoke and mirrors with little genuine product to back it up. Black magic, after all, harmed every practitioner if used too blatantly. Even somebody like Maksim.

"Can you help her?" Darrak asked evenly.

"How did you come by this magic, Eden?" the wizard asked.

Darrak's lips thinned. "Don't you know that, too?"

Maksim glanced at the demon. "It was a spell, correct? Another witch from long ago—she cast a spell upon you." He took a walk around Darrak as if assessing him. "Sex magic. Sleeping with you made her a black witch. And now the same has happened with Eden."

Darrak didn't like this guy, but he couldn't help but be a bit impressed. "Pretty much."

"I can sense the spell. And I can sense your curse as well." Maksim's smile held. "It's a big one."

"I try not to brag."

Maksim now strolled around Eden, who stood stiffly, her arms crossed over her chest. Her gaze flicked to a large oil painting of a nude that looked as if it was a few hundred years old. However, Darrak wasn't much of an art expert.

"How many times have you taken her?" the wizard asked.

Eden snorted at that. "Taken me?"

"Do you not understand the question?"

"No, I—I understand." Eden cast an embarrassed look at Darrak. She hated having their private problems out on the table like this.

Darrak wasn't too happy about it either, especially with the fact this guy knew too much too quickly. But he was hoping it would work out in their benefit.

"Twice," he replied. "But I also believe when I possess her every night at sunset that also triggers the original witch's spell, which has made her magic much stronger than it should be."

Maksim nodded, his attention fully fixed on Eden. "I see. This is why you feel like a furnace of energy to me. And you're also half-angel."

Eden nodded.

"My, my," Maksim said. "Quite a combination. I can see how it might cause . . . complications."

Thus the reason for their visit. Time to move this along.

"There's a tug-of-war going on within her," Darrak said. "The dark magic and the celestial energy are fighting against each other. It's a problem, a big one. And it isn't getting better. Her magic is becoming more difficult for her to control with each day that passes. That's why we need your help."

He hated stating it so bluntly. *Help us, wizard master.*
So weak.

But there was only one alternative Darrak could think of, and he wasn't ready to go there yet. He could go to Lucifer and beg his ex-boss to save both Eden's life and her soul.

Hmm, he thought. *Let's make that Plan Z, shall we?*

He and Lucifer weren't exactly on the best of terms. Last time he'd seen the prince, Lucifer had almost destroyed him. Parts of Darrak still stung a bit from the assault. Mostly his pride.

"How does this tug-of-war between your darkness and your celestial energy feel?" Maksim asked.

She grimaced. "Like I'm being torn in two."

"Does it happen often?"

"Every second day like clockwork."

"And you've only slept together twice."

"That's right," she said with a pointed glance in Darrak's direction.

Yes, well, the decision to keep their relationship platonic was his doing, which was all kinds of hilarious considering he was once upon a time an incubus—a demon who thrived on sucking the life energy out of humans through hanky-panky.

He'd recently become a one-woman demon. Unfortunately, the one woman he wanted was also the one he couldn't touch without potentially hurting her thanks to that pesky sex magic spell. He wanted to protect her from further harm and that managed to nicely trump his libido.

The fact they were being inspected and grilled by a smarmy Eurotrash wizard master was proof positive Darrak was more interested in Eden's future well-being than his own ego-stroking. Or any other kind of stroking, for that matter.

Surprisingly, romance novels had become a nice distraction. Eden had a ton of them on her bookshelf. They were a good enough substitute for the real thing. He was a particular fan of historicals—the hotter the better. Those horny dukes and duchesses really knew how to get it on.

"Okay, enough questions," Darrak said, his patience running thin. His gaze moved around the large parlor that included floor-to-ceiling bookshelves and a leather sofa that looked as if it cost the better part of a small country's annual budget. Then again, so did the wizard's designer suit. "Can you help Eden or not?"

Maksim shrugged. "She is a powerful black witch and

you are a demon. I don't understand why you need any help from me. It sounds like the perfect combination."

Darrak hissed out a breath. "Maybe you haven't been paying attention. Her soul is at risk, get it? Take a look at her amulet. See that color? I don't want it to be a shade darker or she's in danger. The original plan was for her not to use the magic at all, but it's being sparked—sometimes literally—without any provocation. And that the fight against her angelic side causes her any pain at all—well, that's simply not acceptable. Now you're either going to help us directly or you're going to tell us where to get help. That is, if you know what's good for you."

One of his more passive-aggressive threats, but it would have to do. He didn't want to scare Eden by shifting to his demon form and throttling this puny wizard within an inch of his semi-immortal life.

Maksim cocked his head to the side. "You're in love with her."

It wasn't posed in the form of a question.

Darrak's jaw tightened. "Let's stay on topic."

The wizard's brows drew together. "Demons are heartless, cruel, without true emotion other than the glee they might feel at inflicting pain upon another being."

"Stop, you're making me blush."

"But not you. Why?"

"I guess I'm . . . special."

"You love her, don't you?"

"What I feel for her is nobody's damn business but my own. And Eden's."

"Say it," Maksim said. "Or I will do nothing for you."

"That would be a grave mistake." Both Darrak's tone and his mood darkened substantially. Witty, humanity-filled personality or not, he didn't like being pushed.

Maksim's smile looked genuinely filled with amusement. "You'd risk her safety for the sake of your own pride? That does sound more like a true demon. But all I'm asking is for you to admit your feelings, the ones that have made you go out of your way to help her. Say it, and I promise I'll give you the answers you need."

He was messing with Darrak and enjoying it. Testing him. And he seemed unconcerned with the danger this put him in. Darrak had faced many wizards in his existence, pre-humanity-infusion, and those that would dare to piss off an archdemon rarely survived in one happy, magic-wand-waving piece.

Darrak didn't have to look at Eden to know she was watching him, waiting for his reply. They were danger-ous words, dangerous feelings, especially for someone like him. Words held power—a power that even now he strug-gled against.

He supposed he could kill the wizard. Wizards could live for a very long time—just like witches—but a quick twist of the neck would solve that little problem. Unfortunately, he knew a little recreational carnage wasn't in the cards today.

Too bad.

"Yes," Darrak finally said after several tension-filled moments passed. "I tried to fight it, tried to deny it, but I couldn't. It's real and it's big and it scares the unholy shit out of me, but it's true. I love Eden, and I would do any-thing in the universe to save her from all of this. She's the only thing that matters to me."

He finally slanted a glance at her to see her expression was unreadable, but tears shone in her eyes.

"Anything in the universe?" Maksim repeated. "Sounds to me as if the solution to your problem has been right in front of you all along."

"What do you mean?"

"The worry that the fight between her black magic and her celestial energy will destroy her. The seemingly uncon-trollable magic. It's all connected to one very specific thing."

"What?" Darrak asked.

"You. You're the dark object her angelic half is attempting to cast out. You're the reason her magic is unreliable. Her black magic was caused by a spell, but it is a part of her, therefore organic to her core being. You, however, are not."

The news hit him like a punch to the gut. He wanted to deny it, but he knew it was the truth. It was like he'd always known. This was just the confirmation.

"I would do anything in the universe to save her."

He'd said it only a minute ago, and he meant every word. Now he saw the answer written all over Maksim's face—the answer he'd been trying to avoid for as long as he could.

The only way to save Eden was for him to no longer possess her, but he already knew the only way not to possess her anymore was for one of them to die.

The horoscope this morning hadn't mentioned anything like that.

"Awesome," Darrak gritted out. "I just knew coming to see you would be helpful."

"Don't shoot the messenger," Maksim replied.

"Shoot? I had a couple other things in mind, like fire and sharp glass. Bullets are much too speedy."

Not even a glimmer of fear went through Maksim's gaze, which, considering his last unpleasant run-in with a demon, was admirable. "Don't you see, demon? You need to send yourself to the Void. Save the woman you love and sacrifice yourself. Simple."

"That's not going to happen," Eden snapped. "There's another solution."

Maksim turned to regard her. "You think so?"

"Yes."

"So you're determined to do whatever it takes to save both this demon and yourself, are you?"

"One hundred percent." Her eyes narrowed. "And you're going to tell me how to do that."

Maksim glanced at Darrak. "She's spunky."

"She has her moments."

"Another potential answer lies with Selina."

Darrak's eyes snapped to the wizard. "How do you know that name?"

Maksim smiled. "I already told you I know many things.

Selina is the name of the witch who placed the sex magic spell on you. And she's also responsible for the curse that has bound you to Eden now three hundred years after it was first cast."

Darrak struggled to keep his expression neutral. "You don't happen to know what the lottery numbers are going to be this week, do you? Now there's some very useful information."

"Selina could remove both the spell and the curse."

"Too bad she's dead."

"Yes, that is too bad."

Selina was killed by a member of the Malleus, an organization of humans who liked to hunt demons and witches and other things that went bump in the night. Their origins went back to the infamous Salem witch trials. No, the Malleus weren't fun people to be around if one preferred their head attached to their body, more like sanctimonious murderers who saw the world only in black-and-white terms. And red. Red was one of their favorite colors.

Eden had her arms crossed tightly over her chest. "She promised to help me learn to control my magic before she died. She said we were like sisters now."

"More like twins, actually." Maksim moved closer to her, studying her face. Eden stayed very still, her attention on Darrak as the wizard flicked her long, dark red hair back from her shoulder and moved around her slowly as if inspecting her. "If you received your magic from the same source, your magic signatures would be identical, like sharing a fingerprint."

Darrak frowned. "You're saying their magic is exactly the same."

"That is what I'm saying."

"Does that mean I can remove the spell and the curse?" Eden asked, her voice shaky. "Just like Selina would have been able to?"

"It is possible, but not guaranteed."

"Nothing ever is, except death and taxes," Darrak said. "Well, *taxes*."

He watched Eden to see her reaction to this. It did make a crazy kind of sense to him, and he was surprised it hadn't yet occurred to him. Selina and Eden had received their black magic from the same spell—and that was enough to make their black magic identical.

"I don't know." Eden shook her head. "I'd be afraid to even attempt it. I might hurt him."

"Magic is like a muscle," Maksim explained. "With regular use it becomes stronger. It is only the truly destructive magic that will darken your soul. An attempt to do something like this should not tap too deeply into the black magic."

But it wasn't exactly white magic, either.

Darrak wasn't convinced of a word that came out of the wizard's mouth, but Eden seemed intrigued.

"Maybe this is the answer we've been looking for," she said cautiously.

"The spell will be easier to remove and can be attempted at any time," Maksim said. "A curse, however, is made of much denser magic. Take care when you make your attempt on it, and remember it must be made as close to dawn as possible when the bond between you both is at its weakest point."

Eden nodded. "Thank you so much for your help."

He took her outstretched hand and squeezed it. "There's something else, isn't there?"

She frowned. "What do you mean?"

"You have a friend in need. One you're concerned with. You work closely with him and you fear what will happen . . . tomorrow night."

She gasped. "Are you talking about Andy?"

"Yes, that's it."

Andy had been bitten by a werewolf two weeks ago, and tomorrow night was the full moon. Maksim was right on the money. Darrak wondered where he kept his crystal ball hidden, although he did have a few ideas of where he'd like to shove it.

"I have something for you that may come in handy."

Maksim walked to a mahogany desk in the corner, opened the top drawer, and returned with a piece of parchment with faded handwriting on it. "It's a containment spell. Any room he's in when the time comes can be perfectly sealed and cloaked, which will prevent harm to him or to others. Such simple magic, even a human could use it if they have the correct wording. Consider it my gift to you."

Eden took it from him and scanned the Latin words to both cast and remove the spell. "Thank you so much."

"My pleasure."

Darrak resisted the urge to roll his eyes. A gift. Sure. Nothing came for free. He'd just have to wait to see when the bill for this consultation was going to arrive and in what form. "We're leaving."

"You're welcome, too, demon."

"I'll reserve penning any thank-you notes until we see some results—both for Eden and for our soon-to-be furry friend."

Maksim smiled thinly. "Of course. But really, you must ask yourself this—how could things get any worse than they already are?"

Darrak chose not to reply to that.

How could things get any worse?

That was a dangerous question if ever he'd heard one.

⇥ THREE ↞

Ben Hanson couldn't stop thinking about angels.

He'd met one—a real one. He was sure of it. The angel was being kept prisoner right down the hall in the cell with the tiny window on the door. Ben had been staring at that cell for almost ten minutes now.

Ben had quickly realized that the Malleus had a bit of a dark side. To say the least.

But why were they holding an angel prisoner? There had to be a solid reason, something that he could understand.

He needed answers.

Not that he could do a damn thing about it, even if he wanted to. He'd signed over his body and soul when he'd accepted the job offer here. He'd tendered his resignation as a cop nearly two weeks ago and had been faced with questions he couldn't answer. For better or for worse, he was a civilian now. One who worked for the Malleus—Latin for *the hammer*.

There was really only one thing that made this place remotely tolerable. Ben had met a woman named Sandy Matthews, a gray witch. He'd hoped she'd be able to help him forget someone else—a woman named Eden. So far, however, it hadn't worked all that well.

Eden was the main reason Ben had signed up as a Malleus member. She'd helped him see that the world didn't only contain criminals to lock up, but evil monsters as well. And, when the going got tough, Eden had chosen one of those monsters over him.

Things like that weren't too good for a guy's ego.

Ben had been told by his superiors to keep a close watch on Eden and her demon. His boss, Oliver Gale, had plans that had something to do with both of them, but he wasn't exactly all that forthcoming with the details.

Damn it, he needed answers about that angel. It was driving him crazy.

The Malleus worked as a "need to know" organization. If Ben didn't need to know something, he wasn't told. But this was different. For his own peace of mind, he had to know the truth. Oliver was the leader here, the one who'd personally branded Ben's forearm with the fleur-de-lis symbol that, along with the ritual that went along with it, gave him the ability to sense those who are Other and the extra strength needed to fight against them.

The pay wasn't bad, either.

It was too late to change his mind now. He'd been told that once you were a member of the Malleus the only way out was death.

He really should have read the fine print first.

"Hey, Ken doll," a female voice called out to him from the tiny window on a cell to his left. "Come here. I need to talk to you."

"Ken doll?" he repeated.

"You're blond, tan, and perfect. It's as good a name as any."

He glanced in the direction of her smooth voice. He couldn't see anything but dark skin and dark eyes glittering from the other side of the window. The cell itself wasn't lit.

"What do you want?" he asked warily. The Malleus dungeon was filled with evil creatures who were locked up until their ultimate fates could be decided.

"You have to help me. I shouldn't be here."

"If you're in there it's for a good reason, honey."

Her almond-shaped eyes narrowed. "Wrong place, wrong time, that's the only reason for this."

"Are you human?"

"Well . . ." She hesitated. "Not exactly."

"Then you're exactly where you need to be."

"Nice attitude," the woman called after him as he started walking again. "That'll get you far, asshole."

"Nice talking to you."

Her tone turned desperate. "Wait! They're going to kill me. You know that, right? You need to do something!"

Ben's pace slowed and his mouth went dry. "If you want help, you're asking the wrong guy."

He was followed only by silence as his footsteps echoed along the long hall.

He took the stairs to the top floor and came to a halt just outside of Oliver Gale's office when he heard Sandy's familiar voice. Ben hadn't even known she'd be in the office today.

"—won't be much longer," she said.

"And you don't have any new intel?"

"No, I think I need to—"

"What you need to do is focus on your assignment," Oliver hissed.

Ben tensed. Oliver had been rough with Sandy before, given her a black eye when she'd done something he didn't approve of. It had taken everything inside of Ben not to beat the shit out of the old man, but raising a hand in violence against one of the Malleus elders would have resulted in Sandy—and himself—being reprimanded in a much stronger and more unpleasant manner.

"The problem with Ben"—oddly, Sandy's voice held none of the timidity Ben was accustomed to hearing—"is what you see is what you get. He's here because he wants to help rid the world of evil. He has no deeper agenda than that."

"Is he still obsessed with Eden Riley?"

"His connection to her is fading."

"Have you succeeded in making him fall in love with you?"

Sandy cleared her throat. "Love isn't something that can be forced naturally."

"Did he love Eden?"

"He didn't know her very long. I think he might have if given more time. He's still obsessed with saving her from the demon because Ben's fiancée from years ago was murdered. He thinks saving Eden will somehow right that wrong on his conscience."

"How sad."

"He's a noble guy. Stupid, stubborn, and boring, but very noble."

Every muscle in Ben's body was tense. He couldn't believe what he was hearing. Sandy was normally so sweet, so genuine. Or so he'd assumed.

"So you have failed to have him fall for your womanly charms," Oliver said.

"I didn't say that. We are sleeping together."

A smile entered Oliver's voice. "Even though he was told such a relationship between those associated with the Malleus is forbidden."

"There is a rebel inside of him."

"He's too much of a wild card to have here right now. If he loves you, he'll toe the line and won't get in my way. Use a strong spell to make him fall in love with you. Control him, Sandy. Wrap him around your little finger, and, along with the other matter we've discussed, you'll be well rewarded when the time comes. And that time is coming very soon."

"Consider it done," Sandy replied. "He's mine."

There were footsteps on the hardwood floor, but by the time the witch had left her boss's office, Ben was already gone.

Ben had signed away his freedom, his life, in order to do the right thing. And now he was being betrayed by those he trusted. By a woman he was sleeping with.

Nothing made sense anymore. Maybe it never had in the first place.

* * *

Eden stayed quiet on the twenty-minute drive from Maksim's bachelor-pad mansion to the small office that housed Triple-A Investigations as they absorbed the information presented to them by the wizard. Darrak had chosen not to try to get her talking. He wasn't feeling too chatty at the moment anyway.

Something felt off about visiting the wizard, but he couldn't put his finger on it.

Perhaps it was that Maksim had "helped" them without asking for anything in return. Darrak was accustomed to practitioners of magic being on the greedy side. Greed was one of the most popular deadly sins, after all. Right after lust.

It was also one of the most reliable.

"We'll check in with Andy," Darrak said. "Then you and me—we need to talk. In private."

He reached for the door handle to let himself out, but felt Eden's hand on his arm stopping him. He looked at her cautiously. Her beautiful face was tense.

He immediately worried she was experiencing the tearing pain again. "Are you all right?"

She just nodded.

"Then what?"

"What you said back there when he asked you what you felt about me."

"Oh, that."

"I just . . ." She rubbed her lips together, and her gaze flicked up to meet his. "Sometimes . . . I—I don't know what to say."

"You don't have to say anything."

"You didn't have to be so blunt with him. You could have held something back."

"Why would I want to do that? What I said was the truth." He almost laughed at the shadow of doubt in her gaze. "Do you think I was lying to him?"

"No, but . . ." She shook her head. "Nobody's ever felt like that about me before."

He drew closer to her. "Stupid of them, but less competition is not necessarily a bad thing. I'm a little rusty on my sword fighting against other suitors. And pistols at dawn isn't that appealing. I'm not really a morning person if I can help it."

She searched his expression. "You really think this has a chance?"

"What?"

"You and me."

Darrak thought he understood that doubt in her eyes. He wasn't thinking quite so far ahead, but Eden was already looking years into the future to try to figure out if a relationship between someone like her and someone like him had a chance in a world of white-picket-fence dreams competing with a high-divorce-rate reality.

He knew he wasn't Eden's perfect choice in a man. He wasn't even a man, really. Never had been, never would be. Some demons were former humans, with lives and memories and morals that they could cling to even if they'd made a few wrong choices in their lives that caused them to sell their soul to a demon lord or Lucifer himself.

Darrak had been reminded time and time again by the big boss that he was a big fat nothing. A lesser demon created at Lucifer's whim once upon a time with a bit of hellfire and some powerful magic. That he lived, breathed, desired, lusted, loved, wanted, needed, and hungered was only a side effect of that magic.

How could something like *that* aspire to anything more than an eternity of servitude?

But he did. He aspired.

There was a fire inside of him that had nothing to do with Hell anymore. It was a fire ignited by the auburn-haired woman who studied him intently like whatever he said next was going to be some sort of prophecy for their future together.

"Kiss me," he said.

It appeared to be a prophecy that had immediate results. She drew closer, took his face between her hands, and pressed her lips against his with a kiss that would have swelled his immortal soul if he'd been in possession of one. Her tongue slipped past his lips and slid against his own.

The kiss grew heated very quickly and his body responded in kind, hardening with a need he could barely hold back, especially when her hand moved up his thigh to brush against his groin. He didn't stop her; he only managed a dark groan from the back of his throat.

He wanted her. In a parking lot at eleven o'clock in the morning, he desperately wanted her.

And it looked like he could have her as she crawled onto his lap to straddle him in the passenger seat. He moved his hands up to cup her full breasts, slipping underneath her crisp white shirt and bra. He ached to slide inside of her. Feel her heat, her need, make her cry out his name as he took her with long, sweet thrusts.

It seemed as if she was currently a mind reader since she began fiddling with the zipper of his jeans.

"Wait, Eden," he managed. "We can't do this . . ."

"You don't sound completely convinced of that."

"Eden," his tone turned sharper. The woman was insatiable. Twice they'd made love, and both times had been incredible. Maybe he'd inadvertently managed to addict her to his demon loving just a little bit too much.

Sounded conceited, but it could actually be the truth. The spell on him could unconsciously drive her to seek more black magic by any means possible.

"Oh, hell." His mind went foggy when she slipped her hand into the front of his pants and wrapped her fingers around him.

"Did you really mean it?" she whispered. "When you said you loved me?"

There was no parking lot anymore. No chance of being discovered. The world had narrowed to only Eden—sexy, desirable, incredible Eden—the only woman he'd ever truly loved in his entire existence. One who wasn't sure about their future together since there were so many odds stacked against them. A black witch who was part angel.

One he'd corrupted so much that her soul was currently at risk of being sent directly to Hell upon her death.

Damn.

Yes, that thought definitely helped to douse his mindless desire.

He grasped her wrist and pulled her away from him. He turned his head when she attempted to kiss him again. He zipped up his jeans and took her firmly by her upper arms, directing her back to the driver's seat. Her face was flushed and the need in her eyes hadn't left yet.

"Yes," he said very seriously. "I meant every word."

Then he got out of the car and headed into the office on shaky legs.

The black magic made her do it.

It drew her to Darrak like a moth to a flame. While there was a whole lot of celestial energy swirling inside him, more than even he was aware of yet, there was still a large amount of Hell energy, too—the darkest of the dark. And that worked like a magnet for a black witch. And a black witch's sex drive.

She wanted him so badly it hurt, but he'd put on the brakes.

Darrak loved her.

And he'd just soundly rejected her seduction attempt in the parking lot of Triple-A for her own damn good.

She had to focus. Too much was at risk here if she kept losing her mind like that.

A gorgeous, dark-haired, blue-eyed immortal demon had told her he was in love with her. But that same demon was cursed to possess her—and according to Maksim, that was the reason for a great many of her problems.

But she already knew that. Most of it, anyway.

Was it still considered an abusive relationship if the abuse wasn't intended?

There was a time in college when she'd been involved with a man who'd intentionally abused her. She hated looking back at how weak she'd been then, how willing she was to accept a heartfelt apology and shiny gifts to make up for the occasional bruise or broken rib. She knew she'd never be in another relationship like that. Ever.

In fact, it was more than likely the reason she'd shielded herself from love ever since and refused to give up her control. Sure, she'd been briefly engaged since, but only because it had felt like the right time, the right place, the right opportunity. In that relationship she hadn't been abused physically. Emotionally was more like it. Her fiancé had cheated on her on Valentine's Day, originally prompting her to move to Toronto and take over half ownership of Triple-A so she could have a fresh start.

Eden's love life had always been one big fat joke. She couldn't help but be guarded, even now. Even with Darrak.

Maybe it was because of her mother's influence. Caroline had never exactly been a glowing example of someone who had healthy relationships. She'd had a one-night stand with an angel and become pregnant from it. Who did that?

"Morning," Andy McCoy greeted her as she entered the office. Darrak held the door open for her. "Or, rather, *late* morning. Just strolling in now whenever you feel like it, is that how it is?"

Darrak shrugged as he hung both his and Eden's coats up on the rack near the door. "Had to see a wizard about a problem."

"I will assume that's not a euphemism."

"Eden's magic is no euphemism."

Andy nodded gravely. "Tell me something I don't know."

"Well, for starters, you're going to turn into a werewolf tomorrow night."

Andy recoiled slightly. "No, I'm not."

"You are."

"Am not."

"Are."

"Not."

"You can deny it all you like, Andy, but it's going to happen. You got bitten by a werewolf. Mauled, actually."

He shuddered. "I remember that part."

"And that means you're a werewolf, too. I'm not sure why this is so difficult for you to grasp."

Eden felt bad for the guy. He was still in serious denial about what would happen. It was a discussion they'd had several times in the last couple of weeks, but no progress had been made to get him to accept the inevitable.

Maksim had given them a spell that would allegedly help safely contain Andy and cloak the area. Wouldn't want someone to walk by and see a werewolf clawing at the door to be let out.

Apparently werewolves could shapeshift anytime they liked, but when it came to the full moon, they didn't have a choice. It was all werewolf all the time, for one night a month.

She glanced around the office, trying to judge how much damage there would be if they made this the containment area. Seemed like as good a place as any. She'd done some research into werewolves, along with Darrak's knowledge of them, and knew Andy would go one of two ways. Either a rabid, out-of-control beast who had none of his human traits and only wanted to rip things—or people—apart. Or he'd be Andy. In wolf form.

She was hoping for the latter, but planning for the former.

"I am not going to turn into a werewolf tomorrow night," Andy said firmly. "Just stop it. Both of you."

He went to his desk, sat down, and took out a silver flask from his top drawer, draining it in one gulp.

Denial was a thirsty state of mind.

Darrak hadn't looked directly at her since the impromptu lap dance in the car, but they had to talk. If her magic was

truly identical to Selina's, then they had to give it a shot.
First with the spell and then, if they were successful, with
the curse.

Could it really be that easy after all this time?

The bell above the door jingled as someone familiar entered the office. She was short, with bleached blonde hair,
red lips, and a smile that stretched a mile wide. Nancy was
the assistant manager at the coffee shop next door, a place
called Hot Stuff that Andy also owned. She came by with
coffee and donuts first thing every morning, the scent of
which usually made Eden's mouth water.

This morning it seemed to have the opposite effect. She
felt a little queasy, actually.

Great. Word had it that the flu was going around. Getting
sick was the last thing she needed to deal with right now.

"Hello all!" Nancy exclaimed cheerily.

"Nancy, you're back bearing more delicious treats.
Twice in one morning. What's the occasion?" Andy grinned
at her as if thrilled for the excuse to avoid the werewolf
topic. Nancy was blissfully ignorant about a great deal of
paranormal activity in the area. She'd come face-to-face
with some dangerous magic recently at a local singles club
that happened to be possessed by the demon Lord of Lust,
but had recovered nicely. Well, except for one very unfortunate result.

The blonde was currently dating Stanley, the weaselly
wizard's assistant whom Darrak had made cry earlier on the
phone.

Some women had questionable taste in men.

"I saw Darrak and Eden just got here. Had to bring over
more munchies." Nancy held up a paper bag emblazoned
with the Hot Stuff logo.

"You're an angel," Darrak said. "And I mean that as a
compliment, not an insult."

Nancy had a large crush on Darrak for a while, but
thankfully it had subsided. There was a time she'd demon-
strated this crush by making Darrak chocolate donuts in the

blobby shape of hearts. Now they were regular blobby-shaped ovals.

"Here, Eden." Nancy held out a coffee to her.

"Thanks." Eden took it and couldn't help but notice something glitter on Nancy's finger. Her eyes widened. "Wow, Nancy. Nice ring."

"Oh, this?" Nancy held her left hand out to show off the diamond solitaire and then wriggled her fingers.

"You're not . . ." Eden frowned. "Are you engaged?"

She would have thought it impossible, but Nancy's smile shot up another fifty watts. "Stanley popped the question last night."

"Congratulations!" Andy exclaimed.

"Popped what question?" Darrak asked.

"Stanley asked me to marry him, and I said yes." More finger wriggling. "I'm going to be Mrs. Dancy!"

"Nancy Dancy," Darrak said. "It's catchy."

Eden's brows drew together. "I'm glad you're so excited. Don't take this the wrong way, but you've only known him a couple of weeks. Are you positive this is the right thing?"

The brightness dimmed a little at the edges. "Now you sound like my mother."

"I'm just saying—"

"She was all 'Is this going to be like last time? Marry in haste, repent at leisure,' or whatever. But it's not true. It's not like the last time. That wasn't true love. This—what me and Stanley have? It's real. I feel it deep inside of me like nothing I've ever experienced before. It's real and it's lasting and I want to spend the rest of my life with that man. He's the most wonderful person I've ever known in my entire life."

"*Stanley* is?" Eden cleared her throat as Nancy's cheery smile turned into a glower. "I mean, sure . . . he's, uh, great. I'm sorry, I didn't mean to rain on your parade. I'm just practical about this sort of thing. I don't want you to get hurt."

The blonde's expression softened again. "I know. And I

appreciate it. Don't worry about me, Eden. You've always been like an older sister to me."

"I believe I'm a few years younger than you, actually."

"It would mean a lot to me if you'd be one of my brides-maids. Will you do that?"

Eden was at a loss. It felt wrong talking about things like true love, bridal plans, and weddings when she was getting used to dealing with curses, demons, and an unavoidable working relationship with Lucifer himself. "I . . . I would be happy to be one of your bridesmaids."

"Thank you so much." Nancy gave her a tight hug. "Listen, I have to get back to work but we'll talk soon. What fun!"

Then, with her mood elevated again by good wishes and promises of bridesmaids and impending nuptials, Nancy left them to their coffee and donuts.

If anything, Eden felt a bit queasier now than she did to start with. "I just hope Stanley isn't using her."

"When did you become such a Negative Nelly?" Andy said.

"Around the time I was a toddler. And it's called being a realist, actually."

"I think it's wonderful. We could use more good news around here lately."

"Definitely." Darrak bit into his donut, then held the other one out to Eden. "Want some?"

Their tryst in the car came back to her with full erotic strength.

Oh, she still wanted some, all right, and she wasn't talking about donuts. But she'd cooled off from before. Enough to keep her attention fully fixed on the issues at hand.

She gave him a strained smile. "Maybe later."

Andy grabbed his coat. "I need to head out to meet with a client. Glad you two got here so I wouldn't have to shut the office down completely."

"More werewolves?" Darrak asked pointedly.

Andy cringed. "Would you stop with the werewolf stuff, already?"

"It was just a question, not an accusation."

"Then no. Not werewolves. A human client, believe it or not. Wanted me to investigate a missing sister who ran off with a boyfriend without leaving any forwarding address. I already found her living in Vegas. Quick case, nice and easy."

"Well, good," Eden said. "Fine, you go do that. Darrak and I have some business of our own to take care of."

"Oh yeah? Like what?"

"I'm going to experiment with a little spell removal."

"Eden, I thought we were going to talk about that first." There was a warning edge to Darrak's voice.

She ignored it.

"Well, that's great. Good luck with that," Andy said. "But please try not to break anything."

⇉ FOUR ⇇

Andy left.

When Eden looked at Darrak she realized he was staring at her sternly with his arms crossed over his chest, his half-eaten donut forgotten.

"What do you think you're doing?" he asked.

"Just what I told him. Spell removal experimentation."

"I don't think that's a good idea."

She hissed out a breath. "Actually, the more I think about it, I believe it's the best idea I've had in a very long time. You heard Maksim. Me and Selina—our magic is exactly the same."

"According to him. He could have been lying through his shiny white teeth."

"You don't trust him?"

"I can't think of any real reason to trust him, let alone to put your safety in his hands."

She shook her head. "I feel it, Darrak. Inside of me. He was telling the truth."

He paced to the other side of the small office next to the

coatrack and then turned back to look at her. "It doesn't have to be now."

"Why not?"

"We can get a second opinion."

"I don't want to wait that long."

"You can't be *that* focused on sleeping with me again, can you?"

She actually laughed at that. "You think that's all this is? Just some horny witch who needs to get it on with the closest available demon ASAP?"

"Is it?"

"Oh, yes. You're just that irresistible that suddenly I can't control myself. I need you, I want you, I have to have you."

He mock-glared at her. "Sarcasm is not necessary. I'm very sensitive lately, you know."

A smile tugged at her lips. "Who says I'm being sarcastic? I do need you. I do want you. And I do have to have you. Desperately."

He leveled his gaze with hers. "The feeling is entirely mutual, but I'm not sure about this."

She didn't want to argue. She didn't want everything to be a struggle between them. "He seemed to think there was only one other solution if this doesn't work, Darrak, and I don't want you to even think about that. Ever. If I can remove the spell, then I might be able to remove the curse. Problem solved."

He studied her for a moment. "Just because he said it doesn't make it true."

Eden wrung her hands. "Don't you want to be free again? You could have your own body all the time, not just during the day. No more possessing me, no more feeding off my celestial energy. You'd be free to do whatever you want, go wherever you want."

Darrak was silent for a moment. "What if I don't want to go anywhere but here?"

Her heart skipped a beat. "Then . . . well, that would be your choice. But at least you'd have a choice."

His expression turned thoughtful. "What if this doesn't work? What if he was wrong and your and Selina's magical signatures are not identical?"

"Then we'll figure something else out. But we won't know unless we try."

The alternative hung between them like a dark, bottomless pool. She'd resolved herself to having Darrak possess her indefinitely, but according to Maksim, if he was the root cause of her pain, of her erratic black magic, then their days were numbered.

Much like the oncoming bright lights of a truck in the opposite lane, this possibility was too painful to look at directly.

This *had* to work.

"Come on, Darrak." She pushed a confident smile onto her face. "This isn't like you. I'm usually the cautious one, remember? Aren't you a gambler? Somebody who's willing to take a chance, roll the dice for a shot at the jackpot?"

His expression didn't change. "Not at the risk of your immediate safety."

"Then I guess it's a good thing this isn't entirely your decision. Because this is happening. Right now.

"Eden—"

"Shhh. I need to concentrate." She sat down on the edge of her desk. "You can either help or you can get out of my way. What'll it be, demon?" She squeezed her eyes shut.

Darrak approached and gently grasped her wrist. She opened her eyes to look at him warily.

"I'll help," he said, although he didn't look happy about it.

"Good. So I'm open to suggestion at the moment. I haven't exactly done anything like this before."

His handsome face was now set in grim lines. "Okay, well, look at it this way. The spell Selina cast on me when she summoned me out of Hell should still be on me, kind of like a residue. It will be nearly impossible to detect by your average everyday magical practitioner, but it would have remained on the surface. That's the sign of a spell. A curse is deeper, like rust. A spell is more like a light coating of paint."

"Magic for Dummies," Eden murmured.

"Present company excepted. If you share Selina's magic, you'll be able to clearly see the spell, and you may be able to focus on it enough to remove it. But don't delve too deeply into the black magic for this. It's not worth it."

She couldn't disagree with him more. This would be the solid proof of whether her future was bright or dark. It was something she didn't think would even be possible, so she didn't want to get her hopes up. But there they were—hopes up high.

"I can't see anything." She scanned his body as he took hold of her other wrist as well.

He grinned a little. "Well, no. Not with your eyes open. Human eyes are not the best things with which to see true magic."

"Then what do I use?"

"Your soul. And you can best access that sight with your eyes closed. Magic 101, Eden. Class is now in session."

Learn something new every day. "So how do demons and other non-souled entities do magic if they don't have souls?"

"We don't do the same sort of magic as witches and wizards. It's very complicated stuff, trust me."

"I'll have to take your word for it." She exhaled and closed her eyes.

"See past the darkness. I'm touching you, so you should be able to sense me a bit easier on that level. To see me."

He was right. With enough concentration she did see him. He looked different at that level of perception—not like a human form with two legs, two arms—more like a metaphysical presence, but it was still Darrak. She would recognize him anywhere. He was a warm presence who held her anchored to the real world.

"Do you see me?" he asked.

"Yes." She saw shapes and colors shifting together and pulling apart, sort of like what it might be like to swim inside a gigantic lava lamp filled with black water.

"And what about the spell?"

She focused harder, and it felt as if she slipped down another level or two—as if she was in a high-rise apartment and the elevator had sunk down a couple of floors in the lava lamp world. Everything deepened and became more dimensional. She felt pressure—a force that pushed against her on all sides. She concentrated on the being that was Darrak. His form contained equal parts of light and dark—two separate pieces butting up against each other every few seconds like bumper cars at an amusement park.

He didn't feel that light inside of him, she thought, but it was very bright. As bright as the darkness was dark. It was his celestial side, growing brighter every time he absorbed her endless supply of celestial energy. It fed him, kept him from fading away, allowed him to take form when for hundreds of years he'd been stuck bodiless and needed to possess humans. He'd absorbed humanity from those humans, even the nasty ones. He'd developed stronger emotions than what he'd had as an archdemon. He'd developed a sense of right and wrong. It hadn't been a conscious decision, and perhaps he'd always had that sense, but he'd sided with the darkness before. He hadn't been able to feel empathy, sympathy, worry, or compassion. Seeing him like this, the proof before her very eyes that he was changed, was a powerful thing to witness and it made her throat thicken with emotion.

He was different now and he'd never go back to how he'd been before, even if he wanted to. What had changed him hadn't been a spell. It hadn't been a curse. Those things had propelled him in this direction, but it wasn't who he was at a core level.

This—darkness and light combined—it *was* Darrak. And it was there because of her. No demon had ever been infused with celestial energy before. It was like an experiment gone wrong. Or right, depending on how you looked at it.

Eden worried that when Darrak learned of this it would shake his sense of self and his confidence even more than it already had. Darrak liked being a demon. Sure, he'd made his peace with being a demon who had a little humanity to deal with. But being told he was now part angel . . .

He wouldn't be happy about that at all.

That was something to worry about another day.

She focused on the task at hand instead. "I can see it—I *think* I can see it. The spell."

"What does it look like?" he asked cautiously.

"Like a film—a transparent film that coats your entire being. It shimmers and moves and it . . . it feels like pure power. Like you're coated in a perfume of power."

"Does it have a scent?"

She inhaled. "It smells like . . . hmm. It smells really good."

"Sex magic would. It's the whole reason for it to exist. It's like pheromones on crack. Probably explains your behavior in the car. I mean, I know I'm hard to resist, but . . ."

She grimaced. "Let's not talk about that right now."

"Good idea. Much too distracting."

She focused on Darrak's warm skin against hers. "So what do I do now?"

"This I can't help you with. But if your magic is identical to Selina's, that spell you can see belongs to you, too. You might be able to just suck it back up and send it back from whence it came, easy as pie."

"Easy as pie?"

"Well, probably not as easy as pie. Piece of cake, maybe?"

She exhaled shakily. "I'll try."

"Just . . . try your best not to make it any worse than it already is."

She stiffened. "Wait a minute, *worse*? What do you mean?"

"If you make the spell worse, it's possible I won't even be able to touch you at all anymore. That's one of the reasons I'm touching you right now so you can sense if something bad is happening."

"That really could happen?"

"Sex is the extreme. Touching is the safe end, but it's still in the same realm. I have agreed not to have sex with you again for your own good, but not touching you at all for an eternity of being bound together like this would be much too cruel. It would mean I could never kiss you again. Hold your hand. Brush against you. Nothing."

Her breathing sped up. "That would be bad."

"Glad to see we agree about something."

"Can we stop this and regroup?"

"No, it's too late. You're too deep and you've already accessed the spell enough to see it. Keep going, but take as much time as you need."

She'd dived in headfirst without thinking much about it first. Didn't sound like her usual self—that had been much more reckless than she normally was.

They couldn't stop. But she had to be very careful.

Eden concentrated and went deeper still, a few more floors down. She was in this now, for better or for worse. She'd already touched the spell—the gossamer coating that covered his form on this level of consciousness. That was what she focused on.

Go now, she thought. *Leave here. I no longer need you.*

As she thought the command, sending out the magic through what she now knew was her soul, she felt it respond. It was as if the spell had a personality—like a puppy. It recognized her magical signature and wagged its tail. And then it extracted itself from Darrak to return to her and . . . disappeared.

Hocus-pocus.

She inhaled sharply and tried to stand up from her chair, but her knees buckled. Darrak caught her in his arms.

"Eden . . ." he said from what sounded like a great distance. "Eden!"

She blinked, her eyelashes fluttering as she opened her eyes and smiled up at him. "I think I did it."

His expression looked strained, concerned, but hopeful. "You should be teaching Magic 101. I can't help but be impressed."

"Maybe Maksim's advice was too good not to be true."

"Maybe." Darrak looked conflicted by this possibility.

Part of him, though, looked cautiously optimistic. But then his gaze moved to her chest. It only took her a moment to figure out why.

Her amulet.

Damn.

"It's darker," she said. "Isn't it?"

"Maksim said this wouldn't use your black magic in a destructive manner." He swore under his breath. "But he was wrong. It used your magic and your soul at the same time. It was like introducing two horny people on a blind date. They went for each other immediately. It was a direct conduit to your soul for that black magic."

She glanced down at the amulet, taking the cool piece of oval-shaped stone in her hand. It was significantly darker by at least two shades. It was now a medium gray with lines that were the color of charcoal. It was quite pretty, actually, if you didn't know what it really meant.

Instead of panicking, she felt a strange sense of resolve.

"It was worth it," she said, mostly to herself. "Besides, I don't feel any different."

"Not yet." He paced back and forth before stopping and looking at her. "You know, there is a way to take it back a few shades before it gets too much darker."

She shook her head. "No, Darrak."

"You think I like the idea of it? But if necessary, it's what you have to do—"

"Stop it." Her voice cracked on the words.

"Another kiss from Lucifer wouldn't really be so bad, would it?" His eyes burned bright with immediate jealousy, but a dark smile twisted on his face.

"Keep it up, Darrak, and the next time I see him I might not only kiss him."

That helped erase the humorless smile completely.

However, she couldn't exactly argue with his logic. It had already been proven that kissing the Prince of Hell, even a chaste, emotionless kiss, drew the darkness out of her and straight into him. He was the ultimate magnet for evil. But he was a devious, manipulative man. Fallen angel.

Demon. Prince. Prisoner. A split-personality Dr. Jekyll and Mr. Hyde.

All of the above.

She didn't trust him. That her life was now irrevocably intertwined with his didn't exactly help her sleep that well at night.

In a way she felt sorry for him, and that didn't help much either. Lucifer, or Lucas, which was the name she preferred to use for him, felt trapped in Hell. His only desire was to go back to Heaven where he thought he truly belonged, but his darkness was an eternal anchor keeping him stuck in the Netherworld.

Lucas thought he was cursed. Eden couldn't very well say he was wrong about that.

When the prince chose to come to the human world, he did so with one drawback. Here he was mortal. He still had power, especially over beings like Darrak, whom Lucas had created himself, but his mortal body could be killed. And if so, his essence would be sent back to Hell with no chance to escape again for a very long time.

"I'm sorry," she said.

"What for?"

"Everything."

"You're taking my lines again, because I'm the one who's sorry."

"Maybe we're just a sorry pair."

He snorted. "No kidding."

She slid her hands up his chest. "There is some good news, though."

"Oh?"

"Your spell is broken." She smiled. "You can't give me any more black magic than I already have."

"Oh."

"Can you feel it?"

"I think so."

"How does it feel?"

He lowered his face so they were eye to eye. "It feels very good."

"This means we can be together. Whenever we like."

She thought he was going to pull away, tell her to wait, but instead he kissed her, a kiss that didn't hold back anything. It was deep, searching, passionate, and she wanted more. Desire swelled within her swiftly, immediately.

"Here?" he asked.

She just nodded.

A smile spread across his handsome face. "Your wish is my command."

He pressed her back against the desk, his mouth moving down the column of her throat, and then she heard the sound.

A jingle. Somebody had entered the office.

Damn it. They should have locked the door. They were lucky no one had walked in during the spell removal.

She swore against Darrak's lips as he kissed her one more time before releasing her, and they turned toward the door. A young and pretty raven-haired woman stood there looking at them with a hand on her hip and a raised eyebrow.

"Am I interrupting something?" she asked.

Eden cleared her throat and stood up. Her legs felt shaky, and she ran a hand through her long hair to neaten it.

"I'm sorry," she said. "That must not have looked very professional."

Darrak shrugged. "Sometimes I just can't keep my hands off her. She's irresistible."

Eden couldn't help but laugh as she cast a look in his direction. "Anyway, let's start again." She moved toward the woman and stretched out her hand. "I'm Eden Riley. Welcome to Triple-A Investigations. And you are?"

The young woman grasped Eden's hand tightly in hers, her eyes sparkling with happiness. "Honey, it's me."

Eden frowned. "Excuse me?"

"It's me," the woman said again. "Your mother. I'm back!"

⇒ Five ⇐

Eden tried to process what she'd just heard.

Her mother? That was impossible.

This dark-haired woman was barely in her midtwenties and was completely different from her mother. Caroline Riley had looked just like Eden, only with blonde hair rather than the bright red Eden always dyed to a less attention-grabbing auburn.

"I know this comes as a shock, sweetie," the woman said. "But it's true. Maybe you should sit down."

Eden did just that, staggering behind her desk and dropping back into her swivel chair. "What the hell is going on?"

The woman spread her hands. "Okay, so I died."

"I know that part."

"Next thing I know I'm in a holding cell in Hell scared out of my mind. I had no idea why I was there and it truly felt like forever, before they told me I was free. Next thing I know I'm back here, but I had no body. I had to improvise."

"You're a drifter," Darrak said, eyeing her carefully.

The woman eyed him right back. "Is that what I am? Sounds like a good term for it."

Eden's heart sank. A drifter was a bodiless spirit who was able to possess humans at will, pushing aside their consciousness to make way for their own. Unlike Darrak, who was stuck with one human host until their death or his exorcism—or, preferably, his curse removal—a drifter could change bodies as easily as changing their outfit.

Her mother had died three months ago after breaking her neck falling down a flight of stairs in Las Vegas. She already knew Caroline had been sent to Hell. Lucas used her mother as blackmail to get Eden to help him out recently. She'd agreed, albeit reluctantly, and the last she knew her mother's soul had been released.

Eden assumed she'd gone to Heaven.

Instead she'd flitted around until she'd found a suitable body—a young, pretty brunette.

"You look like you've just seen a ghost." Caroline laughed at her own joke. "Listen to me. Still hilarious after everything I've been through. But seriously, thank God I was able to find a body. Otherwise I'd be totally screwed. No way to communicate with you or anyone else. That would be so horrible. You know how much I love to talk."

"Where did you get this body?" Eden said tightly.

She turned in a circle as if modeling a new dress. "She's an aspiring actress. Twenty-three. She's done a little lingerie modeling to pay the rent in the past. Adorable, isn't she? I barely remember having boobs this perky."

"And you just stole her body like it means nothing?"

"Borrowed. There are agencies out there who help set up this sort of thing. Who knew, right? This girl has rented out her body to me for six months. It's not cheap, believe me."

"Are you serious? You rented it?" Eden had never heard of anything like that.

"You think I'd just steal a body? What kind of person do you think I am?" Caroline pouted. "And here I thought you'd be thrilled to see me. Guess I was wrong."

The nausea Eden had felt earlier again rose in her throat. "I don't feel so good."

"Can I do anything to help?" Caroline asked, moving closer.

Eden held up her hand. "You should leave."

"But I just got here."

"Seriously . . . *Caroline*, right?" Darrak said. He'd gone back to finishing off his donut from before. "This is a lot for her to take all at once. It's been a difficult day already."

Caroline's gaze turned sharply toward the demon. "I don't know what your game is, demon, but trust me, now that I'm here you're not going to be able to corrupt my daughter any longer with your evil ways."

Darrak sighed. "Just what I need. A cranky mother-in-law from Hell."

Eden couldn't process this. Her mother hadn't been horrible, but she wasn't exactly a kindhearted woman who'd baked cookies for her only child and been there as a shoulder to cry on or offer up advice when it was needed. No, Caroline Riley was more of a hard-drinking, professional gambler who'd been away more than she'd been at home, who'd paraded a succession of equally unreliable men through their lives as Eden was growing up.

Eden had learned at a very early age how to avoid phone calls from collections agencies, make dinner for herself, and take public transit at the age of ten since Mom wasn't always around to pick her up from a friend's house.

No wonder she had issues with trust and always had a desire for a solitary, peaceful life.

Despite her flakiness, Caroline didn't have a hard or cruel heart. She meant well, really she did. At least, Eden always hoped so.

She eyed the brunette. "Wait a minute. How do I know this isn't some sort of trick?"

The woman frowned. "A trick?"

"I'm just supposed to take this all at face value? Just believe what you're telling me with no proof? I don't think so. I don't know if you're trying to con me by using the grief I feel for my mother—"

"You really felt grief for me, honey?" She looked pleased

by this. "I knew you were angry that we didn't spend much time together anymore. I wasn't sure if you'd be glad I was gone, but you missed me!"

Eden let out an exasperated sigh. "I can't deal with this."

"It's true. I'm here. It's really me. I can prove it . . ." She chewed her bottom lip and looked thoughtful. "You had a teddy bear when you were a kid. You called him Mr. Snuggles."

Eden crossed her arms skeptically. "That's not exactly a huge secret."

"You spilled grape juice on him and I tried to wash him, but he fell apart. You were devastated. We buried him in the backyard and then I bought you that . . . uh, a turtle. A little green turtle."

"And what happened to the turtle?" Eden asked slowly.

She seemed to concentrate for a moment before her expression fell. "Oh, honey. I ran over him with my car."

"And then you tried to pretend that he committed suicide."

She grimaced. "Sorry."

It was enough to prove to her that this woman was her mother possessing the body of a lingerie model. She'd never told anyone what happened to Speedy.

Her mother was back and Eden felt . . . well, Eden didn't know how she felt about that other than feeling a dull ache in the pit of her stomach. She needed time to absorb everything.

Eden directed Caroline toward the door. "We'll get together soon and talk about all of this, I promise. Right now, though . . . I—I just can't deal with a surprise like this."

Caroline looked over her shoulder at Darrak. "I don't know what's going on here, honey. Why are you with this scumbag? Can I do anything? Can I help you?"

"With Darrak?"

"Is that his name? He's a demon, you know."

Eden flinched. "Yeah, well, he's not as bad as you might think."

"Please. I just spent three months in Hell's waiting room.

I think I know a little something about demons. They're evil, vile, disgusting creatures of darkness."

"Stop," Darrak said. "You're making me blush."

"Darrak's different."

Caroline rolled her eyes. "Sure, that's what they all say. So, what? Are you in love with him?"

Eden flicked a glance at him. She had told him she loved him just after she'd nearly lost him forever, but today didn't feel like the right time to say it again. Especially not in front of present company. "We're . . . involved. Deeply."

Caroline's voice lowered to a whisper. "Is he forcing you to do anything you don't want to do?"

She sighed. "No."

"Then what is this? Eden, honey, when did you discover this sordid side of life? Did you summon him for sex?"

That actually earned an amused look from Darrak as he waited patiently for her reply.

"Look, it's not like that. Darrak . . . he—he has a curse. He's bound to me right now."

"Bound to you?" She looked confused and her gaze moved to Darrak.

He crossed his arms. "Yes, your daughter and I met during an unfortunate demonic possession. You know eHarmony? This is sort of the opposite of that."

Caroline's eyes widened. "Oh, my God."

"Not exactly."

"Eden"—Caroline grabbed her shoulders, concern etched into her rented, wrinkle-free face—"what can I do to help you?"

"Help me?" Eden said dryly. "Why would you want to do something like that after nearly thirty years of the exact opposite?"

"Sweetheart . . ."

"This isn't a good time. I'm dealing with a laundry list of problems right now and to have you around, too . . . well, it's not something I need right now. You have to move on. There has to be a way to get you to Heaven."

"I haven't been seeing any tunnels of light. This is it, I think. I'm stuck here in the human world forever."

"Then if you're here forever, we'll have lots of time to catch up later." She hated how dispassionate she felt about this, but she had enough to deal with without adding her estranged mother's presence to the list.

Caroline's mouth thinned to a straight line. "If you think for one moment I'm just going to pretend I don't see what's going on here, and that I don't want to help you, then you're wrong."

"I don't need help."

"You do. You're possessed by a demon." She looked at Darrak. "Strange demonic possession with you standing right there. Didn't know it worked like that."

"It's daylight right now," he told her. "After sunset it's a bit more traditional."

"Disgusting," she spat at him, then turned to Eden again. "How could you let this demon convince you not to exorcise him the moment you had the chance?"

"Oh, I don't know, Mom," Eden said wearily. "Why didn't you tell me my father was an angel?"

Caroline blinked. "Excuse me?"

"An angel? My father—the red-haired guy who came by for a five-minute visit when I was a kid?"

Caroline just gaped at her. "Daniel was a—an *angel*?"

Oh boy. She hadn't known. "Forget I said anything."

"Daniel was a drifter . . . a loser. Nobody I wanted around for long. Sure, he was hot as hell, but it was a mistake I regretted almost immediately." At Eden's sharp look, she added, "Well, I didn't regret *you*. You were a blessing, honey. But that man . . ." She frowned. "An angel? Seriously?"

This wasn't exactly something she'd lie about. "Trust me. He is."

"You've met him recently?"

She shook her head. "Not yet, but the way my week's going, he's probably lurking around the next corner. Look, give me a phone number where I can reach you and we'll get together soon. I promise. We'll figure everything out then."

Caroline grasped her hands. "My daughter, always trying to help other people, putting them before herself."

Eden grimaced. "You make me sound like some sort of saint."

"You are, honey. I never saw it before, but you're truly wonderful. In every way. And you deserve a bright future." She cast a dark look at Darrak. "And anything I have to do to ensure that is exactly what I'll do. Call me, honey. Soon."

Caroline scribbled a phone number down on a scrap piece of paper on Eden's desk and handed it to her. She kissed Eden's cheek and then, shooting an even darker glare in Darrak's direction, left the office.

Eden suddenly felt like having a long nap. For a couple of years.

"So, your mom seems super nice," Darrak said dryly.

She shot him a look. "She's as scattered as she was when she was alive."

"It's adorable."

"No it isn't."

"No, you're right. It isn't. She hates me."

"Don't worry about her. She's harmless. It's a whole 'bark worse than bite' thing."

"Famous last words."

"Let's hope not." Eden noticed he looked disturbed. "You okay?"

"Never better."

"Forget what she said. She doesn't know you."

"She walked in right when I was about to ravish her daughter in the middle of a place of business. Not a great first impression."

"Bad timing, that's all."

Darrak raked a hand through his unruly hair. "I'm going to go next door to see Nancy for another donut and I'll give you some privacy to do your work. We'll talk later."

She was about to argue, but she closed her mouth. He was right. Now was not the right time to plunge back into a ravishment in the middle of the office. The moment had passed.

She nodded. "Later."

Later they'd do many things. One of which, although Darrak didn't know it yet, was for Eden to break his curse first thing tomorrow morning.

Forget "too good to be true." She'd managed to remove the spell with a slightly darker shade to her amulet as the only glitch. She was feeling a renewed sense of confidence.

Maybe their luck was finally on an upswing.

It could happen.

Ben waited at his house for Sandy to arrive. And she finally did, knocking on his front door. He went to answer it and let the blonde witch inside. She immediately threw her arms around him and kissed him.

He'd had a lot of time to think about what he overheard in Oliver's office today. It was possible Sandy was being coerced to act that way. It was also possible she was playing along in order to save her own neck. He was willing to give her the benefit of the doubt.

"How are you?" he asked very seriously, watching for any telltale sign that she was in distress.

"I'm great." She smiled brightly. "I feel like I haven't seen you in ages."

"I guess we've both been busy." Sandy had slept over a couple of nights last week, but this week they'd only seen each other in passing at the Malleus headquarters.

"We need to spend more time with each other."

"I couldn't agree more. You sure you're okay, Sandy?"

She cocked her head. "I honestly can't say I've ever felt better. Things are finally coming together for me, Ben."

"Glad to hear it." So far, even with his trained eye, he couldn't tell if she was being truthful. His gaze moved to her chest. "New necklace?"

She pressed her fingers against the gray pendant hanging on a silver chain. "It's a witch thing."

"Haven't seen it before. It helps you do magic?"

"Something like that." Her smile widened. "But enough about me. I brought you something."

"Oh? What is it?"

"Some soup I made special for you. Chicken noodle."

He took the Tupperware bowl from her. The soup was still warm, filled with chicken, noodles and—according to the conversation he'd heard earlier—a large helping of love potion.

His stomach sank. He'd hoped she wasn't trying to deceive him, but his confidence was slipping with every moment she stood in front of him with that shiny smile on her face.

Her words from earlier replayed in his head:

"He's a noble guy. Stupid, stubborn, and boring, but very noble."

He might be noble, stubborn, and boring, but he was far from stupid.

Ben forced a smile and placed it down on the glass table next to his leather couch. "Smells delicious. Thank you. I'll have it for dinner later."

She nodded. "Good. Make sure to think of me when you take your first spoonful."

"I'm always thinking of you, Sandy."

Her smile widened. "Oh, Ben, what did I do to deserve somebody like you?"

You were assigned the task of making me fall in love with you so the Malleus could use that weakness to keep me in line.

He'd grown very fond of Sandy since he'd first met her, but love was something he didn't feel for the witch. Especially not at this very moment.

Disappointment and betrayal, yes. Love? No thanks.

"Fate," he said instead. "It works in mysterious ways."

She looked back at the door. "I can't stay, I've got so many things to do today."

"Listen, Sandy, before you go, can I ask you a question?"

"Sure."

"The angel in the basement of the Malleus. He's still there—it's been over two weeks now. He has red hair, and his feathers are being plucked daily from his wings. It seems to weaken him. He looks very ill. Do you know what's going on?"

She cocked her head to the side. "Why would the Malleus imprison an angel?"

"Maybe it's an evil angel."

"An evil angel?" she laughed. "I've never heard of anything like that before."

"Well, Eden seems to think her demon is a nice one." Even saying it aloud made Ben grimace. He had major issues when it came to Darrak and had committed himself to destroying the demon at his earliest convenience. So far it hadn't been all that convenient. "If that's true, then maybe it works the other way around."

"Eden is living in a fantasy world. One that is going to inevitably lead to her death. You know that, I know that, and the Malleus knows that."

"I still don't understand why we're not intervening in that matter more forcefully."

"Black witches are dangerous."

He already knew that about Eden from firsthand experience. He'd really prefer to keep his head attached to his body if possible. "But she needs help. Why can't the Malleus help her?"

"Oliver still wants to know how the celestial energy is affecting the demon. He has a lead on more information. Nothing's going to be done until he acquires that information. That's all I can say right now, Ben."

Everything revolved around that damn demon. "So you don't know anything about the angel."

Sandy sighed. "The only prisoner I know about is the shapeshifter we brought in yesterday. And let me tell you, she's a real bitch to deal with."

Was she referring to the woman with the almond-shaped eyes and mocha-colored skin who'd glared at him from the shadows of her cell? "A bitch?"

She nodded. "Evil to the core."

"Yeah?" Bitch, he'd believe. Evil might be a stretch, despite his telling her she probably belonged in a locked room. That unpleasant exchange had stayed with him since he'd walked away from her earlier. "Why do you think she's evil?"

"She has something to do with Eden Riley and that demon of hers. Oliver thinks the shifter has information that could help the Malleus, but she won't talk. She refuses to help us."

"What's her name?"

Sandy crossed her arms. "She won't tell us even that. We tried bribing her, but nothing. My magic doesn't work on shifters to help coax the truth. Tomorrow we're going to have to get more serious with her. Oliver is going to want you there. He wants to introduce you to the more high level intel extraction methods."

He didn't like the sound of that. "I'm supposed to be a part of this?"

"You're involved in the Eden Riley case already. If she talks to you, it won't be too bad for her."

Ben watched her carefully. "And you're okay with that? With these high level intel extraction methods?"

It was a nice, fancy way to describe torture.

She met his serious gaze and he saw nothing in her eyes to indicate any doubt or worry. "It's all for the greater good, Ben."

"Right. The greater good." Ben couldn't believe he'd felt something for this woman who stood before him. It was as if the curtain had been pulled back from in front of his eyes showing the messy stage behind it. He'd thought Sandy was one of the good guys—one of the best of them all, actually.

But maybe she was just another hammer.

What the hell had he gotten himself into?

He had no friends, no one to confide in. A brand on his arm that still itched, that bound him to an organization he'd quickly come to doubt—one that used medieval methods in modern times to prove their way was the right way. The only way.

The greater good.

Ben wanted to do the right thing. He *did*. He wanted to help others more than anything in the world.

But this—it felt wrong to him. So wrong.

"I'll be there, too," Sandy assured him. "For moral support."

"Thanks. I—I appreciate that."

"Eat your soup. Know that I made it with love in my heart."

He nodded. "Can't wait."

"I'll call you later." She went up on tiptoe and brushed her lips against his. Then, with a last flash of a bright smile, she slipped through the front door.

It only took Ben a minute to pour the soup down his garbage disposal.

He'd definitely lost his appetite.

⇒ SIX ⇐

After he left Eden to her busy office-workings, Darrak was a bit surprised to see Stanley sitting at a table at Hot Stuff. Although it did make sense. After all, his brand-new fiancée worked behind the counter.

Two words: free coffee.

Stanley spotted Darrak and immediately turned to study the wall as if looking for a crack to crawl into.

"Relax," Darrak said as he approached the nervous-looking man. Other than Stanley there were a half dozen other customers in the small, delicious-smelling café. "I come in peace."

"Sure. Great." Stanley ran a hand through his thinning hair. "Glad to hear it. Hey, Darrak, how are tricks?"

"Tricks are for kids. Or wizards."

"Oh, right. You—you saw Maksim earlier, didn't you?"

"I did indeed. Believe it or not, he helped us. More than I even thought possible."

"Thank God."

"Or whomever." Darrak cast a glance over at Nancy behind the glass counter filled with pastries, who in turn was sending a look of love and devotion toward Stanley. "So you and Nancy are tying the knot, huh?"

Stanley gripped his coffee mug tighter and leaned back in his seat. "We are."

"Your idea or hers?"

"Mine."

"Really? I didn't think you were that into her."

"Things change quickly. I love her. I know it's crazy and fast, but that's just the way it is. I'm an old-fashioned guy."

"I never would have thought it."

"Maybe you should do the same with Eden."

Darrak frowned. "What?"

Stanley shrugged. "Ask her to marry you. Why not? I get the feeling you're into each other."

That was a thought. A completely insane—if vaguely intriguing—thought. Ask Eden to marry him? Stanley had been drinking one too many espressos today.

"Not so sure about that, but thanks for your opinion."

"When I found the right girl, I knew I'd want to spend the rest of my life with her. Whammo. That girl is Nancy. And here we are."

"Here we are."

"I'm going to leave." Stanley cast a plaintive look toward the exit.

"Don't go on my account."

"Oh, no. This has nothing to do with you. I, uh, have a bunch of things I need to take care of."

"I'm not going to hurt you, Stanley. Seriously. Just chill. What's your problem, anyway?" Darrak was starting to get a complex. If he wanted someone to be scared of him, then that was one thing. A flash of talon or horn from his demonic visage usually did the trick. But this was . . . weird.

So much for making friends and influencing people without even trying. This was more like terrorizing and traumatizing.

"I don't want to go to Hell," Stanley blurted out. "I've done some bad things in my life, but now that I've found Nancy, I've found a reason to redeem myself. Spending time with . . . well, with *demons* isn't going to earn me any brownie points."

Darrak took a seat across from him. "You think I have any pull down there anymore?"

"You're a demon."

"Uh . . . yeah. And your point?"

"I know you're not dragging anyone's ass to Hell at the moment, but that might change at any time."

Interesting point. There was a time, not so long ago, that Darrak had been convinced that this was temporary, this humanity that infused him, making him feel guilty about anything remotely demonic he did. He'd been certain once the curse that destroyed his original form was broken, when he was able to reform himself on a permanent basis, his old ways would return in full force.

But that wasn't going to happen. He had it on very good authority.

Darrak was a changed man. A demon with morals.

Which obviously sucked for way too many reasons to count.

He tried not to think about it. Accepting it was not something he was ready to do yet, but he'd have to eventually.

The main problem was that morals got in the way when it came to life in the proverbial basement. It wasn't such a nice place, depending on how you looked at it, but from a normal demon's eyes, it was business as usual. If Darrak returned to the pit with his new outlook on life, he might start trying to rescue the damned souls who'd been sent there. The ones that screamed the loudest, anyway. That sound wouldn't be quite as melodic anymore. It would actually bother him to hear anyone in agony like that, whether they deserved it or not.

Maybe he'd just try to steer clear of the main hot spots. So to speak.

As if going back to Hell was even an option for him. What a laugh. As soon as he stepped foot anywhere within the Netherworld, he'd be exposed for what he was—a freak of nature. He was now an outcast, a hybrid, a demon with humanity and a bit too much celestial energy he'd digested, thanks to Eden, that he needed to burn off before he could go anywhere near Hell again undetected.

What a mess.

Quite honestly, the only thing keeping him from gnashing his teeth, or whatever, about this situation was Eden.

He knew the love he felt for her weakened him, made him less of a demon. And the craziest thing was he really couldn't care less. He'd never experienced something like this before. Ever. And it made him . . . happy.

At least, when it wasn't making him completely miserable.

Ah, love, Darrak thought. *I could totally write one of those sexy romance novels if I wanted to.*

Hmm. That might be a good idea, actually.

He heard somebody whimpering. He looked up from his thoughts and realized he had Stanley's wrist in a death grip. He let go immediately, no harm done.

"Hey, baby!" Nancy called over from the counter. "Everything okay over there?"

"Oh . . . yeah. No problem. Just chatting with Darrak."

"Cool! Darrak you want another donut?"

"I'm good, thanks," Darrak said. *Good.* Well, that might be an overstatement, really.

Nancy sent another shiny smile their way before she moved to answer the phone.

Darrak cast a look at the man tensely sitting across from him. "Look, Stanley, listen to me and I want you to hear the words coming out of my mouth. I'm not going to hurt you, maim you, eviscerate you, or otherwise bother you. I am not going to kill you and drag your soul to Hell. I do not like green eggs and ham. Et cetera. Get it through your head."

Stanley frowned. "So you're being totally serious with me. The rumors are true that you've changed."

"Uh-huh. Wait, you've heard rumors?"

He shrugged. "A few from, uh, *Maksim*. He called this morning to let me know he was back, which was why I was so surprised to hear from you immediately afterward."

Darrak grimaced. Another mark against him that made him feel like less than his once-powerful self. "Perfect timing."

"Are you going to see Maksim again?"

"Not sure. I got a bad vibe off him, and I don't mean that as a compliment. For his sake, I hope he wasn't screwing around with us."

"Will you hurt him if he was?"

A slow smile snaked across Darrak's face. "You know, everyone always assumes all a demon ever cares about is violence and mayhem and the sound of tearing flesh. But, trust me, that's actually only 95 percent of the time. We do have a few other hobbies, you know."

The look of horror that crossed Stanley's face shouldn't have amused him, but it did anyway. Maybe he was still evil down deep.

It was a comforting thought, actually.

Eden spent the day organizing Andy's files. It was what she typically did on Thursdays, nice mindless work—mostly deciphering her partner's lousy handwriting. She went out midafternoon to Hot Stuff to grab a sandwich, which sat heavily in her queasy stomach.

Stomach flu. Definitely.

She had to look on the bright side—she'd removed Darrak's spell. That was a huge step in the right direction and it made today a wonderful one.

Visit from dead mother and darkening amulet notwithstanding.

Her mother was back. Her dead mother had returned from both the grave and Hell itself to show up on her doorstep. This revelation brought with it conflicting emotions in Eden. On one side she was glad Caroline had survived her trip to Lucas's domain unscathed. It showed that he did follow through with his promise to release her. On the other hand, the last thing Eden·needed right now was a mother set on redemption who wanted to pitch in and help save her daughter from the big bad demon.

She'd deal with Caroline, and of course she'd want to see her again and try to work things out between the two of them. Just not today. Today she needed to deal with the black magic. If only it didn't come at so heavy a price, she would use it for just about anything. Housework would be a breeze, for instance. And cooking. And getting dressed. She'd be Samantha Stephens and Darrak could be Darrin. A happy couple who made the differences between them work, no matter what.

Happy couple.

Was that possible? Did they really have a future together, despite how many odds were stacked against them?

It sounded like a pipe dream at best to a realist like Eden. There were just too many difficulties for her to just ignore.

Love didn't fix everything, even if she really, really wished it could.

But still, she couldn't help but be hopeful.

When it was close to sunset, it was time to shut down the office and go get Darrak and leave before his curse hit and he lost corporeal form. Eden grabbed her coat from the rack near the door and slid it on, grabbed her purse and slung it over her shoulder, then reached into her pocket for her keys. Something else was in the pocket, something small and hard; for a moment she didn't know what it was until she pulled it out.

A marble.

She looked at it. "I don't remember putting you in my pocket."

The marble immediately heated up and she squinted against the bright light it emanated.

"Oh—" she began, but by the time she finished she wasn't in the Triple-A office anymore— "shit!"

Eden was now standing on a beach.

The marble was a summoning crystal given to her a

couple of weeks ago. It always brought her here, to a place that looked exactly like a beautiful tropical beach at sunset, with ocean waves lapping gently against the shore, golden sand, and a warm breeze scented with papaya and lilies.

She'd just been summoned here, to a place that didn't actually exist in real life.

And she already knew by whom.

Another feeling of queasiness went through her, but this had very little to do with a stomach flu. Turning her head slightly to the right she saw him approach from down the beach. He wore white pants and a white shirt. No shoes. He was smiling.

A shiver raced down her spine.

"Hello Eden," Lucas said.

She cleared her throat. "What am I doing here?"

"You're looking well."

"Thank you. What am I doing here?"

"You think I sent for you?"

That's exactly what she thought, and it made her nervous. "Did you predict I'd touch the marble just now?"

"I'm afraid I'm not capable of predicting the future, so no. A gift like that would come in handy, though, I have to say."

"I guess I find it difficult to believe that someone like you doesn't have that ability."

He laughed. "Oh? I guess my reputation gives the impression I'm much more powerful than I really am."

This was one of the biggest problems with Lucas. He was so disarming, so charming, so friendly. Even the way he looked—or chose to look when in Eden's presence— didn't help. Short brown hair, a bit shaggy. Warm brown eyes. A very attractive, but not intimidatingly handsome face. He looked like the perfect guy next door.

He'd also nearly destroyed Darrak with a mere thought the last time they'd been face-to-face. Lucas might be charming, but the Prince of Hell didn't take disappointment very well.

He was powerful, dangerously so, even if he didn't readily admit it.

Eden felt a great need to fill the uncomfortable silence that fell between them. "My mother is back."

"Is she?"

"I think you already know that. She's a drifter now."

"You don't seem pleased by this."

"I'm not. How do I get her to Heaven?"

He studied her. "You don't. She is where she needs to be. Her soul is an in-between case, Eden. Not dark enough for me to keep in Hell indefinitely, but not light enough for her to ascend to Heaven."

"So she stays in the human world forever?"

"The slate is not cleared for Caroline Riley, but this is a chance for her to redeem herself—or damn herself further. Her actions now will tilt her one way or another. And one day she might be given the chance to move on, be it up or down. It's nice to have choices. It's something I never got."

Eden wasn't going to touch that bitter comment with a ten-foot pole. Lucas had issues when it came to his fate. She had no idea how many years, centuries, millennia it had been since the original fallen angel was first sent down to Hell, but he had a chip on his shoulder the size of the planet Jupiter about it.

"Fine. So I guess I'm stuck with my mother."

"You saved her soul. Does she even know that?"

"No. And I'm not planning on telling her."

"So modest." He walked a slow circle around her, and she felt very uncomfortable as his gaze slid leisurely over her.

"Why am I here, Lucas?"

"I like that you call me Lucas. It makes me feel more human."

"No comment."

"But you're right. I did want to see you. Approaching you when Darrak's around probably isn't such a good idea."

She snorted. "Believe it or not, he mentioned you earlier today. Said that I should—"

She clamped her mouth shut before she finished that sentence. Perhaps it was best not to venture into that territory.

"Said you should what?" Lucas's scrutiny was almost palpable as he took another turn around her like a circling shark scenting an injured seal. His gaze finally fell on her amulet. "Maybe I can guess why my name was brought up."

She clamped a hand over it. "Are you a mind reader, too?"

"Another ability that would prove extremely useful. No, Eden, I can't predict the future and I can't read minds. But I've existed for a very long time and my skills of deduction are second to none. Your amulet is darker. You've been using your magic again."

Eden thought about the curse removal she wanted to attempt tomorrow morning. "I need to use it."

"Even knowing the consequences."

"Yes."

Lucas's lips twisted with amusement. "Was it Darrak who suggested you kiss me again so I can take some of that darkness away or was it you?"

Her cheeks warmed. "Neither."

"Liar." Then the humor faded from his expression. "Drinking your darkness goes against my ultimate plan, Eden. I want to get back to Heaven, not push myself farther away."

"Then it's a good thing I'm not asking you for anything." She focused on the ocean and the sunset that didn't rise or lower from its eternal position. "I need to go back now. I have things to do."

"Like attempting to break Darrak's curse?"

She stifled a gasp. "How do you know that?"

"Skills of deduction, remember?" His smile returned. "Have you told him what your delicious celestial energy has done to him yet?"

Eden blanched. "The subject hasn't come up."

"It will destroy what little sense of self he still has left. The ego is very important to demons—especially lesser ones."

"I disagree."

"Then why haven't you told him yet?"

Frustration pricked at her. She turned away from Lucas

to study the calming waves of the ocean. "I have to get back. He'll wonder where I've gone."

"No he won't. I'll return you within the same millisecond that you left."

This earned him a look. "Really?"

He nodded. "Or . . . maybe I should return you a hundred years from now. I might not see the future or read minds, but I do have certain abilities. Keeping you away from him at sunset would certainly help break his ties to you, wouldn't it? He'd be sent directly to the Void if he can't find a new body to possess in time."

There was a veiled threat behind the softly spoken words. He was right. Lucas was in control—he was always in control. He could tear Eden and Darrak apart with only a thought, he had that much power over them.

Eden struggled to breathe normally. "You brought me here for a reason, so let's get to it. Enough small talk."

He studied her for a moment before nodding. "Fine. When we were last together I told you that you worked for me now. You owe me for how things worked out last time."

Lucas had wanted to get his hands on a weapon—a diamond that had been infused with celestial energy called an angelheart. With it he planned to kill his inner beast, the anchor that kept him trapped in Hell. He called that beast Satan. Eden hadn't met Satan—Lucas's split personality—but from what she'd heard, she never wanted to. Eden gave him the diamond, but its power had already been spent and it was useless to him.

To make up for this, she was now his Girl Friday.

"What do you need me to do?" It would be futile to try to deny him or say no to whatever came next. The best thing for her to do was hear him out and then figure out a way to do it.

Lucas pulled a small card out of his pocket. "There's someone I need you to find for me."

She took the card from him. "It's blank."

"I know."

"Why is it blank?"

"Because this person has been cloaked from me. The details are written on that card, but I cannot see it. It will remain blank for as long as I'm near it." His lips thinned. "Which is why I need you."

"Okay." It didn't make sense to her, but she wasn't going to argue. She needed to get back to Darrak before sunset. "Why me?"

"You're a private investigator. I assume you'll be able to find a missing person with a little bit of digging and a couple clues. All I do know is that they can be found somewhere in your city."

Seemed shaky reasoning at best, but she kept her lips sealed. Lucas would have an arsenal of demons to send out to do his dirty work. Why use her?

"Why do you want this person?"

"I want to talk to them."

"About what?"

"That's my own business."

"Just talk?" She looked at him skeptically. "Not torture? Not imprison in Hell? Not use against someone else?"

He held her gaze steadily. "Just talk."

"About what?"

His jaw tightened, but he didn't answer her. He pulled a silver chain out of his pocket and put it in her palm. It looked like a charm bracelet without the charms. "You'll place this on his or her wrist."

"And then what?"

"That's it."

She looked at the chain. "Sounds too simple."

"Are you refusing to do this for me?"

"And if I do?" she asked, then flicked her eyes to meet his. His expression didn't change.

"I suggest you don't."

He sounded so pleasant, but the threat was there. This man—this *thing*—in front of her might not be able to read minds or see the future, but he was the most powerful being she'd ever met. And if she could help it, she'd rather not piss him off anytime soon.

"When does it have to be done?"

"Tomorrow. Right after your attempt to remove Darrak's curse."

She looked at him sharply, but bit her tongue. He couldn't see the future, but he knew way too much about her. It made her extremely nervous.

"Will you do this for me?" he asked.

"I can't believe you're actually giving me a choice."

"You need to say yes, or this isn't a binding agreement. And you need to do so of your own free will."

"Will you destroy Darrak if I don't agree to this?"

He didn't speak for a very long moment. Then finally, "No. But know this, Eden. It's your choice if I'm your friend or your enemy. And trust me, you don't want me to be your enemy."

She had absolutely no doubt about that. "I'll look for your guy tomorrow. I promise."

"Glad to hear it."

She turned away to look at the ocean. "Now I need to get back to—"

Lucas pulled her around to face him and before she could say anything, he crushed his mouth against hers. She gasped against his lips as he kissed her and her hands went up against his chest to push him back. He was smiling when she managed to break away, but his eyes were black—fully black.

"Damn," he said. "Wish that didn't taste so good."

She touched her fingertips to her mouth. "I didn't ask you to do that."

"Good-bye, Eden." He snapped his fingers.

She'd been dismissed.

A bright flash of light and she stood in the Triple-A office. She staggered back a few feet until she felt the edge of her desk behind her.

A moment later, the door jingled open and Darrak walked in. He looked at her standing there in shock, clutching the silver bracelet.

"Did I miss something?" he asked with a frown.

"I—I had a visitor. Sort of."

His gaze moved to her amulet, and his expression turned tense and concerned. Fire flared up—literally—in his previously ice blue eyes. "Lucifer was here."

"Not exactly. He summoned me. He said it was only a millisecond." She glanced at the clock. No more than five minutes had passed. Not a millisecond, but close enough. "He gave me an assignment. Wants me to find a guy for him and put this on his wrist." She raised the bracelet.

He appeared to relax slightly now that he knew she was unharmed, but there was nothing pleasant in his gaze. "Pretty. So was that before or after he stuck his tongue down your throat?"

"Uh . . . before. And there was no tongue."

"Glad you thought my idea to kiss him again was a good one after all."

"I didn't ask for that. He just did it."

"Well, that was nice of him, wasn't it? So helpful, the Prince of Hell. A real swell guy."

"Don't, Darrak," she warned. The desk legs squeaked against the floor as she pushed away from it. "Seriously. I'm not feeling up to this right now. You don't have to be jealous about this. Of all the people in the universe I'd like to kiss, he's not even on the list."

He frowned. "I know that. This is actually much worse than a little jealousy. You've become an object to him. Something he now desires."

She shook her head. "He doesn't feel that way toward me."

"It's not as simple as him wanting to have sex with you. Trust me. That guy could have his pick of anyone in the universe if he wanted. But he wants you. There's something about you he's drawn to. He doesn't do nice things just because. He's freaking Lucifer, Eden. He's up to something. Some master plan. And it has to do with you."

Her breath caught. "What?"

"I don't know. But even with our bond, he has the ability

to snatch you away and I can't protect you. I don't like that at all."

"I can handle him."

"Really? You can handle Lucifer, the Prince of Hell." He didn't sound like he held much faith in that statement. He paced over to the glass door and looked out at the darkening parking lot.

Could she handle him? Maybe it was a good time for a little bit of optimism. "Sure I can. Why not?"

His brow furrowed. "It—it's time, Eden."

"Time for—?"

"What do you think?" Darrak clamped his hand over his stomach and doubled over. He nodded toward the window. Outside the sun had sunk beneath the horizon. Night came early in mid-November.

A moment later, his body shifted from a solid six-foot-tall handsome man to an ominous column of black smoke, which then moved through the office toward her as if she was a magnet.

Eden swallowed hard. "Tomorrow, Darrak. I'm going to break this curse first thing tomorrow morning once and for all. I swear I will."

She closed her eyes when the smoke made contact with her and a gasp caught in her throat as he possessed her.

Being possessed by Darrak had always felt good in the past—warm and oddly orgasmic. Today it felt different. It was cold for a moment, as if she had just walked through a freezer, before the cool sensation moved through her limbs right down to her fingertips and toes.

It had to do with the spell she'd removed. That the sensation of being possessed had changed was only more proof she'd been successful. Realizing for certain that what she'd experienced for the last month was a daily anomaly caused by a malevolent spell brought back her previously queasy feeling.

Queasy was definitely the word of the week for many reasons. Terrific.

So, being possessed wasn't an orgasmic experience anymore. Fine. But it was more proof that she'd be able to successfully break the curse, finally giving Darrak—and her—freedom.

And that was definitely worth celebrating.

"You really think you can break the curse?" Darrak said, his voice now in her head.

"Yes, I do."

He was quiet for a long, tense moment. "One try. That's all. And if there's even a glimpse of anything bad, we stop. Maksim saying it could work doesn't mean a damn thing. I don't trust that wizard."

If it wasn't for Maksim, she wouldn't even have attempted the spell removal. "He was trying to help us."

"Right. Which is pretty much why I don't trust him. Wizards aren't usually the most helpful types."

"But you're not going to attempt to stop me. One try. You said so yourself."

"Yeah, fine. But if anything weird happens, we're pulling the plug."

Anything weird.

That was the story of her life lately. Why should tomorrow be any different?

SEVEN

Someone followed Eden home, and that made her very nervous.

Maybe it was the Malleus—led by Ben Hanson, former crush. They were nasty, horrible people who had conned themselves into believing they were the good guys, but they weren't. Not even close.

It could be Lucas keeping tabs on her, which would explain how he seemingly knew everything without the ability to see the future. However, that was unlikely. If he was the one following her, she doubted she'd even realize it.

It might even be Leena, her ex-roommate, a feline shapeshifter who'd disappeared two weeks ago after a disagreement with Darrak, leaving only a note behind and a key to a locker containing some of her belongings. Her departure only proved that three was a crowd when it came to paranormal beings cohabiting a one-bedroom apartment.

But it was none of these.

It turned out to be her mother—the twenty-three-year-old lingerie model version, anyway. She drove a sports car like some sort of life-size Barbie doll and pulled up right next to Eden in her apartment parking lot.

"So where's the demon right now?" Caroline asked, following a silent Eden to the elevators.

"Around."

"I guess she isn't going to wait for your call," Darrak said from inside of her. "What's it been, six whole hours?"

"Guess not."

"What, honey?" Caroline asked.

"Nothing. Look . . . uh, Mom"—it felt so strange calling this woman that—"we need to talk another day."

"My God. He said at night he . . ." Caroline's eyes widened. "That demon is possessing you *right now*, isn't he?"

Eden grimaced. "It's really not as bad as it sounds."

Caroline hugged her tightly. "Oh, sweetie. I can't believe this is happening to you. I'm so sorry for all of what you've been through."

"It's not exactly your fault. Besides, it's almost over."

"It is? You're having him exorcised?"

"I have a strange feeling I'm not going to win her over with my charm and good looks," Darrak observed.

Eden repressed a grimace. "I'm not having Darrak exorcised."

"How can you be so calm about this? You're *possessed*, honey. By a demon from the fiery depths of Hell!"

Luckily there was no one else in the lobby to overhear her—admittedly true—ravings.

"Calm isn't what I am," Eden said. "But Darrak and I have a mutual understanding. And we're finding a solution. Sooner than you think, actually."

"And how am I supposed to be convinced that he's not manipulating your emotions? Did he seduce you? I know demons. I know how persuasive they can be when it comes to converting one to their sexual deviance. Bondage is meant to be done between two consenting adults, not between a victim and a vile minion of Lucifer."

"Stop her," Darrak said dryly. "I'm getting all turned on."

Eden cringed. "I'm not talking about this, Mom. Not with you."

Caroline's bottom lip wobbled. "I'd do anything for you, Eden, you know that, don't you?"

Anything. Funny, it hadn't felt like that when Caroline had been alive. In her own body. Frankly, it felt as if Eden had been a big burden on her mother's free-spirit lifestyle. Carting a kid around when you never called one place home for more than a few months wasn't exactly ideal to establishing a stable childhood.

Eden exhaled. "Mom, I need you to hear me. Will you listen for just a moment?"

"Of course."

Eden turned to face her directly. "I don't need your help. And I don't *want* your help. I can handle this like I've handled everything else for my entire life. You can't march in here and expect that you can make everything right that went wrong when you were alive. I know you're trying to redeem yourself, but you can start somewhere else. Not with me."

She expected this speech to finally get through to her mother and make her understand. Instead, Caroline's eyes flashed.

"Well, that's too damn bad. Because I'm here. And I'm going to help you whether you like it or not. I might have been a lousy mother—"

"I'm not saying that." Not out loud, anyway.

Caroline raised her hand. "Whatever. I'm not an idiot. I know things weren't ideal when you were growing up. But you turned into a fine woman. I'm not going to say it was my doing, but this is where we are now. I don't know what this demon has been telling you, but it's sick what's going on here. I guess I have just enough clarity to see that. I'm not leaving until I can do something to help fix this. It's all I want, Eden. I want you to be happy."

"I am happy," Eden gritted out. "Ecstatic, in fact."

"Are you in love with that nasty demon? Tell me."

She let out a breath of exasperation. "Would that make a difference to you?"

"It might."

"I care very deeply for him. Yes, I—I love him."

"You don't sound convinced about that."

"I guess I don't like being put on the spot when it comes to discussing my feelings. Especially not with someone who's always had the habit of stomping on them whenever she has the chance."

Finally, Caroline flinched. "I'm sorry you feel that way. Fine, I'll leave. But this isn't over."

She turned and stomped back toward the sports car. Eden watched until she'd driven out of the parking lot, squealing her wheels.

"I think we're making progress with her," Darrak said. "And by progress I mean the opposite of that. What's the opposite of progress?"

"That."

"Yeah."

She was quiet for a long moment. She couldn't help but feel guilt at pushing her mother away, even though she knew it was the right thing to do. There wasn't much more to say. She'd been blunt. Perhaps too blunt.

It was done. And Caroline didn't seem completely deterred in her newfound mission.

Save her possessed daughter.

But Eden was already attempting to save herself. And she might even have the tools to do just that.

"Tomorrow, at dawn, before we go and find the missing person for Lucas, I'm breaking your curse once and for all."

"Is that a promise or a threat?" he asked warily.

She thought it was a promise, but suddenly she just wasn't all that sure anymore.

If it was possible to pace while in a noncorporeal state inside the body of a beautiful, yet frustrating woman, that was exactly what Darrak did while Eden slept.

Pacing. Back and forth.

He might even say he was fretting. He didn't think he'd ever fretted before. It was a word that had only been added to his vocabulary tonight.

Fretting sucked.

She was so damned motivated to try to break this curse. She'd broken the spell relatively easily—so easily it made his head swim. Not that he'd have a head until the morning, but a head was implied.

She wasn't going to take no for an answer. Besides, why would he even say no? This was exactly what he wanted.

Freedom. Something that had sounded like a pipe dream for so long might actually become a reality.

And then what?

Darrak wasn't much of a "look deeply into the future" kind of guy. He liked to live in the now.

Okay. So what *now*?

He had to deal with Lucifer. That wasn't now, but it would be soon. Lucifer was his boss—a boss that Darrak had screwed over once too often. A big lesson he'd learned recently was if you were going to screw over a boss, please try your best not to make it Lucifer, the Prince of Hell.

Yeah. Lesson learned.

Darrak didn't feel the immediate need to head back to Hell anytime soon, of course. He wouldn't be welcomed there anyway until he got rid of the celestial energy churning inside him. He had no idea how long it would take before he would be able to enter the Netherworld undetected. Possibly a very long time. In the meanwhile, he'd have to get used to living here in the human world.

He couldn't help but wonder if Eden would want him around after their ties were finally cut. This was something he tried very hard not to think about much, especially after hearing her awkwardly answer the "Do you love the hell-spawn?" comment from her mother. Eden had answered in the affirmative, which was nice to hear. But it hadn't exactly been delivered with a great deal of enthusiasm.

Ah, self-doubt, he thought. *There you are again. Awesome.*

He hated that he felt this way, that he'd spend even a moment of his energy on this particular problem, but there it was. The uncertainty about whether a woman was head over heels in love with him.

How sad.

Even sadder was the fact that he knew, without a shadow of a doubt, that what Eden really felt about him was only a fraction of what he felt for her. Perhaps it was the fact he'd never been in love before that made his emotions so acute, so strong, so impossible to ignore. He wasn't a puppy dog, ready to roll over and bare his belly the moment he thought she might give him a scratch. He wasn't *that* whipped. But he knew he'd do just about anything for her.

And if, when all was said and done, she wanted them to part ways, then that was exactly what he'd do. As the saying went, if you love someone you should let them go, and if they didn't return you should hunt them down and . . .

No, wait. That was a different saying. The original one was that if they didn't come back then they never were yours to begin with.

Thus, the fretting.

Even Stanley, of all people, had been hit by the love stick when he'd least expected it, and it had changed the direction of his life forever. Well, Nancy did know how to make an excellent donut, that was for sure.

All Darrak knew for absolute certain was that he cared for Eden more than anything in the world. And the fact that she'd become a person of interest to Lucifer didn't sit well with him. Lucifer might have a very disarming face here in the human world, but that didn't make him any less dangerous.

He just wished he knew what to do about that.

It felt like a very long time before the sun began to rise. He knew the moment it happened, because it hit him like a lightning bolt before surrounding his incorporeal form like a clawed hand, tearing him from the darkness and wrenching him up through to the physical world.

Eden gasped in her sleep as he was expelled from her body. Immediately he began to take form, his essence rebuilding itself in the image of whom he'd been before, so very long ago. Tall, demonic, and handsome, limbs in all the right positions. It was effortless and yet exhausting at the same time.

A few moments later he found himself lying next to her on her bed. A feeling of relief and calm swept over him.

Eden appeared to smile in her sleep, and she slid a hand over his bare chest. He covered it with his own hand, not wanting to break the moment. It did surprise him that she was able to sleep through this every morning—*almost* every morning, unless she was already awake.

"Today is special, I feel it," he whispered to her. "It's the beginning, not the end."

She grunted a soft reply, but didn't stir further. In her sleep she wasn't consumed with worry or anxiety over their unusual situation. Eden slept very soundly for a woman who had to deal with an unwanted demonic possession and a million other problems since he'd come into her life.

Today could go very well. Darrak tried to hold on to that thought.

It was an important Friday. First he'd walk her through the curse breaking. One way or another, after that they would find Lucifer's missing person to check that chore off the list and get him off their backs for a bit longer.

And tonight was also the full moon.

Andy was scheduled to turn into a werewolf at approximately the same time Darrak would next lose form. That was, if they were unable to break the curse this morning.

Let's think positively, he told himself.

"Darrak . . ." Eden whispered, her eyes still closed.

She often talked in her sleep, saying all sorts of interesting things.

He drew closer, bringing his head to rest on her pillow. "Yes, Eden?"

"What am I going to do . . ."

"What are you going to do . . . ?" he prompted when she trailed off.

". . . without you?"

"I'm not going anywhere." He frowned at the strange statement and studied her face. "Do you love me, Eden?"

His breath caught and held as he waited for her answer as if he was a teenage human boy looking for the girl he liked to confirm she would go to the prom with him. She was very honest when she was asleep.

"I want you," she murmured. "I need you . . . yes . . ."

"All good to know. But what about . . ." Oh hell, what was he doing? Trying to coax some sort of oath of love and devotion from an unconscious woman? "Forget it."

"When you're gone I'll be all alone again . . ."

"Gone?" He frowned again. "Where am I going?"

"I love . . ." she whispered.

His attention grew fixed on her again. "Yes? What do you love?"

"When you . . . make love to me. Want it . . . please . . . again . . ."

Okay, so she wanted him for his body. It was nice to know. But oddly empty. Nice. But empty. Kind of like how he felt after eating one of Nancy's chocolate donuts.

"You want me?" he said.

"Yes, so much . . ."

"There's no more spell to stop us anymore."

Her hands slid over his chest to his shoulders. "No more spell."

"Wake up, Eden." He stroked the long strands of dark red hair off her forehead. He studied her face, as if committing it to memory. Every part of her, right down to the very faint and adorable freckle just under her right eye, burned into him for the rest of his existence—a scorch mark where his soul would be if he actually had one.

Instead, she had become his soul.

Damn. He really *should* start writing those romance novels. He'd kick ass at it.

Her eyelashes fluttered, and her sleepy gaze took in the sight of him lying next to her. This didn't happen anymore, not since he'd been trying to be well behaved. Too dangerous to be this close when there had been nasty spells to contend with.

"Darrak . . ." she whispered.

"That's my name."

For a moment he thought she'd pull back from him. It was what she'd done in the beginning, when she'd woken to find her unconscious self had been getting a bit too close for comfort with a naked demon.

But she didn't pull back. Just the opposite, actually. She pulled his face closer to hers and kissed him hard and deep. He didn't try to stop her.

Eden loved him for his body, for how he made her feel when they had sex.

That wasn't all this was. It wasn't.

Come on, Darrak, he admonished himself. *Can't you just enjoy the ride and stop second-guessing everything?*

He could enjoy the ride. Sure he could.

Her cold amulet pressed against his chest as her lips moved down his throat. Lucifer had kissed her behind his back, sweeping her away to some alternate dimension so he wouldn't be around to disrupt them. It bothered Darrak a lot, and it wasn't because he was jealous.

Then again, jealousy wouldn't be completely unheard of. Lucifer might be the ultimate hellish asshole, but he *was* a prince. Influential, powerful, and if he really did have a thing for Eden, the things he could give her . . .

Oh, this was not good at all. Thinking about his ex-boss was deflating more than just his ego.

"Is there a problem?" Eden asked.

"Problem? No, of course not."

"I thought you wanted us to . . ." She cleared her throat, her expression now uncertain.

Thinking about Lucifer was pretty much the equivalent of taking an ice-cold shower. Not exactly firing up his libido. Quite the opposite, in fact.

How embarrassing. An ex-incubus who couldn't get it up.

"It's not you," he assured her. "It's Lucifer."

Her eyebrows raised. "Oh?"

"Thinking about him isn't exactly helping matters."

"Then stop thinking about him."

He flicked her amulet. "A bit difficult to do. I feel like there's three of us in this bed right now." At her amused expression, "Don't get any ideas about having a ménage à trois from Hell. He's really not my type."

"As if I would." She shook her head. "You're funny."

"So hilarious I forgot to laugh."

She took his face between her hands. "Sometimes you just prove to me that you're so much more than just a demon. Sometimes you're practically human."

"Let's not get insulting."

"Not an insult. You have doubts, worries, issues."

Darrak groaned. "This is not an issue that's going to be long-term. Seriously. Just give it a moment. This has never happened to me before." He glared at her. "Okay, you look way too amused right now."

She was grinning at him. "You're amazing, you know that?"

"Maybe once upon a time, but not anymore."

She nodded. "Let's do this."

"I thought I already explained in flaccid detail that it's not going to happen. Ten minutes. Give me ten minutes. I need some peanut butter or something. Protein."

"I mean the curse." Her expression had grown serious very quickly. She shifted so she pushed him onto his back and straddled him. Even though she was wearing full flannel pajamas, he found that his issues were disappearing as quickly as they'd arrived. The woman could make even flannel sexy. He ran his hands up her thighs.

"This is much better," he said. "I can work with this."

He pulled her down and captured her mouth again.

Eden pushed back from him. "I want to break the curse. Now. Let's get it over with. Why would we want to wait another minute?"

He eyed her warily. "Now? You're sure?"

"I've never been more sure about anything in my life."

"That's pretty sure."

She pressed her hands against his chest. "So should I approach this the same as the spell? Maksim said a curse is made of denser magic and I was supposed to be careful with it."

"Yes, you definitely want to be careful. And he was right. A curse will feel different than a spell on that level. It's stronger, tougher. Think about gum stuck to someone's shoe. Only it's not gum and no shoes are involved."

Eden's expression was filled with enthusiasm, hope, and sheer determination. He didn't want to say anything to break this mood. He liked seeing the worry gone from her green eyes.

"I don't want to hurt you," she said.

He almost smiled at that. He was more concerned for her, not him at this moment. "The spell could have gotten worse, but a curse is as bad as it gets. Not sure you could do more damage than was already done."

Eden nodded. "Then kiss me again for good luck."

"I can definitely do that." He flexed his abdomen and sat up, doing just as she asked. She tasted good. Addictive. His body responded immediately.

Sure, *now* it responded. What happened to this surge of desire five minutes ago?

Stupid Lucifer.

He slid his hands under the edge of her flannel top to trail up the length of her spine.

"Should touch you skin to skin again," he said. "It will help."

"It's helping."

"Now try to concentrate, Eden, and break this damn curse once and for all. One shot. That's all we're doing right now. Just a test of the emergency broadcast system."

"Just a test." She kissed him one last time, then closed her eyes and pressed him back down to the mattress. "I can do this."

Darrak watched her guardedly. There was no change for a moment, but then she frowned, her eyebrows drawing together. "What's wrong?"

"Nothing . . . but I—I think I can see something. I think it's your curse. It's . . . it's so dark and horrible."

He did hope that was the curse she was seeing, not simply his true demon self. "Tell me exactly what you see."

"The darkness is filled with evil like a black hole. It scares me."

"What else?"

She hesitated. "On the other side there's a glow, a—a brightness. Filled with light and life and goodness."

That was probably the celestial energy he'd absorbed from her like an undigested candy bar in his gut. "Focus on the dark part. Try to grab that darkness and test it out—you'll be able to see if it's really the curse then or if it's, uh, just a part of . . . yours truly."

"Okay, I can do that." She was silent for a long moment, her forehead creased with concentration. "I'm almost there. I can move it—right now . . . it's hard to budge . . ."

Something was wrong, he sensed it deep in his gut. "Eden, wait a minute. Something about this doesn't feel right. We need to hang off for just a—"

And then he felt it. Pain—a searing agony more intense and acute than he'd ever felt before crashed over him like a tidal wave. It was quite possible he literally screamed. He pushed Eden off of him and rolled off the side of the bed. And then, suddenly, his body was gone, and there was only smoke.

This is it, he thought past the white-hot pain tearing through his entire being. *The end. It's over. It's all over . . .*

⇒ EIGHT ⇐

Eden panicked, scrambling off the bed so fast and hard that she bruised her knees. "Darrak! No . . . no! Please!"

He was gone; only black smoke remained for a long, horrible drawn-out moment.

And then his body returned. Darrak lay on his back on the carpet, next to an old copy of *Glamour* magazine.

"Oh, my God!" She grabbed hold of his shoulders. "I didn't mean to hurt you! I'm so sorry! Darrak . . . are—are you okay?"

He blinked, then squeezed his eyes shut for a moment before opening them and meeting her gaze. "How do I look?"

"You . . ." Eden gulped and scanned his body—currently in all its naked glory. "You look fine. Great. Normal. How do you feel?"

He forced himself into a sitting position. "*That* was extremely unpleasant."

"I didn't mean to hurt you." Hot tears streaked down her face. "And I don't think it even worked. I had to stop before

I could really try to do anything else. I didn't want to make it worse."

He touched her face to push the tears away. "I'm fine now. But you're right, the curse is still with me. I feel it. Nothing's changed."

"I know. I'm sorry." She'd tried, but she knew it hadn't done a bit of good. The bright light had blocked what she'd tried to get at—that dark, nasty sludge that she was certain represented the curse on a metaphysical level. As soon as she'd tried to separate the light from the dark she'd sensed Darrak's distress. It had come across to her loud and clear.

"Don't be sorry," he said. "We tried. It was enough to know it's not nearly as simple to remove as the spell."

Darrak was still bound to Eden, as much as he'd ever been.

But she wasn't disappointed she'd failed. She was filled with relief that he was okay. For a horrible moment there, she thought she'd lost him completely.

Looked like Maksim's advice *had* been too good to be true after all.

"So . . . it looks like you're stuck with me," Darrak said cautiously.

She leaned back against the side of her bed. "Looks that way."

"We can go see Maksim again if you like. Get some more advice from the Wiz."

"Maybe another day. But today we have other plans if you're up to it."

"I'm up. Or I will be momentarily."

She finally let go of him. The near-romance of earlier had momentarily passed. Nothing like wrenching pain and a near death experience to help spoil the mood.

For now, anyway.

"What was the guy's name again?" Darrak asked.

"Good question. Lucas gave me a card that has info on it, but since the guy is magically cloaked from him the card was blank. I'll check it in a minute."

When he didn't reply, she glanced over her shoulder at him. He was pushing himself up to a standing position, and in three seconds flat had conjured clothing to cover his body. He gave her a quizzical look.

"What?" she asked.

"You don't like calling him by his real name, do you?"

She swallowed. "I don't know."

"Makes you feel like he's not as dangerous, maybe?"

"What's the difference?"

Darrak shrugged. "Nothing, I guess. Call him Gertrude if you like."

"He might not answer to that."

"Where's the famous summoning crystal?"

"Why?"

"Maybe I should hang on to it for you so there are no more unplanned trips."

"I don't think that's such a good idea." Her eyes narrowed at his pinched look. "Lucas isn't interested in me. I mean, come on. I'm a nobody in the grand scheme of things."

"Right. Nobody. You really think that, don't you? Just Caroline Riley's daughter, the slightly psychic loner who doesn't let anyone get close to her."

Eden cringed. "I wasn't asking for a psychological evaluation. Besides, today's not about me. Or you. We gave it a shot just now, and it didn't work. Now we need to find this blank card guy, and then we have to focus on Andy. Our problems will wait for another day."

Darrak nodded. "You're right. You're always right."

He left for the kitchen. He didn't sound completely sincere, and Eden tried not to think about that.

They had to get along. Fighting or major disagreements wouldn't serve them at all. Besides, she'd just proven to herself that the two of them were stuck together. And she had no idea how long she had to find another solution for them.

* * *

The moment Eden pulled the previously blank card out of her coat pocket, she realized it wasn't blank anymore. After all, Lucas wasn't near it anymore.

BRENDANFRANKS
55BL__RST__E_W___

She could read the name, but whatever it said beneath it wasn't very helpful. Letters were missing, smeared or blurry, or just totally unreadable.

Well, the name was a good start.

"Okay, Brendan Franks," she mumbled to herself. "Little do you know, but you have a conversation with Lucas coming up very soon."

Just a conversation. He'd promised her that.

And she trusted him, right?

Yeah, right.

They left for Triple-A. If anyone could help them locate Mr. Franks, it would be Andy.

"Well, let's have a look-see," he murmured as he ran the name through the special government database he had access to on his office computer. Eden didn't think the access came courtesy of the government itself, but through some talent Andy had for hacking into places he shouldn't be. Eden didn't ask for details. She really didn't want to know. "All right, I've found one hit on that name here in the GTA."

"But what about what it says underneath?" Darrak asked. "I'm no Magnum, P.I., but I'm thinking that's a clue."

"You're right. My guess is it says 55 Bloor Street West, which is the Manulife Centre, but no Brendan Franks came up there. But maybe it's where he works."

Eden blinked. "You *guessed* that?"

"I'm killer at Hangman. You have no idea."

"I'm impressed." She nervously played with the silver bracelet in her pocket. It remained cold as ice, not warming to her body temperature—one of the signs of its supernatural qualities.

Lucas wanted her to put this bracelet on Brendan Franks so they could have a conversation. Sounded so easy. *Too* easy.

She knew that likely meant it wouldn't be.

And Darrak was right, she did prefer to call him Lucas even knowing exactly who he really was. What did that say about her? Was she ignoring reality?

As much as humanly possible, thank you very much. But it didn't mean she wasn't still painfully aware of it.

"How are you feeling today, Andy?" she asked, exchanging a glance with Darrak.

"I'm just fine and dandy. Never better. Why do you ask?" At her pointed look, he held up his hand. "Don't you start with the werewolf thing again."

"Andy—"

"No, Eden, I'm serious. I don't want to talk about it anymore."

Frustration welled within her. "Denying it isn't going to change anything. You're the one who's going to change. *Tonight.* Don't be a fool."

Andy pointed at the door. "You're fired!"

Eden almost laughed, but managed to repress it. "You're not my boss. We're partners."

He slumped forward on his desk. "Why must you torment me about this? I'm not a damned werewolf."

"So prove it," Darrak said.

Andy tensed. "What?"

"Prove it. Tonight at dusk."

"And how am I going to do that?"

"Let us lock you up right here," Eden said, glancing around at their one-room office. "If you don't change into a wolf, then you're right and I'll eat my words and apologize profusely every day for the rest of my life. But if I'm right, then you'll be safely contained in here and you won't hurt anyone."

He made a face. "Contained? I could easily bust down that door with a well-placed kick."

Darrak shook his head. "Normally I'd agree with you, Chuck Norris, but we happen to have a spell that will, allegedly"—he glanced at Eden and she saw the doubt about Maksim in his eyes. After what happened this morning she couldn't really blame him there—"seal this place up nice and tight. Also, no one walking by will be able to see anything hairy going on in here. Literally."

"*Here*," Andy said skeptically.

"Yup."

He sighed, and it sounded shaky. "How long do I need to be locked up before you two realize this lycanthropy thing doesn't apply to me?"

"An hour," Eden said.

"An hour. That's it?"

"Yes." She held her breath, hoping he wasn't going to keep arguing with them. She had enough on her plate today already without this discussion going around in endless circles.

Andy reached into his desk drawer and pulled out his silver flask, unscrewed the cap, and took a long drink from it before putting it back. "Fine."

Eden raised her eyebrows. "Really?"

"Yes, really. You have my permission to lock me in here at sunset tonight for exactly sixty minutes and not one second longer. That's it. That's all. And then we can finally move on from this ridiculous topic of conversation. Agreed?"

"I think we can agree with that," Darrak said. "And, FYI, it's really not all that ridiculous."

"It is."

"It isn't."

"It is!"

Eden sighed. "We're not arguing with you. It's impossible."

"*You're* impossible," Andy countered.

"Good comeback."

Andy grabbed the printout from his Brendan Franks search and glanced at it. "Who is this guy, anyway?"

Eden took hold of the list of two addresses from him. "Just somebody I need to find."

"For who? A client?"

"No." She hesitated. "Actually, it's for . . . Lucifer."

Andy let the paper go so abruptly she staggered back a step. "Do I even want to know anything more about this?"

"Probably not"

"Then I won't ask."

"Good idea. We'll be back later." She looked at him sternly. "And don't even think about leaving after work. You need to stay right here."

He saluted. "Yes, ma'am."

That was what you got when you tried to help people out these days. Shameless mocking.

So they were off on their Lucas-related assignment. Eden prayed it would go smoothly.

It was worth a shot.

Ben tried to make peace with the idea he'd be called upon to torture a woman for information later tonight. Not so strangely, that peace didn't come.

He didn't like to harm women. Ever. For any reason. He was old-fashioned that way.

If he stooped to the Malleus's level to that extent, then he was no better of a monster than Darrak.

Ben wouldn't be able to live with himself it if came to that.

There had to be another solution. And that solution was to get the shapeshifter to talk without any unpleasant means, and Oliver would be satisfied with whatever answers he was looking for. Only Ben would have to get those answers without first asking his boss for permission.

Say what you would about the Malleus and their airtight rules and employees who'd handed their very lives over to the "cause," sometimes a little money worked as well as any magic ever could.

Especially to the guards who held the keys to the prisoner cells.

One of those greedy guards in question slipped his key into the shifter's door.

"You have five minutes," he gruffly informed Ben. "That's it."

"Do you think she'll try to escape?"

"Not with that metal band on her wrist. It stops her from shifting, giving a hell of a shock if she even plays with it. She's trapped here whether she likes it or not."

"Handy."

"Five minutes," the guard reminded him.

It would have to be enough. This was a little talk that wasn't sanctioned by Oliver. And he'd been avoiding Sandy ever since she delivered the tainted chicken soup yesterday.

He was on his own.

Other than a small cot and a toilet, there wasn't much else in the ten-foot-square room but her. The woman crouched in the shadows in the corner.

Ben was met with a glare sharp enough to cut glass.

"What the hell do you want, Ken doll?" she snapped.

He gave her a smile that might have looked more like a grimace. "The name's not Ken. It's Ben."

"Hooray for you. Leave me alone, jerk."

"Jerk? You don't even know me."

"I know enough. You're one of them." She thrust her chin toward the door. "Locked me up in here like an animal."

"Well, you *are* a shifter. So you're an animal part-time, anyway, aren't you?"

"Bite me."

"Not in my plans. Sorry." He glanced at the door, then moved toward it to look out the small window. The guard had moved down the hallway. They had a bit of privacy to speak.

When he looked back at the woman, she was already in front of him, her right fist aimed toward his jaw. He deflected the punch before it landed and wrenched her arm behind her back, pushing her up against the wall like he'd done hundreds of times before with common criminals who'd tried to escape.

"Be nice," he warned.

"Why should I?"

"I'm not the bad guy here."

"Sure," she growled. "I believe it."

"Have they hurt you?"

"No. But you're hurting me right now."

He let go of her. She scrambled away from him, returning to the opposite corner but staying on her feet. He swept his gaze over her. She was somewhere in her twenties, about five seven, with skin the color of cocoa and eyes like bright amber. Her black hair was long and sleek and swept back over her shoulders. The silver cuff circled her left wrist. She wore a simple white T-shirt, which looked a size too small, making her breasts strain against the jersey material.

He felt something stir within him.

Great. The last goddamned thing he needed right now was to find himself attracted to a prisoner. And a bitchy, unhelpful one at that.

"How do you know Eden Riley?" he asked bluntly. The sooner he could get out of here the better.

The woman's eyes widened as if he'd surprised her, but then they narrowed. "No idea who you're talking about."

"How about Eden's new boyfriend, Darrak? The one that's going to suck the life right out of her. Do you know *him*?"

Her jaw tightened.

"I know you do," he said. "And I have a funny feeling that you just might care what happens to Eden enough to offer up some helpful info."

"Did you say your name was Ben?" she asked. "That wouldn't happen to be . . . Ben *Hanson*, would it?"

This time he took a step back. "You know who I am?"

"I've heard things."

"How about you tell me what they are?"

She gave him a thin smile. "How about you go screw yourself?"

He studied her for a moment. "Does the tough chick act usually work at making people back off?"

She snorted. "Works like a charm, actually."

"It won't with me. Believe it or not I'm trying to help

you. These are answers we need, and if you don't want to give them to me right now, just chatting like this, then there are going to be consequences."

"Story of my life."

"I can help you." He pressed back against the cell's cold wall.

"I've heard that line before, handsome. I've realized the hard way that the only person who's ever going to help me out of a jam is myself."

"That's not true."

"It is."

"Hard life?"

"It's had its moments."

"No knights in shining armor?"

"I'm not the type who believes in them." She swept her gaze over him. "Why? You offering to suit up?"

"No. Not me." He extended his arm to show her the brand that bound him to the Malleus body and soul. "My choices are limited when it comes to rescuing damsels in distress these days."

"Too bad."

"Just tell me one thing . . ."

"What?"

"Darrak . . . he's bad news, isn't he?"

She hesitated, but then her jaw clenched. "He's an arch-demon. That's the worst kind of demon there is."

"What about any changes to do with him absorbing Eden's celestial energy? Did you ever notice any change in him because of this?"

"Not really. He puts up a good front that he's a decent guy now, but I don't believe it. I've seen too much in my life to believe he's in this because he really loves her. Call me a cynic."

Oliver thought she had more answers than that. He was fixated on the nephilim energy potentially changing the demon. This bit of info wouldn't be enough to satisfy him.

"I need to go," he said. "I'm sorry I can't help you. Really."

She let out a long shuddery breath. "If you can't rescue my sorry ass, then do me a favor and rescue Eden. Before it's too late."

"I'll try my best." He turned from her and rapped on the door to get the guard's attention.

The door opened a moment later, and he felt the woman's warm hand on his shoulder. He glanced back at her warily, but this time she didn't look ready to claw his eyes out. She looked sad and vulnerable.

"That mark on your arm? It's just a scar unless you believe differently."

"I wish you were right."

He left her, feeling like hell that she didn't know enough to save her own neck and knowing he'd likely have to see her again later that night under less than pleasant circumstances. But one thing the beautiful shifter had reminded him about was his original goal.

If he could save Eden from the demon who possessed her, then everything else in his life just might start to make sense again.

Eden peered through the fence at their first stop, where Andy said they'd find the only confirmed Brendan Franks in Toronto. After this, all they had was the lead on the address at the Manulife Centre downtown.

"That can't be him," she said.

"I disagree," Darrak replied. "He looks like someone Lucifer might want to have a chat with."

Brendan appeared to be about six years old and was currently on recess at a local elementary school.

"I don't think so."

"Come on, Eden, don't be naïve. Demonic children are a dime a dozen in the Netherworld. Need I mention Children of the Corn? Damien? Justin Bieber?"

Brendan ran toward the entrance to the school when the bell rang and succeeded in tripping and falling. He sat there for a stunned moment before he started to wail. A teacher came over and helped him to his feet, patting him comfortingly on the top of his head.

"Well . . . maybe you're right," Darrak conceded. "Lucifer isn't a big fan of crybabies. I know this from personal experience."

The other location was looking more promising with every passing moment.

Eden knew she had to concentrate, but her mind kept wandering. Why did this have to happen today? Couldn't Lucas wait till next week? Next month? Exactly what kind of conversation did he want to have, and why hadn't he been more forthcoming with the details?

She could ask a million questions, but it wouldn't change a damn thing. She had to come through on this. Lucas hadn't specifically threatened Darrak, but the prince simply had too much control over her demon in residence. After how close she'd come this morning to losing him, she hated that Lucas could use him as punishment if she messed up a job for him again.

"We do need to see Maksim again," she said. "First thing tomorrow. I don't want to put it off any longer after what happened earlier."

"No harm done."

"Wrong. Harm *was* done. Just because you're okay now doesn't ease my mind a fraction."

He nodded as they returned to the Toyota. "Fine, if you absolutely insist. I'll stifle my dislike of that guy for another day. But don't get your hopes up. He already told you what the other option is if we can't break the curse." He said it lightly, but his expression was tight.

Her stomach twisted with part flu, part nerves. "That's exactly what I'm trying to avoid."

He didn't reply.

"And we're *going* to avoid it," she insisted.

"Of course we are."

"Nothing bad is going to happen to either of us. I promise."

He eyed her. "You're still after that happily ever after, are you?"

"I'll settle for nothing less." She did wish she could coax a bit more confidence into her voice. "Tomorrow is another day."

"Yes, Scarlett."

She'd felt as if she'd been close to breaking the curse this morning. *So* close. That she'd failed so epically was a bitter pill to swallow.

But maybe she'd been wrong. Maybe that black blob she'd seen wasn't anything more helpful than one of Nancy's malformed chocolate donuts.

A mere fifteen minutes later they walked into the lobby of 55 Bloor Street West, a shiny office building and shopping mall.

"Andy's probably right," she said. "Brendan could definitely work here."

"Then why didn't that come up on his search? I mean, he was able to find the location of a little kid, but not some guy with a job right in the heart of the city?"

She shook her head. "No idea."

"So slap that bracelet on this guy's wrist, send him directly to Hell, and we head back and deal with Andy."

She froze, nearly going over on her high heels on the shiny floor. "Excuse me?"

Darrak looked at her. "What?"

"Did you say, send him to Hell?"

He frowned as if not understanding her confusion. "Well, yeah. What do you think that set of handcuffs there does?"

"These are handcuffs?" She yanked her hand out of her pocket where she'd been touching the cold silver of the bracelet again. "I—I didn't really think about it."

He grimaced. "Well, forget I said anything."

"How am I supposed to forget about that? I'm going to send someone to . . ." She lowered her voice. "To *Hell* if I clamp that thing on their wrist?"

"Likely the reason this dude has the cloaking spell on

him so Lucifer can't find him and drag him there before this."

"He told me he just wanted to talk to him."

"Well, what else was he going to say to you?"

"Why would Lucas lie to me?" Her voice sounded strained.

Darrak raised a dark brow. "You do know we're talking about *Lucifer* here, right? Not Abraham Lincoln."

She sighed shakily. "He couldn't possibly think that I'd be okay with this."

"If it's any consolation, I bet this Brendan guy is bad news. If he's hiding from Lucifer, what else could he be?"

"How can you be so calm about this?"

"Just another day at the office, Eden. Only I haven't actually been at my desk for over three hundred years."

She tried to breathe normally, but it was a struggle. There was no reason, in her opinion, why Lucas would have lied about this. If he wanted to drag an evil soul to Hell, then there were other means to facilitate that that didn't include her. He'd know by now that Eden, despite being a black witch, had issues with being evil. She didn't want to cause anyone harm unless they really deserved it.

The longer she thought about it the more she realized it was too late to change her mind. She knew Darrak's well-being—her *own* well-being—was at risk right now. Lucas might be nice and personable and easy on the eyes, but she wasn't ready to cross him today. Not over something like this.

She sighed. "Fine. Then let's get this over with. How are we supposed to figure out if he's even here?"

Darrak scanned the lobby, his gaze coming to rest on the security desk near the elevators. "When you're lost, it's a good idea to ask for directions."

"Most men wouldn't admit something like that."

He grinned at her. "I'm not most men."

"Touché."

He approached the guard. "Hey, there. We're looking for somebody who works in this building. Can you help us?"

"What's the name?"

"Brendan Franks."

"What do you want with him?"

Not a question they should answer honestly, to say the least. But Eden was at a loss of a good excuse to use.

Darrak, however, was not.

"We're with Publishers Clearing House," he said smoothly. "Mr. Franks has won our latest sweepstakes, and this is our initial contact visit. It's very exciting for everyone. Do you feel the excitement, good sir?"

The guard regarded him skeptically. "For real?"

"The realest. Three million dollars. A trip around the world. Uh . . . a whole mess of balloons. There's even a cake. And a party. It's going to be amazing. My lovely associate and I just need to talk to Mr. Franks and have him sign some release forms and then we do the whole presentation with the big check and confetti."

Eden didn't think their reason behind looking for Brendan Franks needed to be this elaborate, but the guard seemed very impressed.

She was also impressed. Darrak was a fantastic and very creative liar.

She stepped back a little to give him space to keep talking with the guard, who was now checking the employee database.

The guard frowned. "Sorry, but I'm not finding that name."

"Keep looking," Darrak suggested. "He's got to be in there somewhere."

A dark-haired woman on her way toward the elevators slowed and glanced at Eden. "Is that right? Someone in this building won a major prize?"

Eden cleared her throat. "Looks that way, doesn't it?"

"Who is it, if you don't mind me asking?"

"Brendan Franks. You don't happen to know him, do you?"

The woman frowned. "I'm afraid not."

Damn. This wasn't going to be an easy assignment, but she already knew that.

Darrak waited, leaning against the security desk. He glanced over his shoulder at Eden and gave her a thumbs-up.

At least one of them was staying positive about this.

This was ridiculous. They had better things to do today than chase after half-baked clues for Lucas. If it took much longer, it would have to wait for another day.

Something caught Eden's eye then. Darrak wasn't leaning against the desk so much as he was hanging on to the side of it. His shoulders were slumped and a trickle of perspiration slid down his temple.

He wasn't feeling well.

She'd think he might have contracted the flu, just as her symptoms were coming on slowly but surely this week, but there was just one very important thing . . .

Demons didn't get sick.

Then what was going on? Or was it just her imagination?

"Darrak—" she began. She was going to suggest they leave and try again tomorrow. Lucas would just have to understand that all good things came to those who waited— even if they were the Prince of Hell. Triple-A didn't offer twenty-four-hour turnaround for anybody.

"You don't mind if I wait here, do you?" the dark-haired woman interrupted her. She hadn't budged a step from where she stood next to Eden, gazing at the security desk. "I'd hate to miss any of the excitement."

"We're probably going to go soon. I don't think they can find his name on the employee list."

"Brendan Franks," she repeated. "You're sure about that?"

"Do you work here?"

"Tenth floor. I know this place like the back of my hand."

"Do you mind if I ask you a couple of questions?"

"Not at all. I'd be happy to help if I can."

Eden wanted to leave, but she couldn't turn down a solid lead when one presented itself to her. This woman might know where to find Brendan. And if she could get to the bottom of this minor mystery today, then it was one less thing to think about and she could focus on Andy's werewolf dilemma tonight and seeing Maksim again tomorrow.

So much to do, so little time.

"I definitely don't have a Brendan Franks," the security guard told Darrak to their right. "Sorry about that."

Damn. That wasn't very promising.

"However . . ." the guard continued.

"What?" Darrak prompted.

"I do have a . . . uh . . . a Brenda N. Franks. Do you think that might be it?"

"*Brenda?*" Darrak repeated. "Are you sure?"

"Positive. I can see why there might have been an error made. One little dot can make a whole lot of difference, can't it? Do you think Brenda's the winner you're looking for?"

Darrak turned his head in Eden's direction just as she felt an arm clamp tightly around her.

"Middle name's Natasha," the woman purred into her ear. A whisper of sharp steel pressed against her throat. "Nice to meet you. Now what the hell do you want with me?"

⇢ NINE ⇠

The moment the woman pulled the knife, flames rippled down Darrak's right arm and covered his hand. All archdemons had an element to call, and his happened to be fire. He didn't have a ton of power left in reserve—plus, he was feeling strangely weakened ever since the curse removal attempt—but he had enough to reduce this woman to a pile of ash if he was properly motivated. And seeing her press a knife against Eden's throat was more than enough to properly motivate him.

He didn't want Eden to tap into her black magic, but he knew it was only a matter of time. By the shade of her amulet, she couldn't delve too deeply. Unfortunately, life or death situations like this called for a bit of delving.

"Who are you?" Brenda's gaze shot toward him.

The guard stood up from behind the security desk. "What are you doing?"

"Mind your own business," she hissed.

"Okay." The guard's eyes glazed over and he sat back down to begin fiddling with his computer.

"You've got some tricks up your sleeve," Eden managed.

"A few. Now in case you didn't hear me before, who the hell are you and what do you want with me?" The blade pressed closer, and Darrak was afraid to move too quickly or he might spook her. Black witches, even reluctant ones like Eden, were as easy to kill as a regular human. He wasn't willing to risk her life.

Eden met Darrak's gaze and concern tore through his gut. He hadn't expected this, although he should have. If this chick was someone Lucifer wanted, that meant she was extremely dangerous.

"I'm Darrak." He forced his tone down to one much calmer than he felt. "That's Eden. A pleasure to meet you. Now, let go of her right now or I'm going to introduce you to Mr. Third-Degree Burn. He's not so friendly."

"Why are you looking for me?" she demanded. "And don't tell me I just won the lottery."

"Publishers Clearing House Sweepstakes," Darrak corrected. "Much cooler than any boring lottery. Did I mention there was going to be cake? Then you had to go and ruin all the fun."

Her eyes narrowed. "Start talking or I'm going to slit her throat."

The heat of his fire increased along with his temper. "You really don't want to do that."

"Maybe I'm feeling like I don't have many choices here."

"You're right, you only have one choice and that's to let Eden go. Not to quote from old TV shows, but you really don't want to see me when I'm angry."

People continued to walk steadily through the lobby, but were completely ignoring their standoff. This Brenda woman was able to work some sort of cloaking magic— much as she'd done to hide herself from Lucifer, he was sure, but on a smaller scale—and also she had the power of verbal influence over humans. Handy tricks, actually.

Suddenly, Darrak's fire energy flickered and nearly went out.

Damn it, not now.

He was having difficulty maintaining what little power he had left. He wasn't sure why he felt so off today. Demons didn't suffer from ailments or illnesses. If they were injured, they healed quickly. But this didn't seem as if it was from any specific injury.

The pain began in the center of his chest when they'd first arrived here and had slowly radiated outward. He barely noticed it until it now made it difficult to concentrate. Then it accelerated and felt as if something was attempting to claw itself out of his chest, tearing him in two pieces from the inside out.

Another wave of agony followed the first in rapid succession and was equal to what he'd felt that morning when he'd lost form. It knocked him right to his knees, and he braced his hands against the smooth marble floor. He gritted his teeth and tried to see past the white-hot flash before his eyes.

"Darrak!" Eden shrieked.

The other woman screamed as a wave of Eden's black magic hit her and she flew backward across the lobby. A pain-filled glance up showed more dark veins spreading across Eden's amulet.

Not good.

Also not good was the sensation that he was going to turn to smoke again at any moment. It took a lot of energy to maintain his corporeal form during the day, even with Eden's celestial help. But he felt he had nothing in reserve. The well was dry.

He looked down at his hand, previously covered in fire from fingertip to elbow, as it turned to smoke before his eyes. This time, however, the smoke wasn't only black. It was black and bright white—swirling together like a tornado.

What the hell?

A moment later the tearing pain eased off completely and his hand reformed.

The woman's eyes widened as she took in the sight of him. "What the hell are the two of you?"

"Complicated," Darrak replied wearily.

"Darrak, are you okay?" Eden stood between him and the woman, her fists clenched at her sides. He could see the static charge of her magic running down the length of her arms like small lightning storms.

"Never better," he lied.

"You're a witch." Brenda eyed Eden from her position crouched on the floor and looked ready to spring if anyone came close to her. "But I sense something else . . . I sense—angel?"

Eden glared at her. "How do you know that?"

"I know lots of things whether I want to or not. Who sent you to grab me?"

Eden held her gaze steadily. "Lucifer. Ever heard of him?"

Brenda gasped, then swore under her breath. "I knew it."

"He wants to have a little chat with you. I'd been feeling a bit guilty about helping him facilitate that chat, but you know what? I'm over it now."

"I don't want to talk to him. I don't want anything to do with him."

"Oh?" Darrak couldn't help but be intrigued. "Do you know what he wants with you?"

"I think he wants to make me a job offer."

His brows went up. "Excuse me? *You?*"

She exhaled shakily. "It was prophesied since I was a child that I was meant to be involved somehow with Lucifer."

"Let me guess, you're Toronto's answer to the Antichrist."

"Something like that. And it's something I've been try-ing to avoid my entire life. Just because I've got a lousy prophecy attached to me doesn't mean I'm willing to ful-fill it. I work for a children's charity and have for ten years. What more do I have to do to prove that I'm a good person?"

"Oh, I don't know. Maybe for starters, stop pulling knives on people in office lobbies?" he snarled.

"It's called self-defense. And come near me again and I'll destroy the both of you."

He took a couple of steps closer to her. "Maybe you're bluffing."

"Maybe I'm not."

"You couldn't take both of us on. Trust me on that."

She clutched her knife tightly, and he saw a shadow of fear finally slide behind her eyes. "I don't even know how something like you can exist. It's unnatural."

"Gee, you sure know how to compliment a guy. I appreciate it."

"Wait," Eden said warily. "You could see what I am. Can you see what Darrak is, too?"

"Yes." Brenda didn't tear her gaze from him for a moment. She seemed confused. "I thought you were a demon."

"Good guess," he said. "But you still don't get any cake."

"But . . . I sense angel, too. A lot of it. I don't understand how that's possible."

"I've been drinking some angel juice for about a month. It's a temporary infusion of sparkle to my regular diet."

"No, it's not only that," she whispered, staring at him with shock. "You're half-demon and half-angel . . . all at once. It's the most incredible thing I've seen in my entire life. You shouldn't exist, not like this. How do the two opposites exist in the same form without destroying each other?"

Darrak felt himself pale. "You're wrong. It's just some energy I need to burn off."

"No, it's not. You must feel it. How can you not? You're filled with light—and it's equal to the darkness. Your pain before . . . the different parts are tearing you in two."

"You're crazy." His gaze flicked to Eden to share a moment of "this chick is wacko," but the look on her face was enough to steal his breath.

Pure shock and an edge of fear.

"Eden . . ." he began.

She shook her head. "I'm so sorry. I—I didn't want you to find out like this. Not from someone else."

"What are you talking about?"

"She's telling you the truth."

His brain had stopped processing information. "It can't be true. I'm a demon, I'm not a . . . a . . ."

Her face had paled. "Half. You're half-demon and half-angel now. The celestial energy—it's not a temporary thing. It changed you . . . permanently."

He wanted to make a joke and laugh it off, but nothing came out. Just the stunned realization that he couldn't deny this, because on some level he'd already known the truth.

The angel juice he'd been absorbing from Eden from day one, the same stuff that gave him the ability to take form during the day after hundreds of years of being nothing more than black smoke trapped inside a succession of human hosts . . .

It hadn't only tainted him by enhancing his already messed-up humanity-tainted archdemon form. It had literally changed part of him to angel.

Holy shit.

"You already knew," he bit out. "And you never told me?"

Eden looked distraught. "I should have. I didn't want you to freak out. Please don't freak out."

Freak out? That was the shallow end of reactions he could have to this revelation, actually.

In one single sentence, his entire existence had just taken a swan dive directly into the Void. That was the only place he could end up now. He knew without a single doubt he'd never be accepted in Hell again. Not like this.

And Heaven? As if he'd want to stroll through those pearly gates even if he had the opportunity. Not a chance in . . . well, wherever.

It was over. It was all over.

And, no, he wasn't overreacting. He'd witnessed much worse than the Void as a result of way less. For a time he'd even been one of those responsible for doling out punishments to those Netherworld beings deemed unworthy or flawed or . . . tainted.

Talk about karma.

Eden pulled the silver chain out of her coat pocket. "Okay, Brenda, enough stalling. I don't know your real story, but I was sent here to do a job and I'm going to do it. Lucas . . . *Lucifer* wants to talk to you and you need to have that talk.

Say no if he offers you a job downstairs, but you have to see him. I'm sorry, really, but I have no choice."

"Me neither," Brenda replied.

She turned and ran out of the lobby.

Eden immediately chased after her.

"Eden!" Darrak began to pursue them, but another wave of pain crashed over him, halting him in his tracks. This time it was accompanied with dizziness. His entire world devolved into a Tilt-A-Whirl from Hell.

Eden wouldn't get too far without him. Their hundred-foot tether would stop her the moment she reached it.

Or maybe not. He raised his hand before his face, again disturbed to see it shift to the white and black swirling smoke.

Pure light and pitch-black.

Now he knew why it had shifted to that color combo. It was pure evil with a side order of sparkle dust.

It was . . . *him*.

Quite honestly, if this didn't mean the beginning of the end of everything he'd ever known, he'd think it was freaking hilarious.

"Please stop!" Eden grabbed the woman's arm before she reached the exit. She felt a twinge of pain here—she was at the farthest point she could be from Darrak. Another few steps and she would have had to give up the chase completely.

Brenda's muscles were tense. "Did you just say 'please'?"

"I can't help that I'm polite." Eden glanced at the knife the woman still clutched, and with a mere thought it rocketed out of her hand and imbedded itself into the wall next to them.

The woman didn't seem particularly strong, despite her other gifts. Eden was able to hold her in place without too much effort.

"Let go of me," she snapped.

"Can't do that." Eden pulled the silver chain out of her coat pocket. "You tried to kill me."

"I wouldn't have killed you."

"Sorry if I don't automatically believe that. That's quite a knife to carry around during the workday."

"I'm too busy to learn kung fu. A girl's got to protect herself somehow."

"You think that would help you against Lucas?"

"Who?"

Eden gritted her teeth. Damn it. *"Lucifer."*

"I'm cloaked from him in the human world—totally. He can't find me without help." Brenda gave her a dirty look.

"Maybe you should think of it as an honor. Any job he wants to offer you might be a good one for somebody like you."

Brenda stared at her incredulously. "I don't want anything to do with him."

Everything this woman said was confusing Eden. She'd been so focused when she'd arrived here, but now she was distracted and doubting herself. Plus, having the truth about Darrak come out so unexpectedly had thrown her completely off guard.

Darrak.

What was wrong with him? He hadn't followed after them, which meant he might be in trouble. She had to get this over with so she could check on him.

"Enough," she gritted out. "Lucifer wants to talk to you and I'm going to—"

"No, Eden. Please listen to me." Brenda shook her head. "You can't do this, and you know it. You're a good person."

Her throat tightened. "I'm a black witch. Take a good look at my amulet. Does that seem like a good person to you?"

"You're a good person who's had a few hard knocks. Like me. You do what it takes to survive, to get through day to day. Don't do this. If you put that thing on my wrist you're going to be going against your better judgment. You *know* this is wrong."

Eden hissed out a breath. "Stop it."

"See?" Brenda brightened as Eden's grip on her loosened a fraction. "We're in the same situation, you and me. I have a prophecy telling me my destiny is set. But I know I can fight it. I choose what I want to be and, let me tell you, it's got nothing to do with Lucifer or Hell. I want better than that for myself. And whatever I have to do to keep myself away from him is exactly what I'll do. He can give that job that's up for grabs to somebody else."

"How can you see the truth? How did you know what Darrak is so easily?"

"I don't know. I just can. He needs you, Eden." Her brows drew together. "He needs you, more than ever, to make the right decisions—for both of you. And there's more at stake now than the two of you, you just don't know it yet."

"What are you talking about?"

Brenda's gaze clouded over as if she was focused on something a long way from here. "Some things I can't tell you. Some things are just whispers in my head, but I know you're going to have to be strong. You're going to have to do the right thing in the darkest situation. You have to prepare for a journey that will change everything."

Eden hissed out a breath of frustration. "You sound like a fortune cookie."

Brenda's eyes cleared and she laughed, but it sounded a bit bitter. "I know."

Eden couldn't help but ask. "This journey, this dark situation . . . will everything work out okay in the end?"

Brenda shook her head. "I don't know that."

"Lot of good you are."

"Sorry."

"Lucifer wants to talk to you, and I don't think he's willing to negotiate about that." Eden's grip on the chain grew tighter.

"Talk? You really think anything to do with him is that simple?" Brenda looked stressed. "Please, Eden, look into your heart. Do the right thing for you, for Darrak, for . . . for *everyone*. Let me go."

Where was Darrak? Why hadn't he followed her out here yet?

This woman had nearly killed her, Eden had no doubt about it. When it came to self-protection, if Brenda was that dead set against ever having this "talk" with Lucas, then she might have been willing to do anything to avoid it.

Eden didn't know the whole story. All she had was a request from Lucas on one side and this woman begging her to let her go on the other.

In the end, all she really had was her gut instinct.

"Fine." She let go of Brenda's arm. Magic still sparked off her fingers, charged and ready to be used, but she wouldn't need any more of it today. Today was proof that the more she used it, the more control she had over it. It was only when she tried to ignore it that it began to control *her.* "Get out of here before I change my mind."

Brenda's eyes widened with surprise. "Really?"

"Why are you still standing here?"

"Thank you! Thank you so much!" Brenda N. Franks then pushed through the glass doors and ran down the sidewalk until Eden couldn't see her anymore.

It was the flu that made her do it. It was obviously messing with her brain as well as her stomach this week.

Lucas wasn't going to be happy with her. Not at all.

⇉ TEN ⇇

Eden didn't stand there another moment; she turned and ran directly back to Darrak. He sat with his back up against the front of the security desk. Brenda's cloaking magic still seemed to be in effect since no one seemed to notice. Either that, or nobody cared.

She knelt next to him and grabbed his hand, which felt disturbingly cold to the touch.

"Let me take a wild guess," Darrak said. "You slapped the chain on that chick's wrist and sent her ass straight to Hell like the coldhearted assassin I know you to be."

She snorted. "Sure, that's exactly what I did. I'm such a badass."

His answering laugh sounded pained. "No, you let her go. You believed her sob story, bought the whole 'I'm a nice girl in a tough situation,' and let her scurry away."

"You really think I'm that much of a sap?"

"Not a sap. But for a black witch who could level this city, you're a hell of a softie."

Her eyebrows raised. "You really think I could level this city?"

"Maybe just the downtown core. Use the CN Tower as a

big-ass cigarette and the Rogers Centre like an ashtray. It would be epic."

Eden got to her feet and held a hand out to him. "Let's go."

"Cigarette and ashtray time?"

She shook her head. "See Maksim the wizard time. What happened before with you—it scared the hell out of me."

His expression wasn't filled with humor anymore. "Why didn't you tell me, Eden?"

Her chest felt tight. "This isn't a good place to discuss this."

"Damn it, Eden, talk to me."

She swallowed hard and felt tears burn her eyes. "I was going to tell you."

"When was that? Before or after I found myself torn into two separate but equally annoying beings of light and dark?"

"We need to see Maksim. It can't wait till tomorrow, not if you're feeling like this. Whatever I did earlier triggered something bad."

Darrak slowly got to his feet, using the security desk to help him up. "How long have you known?"

He was angry with her. She couldn't very well say she didn't deserve it. "Two weeks."

He actually laughed at that, but it sounded bitter and unpleasant. "Two whole weeks? And you figured this out all by yourself?"

Might as well get it all on the table now. "No. Actually, Lucas told me."

"Oh, this is terrific. Just terrific." He swore darkly under his breath. "You should have told me, Eden. I should have known it wasn't just an acorn. The sky is literally falling."

A spark of anger fought against her guilt. "Why? So you could overreact like this? We'll figure out what I did to screw you up this morning, Darrak, but this isn't the end of the world. So you're part angel. So what?"

Eden went to reach for him, but he shrugged away from her.

"Not the end of the world," he repeated. "No, to you this is probably great news. I'm not a scum-sucking, bottom-dwelling demon anymore. I've been given a little additional sparkle at the edges like a fancy doily. But it doesn't work that way, Eden. I *can't* be both demon and angel. It's impossible on too many levels to count."

Eden raked a hand through her hair and paced back a few feet before turning around to face him again. She understood his anger. She'd been wrong to keep this from him for so long. "You *can* be both. That you're standing . . . err, *leaning* . . . right in front of me right now proves that."

"You just don't get it, do you? This will destroy me. That—what happened before? It was only a taste test of the pain to come. I'm headed directly for the Void like this, Eden. But, hey, look at the bright side. At least you'll be rid of me forever."

She just gaped at him.

"Excuse me," the security guard piped up from behind them. "You were looking for someone, weren't you? Something to do with a sweepstakes? What was that name again?"

"Forget it," Darrak said, his lips twisting into a humorless smile. "Looks like the party's canceled. Permanently."

Eden drove immediately to Maksim's mansion and knocked on the door until her knuckles hurt. The butler finally answered to tell her he wasn't home. He hadn't been seen since their meeting with him yesterday, and the butler didn't know when he'd be back.

"Tell him Eden Riley needs to speak with him as soon as possible," she said, trying to control the sharp edge of panic in her voice.

So much for wizard intervention.

Darrak had waited in the car. He hadn't said a word since leaving the office building. She thought for a time he was just being sullen, but then she realized he was dealing with the tearing pain inside of him.

He needed to be comfortable and her apartment was the first place that came to mind. He didn't resist when she helped him into her bedroom and into bed.

She'd worry about failing Lucas's task later.

"Tell me what you need," she asked, stroking the dark hair back from his forehead.

"I need you to cut the angel parts out of me. Stat."

"Can't happen."

He squeezed his eyes shut. "Then just leave me to die."

"Don't be so damn melodramatic, Darrak. This isn't that bad."

His eyes snapped open. "You know, your bedside manner leaves a lot to be desired."

Eden's heart twisted to see him in this much pain, but she refused to believe this was the end for him. She'd dealt with complications, too, that fight between her angel side and her black magic—although Maksim seemed to think it was the demon who possessed her that had caused her imbalance. The jury was still out on whether he was right.

This, what Darrak was dealing with, was an imbalance as well. However, it was recent. If he'd been half-angel for a while, then this should have been an issue all along. But it wasn't.

"If it wasn't for the angel part, you wouldn't be who you are," she reasoned.

"Small comfort."

"You're going to be fine."

"I hate angels. Despise them." He stared up at the ceiling. "And I'm not just being cranky. I'm *supposed* to hate them. I'm a demon. It's a balance thing. I hate angels, so I stay away from them as much as possible. They hate demons so they stay away from us, too. Everything's all equal and proper on the universal playing field. But now I have an angel inside of me clawing to get out."

"It's not inside of you like an alien in a movie. It *is* you."

"Are you trying to be helpful or make me feel worse?" He took a deep breath and let it out slowly. "I think I have a solution to this problem."

"What?"

"Slap that chain on my wrist and send me directly to Hell. Maybe the angel bits can be burned right out of me if I jump into a pool of hellfire."

"Don't be an idiot, Darrak."

He glared at her. "That bedside manner? Not improving."

How could she fix this? Trying to reason with him seemed pointless when he was dealing with this pain. It was manifesting itself physically, rather than just emotionally.

"We'll fix these unpleasant side effects," she assured him. "But then you're going to have to look on the bright side."

"There's a bright side?"

"Sure. You felt fine this morning. You had no idea anything was even wrong."

"*Fine* has taken on a whole new definition for me lately. I used to be a strong, powerful archdemon, and now I'm an inconsequential leech on the world. Yeah, sounds fine to me."

She grabbed hold of his hand, which felt even colder than it had before. That wasn't a good sign. His skin was normally warm, even warmer than a human's. "Selina showed you to me in that vision of the past, you know. How you were back when you were that strong, powerful archdemon before you were cursed. You were absolutely horrific."

Darrak pressed back into the mattress. "I appreciate the compliment, but fond memories of who I used to be aren't helping."

She knew he was trying to be amusing, even now. "That wasn't supposed to be a compliment."

"But it was. Demons . . . we're supposed to be fearsome. Powerful. Scary as hell. It's our whole raison d'être. I mean, you've seen my demonic visage. All horns and talons and fire. I can't accept the possibility of wings and halos. I just can't."

She grimaced. "Got to say, I prefer the Darrak who has humanity and a pinch of angel running through him. Personally, I think it's an improvement on the original."

A glimmer of a smile played at his lips before it faded away completely. "This is the beginning of the end, Eden."

She shook her head. "No it isn't."

"You really think we can stay this way forever? Playing house in your little apartment in the sky while our lives fall apart all around us? We've been fooling ourselves."

Her throat felt thick. "Don't say that."

Darrak's dark brows drew together. "You really think this has a chance in hell of working out? You and me? Even if the curse is lifted, it doesn't change anything else. I'm a demon/angel hybrid freak and you're a half-angel who can do black magic. Sounds completely nuts, that's what it sounds like."

A moment later, his expression shuttered off, his forehead creasing. He didn't make a sound, but she knew he was feeling the tearing pain again.

Enough of this. Enough damned waiting.

She stood up from the side of the bed. "I need advice."

Darrak gasped for breath. "But you said Maksim's gone AWOL. Again."

"Not from Maksim." She turned and left the bedroom headed toward the hall closet. She grabbed her coat and reached into the pocket to pull out the marble.

Desperate times called for desperate measures. She'd tried to deny everything, but what Darrak told her had gotten through to her in one very important way. She knew he didn't have much time left—not feeling like this. She'd seen him shift to smoke this morning for a horrible moment. If he did that and wasn't able to possess her, wasn't able to take form again, he'd be swept away to the Void. She'd lose him forever.

She wouldn't let that happen.

Eden had failed to send Brenda to Lucas for his hellish job interview, but she had to see him. She had to get him to help her. Help Darrak. She couldn't think of another answer.

Her hand closed on the marble just as Darrak's grip clamped around her wrist. She looked up into his now fiery eyes.

He was pale and looked ill, but he'd dragged himself out of bed in order to stop her. "Don't do this. I don't want to owe him anything."

She shook her head. "I'll be back as soon as I can."

"No, Eden, don't—"

She squeezed the marble. *"Lucifer."*

Bright light flashed in front of her and her apartment disappeared, replaced by the familiar beach. However, it was darker this time and a cold breeze blew across the sand. The sun could barely be seen on the horizon. Instead of a wash of pink, purple, and orange, it was indigo and black.

Something felt wrong here.

But this place didn't really exist. It was made up out of Lucas's imagination. A pleasant getaway compared to his usual home base in the fiery pit.

A chill went through her as she turned, trying to see where he was. If she was here he had to be, too. Somewhere.

Eden spotted a form on the sand fifty feet up the beach. She swiftly moved toward it to find that it was Lucas, lying on his stomach. She gasped and dropped to her knees next to him.

"Lucas!" She tentatively touched his shoulder.

He didn't move.

What could have happened here? She rolled him onto his back so she could inspect him better. No wounds. No blood. She wiped the sand off his face and felt at his throat for a pulse, even though she knew he wasn't human. There was a faint pulse, but his skin was cool.

Had he somehow been affected by what had happened to Darrak? It seemed impossible, but she knew they were connected. After all, Lucas had been the one to create Darrak in the first place.

Her hands trembled. If she had to guess, she'd say Lucas was dying. But the Prince of Hell couldn't die, could he?

"I don't know how to help you." She grasped hold of her amulet and squeezed it. "I can't heal, I can only destroy with my magic."

Eden didn't like him, didn't trust him, but the thought

that he was hurt or gone forever bothered her. If he was gone he couldn't help her fix Darrak.

She pressed her hands to either side of his face. "Please, don't go. I need you. Wake up. Say something."

Faster than anything she'd ever seen before he grabbed her arms and twisted her over to press her against the sand. His hands closed around her throat.

Lucas's eyes didn't blaze with fire like Darrak's did. Instead, his were filled with bright white light. This, strangely enough, was much scarier.

"You defied me, Eden." His voice was calm, but filled with menace. "Didn't you? And now you come here looking for my help? Are you gutsy or just plain stupid?"

Definitely stupid; she knew that coming into this but she'd done it anyway. She struggled to breathe. "Lucas, let go of me!"

"Why should I? I know you didn't follow my orders. You failed me, yet again. And what am I supposed to do now? Forgive and forget?"

It was on the tip of her tongue to try to lie, but she knew it was futile. "You must have known I couldn't go through with it. Maybe you're the one who's stupid."

Oh, that was smart of her. Call Lucifer stupid. Great.

She must have a death wish.

Time to be proactive. She clenched her fist and tried to summon her magic, and was surprised when nothing happened.

Lucas smiled. "Remember, this is my domain, Eden. Your magic doesn't work here."

"So I'm at your mercy, is that it?"

"I've never really been known for my mercy."

"Then why haven't you killed me yet if I defied your undefiable order? Because I'm right, aren't I? Because you didn't think I'd be able to do it at all. Besides, she doesn't want to talk to you."

He raised an eyebrow. "She?"

That was right. He didn't know anything about the person named on that card. Brenda had been cloaked to him and still was. "Let's just say, she's not interested in working for you."

"Not *for* me, exactly. And it doesn't really matter in the end. She was only an alternate. I have someone else lined up who is much more eager for the opportunity."

Relief filled Eden, but she didn't dare move just yet. "So no harm done."

"You still defied me. And now you come here seeking answers to fix your demon boyfriend."

Tears burned her eyes. "He's in trouble."

"What else is new?"

"It's my fault. I did something by mistake that hurt him, made something shift inside him. You have to help me."

Lucas laughed at that and pushed up off the ground. "Help you? Why would I want to do that?"

"Because you need me."

He cocked his head and studied her curiously. "You think so, do you?"

Darrak thought Eden was part of some master plan on Lucas's part. She knew the prince wasn't in love with her, so why else would he put up with her mistakes, her arguments, and all the difficulties she'd caused him since they'd first come into contact?

And yet, he kept sniffing around.

Lucas wanted something from her, but he wasn't ready to ask for it yet.

This didn't help ease her mind one tiny bit.

"Yes, I think so, Lucas," she said evenly. "Whatever you need from me, I'm willing to help out. Within reason. But you have to help me in return."

"Do I now?" He smiled and closed the distance between them to grab hold of her amulet, and he looked down at it before his gaze flicked to hers. "You're the strangest black witch I've ever come across. Filling up with darkness on a daily basis, but unable to resist helping someone in need. Be it this woman today, or Darrak, or even me, seemingly injured on a beach. Your charity may one day lead you down a very dark path."

His proximity made her tremble. There weren't too many paths that would lead her anywhere darker than this. "Tell me how to fix Darrak."

"To truly fix him? You'd have to remove the angelic side, which I'm sure he's just thrilled about. But that's impossible. There are no take-backs." His lips thinned. "Do you know that one word from me would set Hell on him like flies to honey? There are many demons who hate anything angelic so much they'd relish the chance to tear an anomaly like Darrak apart. Others, however, would prefer to dissect him slowly. Demons aren't quite as altruistic as you are."

Fear raced through her and she struggled to keep her voice calm. "Please don't do that."

"We'll see."

"Whatever you need from me, you can't get it just by threatening me."

"When have I ever threatened you, Eden? Never. Not once."

A nervous laugh bubbled in her chest. "You had me in a choke hold a minute ago, in case you forgot."

"That was just playing around." He stroked a long lock of her auburn hair behind her shoulder, and she couldn't help but take an automatic step back. This made him smile. "So many women would literally kill for me to touch them. To do whatever I like to them."

"Is that what you're looking for? For me to want you like that?"

"No, in fact I prefer that you don't. What I want from you is very specific, but you're not there yet, Eden. So very soon, but not quite yet. There's too much at stake for me to strike before the iron is hot, as the saying goes." His gaze moved down the length of her. "Besides, I know you already belong to him. He has staked his claim in ways that surprise even me."

She had to get back. Darrak was getting worse with every minute that passed. "Darrak needs—"

"He needs something I won't be providing. Quite honestly, I don't care if he lives or dies. But he matters to you." His eyes lit up again. "The answer is as simple as they come, Eden."

She went silent, waiting, willing her impatience to back off. It wasn't helping right now with this hellishly frustrating man. "I need to get back."

"Of course. For Darrak. And for your friend . . . the werewolf."

She inhaled sharply. "You know about Andy?"

He nodded. "You have obtained a spell to contain him tonight."

"How do you—?"

"Not everything is cloaked to me, Eden. I know the things I need to know. It's all a part of the whole."

Now he was talking like a fortune cookie, too. "Please tell me how to help Darrak."

"Like I said, it's simple." He grasped her chin and looked into her eyes. "You broke him, so you need to fix him. I'll see you again, Eden. Very soon."

He snapped his fingers, and the next moment she wasn't on the beach any longer. She was back in her apartment.

Darrak stood directly in front of her, holding on to her wrist. "I'm serious, Eden. You can't see Lucifer again. It's too dangerous. Put that damned summoning crystal down, will you?"

Lucas had returned her within the exact millisecond she'd left. Darrak had no idea she'd even been gone. She put the marble back in her pocket and hung her coat back up in the hall closet.

He sighed with relief. "That's better."

"I need you back in bed," she commanded.

He leaned against the wall. "I appreciate the interest, but I'm not feeling all that frisky at this precise moment."

She grabbed his arm and pulled him along with her to the bedroom. He didn't argue again as she put him back into bed and sat on the edge with her hand on his forehead.

"It's okay," he said. "It doesn't hurt that much."

"And here I thought you were a good liar."

"It's over, Eden. I can feel it."

"No it's not. Not even close."

She didn't need to be a rocket scientist to get what Lucas had told her. She'd made this mess, she'd done something, shifted something, messed with something that shouldn't have been messed with when she'd tried to remove the curse. Nothing else had changed in order for him to feel this lousy.

This wasn't his inner angel and demon doing battle inside him. This was merely a glitch.

She looked down at his pale face as he looked up at her uncertainly.

"I'm going to fix you," she said. "So get ready."

⇛ eleven ⇚

"Not that I don't have every confidence," Darrak began, "but are you sure you know what you're doing?"

"Do you trust me?"

He eyed her. "Should I?"

"Do you?" Eden asked again.

"I don't want you to use your magic again for this."

"Tough. It's the only way. I need to go back in and shift things back to the way they were before. When I tried to remove the curse, I rearranged the furniture in there. I know what I did wrong—I shifted the light and dark sides of you when they were already in perfect feng shui position."

"So you're trying to say you did an Extreme Home Makeover on me?"

She snorted. "Pretty much."

He leaned back against the pillow. "Fine. Do your worst."

"I think I already did that."

"Andy's got less than three hours before sunset."

"I know. Now, shhh."

Eden pressed her hands against his chest and closed her eyes so she could concentrate. This time it didn't take long

at all to sink down to the metaphysical level. She wouldn't
be able to explain it to somebody else, only to say that it felt
very natural. Very right. If it didn't do damage to her soul
while she was down here fiddling around, it would prove to
be a very useful talent.

She scanned Darrak's being, and yes, the light and the
dark were bumping up against each other violently now. Of
course. How couldn't she have noticed that before? It was
like two lions infringing on each other's territory, both
equally powerful but very, very different.

A turf war was going on in Darrak's body between who
he was and the new part of himself he refused to accept.

Something else caught her attention. She hadn't noticed
it before. She'd been too distracted thinking the pure darkness was the curse, when really it was his demonic side. But
now she saw it hiding at the edges, staring out at her. His
curse. It was slimy and evasive, and one look at it told her
it would devour her if she even attempted to reach toward it.

If the spell from before had been like a puppy returning
to its master at its first opportunity, this was a snake, wind-
ing around everything, both light and dark, until it was too
tangled to untie.

One day, she might try again. But not today. She instinctively knew that grabbing hold of it now would only do
more damage.

Darrak gasped out loud as she shifted the light and dark
parts of him back into their comfortable positions. The rag-
ing jutting turf war stopped immediately.

Putting Darrak back together was a lot like putting IKEA
furniture together. Only this didn't come with instructions.

Eden opened her eyes to see Darrak was staring up
at her.

"Done," she said. "How do you feel?"

"Better."

Relief flooded her. "Thank God."

"If you say so." He grinned and slid his fingers into her
hair. "Yeah, I feel way better now."

"Things don't seem as bleak?"

"Oh, things still reek of bleak. Just without the bonus prize of sheer agony."

She pulled back. "I should have told you. I'm sorry."

He sat up. "Yeah, well, I'm sorry for not taking the news like a champ."

Her guilt from before prodded at her again. "You had a right to know earlier than today."

"How about we renew our agreement to be honest with each other? Or I might start borrowing your body again to do my errands at night."

"Blackmail. I can respect that." She hadn't told him about her meeting with Lucas, but she'd been returned so quickly that she honestly didn't see a reason she needed to share that with him. She didn't want to spoil his improved mood by mentioning his ex-boss.

Eden looked down at her amulet. "Not much damage done."

"Anything is too much."

"It was worth it. I'm so glad you're feeling better."

"Angel." He blinked. "I'm half-angel. Maybe if I keep saying it out loud it won't feel so utterly insane. Which half is angel, though? That's the question."

She almost smiled. "I think it's your right half."

He snorted. "It was a rhetorical question."

"I could see it, you know. Two separate pieces that aren't too thrilled about taking up the same space. The right"—she took his right hand and brought it to her lips, kissing it—"and the left." Then she did the same to the left.

Darrak watched her carefully. "Well, I can tell you that both sides like that a lot."

He was wrong. This wouldn't be the end of him. She'd fixed the pain and she could fix everything else if given enough time. "You're going to be okay."

"You know that for a fact?"

She nodded. "Yup."

"Beauty, brains, and the ability to soothsay. I'm very impressed." He frowned. "You're looking at me strangely right now."

Desire had replaced the concern she'd felt before. She slid her hands over his shoulders. "Am I?"

"You are."

"How are you feeling?"

"Better, like I said."

She leaned forward and brushed her lips against his. "How much better?"

His gaze darkened with passion. "One hundred percent."

Then, as if a well had broken, he pulled her against him and kissed her hard and deep on her lips.

She grinned. "So you are feeling frisky now."

"Never friskier."

His mouth covered hers again, his tongue sliding against her own. She couldn't remember him ever kissing her with this kind of abandon before, not even the time they'd been given a lust elixir. There had always been something to stop them—worries about her black magic, Darrak's spell that might make it worse, or not admitting her true feelings about the demon in the first place. They'd always fought against what felt so right.

Sure, they had plenty of problems stacked up against them like a tall, impenetrable brick wall, but nothing remained to keep them from giving in to their passion for each other.

"I want you, Darrak," she whispered against his lips.

His eyes blazed with need. "You know how much I love you."

"Show me. Make love to me."

It was all the encouragement he needed. He gathered her into his arms and turned her around to press her down against the mattress. She worked to remove his T-shirt and jeans, running her hands over his hot, bare skin.

He kicked off his shoes and unbuttoned her blouse, sliding her pants down her legs. His mouth moved over her curves as he went, filling his hands with her breasts so he could slide his tongue over them, making her arch her back and gasp with pleasure.

She wouldn't think about their problems. She wouldn't

think about anything but this moment. She'd do like Darrak always suggested and live in the now. The future was not invited.

"I love you," he whispered again after he'd explored her body inch by inch.

"Darrak, I—" But anything she would have said next was swept away by the feeling of him filling her in one deep thrust. It swept away her thoughts, her words, her entire universe.

Eden clung to him as he moved inside of her and she captured his handsome face between her hands, staring deeply into his ice blue eyes—such a cool color to be filled with so much heat. He felt so good, smelled so good, tasted so good.

Darrak made her feel better than anyone ever had in her entire life.

People like Ben, like Leena, like her mother, thought what they had between them was wrong. That it was impossible for her to care this deeply for a demon and for that demon to care about her in return.

But Darrak wasn't exactly a demon anymore, was he? He was special. He was unique.

He was hers.

She arched against him as it felt as if she exploded into a million pieces of pleasure and couldn't help but cry out against his lips. A moment later, her name left his lips in a harsh, raspy groan as he experienced his own shattering moment of completion.

They lay naked on her bed, side by side, the covers tossed off and the shadows of the dark room playing across their bodies. Darrak held her hand tightly in his, their fingers entwined, and stared into her eyes as she relearned how to breathe.

"Yes," she whispered, trailing her fingertips down his bare chest. "That was very good."

He pulled her closer, his lips tracing the contour of her jaw. "No spell."

"Gone for good."

Darrak slid his hand over her hip, then around to her back where he played up the length of her spine. She nestled closer to his warmth, which had thankfully returned now that everything was back in proper alignment.

"I think I could get used to this," she said.

"You, me, a messy bed."

"To hell with everything else."

A smile played at his lips. "I have a feeling you'd need food. Eventually, anyway. We could always send out for chocolate donuts."

"You know the way to a girl's heart."

He slowly trailed his fingers over her face, then down her throat, collarbone, and breasts. He swirled his thumb around her nipple, which made it extremely difficult to think properly.

She wanted him again. And again.

"Darrak, please . . ."

"Please what?" He was grinning now.

She eyed him and couldn't help but smile as well. "Don't be so smug, demon."

"Smug? Moi?" He leaned forward and kissed her shoulder, but his fingers didn't stop playing with her sensitive flesh until he replaced them with his tongue. Her mind went white. "You want me, Eden?"

"No, you absolutely disgust me." She grinned and captured his mouth, kissing him deeply. "Yes, I want you."

"And you need me?"

"Oh, yes."

He leaned closer to whisper in her ear. "And you love me?"

She took his face between her hands and stared deeply into his eyes. "Of course I do."

He pulled back, locking gazes with her. A frown creased his brow. "I've been thinking a lot. You know, between the bouts of agony and confusion."

Eden raised an eyebrow. "Should I be scared?"

"Possibly."

"What have you been thinking about?"

"Stanley."

"You've been thinking about Stanley? Before, during, or after we had sex?"

He laughed. "Not now, trust me. No, I've been thinking about him and his decisions lately. Especially when it comes to Nancy. He and I had a little talk about his proposal to her."

"Oh yeah?"

"Stanley was a selfish loser, never thought much about anyone but himself and his next conquest."

"I remember. But what's your point?"

"I was like Stanley, sort of. Way better looking, of course." He flashed her a wry grin. "Less balding, anyway."

"No argument here."

"But when it comes to faulty starts, him and me—we're a lot alike. Until we met a couple of very special women. Stanley met Nancy . . . and I met you."

Darrak looked so serious right now it almost made her laugh. By the looks of things, his brush with mortality had given him much to think about. "You did. So what's your point?"

He met her gaze and held it. "Eden, this is going to sound crazy, but it feels right. Especially now. I . . . I just . . ."

She stroked the messy dark hair off his forehead. What was this all about? "Just say it. It's okay."

Darrak sat up completely and brought Eden up next to him, clasping her hands in his. His eyes were so full of sincerity she had a moment of fear about what exactly he wanted to tell her, what confession he suddenly wanted to make.

"What, Darrak? Talk to me."

He searched her face. "Eden . . . marry me."

She blinked. "What?"

He squeezed her hands tighter. "We've been through so much together and . . . I know it's a human concept that doesn't normally apply to demons, well, like *ever*. But it feels right. I want to be with you for however long we have together. I know it's not ideal, and our lives aren't anything remotely resembling a fairy tale, but . . . I love you. And I want to marry you because it's a symbol of how we feel. How *I* feel." He laughed a little. "Damn, I sound like I have no idea what I'm doing here, but I'm doing it anyway. Eden Riley, will you marry me?"

She gaped at him for a long moment before she tried to speak, but nothing came out. Her mouth had dried up like a box of sand.

What was he doing? Just what exactly had she clicked into place when she'd been shifting his dark and light jigsaw pieces apart before?

"Darrak . . . I—I don't know what to say. I'm surprised you'd ask me . . . this. It's just, I . . ."

A shadow of doubt entered his expression. "It was stupid, wasn't it?"

"No." She gripped his hands. This was so unbelievably sweet and unexpected and . . . she didn't know how to deal with this. A wistful sensation passed through her wishing things could be different than they were. Wishing they were remotely normal and could discuss things like this seriously. "Not stupid. Just not—Darrak, I . . . it's just not something we should even be thinking about right now. There's too much to deal with. I mean, at the very least you don't even have a birth certificate. Or a driver's license. And . . . and we've only known each other a month. One month!"

Clarity washed over his expression. "Forget I said anything."

Her stomach twisted. "No, I don't want to forget it. Just . . . maybe ask me again when things are better. But right now—you can't honestly think this is a good time for this, do you? Besides, we have to go deal with Andy." She glanced at the clock on her nightstand. "We really have to get moving right now."

New clothes flowed over his skin, and he let her go completely. "Of course. Andy. I forgot about him for a minute there."

Eden grabbed at the bedsheets to cover herself. She suddenly felt extremely naked. "Darrak, I mean it. We'll talk about this later, I promise we will."

He got up off the bed, averting his gaze. "No problem. I'm going to let you get ready. I'll give you some privacy."

He left the bedroom and the door closed behind him with a soft click.

It felt very quiet all of a sudden. She could even hear the pounding of her heartbeat in her ears, loud and fast.

Darrak had just asked her to marry him. *Marry him.* And she'd all but replied with a hell no. The last thing she wanted to do after all they'd been through was to hurt him, but what was she supposed to say? And what in the world had possessed him to ask her that in the first place? Had he really been inspired, of all things, by Stanley Dancy, minion to wizards and demons alike?

The full moon was making everyone go wild this month.

So, that couldn't possibly have gone much worse than it did.

Darrak wished for a button to press that could undo the dumber things he attempted. It would have helped many times over the years.

This, quite possibly, had been the dumbest.

"Eden Riley, will you marry me?"

He covered his face with his hands. "What do I think this is? *The Bachelorette*?"

Sex didn't normally make him lose his mind like that. First time for everything.

It was sort of humorous, actually. A cursed archdemon asking someone to be his wife in holy-freaking-matrimony. And the entire idea had been put into his mind in the first place by the romantic lothario Stanley, of all people.

Hilarious. Maybe someday he'd be able to laugh about it.

That day was not going to be today.

Fine. So the proof was in the proverbial pudding. He had sensed it all along, but now he knew for sure. What he felt for Eden was not returned in full. She cared about him, she lusted after him, she might even love him a little. But it wasn't nearly the same as how he felt about her.

Point taken. He didn't need any further embarrassment, thank you very much. He could take a hint when it hit him in the face with the force of a city bus.

He caught a glimpse of himself in the oval mirror attached to the wall. "This is what happens with all that angel inside of you. It's turned you into a romantic dope."

He was soft, sensitive, and making offers of marriage.

It was the beginning of the end, just as he'd predicted for himself.

Lucifer must have been laughing his ass off about his least favorite ex-employee. Darrak was nothing more than sentient hellfire with a soft side.

There were bigger issues to be concerned with at the moment; he knew that. Much, much bigger.

But still. How embarrassing.

⇻ TWELVE ↤

Ben was getting better at lurking. Practice made perfect.

He currently lurked outside of Eden's apartment building. He hadn't been here for a while, but he was determined to do something now—something that would redeem him from his recent lousy decisions. He'd gone into everything with the Malleus because he wanted to save Eden from the demon who possessed her, and that was exactly what he'd do.

The only question was *how*.

Do this and everything goes back to normal.

Yeah. Unlikely at best, but it was a nice thought.

The chill in the air made him draw his coat closer. He'd been standing there staring at her building for nearly a half hour now trying to concentrate, but his mind kept going back to that shapeshifter.

Big trouble, that one. Her being locked up in a cage wasn't necessarily a bad thing.

Still, something about her situation had struck him as wrong. She was locked in that cell because she had information Oliver wanted. She was also locked up because she was a shifter, since the Malleus deemed anything Other to be evil. Just like the police, the Malleus had rules and guidelines that governed their actions. They were trying to make the world a better, safer place.

He'd honestly believed that in the beginning.

"You look troubled."

Ben glanced next to him with surprise. He hadn't seen the man approach, now leaning against the car next to Ben's. He was tall, with short messy brown hair and an ill-fitting suit that looked like it could use an ironing.

"Do I?" he replied.

"Definitely."

"Who're you?"

"Just a concerned citizen. I want to help you . . . if you want my help, that is."

"You can help me? You don't even know me."

"I know enough, Ben. Enough to know you're a good person who wants to do the right thing. Just like her." The man nodded off to their left.

Ben was taken aback that this guy knew his name, but he turned to see that they weren't alone in their survey of the apartment. There was a pretty, dark-haired young woman sitting in a Corvette nearby, her gaze fixed on the building.

"Who's she?" Ben asked.

"Someone like you who's looking for redemption. Her name's Caroline. You two have a lot in common."

"Like what?"

"You both care about the ultimate fate of Eden Riley."

Ben tensed. "What do you know about Eden?"

"A fair amount."

"Who are you?"

"A friend."

"I don't need any more friends."

"No? Could have fooled me. Here I thought you currently have"—he cocked his head to the side—"exactly zero friends, right? At least ones you can count on in a pinch. You know what they say, a friend can help you move. A good friend can help you move a body. It's all very true."

"What the hell are you talking about?"

He nodded toward the parked car. "You and Caroline should become friends. Together, I think you can help Eden. After all, that's what you both want: to help her. And you both think you know how to do that."

Ben took all this in. "She knows about . . . Darrak? Do *you* know about Darrak?"

"I can't directly help you, but I can give you some advice if you want to hear it."

"What do you want in return?"

"Nothing. Not from you, anyway."

"Who the hell are you?" Ben demanded again.

The man's expression didn't change. He didn't move closer. He just sat against the car's hood and looked up at the building. "Like I said, a *friend*."

"Whose friend?"

Finally the man cast a glance in his direction. "Do you want the advice I have to give you or not?"

Ben didn't like not being in control. He didn't like not having his questions answered. But at the end of the day he'd come here for one reason—to help Eden. And he currently had no damn idea how to go about that.

"Yes," he said. "I want the advice."

The man's smile grew. "Somehow I just knew you were going to say that."

A sense of foreboding followed Eden when she and Darrak left the apartment and headed toward her car. It passed, but it was unpleasant, like walking through a thatch of spiderwebs.

Darrak was trying to act like everything was fine, but she knew it wasn't. She'd broken something between them— something she didn't know was breakable.

Why did he have to go and ask her to marry him? Why now when there were a million other things to concern themselves with?

"So, did you buy a leash for our new puppy?" He was

trying to make a joke as he got into the passenger side of her car, but his lips were tight as he smiled.

She put the key in the ignition and pulled out of her parking spot. "Didn't get around to it. It's on the list."

"You don't have to worry. Even if he's a mindless, vicious werewolf, it's only one night a month. We can contain him with that spell. Andy's just lucky he has you looking out for him."

She had Maksim's containment spell tucked safety into her coat pocket. He said even a human could do it, so she didn't think it would require her tapping into her black magic. She'd just have to read the incantation aloud when the time came and the office would be sealed up nice and tight until she decided to remove it again.

And according to the wizard it would also work as a cloaking spell, so no one who wandered past would see anything weird going on.

"Tomorrow I'm going to track Maksim down and we'll see him again," Darrak said. "There has to be some other options for us."

"You really think so?"

"Sure. In the beginning, we thought it was only Selina that could help us, but now we know for sure that you share her magic. Just because the curse removal didn't work the first time doesn't mean that something else can't be done to help us."

"You sound so positive today."

"That's me. Sunshine to go." A bitter smile stretched over his face. "It's probably the angel half."

She didn't want to broach the subject, but it was still five minutes till they arrived at the office. She returned her attention to the road. "Lucas said that other demons would come after you if they found out. Maybe we can find a way to cloak you from them."

As soon as the words left her mouth she regretted it.

"Oh?" Darrak said. "And when exactly did *Lucas* tell you this?"

She remembered her recent promise to tell Darrak the

truth and not to keep anything back. Time to hold true to that. "When I touched the marble earlier, I saw him, but he sent me back so fast you never realized I was gone."

There was silence in the car for a moment.

"Well, that was convenient, wasn't it?" His gaze fell to her amulet. "Same color as before. Guess there wasn't any tonsil hockey going on this time, was there?"

She looked at him sharply. "Sorry to disappoint."

"What do you think would happen if you slept with him? Might suck the evil completely out of you."

"Darrak, don't go there." Her tone held an edge of warning.

"I guess I understand the 'let's wait' reply to my question now. Got to keep your options open in case a better offer comes in."

"I swear to God, Darrak, stop it."

He eyed her. "You swear to *God*? Why? Are you dating him, too?"

Anger rose in her throat, but she swallowed it down. "I know I hurt you—"

"You didn't hurt me." He waved a hand flippantly. "Just helped to put things back into perspective. I should thank you. Lesson learned."

"Oh, what lesson is that?"

He hissed out a breath. "I don't want to talk about this."

"That makes two of us."

He turned his attention to the roadside swiftly moving past them. "Maybe if I wasn't so connected to you, I'd be able to gather my balls back together and be less of an emotional basket case." He snorted. "It's funny, actually. I keep blaming myself for everything I've done to you—made you part evil, ruined your life, destroyed your immortal soul . . . I keep forgetting just how much you've messed me up in return."

That hurt, but she couldn't say he was wrong. Tears burned in her eyes, and she gave him a sideways glance as they pulled into the parking lot.

"Then I guess we're even, aren't we?"

He didn't look directly at her. "Guess so."

"So you hate me now, is that it?"

Darrak was silent for a moment before he laughed out loud. "I don't hate you, Eden. I love you. But I get that that emotion isn't returned in full. Let's just forget about it and go deal with werewolf boy."

He got out of the car, slammed the door behind him, and started walking to the front door of Triple-A.

Damn it. She so didn't need this right now. Any of it.

If she had one wish at this very moment, she'd wish that she wasn't bound to Darrak. At all. She needed her freedom, her space, her privacy.

She'd never asked for any of this to begin with. Who the hell would?

Darrak had given her unwanted black magic that put her soul at risk. He'd taken away any possibility for privacy. He was frustrating and vain and self-involved.

He was also funny and sexy and fiercely protective of her. She enjoyed his company. He challenged her, made her laugh, drove her crazy with desire. He was truly the best man she'd ever known. One she knew she could trust her secrets to.

And maybe her heart, too.

Something continued to hold her back. There were too many problems, obstacles, and challenges. How could she possibly allow herself to fall for him completely when they had so many issues to deal with on a daily basis?

She honestly had no idea. But right now she had to deal with Andy.

Eden marched into the office. Andy sat behind his desk looking oddly serene.

"Everything okay?" she asked.

Andy eyed the clock. "You know, the last time I checked, you still worked here. I know you're not my employee, but we're partners, right?"

"Right. Of course."

"And I bought you that BlackBerry so we could stay in touch. I've been texting you all afternoon and I haven't heard back from you once."

"Oh, right. The BlackBerry." She bit her bottom lip.

"Eden destroyed that," Darrak said. He leaned against the wall right next to the glass door surveying the small office space. "Her black magic made it go boom."

"When was this?" Andy's voice went a bit pitchy.

"Yesterday morning. Didn't she mention that to you? Not surprised about that. She likes to keep things to herself."

Andy's brows knitted together. "I sense that you two aren't exactly in a good mood. What's the problem?"

"We're fine," Eden said, with a pointed look at Darrak. "Aren't we?"

"Stellar." He shrugged and focused on Andy, his expression now turning concerned. "Forget about us. How are *you* feeling right now?"

"Me?" Andy pointed at himself. "I'm fine. I feel fantastic, actually."

"You would. Lycanthropy usually brings with it a renewed life force, kind of like a sip from the fountain of youth."

Andy's jaw tensed. "I hope this evening will prove to the two of you once and for all that you're wrong about me."

Even though his words were firm, there was now a sharp edge of worry that slid behind his eyes. They were close now. That had to be scary when he didn't know what to expect.

"It's going to be okay, really. The moment I sense that you're changing"—Eden held up her hands at his immediate bristle—"*if* that happens, of course, Darrak and I will leave, and I'll read the spell from out in the parking lot." She glanced over her shoulder at the sunset. "We don't have too long to wait."

"Great." Andy stood up and began to pace. "This just . . . it feels wrong. It's not going to happen. I can make the choice *not* to be a werewolf."

Darrak shrugged. "You can try."

Andy walked to the glass door and then back to his desk. Twice. "I'll be fine."

He was keeping up a good front, but Eden knew him well enough by now to see it was all fake. He was scared. He hadn't mentioned much about the attack, but it had been bad. He'd been bloody, torn up, and if he'd been attacked by a regular wolf, there was no doubt that he would have died from his horrible injuries. As it was, they healed up quickly, leaving him with no scars.

There was no doubt in Eden's mind what was going to happen after the sun went down. All she could do was try to be here for him and contain the situation.

Control it.

She smiled wryly as that word flitted through her head. Everything could be controlled with the right amount of will. And a little bit of magic didn't hurt.

After all, she'd controlled the Malleus situation. Last time she'd been face-to-face with Ben, his boss Oliver Gale, and his new witchy girlfriend Sandy, Eden had unleashed her black magic as self-protection. It had practically killed them, and at the time, she hadn't cared if she had.

It was as disturbing as it was empowering. She might still look like a nice girl, but underneath . . . she knew she wasn't. Not anymore. Eden didn't want to hurt anyone, but if they tried to hurt her first, what choice did she have?

Just the thought scared her. She pressed her hand over her amulet, feeling the cold stone surface like ice over her heart.

She sensed Darrak watching her and she looked at him, surprised to see the concern in his gaze.

"You okay?"

She nodded. "Yeah, I'm fine."

Other than the flu still circling her like a vulture waiting to swoop in, and a tendency to latch onto black magic at the drop of a hat, she was fine. Sure she was.

She held his gaze. "I'm sorry about . . . well, I—I'm sorry, Darrak."

He nodded. "Me, too."

Well, that was a start. Just because they argued, or disagreed, or got angry with each other, didn't mean much in the grand scheme of things. It wasn't like they could break up—not like normal couples could, anyway. They were bound together whether they were romantically involved or not.

She really would prefer to have a choice about that. But, much like who her mother was, fate hadn't given Eden much of a choice in anything in her life.

So be it. She'd deal.

There was a jingle as the door opened, and Eden glanced over her shoulder.

Great, she thought. *Speak of the devil.*

Caroline Riley peeked her head in. "Hey there."

"Hello," Andy greeted her cheerily. "Come in. We're about to close, but we have a couple minutes left."

Caroline grinned. "Andy McCoy." Her gaze slid down the front of him. "You're still looking rather delicious, even after all this time."

His eyebrows went up. "Why, thank you. I have to say that the feeling is utterly mutual." He held out his hand. "And you are?"

She smiled and took his hand to squeeze it in hers. "Let me give you a clue. Vegas. New Year's Eve, five years ago. Strip poker. You lost."

He blinked. "But, I—uh. That was . . . I mean, I remember . . . vividly . . . but . . ."

Eden wanted to move this along. "Yeah, that's my mother, Andy. She's back from the grave and renting the body of a lingerie model."

Caroline looked at her sharply. "Aspiring actress, actually."

"Whatever you say."

Andy gaped at her. "You're kidding me. Caroline? Is that really you?"

"In the flesh." She turned in a slow circle.

"Christ on a cracker!" Andy exclaimed. "You're alive!"

Caroline grimaced. "Sort of. My original body is gone for good. I'm stuck on earth until I redeem myself. It's proving to be a challenge. Apparently, I was more of a bad girl than I ever gave myself credit for."

"But . . . but this is wonderful. Just wonderful!"

"I'm glad someone finally thinks so."

Andy always had a thing for her mother. It had never really been discussed between them, but Eden was fairly certain there had been more than just a poker game during the fateful night when Andy had lost 49 percent of Triple-A to her, which she'd left in her will to Eden.

But *strip* poker? There were some things she really didn't need to know.

For Andy it might have been love. For her mother—it had been yet another fling with a man who paid her some attention.

Frankly, Eden wanted better for Andy than that.

"Mom, what are you doing here?"

"I want to talk to you," Caroline said, then flicked a disapproving glance at Darrak. "In private. Can you do that for me, honey? Five minutes of your time is all I'm asking for. Please."

Eden looked at Darrak, who nodded.

"It's okay," he said. "Let her give you an earful about why you should have me exorcised at your earliest convenience. I'll keep Andy company."

"Five minutes," she assured him. "Then I'll be back and we'll . . . you know . . . do what we have to do."

"Sounds good."

There was still a lot left unsaid between them. Later that night they would have a serious conversation and Eden would force herself to get into it. She'd tell Darrak why she wasn't able to give her heart to him completely. He'd understand. He'd give her time to get comfortable with everything. After all, time together was one thing they could count on.

She looked at her mother. "I'll buy you a quick coffee. Have your say. And then I'm really sorry but I have other important business to deal with."

Caroline shook her head. "My daughter, always so serious. Must come from her father's side." At Eden's sharp look, she huffed out, "What? It's true. I'm way more laid-back than you are. Always have been."

"*Too* laid-back, if you ask me," Eden mumbled as she did her coat up.

"Bye, now. Have fun with mommy dearest," Darrak said dryly.

She met his gaze. "I'll be back."

"I don't doubt it."

She reluctantly left the office, leading her mother right next door to Hot Stuff. Nancy quickly prepared their coffees, and they sat down at a booth.

Eden looked across at her mother's borrowed face. "Okay, we're here. You have the floor."

"You know how much I love you, Eden," Caroline began.

Eden sighed. "I know. And I know you mean well, but you don't know Darrak like I do."

"He's a demon from Hell."

"This is an argument that is going to go in circles, so let me stop you right there. He's great. He's wonderful. If he was a human guy I'd just met on the street I'd be damn lucky if he'd even look in my direction."

"But you're not happy, are you?"

"My current level of happiness actually has very little to do with Darrak himself. It's complicated. I know you're trying to help, but you have to give me space to deal with this." She glanced at her watch. "I don't have much time. What's your plan? Are you going to stay here in Toronto?"

"I haven't decided yet." Caroline took a sip from her coffee, black with two sweeteners, just like Eden remembered.

Her mother had always been on a diet to keep her figure as fat-free as possible. She'd saved up money when Eden was just a little girl to buy herself breast implants. She'd looked exactly like a Vegas showgirl, blonde and glamorous—everything that Eden knew she herself wasn't.

Not that she ever wanted breast implants. And Eden never had a great desire to be a size zero. She was a six.

Sometimes an eight. She didn't overeat, but she didn't really pay too much attention to it. She figured if she did pay too much attention she might become like Caroline, concerned with every calorie. Finding her pleasure with a diet of cocktails instead of a good meal.

It wasn't exactly a surprise that Caroline had chosen the svelte, beautiful, *young* body she had. Eden would have been able to call that particular decision from a mile away.

Caroline had always valued beauty and her outward appearance because it bought her what she needed—men to take care of her when the tables didn't pay out right. Beauty was a commodity, and she'd had it in spades. Eden knew, at the time of Caroline's death when she'd been pushing fifty, that her fading beauty was an issue for her.

"So now what?" Eden asked when Caroline didn't say anything for a moment. "Do you need money?"

Caroline laughed. "I can take care of myself."

"Half of Triple-A is yours. Maybe you want it back."

"No, I don't want anything from you, Eden." Her expression shadowed. "I know I was a lousy mother. It's time for me to make up for that. I'm here for you in your greatest time of need."

Eden reached across the table and took Caroline's hand. "Things weren't always the best between us, but I know you meant well. And I was really sorry to lose you like that, especially after we hadn't spoken in a while."

"That was totally my fault." Caroline shook her head and took another sip of her coffee. "I should have stayed in touch. I got mixed up with an acrobat from Cirque du Soleil. Half my age. He was very . . . flexible."

"Sounds interesting."

She grinned. "It had its moments. And about your father . . . I honestly didn't know what he was. I had no idea about anything supernatural in the world until after I died."

Eden grew concerned again. "Were you okay? I know you were in . . . in Hell for a while."

"I was fine. I felt like I was sheltered—like someone was looking out for me, protecting me. Then I was returned here with the knowledge that I had to redeem myself for the mistakes I'd made in life before I'd have the chance to go to a better place. It could take me a long time to do that."

Eden knew who'd been protecting her mother. Lucas had. But only because he was using Caroline's soul as a bartering tool to get Eden to do what he wanted. Still, she was glad her mother hadn't had to suffer. She stood up, knowing they had to wrap this up. The sun was setting. "You know I'm here for you."

"I know, honey." Caroline stood as well. "I'd like to spend more time with you while I'm here. If that's okay with you."

"I think that could be arranged. But you're going to have to let the subject of Darrak go. Him and me—we're together. For better or for worse." Eden inwardly cringed. That phrase made her think about his proposal again.

She threw her coffee cup in the garbage as they made their way toward the door. She waved at Nancy and saw the sparkle of her engagement ring as the barista waved back at her. She looked so happy.

The air felt cold on her face as they left the café.

Caroline looked disturbed. "You deserve better than to be possessed by a demon, Eden. It's nothing I ever would have envisioned for you."

"Sometimes life doesn't always go the way you envision it. It's a lesson I've recently learned."

Caroline grasped Eden's hands in hers. "This is bad, Eden, and it has to end. I can see that even if you can't."

"Mom, please. I need to get back." It was the same thing over and over and her patience was wearing thin. By the look of that sun, Darrak was going to start to lose form very soon.

"I'm not the only one who cares about you, Eden," she said tightly. "This—what's happening right now—this is an intervention."

She really didn't like the sound of that. "What are you talking about?"

"Eden," a familiar voice said from behind her. "Don't get upset."

She swiveled to see Ben Hanson standing ten feet away.

Shit. This was the last thing she needed right now.

"What do you want, Ben? I thought I made it very clear the last time I saw you that—"

He cut her off. "I know. I approached everything the wrong way then. I was motivated by my own hurt feelings. But Eden, this is so much bigger than that—I see that now. It's made me change my life, and I wouldn't do that simply out of some misplaced emotion toward a woman I'd been on a single date with. It's just taken me this long to get the right kind of focus."

Eden hissed out a breath of frustration. "I swear, Ben, don't come another step closer to me. I think you know what I can do if you push me too far. I'd rather not go there, especially not here."

Actually, there weren't that many cars in the lot. And the café had been practically deserted, apart from Nancy, the baker in the back kitchen, and maybe one other customer. No witnesses nearby if she had to use a little bit of magic to protect herself.

"So what is this? You and my mother have hooked up in order to grind some sense into me about Darrak, right?" She looked back at Caroline. "You know Ben's with the Malleus, don't you? They're not all that friendly toward drifters like you. I've seen a Malleus member take one out before. No redemption for you, then. No fluffy set of wings and a chance to hang out with my father again. Just a one-way ticket to the Void."

Caroline shook her head. "Ben and me—we want the same thing. We want to help you."

"I guess you don't understand what I've been telling you, so let me go ahead and spit it out one last time." Eden glared at Ben and felt the crackle of black magic move down into her hands just in case he tried anything funny. "You need to leave me alo—"

She gasped at the sharp stabbing pain in her shoulder and staggered forward. She'd been thinking it would be Ben who tried something. He'd shot her full of tranquilizer a couple of weeks ago so he could kidnap her and present her to his boss for an unpleasant Q&A. But Ben didn't have the tranquilizer needle this time.

Her mother did.

Caroline's eyes filled with tears. "I didn't want to hurt you, but this is for the best, honey. When you wake up, you'll realize that."

"No, wait . . ." Eden fell forward, but Ben was there to catch her before she hit the ground. "You don't know what you're doing."

"Your mother's right," he said. "This is for the best."

And then the world disappeared.

⇾ THIRTEEN ⇽

"I'm going to find that goddamned werewolf who mauled me," Andy said, taking a deep gulp from his silver flask. Darrak had no idea what he kept in there, but it seemed to be working. The man was quickly getting plastered. "And I'm going to make him into a rug. A nice furry rug for in front of my fireplace."

"You don't have a fireplace."

"I'll have one specially installed." He paced back and forth and pointed at Darrak. "This is all your fault."

"Probably. Everything else is, why should this be any different?"

Andy stopped pacing. "You sound kind of whiny today."

"I know. But thanks so much for mentioning it."

"You got it all, you know that? No reason for you to be a baby about it."

Darrak laughed dryly. "I'm feeling sensitive at the moment. You're going to make me cry if you keep being a meanie like this."

"What's the problem?"

"I think you have more important things to think about than my issues, Andy."

"Maybe, but I'm trying to take my mind off them. What's up?"

"Nothing, really." Darrak stared out at the sinking sun over Eden's parked car. "I went from being a fearsome arch-demon with a plan of one day overthrowing Lucifer, to being the amusing sidekick for an unlicensed female private investigator. The woman I'm in love with is feeling a bit blah about me, and I can't say I blame her. What do I have to offer someone like Eden? Pain, frustration, misery . . . maybe some hot sex now and then—"

Andy held up his hand. "I don't want to hear about it. Seriously."

"Sorry. But it's true. I'm already a big fat nothing, and I'm slowly coming to the realization that it's all downhill from here."

"I'll tell you exactly what you need to do, Darrak."

"Yeah, what's that?"

Andy sank down in his chair. "Damn, I don't know. I'm not good with giving advice. Sorry."

"Helpful. Thanks."

"Women." Andy took another swig from his flask. "More trouble than they're worth."

"You said it." Darrak focused on him for a moment. "It's going to be okay, you know. You don't have to be scared."

"I'm not scared."

"You're terrified."

"A real man would never admit something like that."

"I can guarantee you that nothing bad is going to happen. Well . . . other than turning into a werewolf, that is. Any minute now."

Andy paled. "That's pretty bad."

"I have a feeling you're going to be one of the good ones. This is not the end, it's only the beginning. It's not what you are, it's what you make of it." He grinned. "Make the most of it, Andy. Being a werewolf is going to give you a hell of a lot more than it takes away. Werewolves are cool."

"Really?"

"Sure. Nobody tells you what you are, you define your own rules. Your own guidelines. You're a good man, I already know that. There's no way you're going to hurt anyone. That's what you're the most afraid of, aren't you? Doing to someone what that bastard did to you."

Andy looked at him bleakly. "Yeah."

"Besides, Eden'll lock you up nice and tight in here the moment she gets back from her mommy/daughter powwow. Triple-A will be like a kennel once a month. Fun times."

His knuckles whitened on his flask. "Is it going to hurt? I mean, *if* I change."

Darrak's jaw tensed. "Probably a bit. But life is pain. Trust me on that."

"You give some good advice, if a bit on the unpleasant side. You should take some of it, too."

"What?"

"You're so wrapped up in what you're not—what you've lost—you don't realize what you have."

"Oh? And what's that?"

Andy shrugged. "You have Eden."

Darrak tried to summon a smile, but failed. "Only because she has absolutely no choice in the matter."

He flinched as the first pain hit him. Nothing remotely like what he'd felt earlier that day when his yin-yang, or whatever, had been out of whack, but still enough for him to take notice. It was a warning signal that he was going to be losing his corporeal form very soon.

Just another day at the office.

"She must be having a good chat with her mother. She's forgetting the time. It's been more than five minutes by now."

"Caroline Riley." Andy grinned. "So hot, you have no idea. I would have sold my soul for her at one time in my life."

"You really shouldn't tell a demon something like that. I might get ideas."

Andy shook his head. "Maybe once, but not now. I would have done a lot of bad stuff once in my life, but

I'm different now. Older, wiser. I'm not the smartest guy around, but I know what I want and what I don't want. You're the same. Whatever you were back in the day, that Darrak's gone for good. You hold on to him because you've let him define you, but you shouldn't. I have a feeling he was a real asshole."

"So what am I now?" Darrak asked quietly.

"Better."

"By whose definition?"

Andy shrugged. "Mine. What more do you need?"

Darrak laughed and flinched again. "Nice to see Eden's keeping a close eye on the clock. She's probably trying to get back at me for a little disagreement we had earlier."

"About what?"

"I accused her of wanting to date both God and Lucifer at the same time."

Andy blinked. "Women are moody sometimes."

"My thoughts exactly. I better go fetch her. Pardon the expression."

"Yeah, you go. Wish me luck with my . . . well, you know," Andy said, his tone turning serious.

Darrak turned to face him and took Andy's outstretched hand, shaking it firmly. "You won't need it. But good luck."

"Thank you."

Darrak turned toward the door, twisting the handle and pushing forward, but it didn't budge.

"What the hell?" he mumbled. He checked the lock to see if it had been turned, but it wasn't. "The door's stuck."

"Use your demonic superstrength."

"Right." Not exactly as strong as he once was, but he could probably take at least twenty humans on in a fight if he had to without resorting to firepower. He pushed the door as hard as he could.

Nothing happened.

He frowned deeply. "I don't know what's going on."

Andy was at his side and he tried the door. "It's sealed shut."

"Sealed?" Darrak shook his head. "But Eden hasn't done the spell yet. She wouldn't do it with me still in here."

Andy shrugged. "She'll be back any second. If she hadn't destroyed her stupid BlackBerry we could give her a quick call."

No, something was very wrong. "I need to break this door open."

"Do you know how much it costs to fix something like that?"

"I'll repay you."

"With what? Uneaten donuts?"

But Darrak had already grabbed a chair. Another wave of pain shuddered through him as he slammed it against the door. It would normally be more than enough to shatter the glass.

But nothing happened. It barely rattled.

He swore under his breath.

"It's the spell," he confirmed. "It's working exactly how Maksim told us it would. But where's Eden? Why would she do this already? Doesn't she know that it would trap me in here with you? We don't have time for games."

"Not good." Andy sounded worried. "You'll be trapped in here with a werewolf. A *potential* werewolf."

"Believe me, Andy, you turning furry is the least of my worries at this exact moment." He moved toward the phone on Eden's desk, grabbed the receiver, and pecked out the numbers to Maksim's house. It went directly to voice mail.

"Damn it." He slammed the phone down.

Fine. He would just be strong for as long as this took—until Eden returned. But he felt the sun slip fully behind the horizon moments later. He knew when it happened since the pain blossomed out from inside of him.

Light and dark. Just like what was going on inside of him. The light helped. The dark hurt.

Based on his history, it seemed like the wrong order to things.

Andy moaned, a long sound that ended in a tiny wolflike

howl. He clamped his hands over his mouth. "Oh shit! Was that me?"

"This is not good," Darrak muttered. "You're starting to shift. Go with it, Andy. Don't try to fight it."

"Like what you're doing?"

"I have no choice. I have to fight this. I have to wait till Eden gets back. Where the hell is she?" He went to the glass door and pounded on it. "Eden! Damn it! Where are you?"

"So if she doesn't get here soon, if you're trapped in here and can't get out because this place is sealed up tighter than a nun's panties"—Andy's voice shook—"you won't be able to possess her."

Darrak's jaw clenched. "Exactly."

"So what then?"

"Then . . . then I'm in serious trouble." He gasped for breath. "Why would she do this to me? Did she say anything to you?"

"No, nothing!" Andy shook his head violently. "Something must have happened to her."

Yes, of course something happened. Her mother is what happened. She'd wanted to get rid of Darrak from the first moment she strolled her shiny new body in here. Caroline had known what Darrak was without asking any questions or being told anything at all. She'd just known he was a demon.

Was Eden okay? Was she hurt? Had Caroline done something to her? Maybe convinced her to get rid of Darrak once and for all?

No, that couldn't be it.

Fury rose in his chest that Eden might be hurt right now, unable to return to him, but anger wasn't going to help him. There was no way he was escaping from this room. The spell had worked perfectly. Nobody was getting in, and nobody was getting out. It had been meant for a werewolf, but it worked on a demon just as well.

Just what kind of a spell was this?

Andy began to shift to werewolf, but he still looked

more worried about Darrak. His nose grew longer, turning into more of a snout. His fingernails became long and sharp. His ears bigger and pointier. A thick layer of fur sprouted on his cheeks.

"Darrak—" His voice was a half growl now. "Possess me, if you need to. It's okay, I don't mind."

Darrak's throat felt thick. "I appreciate the offer, but shifters can't be possessed."

"Maybe I'm not . . ." Andy looked down at his hands. "Oh crap. It's true!" He looked at Darrak. "I'm so sorry."

Darrak gripped the side of the desk. "You'll be okay, I swear it. Just do me a favor."

"What?"

"Tell Eden . . ." He shuddered and slid down to the floor. "Tell her that I—"

But it was too late. He couldn't hold back another moment. His solid form morphed to the swirling mix of black and white smoke as his curse kicked in as it did every single night. His weeks of being able to take form half the time had been a gift. He'd quickly gotten used to it and taken it for granted.

This was who he really was now thanks to that centuries-old curse. This formless creature who couldn't speak, couldn't touch anything and was only able to possess and feed and drain and kill.

And he was trapped in a room with no way out. He instinctively moved toward Andy, even though he knew it wouldn't do any good, and was immediately repelled, glancing off the shifting werewolf's skin like a tennis ball thrown against a brick wall.

Andy continued to shift form. He howled and fell to the floor, his eyes still filled with a strange mix of fear for himself and for Darrak. Andy had never seen Darrak in this unnatural, incorporeal form. Maybe he'd thought that Darrak was someone to trust as much as a human, as evidenced by his little speech a couple of minutes ago.

But Darrak wasn't human. He was nothing close to human—even with the recent angel infusion. He had a great deal of humanity in reserve, but that was as close as he got to the real deal.

Would that humanity last? Or would it be taken from him along with everything else?

He already knew the truth. *Everything* would be taken. Everything that he thought he resented, everything that he thought he didn't want. The Void would strip away everything and leave nothing behind. Nothing at all.

All gone. His humanity, his emotions, his memories, even his angel side. Funny, it didn't seem so bad anymore. It was embarrassing for a former archdemon who'd laid waste to many a town in his existence, a former incubus who'd personally helped stock Lucifer's harem full of willing souls for him to sate his many hungers.

Part angel.

But now he wasn't even that. Now he was only smoke swirling around a magically sealed room.

He tried the door, tried to seep through the tiny cracks in the walls, the heater grate, anything.

Nothing worked.

Andy now raced back and forth in full werewolf form, claws scratching against the floor, looking very much like a large wild dog, his eyes still so much like Andy's, full of concern, full of fear.

But Darrak knew Andy didn't fear for himself anymore. He feared for Darrak.

Darrak always knew it was only a matter of time before this would happen—he'd just thought it wouldn't be quite this soon. Quite honestly, this was for the best. Eden would finally be free of him. The dark and light that fought within her would have one less daily struggle.

She'd be better off without him.

But he'd miss her. So much.

An exorcism could have harmed her. This way, she wouldn't have to feel a thing.

That was one of Darrak's last thoughts as he began to dissipate. This form could only last so long without a human host, and his time was finally up.

The last thing he heard before he vanished completely was the sound of a werewolf howling very loudly.

Nice puppy. Stay and take care of Eden for me. Keep her safe.

No . . . he thought. *I don't want to go, not like this. There's still so much I need to—*

And then he was gone.

⇴ FourTeen ⇷

Eden had a hell of a hangover. Somehow, somewhere, she'd drank way too much and now had to pay the price.

Her eyelashes fluttered as she opened her eyes.

"Eden, sweetie," her mother's brand-new voice said softly. "You're awake. Good."

"Give her a minute," Ben said. "She'll be woozy for a bit."

Her throat felt like sandpaper. "Wh-what happened? Where am I?"

"You're safe."

She was confused, but her vision began to come into focus. "You . . . have you taken me to the Malleus?"

"No, of course not," Ben said. "This doesn't have anything to do with them. They don't need to know about this. It's safer that way."

Safer. Sure, now he gets cautious when it comes to those jerks. Maybe he'd learned a few things in the last little while.

Wait a minute.

She tried to push herself up and looked around the small enclosed space. "Where am I?"

"In a van I rented," Ben said.

"A van. So you . . ." She felt her shoulder where the injection went in. "You drugged me and threw me in the back of a van?"

Her mother's currently young and beautiful face loomed in front of her. "Seemed like a good gathering spot on short notice."

"And what is this? Your intervention?"

Ben cleared his throat. "Yup. Kind of amateur, I'll admit it, but it worked well enough."

Unbelievable. How many times did she have to say she didn't need anyone's help before they'd leave her the hell alone?

"I don't have time for this." She glared at them. "You have no right to approach me ever again, you hear me? I swear to God, if you do then you're both going to be sorry. I don't want your help or your stupid intervention."

"It had to be done," Ben said. "You'll see that eventually. Maybe not today, but soon. And you'll thank us for this."

Her eyes narrowed on him. "You know, I once thought you were a really nice guy, Ben. Someone who wanted to do the right thing, even at a cost. I heard you'd left the police force."

"Couldn't balance things as well as I thought. Had to choose."

"I guess that brand on your arm made that choice nice and simple for you."

"I know you think the Malleus are evil, but they're not. Not all of them, anyway." His jaw clenched as if he didn't entirely believe his own words.

"Let me out of here. Now."

They exchanged a look. Great, Ben and Caroline had forged a bond of some kind. United to save Eden from the big bad demon. How did they even meet?

She felt magic spark in the palms of her hands, ready, willing, and able to be used whenever she liked. "You have three seconds to get out of my way. Three, two, one."

When they didn't do anything, she cast a focused look at

the back doors of the van and they swung wide open. She
scooted toward the exit before she noticed something that
made her gasp out loud and her heart start pounding hard in
her chest.

"Why is it dark out?" She didn't get an immediate reply
so she turned to look at them. "What time is it? How long
was I out?"

Caroline pressed her lips together and glanced away.

Ben held Eden's gaze steadily. "It's six o'clock. You
were out for a little over an hour."

Eden began to tremble. "No . . . but—but I need to—"

She leapt out of the van and scanned the parking lot.
They hadn't gone anywhere. They were still here, next to
her Toyota. Next to Triple-A. She ran so fast she nearly
twisted her ankle. The door was locked and she yanked on
the handle so hard it hurt her hands.

Fumbling in her pockets for the spell, she realized with
a horrible sinking feeling that it wasn't there anymore. Suddenly, Caroline was next to her, the paper clutched in her
hand.

"We had to do it to save you, Eden," she said, her voice
shaky. "It's going to be better now. You'll see."

Tears blurred her vision, and she snatched the paper
away, quickly speaking the Latin words to break the spell
that had sealed the office up. There was a slight swell of
light to show it worked.

She grasped the door handle and pulled, bursting into
the office. "Please, *please* still be here."

A large doglike creature scrambled toward her, and she
reacted instinctively, balling her hand, ready to unleash
magic to protect herself if the werewolf attacked. Instead,
it sat down on its haunches in front of her and whined, raising its front leg to paw at the air.

"Andy . . . what happened? Where's Darrak?" She turned
in a circle. "Darrak! Where are you?"

Andy tilted his muzzle back and howled mournfully.

And then she just knew.

Darrak wasn't here. He'd been trapped inside the office

by the spell. He couldn't possess Andy since he was a shifter. Darrak had nowhere to go when he lost solid form.

He was gone and she hadn't felt a thing. Nothing. She'd felt nothing. Not even when she'd woken up—not even a twinge of pain to signify what had happened.

But she felt the pain now.

"Sweetie," her mother said from the doorway. "Come on, let's leave. Get a good night's sleep. Things will be better tomorrow."

"Things will be better tomorrow?" she managed. "Do you have any idea what you've done here?"

"Yes," Ben said. "Something that should have been done weeks ago."

"It'll be okay now," her mother soothed. "And . . . uh, why's there a big scary-looking dog in here? Where's Andy?"

A moment later, the glass door shattered into a million pieces. Caroline shrieked.

Eden turned to face her mother and Ben, the two people who'd taken Darrak away from her. They'd decided to save her from the demon who possessed her and they'd gone ahead and destroyed him.

"I'm going to kill both of you. Right now."

Power surged into her hands. Lucas once told her that using black magic to kill a mortal would turn her soul jet-black. She'd be hellbound with no chance for redemption.

At this moment, she honestly couldn't care less. Darrak was gone, and it felt as if her heart had been torn right out of her chest.

She *did* love him—utterly and completely. But she'd been afraid to admit the depth of her feelings for him, even to herself. She hadn't known how she'd truly felt until it was too late.

He was gone, and nothing else felt like it mattered anymore.

"Don't, Eden." Ben held his hands up. "We did this to help you!"

"I loved him. And you took him away from me, you self-righteous son of a bitch. I want you to suffer. I want to watch you bleed."

"Eden!" Caroline snapped. "Don't do this. He was a damn demon who'd corrupted your soul. How could we not do anything we had to do to help you?"

"He wasn't just a demon. Not to me." Her voice was eerily quiet. The flood of black magic had given her that much—cold, emotionless resolve. "He was everything. He was a part of me. And now there's a hole where my heart used to be—a wide, gaping chasm of darkness."

"Oh, don't be so damn melodramatic," Caroline snapped. "And don't aim that nasty magic toward us. I raised you better than that."

In another life, another universe, that might have made her laugh.

Andy whined, and gently tugged at the corner of her shirt. It was enough to snap her slightly out of her blood-thirsty and mindless need for vengeance.

Tears slid down her cheeks. "See? I knew you were going to make a nice werewolf."

He nudged her magic-filled hands with the top of his furry head.

She shook her head. "I can't help it. I need to do something or I think I might die over this. All I have left is my magic."

He nudged her again.

Andy didn't want her to do anything she was going to regret. Using this magic, feeling the way she was, it wouldn't end well. For anyone.

"Damn it." She took a deep breath and pushed back against the power at her disposal, the darkness that threatened to overtake her if she waded too much deeper into it. The moment she did, the steely, calm reserve she'd had a tentative hold on peeled away and all she felt was raw pain.

Her stomach lurched violently. She managed to make it to the washroom before she threw up. The flu had been waiting for this exact moment before it decided to make its presence known in full force. One more thing for her to deal with.

It took her a while before she cleaned herself up, ignoring her churning gut and her puffy, red-ringed eyes in the mirror. She expected to be alone when she entered the office again, the cold wind moving in through the broken glass door. Ben was gone now—smart guy—but her mother still stood there.

Eden cast her a dark look. "Go away if you know what's good for you."

Caroline wrung her hands. "You just puked."

"The flu's been circling me for days. I hardly ever get sick like that."

"The only time I ever had bad nausea like that was when I was pregnant with you."

She wanted to be alone. "Not really in the mood for a walk down memory lane right now."

"So what do you think you're going to—?"

"Leave," Eden growled. "I don't want to see you again. Ever. Get it? *Ever.* I hate you."

Caroline flinched as if she'd been hit, but she wasn't stupid. She finally got the hint and slinked out of the office, leaving Eden and Andy alone. Eden's knees gave out and she crumpled to the ground, cold and empty and not sure what she was supposed to do next.

Andy sat down next to her. She could feel the heat from his large furry body.

A hot tear slid down her cheek. "I loved him, Andy. I didn't even realize how much. More than anything. *Anything.* And he's gone forever."

He whined again and pawed at her leg.

Eden slid her hand over her stomach, hating the thought that she was getting sick, especially now.

Then she went very quiet. There was no sound at all except the thud of her heart in the cool, silent office.

"The only time I ever had bad nausea like that was when I was pregnant with you."

It couldn't be. It *couldn't*.

But Eden suddenly knew with total and complete clarity that it was true. She wasn't nauseous because she was coming down with the flu.

"Oh, my God," she said out loud. "I'm pregnant."

Ben wasn't sure what he'd expected. Maybe shock for a bit, followed by an outpouring of gratitude as Eden realized she'd been saved from a fate worse than death by two people who cared about her.

He was such a fool.

"I need to go," he said to Caroline outside of Triple-A. The front window of the van was cracked down the center from Eden's surge of magic that had made his blood run cold with fear. The rental agency wouldn't be happy about that but at the moment he couldn't care less.

Despite his initial reluctance, he'd teamed up with this drifter—a wandering soul inside a stolen human body. Together, with the same goal, it had felt so right. But now it felt wrong.

Everything felt wrong.

"It wasn't a mistake," Caroline told him. "She'll see that in time."

Even she didn't sound so sure about that anymore.

Ben's throat felt thick. "I have your number. I'll call you later to make sure you're okay."

He drove away, barely able to focus on the road. All he saw was the look on Eden's face when she realized Darrak was gone. She'd been a study in grief, in rage. He'd seen emotion that strong before. It was when someone lost a loved one in a senseless tragedy.

There was no arguing with it anymore. Eden had loved Darrak. Truly *loved* him. And that love had not been forged out of something vile or impure as Ben had always believed. It was as real as anything he'd ever witnessed.

Eden had been ready to kill him and Caroline on the spot

for what they'd done, but she'd let them walk away. He was still surprised by that.

Ben drove to the Malleus headquarters. He had a meeting with Oliver.

"I'm glad you're here," Oliver said. He had a large, richly decorated office, done in shades of gray, silver, and black, and he was seated behind a large black lacquered desk with his fingers templed in front of him.

"Where else would I be?"

"Are you well? You look distracted."

"I'm fine. What do you need me to do?"

"Fetch the shifter. Bring her to interrogation room three. Tonight we'll get to the bottom of everything. Find out exactly how she and Eden Riley are connected. See if she can give us any insight on the demon and how the angelic energy has affected him during the possession. I need answers."

Ben nodded. "Fine."

"You will take the lead in this questioning, Ben," Oliver said. "And you are to use any means necessary to extract the truth from her. It can't wait another day. Do you understand?"

"I understand." Ben was once a man, but now he was a monster. Might as well prove that just a little bit more than he already had. "Can I ask you about something, sir?"

"What is it?"

"I want to know about the angel you have imprisoned downstairs."

Oliver's composed expression didn't give anything away. "An angel?"

"Yes." Ben's gaze wanted to move to the single white feather that lay on the floor next to Oliver's desk, but he forced himself not to look.

While he waited for a reply, the office felt as if it chilled a few degrees.

Oliver fixed him with a steady smile. "You're working too hard and beginning to see things that don't exist. There are no angels downstairs. That makes no sense at all. Why would I imprison an angel?"

"That was what I wondered."

"Soon I'll be able to authorize a two-week leave for you, Ben. I think you need a vacation. But there are important matters to deal with first. Go get the shifter."

He knew better than to argue. No one wanted to tell him the truth about what he'd seen, so much so that he was beginning to question his own memories.

Ben went downstairs and his hard-soled shoes made an echoing sound against the floor. The walls were narrow down here. A guard accompanied him. He glanced down the hall at the silent cell that held the winged man to whom he'd spoken only once.

No time to think about that. He had other matters to attend to.

"She's pretty hot," the guard said. "Maybe after you're finished with her later, I can play a little bit."

Ben's lips thinned. "Maybe."

The guard slipped his key into the lock and swung the door open. "Hey, little shifter. Looks like your time is finally up."

The woman cowered in the corner, her knees drawn up to her chest. Everything about her signified that she was afraid . . . except her eyes. They blazed with indignation. With challenge. With pissed off fury.

She wasn't going to give up without a fight.

Quite honestly, Ben gave her five minutes max before she started telling them anything they wanted to know—and then some. He'd already been shown some of the interrogation tools the Malleus deemed worthy for use on prisoners. Not much had changed since the Salem witch trials hundreds of years ago.

"She's all yours," the guard said.

"Thanks."

Ben slammed his fist into the guard's face, then grabbed him and whacked his head against the metal door. That was more than enough to knock him out cold.

Then Ben looked in at the woman in the corner—this so-called evil creature he was scheduled to torture for information in a few short minutes.

"What the hell are you doing?" she demanded.

He held his hand out to her. "We need to get out of here. Now."

⇢ FIFTEEN ⇠

Eden sat on the floor of Triple-A for what felt like a very long time. It was cold, with the broken door letting in the chill of the mid-November evening, but she barely felt it.

Darrak was gone forever.

And she'd just realized she was pregnant with his baby.

He'd told her demons didn't carry human diseases, so she was safe with him when they'd slept together. The only unexpected side effect had been her black magic.

She'd assumed—well, hell, obviously she hadn't given it any thought at all.

If she felt morning sickness now, that meant it likely happened the very first time they'd been together.

She was one month pregnant.

"What am I going to do?" she whispered.

Darrak had been sent to the Void—a place of endless nothing. Death for demons and other soulless creatures. The end of everything with no chance to ever return.

It was the absolute worst thing that could have happened.

Andy whined.

"He's gone," she told him, her voice quiet and broken. "It's too late."

She'd never felt so incredibly helpless in her life. The control, once and for all, had been completely taken out of her hands. She'd wanted to break his curse in order to obtain her freedom and privacy again, but not at this cost.

Destroying him managed to do the trick. The curse was officially toast.

Damn Ben and Caroline for doing this without her permission, for not even giving her a choice.

That was the negative side, the dark side that was ready to give up and just cry, yell, and break things.

But Eden had another side, one that was screaming for her to get up off the floor, to let go of the werewolf she was clutching, and to bloody well do something to fix this.

"What am I supposed to do?" she whispered.

Something. Anything. She couldn't just accept this. It *wasn't* too late.

"It *is* too late."

No, it wasn't. It couldn't be. She wouldn't let it.

Darrak had been swept away to the Netherworld, to the Void, and he'd always told her that meant the end of everything.

But maybe it didn't. Maybe there was still a chance to save him.

After all, Eden did have friends in important places.

Friends who wanted something from her, but it hadn't been the right time. She hadn't been taken to the very point of desperation before. Not like this.

Lucas could fix this—he was the Prince of Hell. He might not be able to read minds or see the future, but he ruled the Netherworld and had for an eternity.

Darrak thought Lucas had a master plan that involved Eden, the reason why he was willing to forgive her slipups, her excuses for not following through on her previous assignments for him. The quest for the angelheart and the attempt to slap the silver chain on Brenda for her hellish job interview had both ended in failure.

And yet Lucas was still willing to take some of her darkness away from time to time so her soul wouldn't be too damaged. It was still gray, even after all the black magic she'd burned through.

Thanks to Lucas.

Eden had to talk to him, and it couldn't wait another minute.

She scrambled to her feet so fast it made her dizzy. Darrak was gone, no question about that, but it was possible he wasn't gone for good. She might have a window of opportunity here—a very small one. So small she hadn't even noticed it before.

This had to work.

Her hand shook as she slid it into the pocket of her coat to find the marble.

Nothing was there.

She reached deeper, then tried the other pocket, patting down the lining of the coat in case it had dropped through a rip in the seam.

Dark panic returned, chasing away her momentary glimmer of hope.

"Where is it?" she choked out.

Her mother and Ben had stolen Maksim's containment spell while she'd been unconscious. Had they taken Lucas's summoning crystal, too? It was all she had—the only way she could contact him.

She tried the pockets one more time as if the marble might have magically reappeared. "Why the hell isn't it here?"

Then, shaking, tears streaming down her cheeks, she sank back down to the floor and grabbed hold of Andy as an anchor. He rested his currently furry head on her shoulder and whimpered.

"It's too late. I can't find it. I don't know where it went. It was my only hope."

Andy's mournful whine turned into a dangerous-sounding growl, low in his throat. Eden froze, then slowly swiveled to glance over her shoulder.

Lucas stood behind her, his palm outstretched. On it lay the marble. "You wouldn't happen to be looking for this, would you?"

"Wh-what are you . . . ?" She was so stunned she could barely form words.

He cocked his head. "I guess you were distracted earlier. You didn't see me sitting in the corner of the café drinking a latte. Looked as if you and your mother were having a lovely family reunion. Warms the heart."

Magic immediately crackled down her arms, begging to be used. "So you saw what happened to me and didn't do anything?"

He seemed unimpressed with her show of anger. "No, I didn't intervene. Sometimes it's important to let nature take its course."

He'd just been watching her get tranquilized and thrown in the back of a van while Darrak was trapped in here? "Was this all your doing, Lucas? Did you destroy Darrak?"

"If I wanted to destroy him, I would have done so a long time ago, Eden, and no adorable displays of magic would be able to stop me." He slid the marble into the pocket of his rumpled jacket.

She wondered, not for the first time, why this was the form he chose to use here in the human world. From what she understood, he could look like anything he wanted. And yet, this disarming, brown-haired, brown-eyed man was his look of choice.

"You have to help me." She forced the words out. "You have to bring him back."

Andy stayed right next to her.

"But don't you feel relieved that he's gone? You're finally free from him. You can admit it to me, Eden. I won't tell anyone."

"Do I look relieved to you?"

Lucas swept his gaze over her. "Not particularly. Honestly, though, it shouldn't be such a big loss to you. He was trouble, he brought bad things into your life from the first moment he possessed you. I've told you before, Darrak was just some hellfire I decided to give a personality to once upon a time. Nothing worth shedding tears over."

Yes, she'd heard this before, but she still didn't care. Darrak came from lowly beginnings—so did a lot of people. Maybe not quite so literal, but it didn't matter to her who Darrak was, how he'd been created, or how he'd spent the first portion of his existence. All she cared about was the man—yes, the *man*—she'd grown to know and love with every ounce of her being. He wasn't simply hellfire with a personality. Not to her. Never to her.

Lucas cast a glance through the small office space. "You broke the door."

"Screw the door."

He touched the frame and it mended itself before Eden's eyes, the shards of glass reforming so there wasn't even a crack left to show what had happened to it. "There. I've saved you and your partner a few hundred dollars at least." He glanced at Andy, whose muzzle was drawn back from his sharp teeth. "You're welcome."

Eden shook her head. "Bring Darrak back."

Lucas stood by the door he'd fixed and stared out at the parking lot, likely a very bland sight for someone like him. He said nothing, and it was driving Eden literally insane with every moment that passed and nothing changed.

"It's not that simple," he finally said. "The Void is a one-way trip. None have ever returned from that region of the Netherworld. You must come to terms that he's gone and get back to the rest of your life. You have more important things to concern yourself with now."

"Lucas, *please*."

That earned her a look. "Are you so desperate that you're actually begging for my help?"

There was no time to play games. "I'll beg if I have to."

"He's gone, Eden. And it won't be long before he's lost to you forever."

Harsh words, but they worked exactly the opposite of how he'd likely meant them. They gave Eden a glimmer of hope. "*Won't be long*. But that means there's still a chance."

This earned a laugh from the prince. "You're very determined. Pregnancy becomes you. You have that special glow."

A breath caught in her throat. "You knew?"

"I sensed it the last time we spoke."

"You didn't say anything."

"What was I supposed to say? Demons like Darrak—those who were never human to begin with—shouldn't be able to father a child. I guess he's changed more than even I realized."

"I guess he has."

Andy paced in front of Eden, as if marking the line Lucas wasn't allowed to cross. Lucas glanced at him with humor. "The werewolf is very protective of you."

She willed herself to remain calm and inhaled slowly. "What do you want from me?"

He looked at her curiously. "Pardon me?"

"You want something from me. Something you haven't asked for yet because you said I wasn't ready." She blinked. "I'm ready. Ask me."

He approached her, ignoring Andy's warning growl.

"You're right, Eden, I do want something from you. And if you agree, then it's possible I might be able to help you find Darrak before it's too late."

Hope grew inside of her, tempered with worry. "What is it?"

He slid his hand into her dark red hair and pushed it off her face. She watched him warily, as he leaned closer to whisper in her ear. "I want your angel half."

Eden pushed back at him with surprise. "What?"

Lucas's gaze was steady on her. "I want your celestial energy, that which has sustained Darrak and given him more power than he's had in three hundred years. The energy that's changed him into something else, something that's never been seen before. You have to give it freely to me. And I want it all."

She wasn't sure why this came as a shock. "But . . . but why?"

His expression grew pained. "I want to return to Heaven,

but I'm weighted down with too much darkness. The celestial energy inside you would burn that darkness away enough for me to unshackle myself from Hell once and for all. A nephilim must give that energy to me of her own free will, every last piece of it, and I can accomplish my one and only goal."

Eden paled with every word he spoke. She already knew Lucas wanted to go back to Heaven. He'd tried other solutions to this age-old problem of his. This, though . . . this was new.

"Have you tried this with another nephilim?"

"All nephilim have been cloaked to me in the past here in the human world, and now I know why. It's an angel thing. Your black magic helped remove part of that angelic cloaking from you and I was able to see you for what you are." His lips twisted wryly. "This is a solution to my problem that I began considering the same time the angelheart was in play. I've been trying to find a way to kill my darkness, but my darkness is immortal. To rid myself of it forever, I must give it to another."

"The job interview," she said, putting it together. "You're trying to find your replacement for when you leave Hell."

"Yes. I might be a selfish bastard, Eden, but I know I can't leave Hell without another to take my place. That someone must control the darkest shadows of Hell—and only someone with true, pure goodness inside them can do that."

She gaped at him. "You're trying to tell me you have goodness inside you?"

"I was an angel—the brightest and best of them all."

"And the least modest."

Lucas smiled. "My target from earlier today was only one possible candidate. There is another I have lined up who has already enthusiastically agreed to take my place." He crossed his arms. "Tick tock, Eden. Darrak has very little time left. Time works differently in the Netherworld. You said you'd do anything for the chance to save him. Are you willing to give me your celestial energy for that chance?"

She hesitated and slid her hand over her stomach.

Lucas noticed. "I can make you one solemn promise. Your child will be fine. I'll personally guarantee it."

That was . . . reassuring. A promise from Lucifer himself.

Eden's mind swam, but she didn't have that difficult a time with this question. Was she willing to give up her angel side—a side that had given her nothing her entire life but a bit of unreliable psychic insight thanks to an absentee father? Would she give that up in order to rescue the man she loved—the father of her unborn child?

"Yes," she said. "I agree."

"Say it again."

"You can have my celestial energy. All of it."

"One more time."

"You can have it, Lucas. Yes."

His warm smile widened. "Thank you."

She crouched down, watching him warily, and put her hand on Andy's furry back. The werewolf had gone very quiet, watching the two of them as though witnessing a tennis match.

"Now bring Darrak back," she said firmly.

Lucas ran his index finger over the edge of her desk as if looking for dust. He probably wouldn't be disappointed. "Well . . . that wasn't exactly what you just agreed to."

"What?"

"Remember, Eden, the wording is important. I don't have the ability to snatch Darrak right out of the Void. Nor do I have any desire of going anywhere near that place. It's very dangerous there, even for me. No, what I said was that I could offer you a chance to save him."

Fury rose inside her. "You asshole. You tricked me."

"Not a trick. It's not my fault your head is not in the game."

"A chance? That's it?"

"Yes. I will grant you entrance to the Netherworld. Mortals, even if they're witches or nephilim, or both, are still vulnerable there. Without my permission you would burn up the moment you entered my kingdom. But tonight I'll let you in so you can seek your demon at the very edge of his ultimate doom."

She swallowed hard. "You're sending me to Hell."

"You don't have to go at all, if you don't want to. However, I should warn you, our deal holds no matter what your decision is. I will, however, ensure your safety and your child's safety . . . but Darrak, well, he's the wild card in this scenario. No money-back guarantee."

Her nausea came back in full force, but she tried to ignore it. "Fine. I'll do it. I'll go."

"Just one more thing. You need a guide." He smiled down at Andy. "Would you be willing to protect your lovely business partner tonight? She needs someone who cares about her. I don't think I'd trust anyone else to help her in this quest."

"Andy, wait . . ." Eden began.

But Andy barked.

"I'll take that as a yes." Lucas held out his hand. Andy walked over toward him and Lucas grasped either side of his head. The next moment, dark light slid along Andy's werewolf form and he whined.

Eden grabbed Lucas's arm. "Stop it! You're hurting him!"

Lucas shook his head. "He's fine. Better than ever, in fact."

Andy looked different now. His fur had quickly changed to become black, short, and wiry. He was at least fifty pounds heavier than he'd been before. And his eyes were now red, with slits for pupils more like those of a cat. He looked like a cross between an otherworldly black panther and a Rottweiler.

Eden gasped. "What did you do to him?"

"Consider it an upgrade." Lucas stood up and brushed his hands off on the front of his pants. "He was a werewolf. Now he's a hellhound. They're the best guides in the Netherworld."

Eden stared with fear at the muscular black monster that bared its sharp teeth at her.

"Christ on a cracker!" a voice proclaimed in her head, but the hellhound's lips didn't move. *"I need a drink!"*

Her mouth dropped open. "Andy, I can hear you. How . . . how can I hear you?"

"You can hear him because he's the first and only were-hellhound. Now, you best get going. He'll return to his human form at dawn, and he won't survive more than a couple seconds if you're still in the Netherworld." Lucas's smile returned. "Again, you're welcome."

Eden hadn't said thank you. She wasn't prepared to say it yet, not with the heavy price tag associated with this literal deal with the devil.

Lucas walked toward the door and pushed it open.

"Wait!" Eden called after him. "How do I get there? Is there a gateway nearby?"

"You won't need one. You already have the keys to my kingdom at your disposal. Darrak's ultimate fate is in your hands now, and I suggest you don't delay. I'll be in touch soon to collect on our bargain. Good night, Eden."

Before she could say another word, he left the office. She ran to the doorway and scanned the dark parking lot, but Lucas was nowhere to be seen.

Feeling completely stunned, Eden looked down at Andy the werehellhound.

"Don't look at me," he said, or thought, or however he was able to communicate with her. *"I have no idea how to get there. Was that really Lucifer? He looked so . . . normal. Quite frankly, I'm really hoping this is all just a crazy dream."*

This was no dream.

"Keys to the kingdom," she whispered, wracking her brain for the answer.

But then it came to her. Of course that was what Lucas had meant. What else?

She grabbed her coat and slid her hand into the pocket, pulling out the silver bracelet Lucas had given to her—the one he'd meant for her to put on Brenda that would have taken her to a job interview in Hell. She stared at the chain in stunned silence, feeling resolve fill her.

There was no time for regret or second thoughts. Now was the time for action.

She eyed Andy. "Are you ready?"

He cocked his head and stared up at her with those spooky red eyes. *"I expect to wake up in my warm bed any moment. But until that happens, let's go get your boyfriend and hope for the best."*

Eden had agreed to go to Hell itself to rescue the demon she loved. Hoping for the best sounded a bit presumptuous. "Fine. Let's do this."

She grabbed hold of Andy and slipped the chain over her wrist.

⇴ SIXTEEN ⇷

"Last call, demon. You want another drink, or what?"

Darrak raised his head off the hard wooden bar where he'd dozed off for a moment and eyed the empty shot glass in front of him. "No, no more."

Where was he?

He glanced to his left around the dim interior of the empty bar. Looked like something out of an eighties sitcom. There was a lot of wood paneling and vinyl. Definitely the Netherworld, though. He ran a hand through his hair to check himself. No horns. He was in human form. At the moment, anyway.

He didn't remember how he'd gotten here. Usually when he went to bars they were in the human world, not here. Why bother? Drunk humans were way more fun to play with than drunk demons.

Strange.

He wondered how long he'd been out. He'd had one hell of a dream—a long epiclike dream full of adventure and danger and . . . huh. It was already slipping away.

He wished he could write it off as nothing, but two things troubled him deeply.

First, demons didn't dream.

Second, demons didn't sleep.

It didn't take a genius to notice that something was strange about that.

Maybe it wasn't sleep. Maybe he'd just zoned out for a while. Yeah, that had to be it.

Funny, though. It had felt different than zoning.

"You sure you don't want one last drink?"

He looked to his right to see his friend Theo sitting there, which struck Darrak as odd—on top of everything else— but he wasn't sure why. He and Theo always hung out like this when business didn't have to come first.

"Why did you let me drink so much?"

"Because it's fun."

Darrak eyed him. "You know, it feels like I haven't seen you for a while."

"Me?" Theo pointed at himself. "You really have had too much to drink, haven't you?"

Theo had started his existence at almost exactly the same time as Darrak, created from hellfire by a very industrious Lucifer. Both had been incubi for centuries before their promotions to archdemon.

They'd scorched a path of destruction and good times across the human world in their day. Very few knew how to party as hard and as well as an archdemon with power to spare and the good looks of an ex-incubus. There were very few who could resist the pair of them.

Theo was tall, broad shouldered, with long dark hair that he kept held back with a leather strap. His almond-shaped eyes gave him an exotic appearance, like a prince from a faraway land or, possibly, a surfing instructor from Hawaii. It worked for him. The ladies loved it.

If there was one demon in the entire Netherworld that Darrak considered family, it was Theo.

This sentiment, however, was not something that demons tended to share with each other. Emotion, anything that might make them seem soft or too humanlike, was strictly avoided. But Darrak had always thought his friendship with Theo was more helpful than harmful. It was good to have one other being who you could turn to if you were in trouble and needed help.

So strange, though. A feeling was churning through his gut—one he didn't recognize.

"What's wrong?" Theo asked.

"Don't know." Darrak placed a hand on his abdomen. "I feel like I've lost something."

"Too many shots of vodka, that's all."

"Where are we, anyway?" Darrak glanced around again at the vacant bar, empty apart from the two of them and the bartender. "I don't feel like I've ever been here before."

"Yeah, this place? It's the best. Not tonight though. Dull night. Another night would be better. Entertainment, women, it's a nonstop party."

"Sounds great. So why are we here tonight?" Darrak narrowed his eyes at a couple of male fairies that walked through the door and cut an unfriendly glare in his direction. They weren't quite as lovely as they were in the human world, where they hid their true natures with glamours. Here in the Netherworld they were regular fairies—fearsome dark-skinned creatures with sharp teeth and pointed ears and eyes that could burn a hole straight through your soul. Literally.

Luckily, Darrak didn't have to worry about that.

He remembered a glimpse of his dream. *Something about somebody's soul.*

Impossible. He didn't dream.

Wow, he was seriously messed up. Time for a vacation, maybe. He'd been working hard for Lucifer for so long that he had forgotten to stop and smell the brimstone.

"Let's go," Theo said. "We have somewhere we need to be. May as well not put it off any longer."

"Oh yeah? Sounds deliciously ominous."

"You have no idea."

He followed Theo to the exit and emerged onto the main

street. It was dark outside, but it was always dark in the Netherworld.

"Can we phase?" Darrak asked, referring to the method demons used for easily transporting themselves from place to place.

"No, we're walking today." Theo smirked. "It's not very far from here."

Darrak frowned. "I feel like I'm forgetting something."

"Yeah? Something important?"

"Seems that way. I don't know."

"Well, if it's *that* important, it'll come back to you. If it isn't, then it won't."

Theo had a way of reducing most problems down to their base parts. "Good point."

Darrak rubbed his temples. He didn't feel the effects of whatever amount of booze he'd drunk tonight, but he still felt off. Kind of bruised and broken, as if he'd survived some sort of major stomping. It wasn't an unfamiliar feeling. Darrak didn't *always* win the fights he got into— just most of them. And usually those he beat didn't walk away feeling bruised and broken. They were sent to the . . . the . . .

Somewhere. Where were they sent?

Something that started with a *V*. It was on the tip of his tongue . . .

"Shit," he mumbled. "I'm seriously messed up."

"Just relax," Theo said. "It'll be easier that way."

"Easier? What will be easier?"

"Everything."

"You know, I'm trying to remember the last time I saw you."

"Don't try too hard. You might break yourself."

Darrak snorted, then sobered. "Wait, I think I remember something."

Theo stopped walking and turned to look at Darrak. "What's that?"

"I was . . . summoned. By a witch. She summoned me to

the human world and made me give her an extra serving of power. Then she tried to destroy me."

"You remember that?"

"Yeah . . . it's fuzzy, though. Has Lucifer been messing with my head again?"

"It's possible. He can do that."

"Hate that guy." Lucifer hated him, too. Even though the Prince of Hell had created Darrak out of nothing, given him life, so to speak, and power and strength—then upgraded him to archdemon—he knew Lucifer still resented him. Darrak liked to believe it was because Lucifer feared him. A little. Now and then.

Yeah, right. What a laugh. Lucifer could smite him with a single thought. Ashes to ashes, dust to dust. A couple of seconds later Darrak would be a handful of hellfire again, only lacking the good looks and charming personality he had now.

Something moved up ahead, something dark and formless.

Darrak tensed. "What was that?"

"What?"

"That thing—it looked like a wraith."

He would have preferred not to say it out loud. Wraiths were not the kind of creatures you wanted to come across in the Netherworld. They were energy suckers. If one latched onto you they could drain you dry in a very short amount of time.

Not fun.

"What the hell are they doing here?" Darrak mumbled, feeling more annoyed than worried. "Who sent them?"

Wraiths weren't just arbitrary beings that wandered wherever they liked. They were creatures with a job to do—to target someone specifically and get rid of them. Seeing a wraith was not a sign one's day would be pleasant.

"Don't know." Theo didn't sound too concerned.

"Let's head to the human world," Darrak suggested.

"Nah, let's not."

"If you want to stay here and give them the chance to creep up behind you and give you a nice wet kiss, feel free. As for me, I'm out of here." Darrak concentrated on phasing somewhere else—anywhere else. However, nothing happened.

He frowned very deeply. "I can't phase."

"Oh no?" Theo cocked a dark eyebrow.

That weird feeling Darrak had gotten since he first woke up grew much larger. He now realized it was paranoia. "What's going on, Theo?"

Theo shrugged. "Stuff."

"Can you be any less helpful?"

"Probably. If I tried harder."

Darrak scanned the street again. The wraiths were gone, which eased his mind some. Then he saw something else. It looked like a woman with long auburn hair who disappeared behind a corner up ahead.

He wasn't sure why, but he started walking, quickly, after her.

"Where are you going?" Theo asked.

"I need to talk to her."

"Who? I don't see anyone."

"Her . . . uh, I don't know. There was a woman over here." He reached the corner and looked around it, but nobody was there. He swore under his breath. "I am really messed up tonight. I'm seeing things."

"Who did you think you saw?"

"Somebody, I—I'm not sure." He frowned hard. "I thought I recognized her, but I have no idea who she is."

"Sure, that makes sense."

It didn't make any sense at all, which was why he was starting to get more concerned about his current disoriented state. Maybe he'd been drugged or bespelled. But who would do that to him? And why?

Something was off, and he had a feeling it had to do with the woman he'd seen—or, rather, that he'd *thought* he'd seen. He'd felt a desperate need to catch up to her, to grab her arm and pull her around so he could see her face.

Women. More trouble than they were worth. Especially the ones here in the Netherworld. For all he knew, it was some apparition sent to lead him to his doom.

He glanced around the unfamiliar street. The Netherworld had the appearance of the human world, depending on where you were. You either got this type of urban setting—always night—or you got the inferno. And, no matter your location, it always felt like the hottest day of summer.

He didn't tell anyone, but he preferred spending time in the human world. At least there was a little more variety up there.

This area didn't look familiar to him. It was deserted. A lot of the Netherworld was very busy, bristling with activity, but not here.

This didn't feel right. At all.

Darrak turned around in a circle, trying to see something that might strike a chord of familiarity in him, but nothing did. "Talk to me, Theo. Tell me where we are."

"We're exactly where we need to be."

"And where's that?"

"You could call it a waiting room."

He hissed out a breath of frustration. "A waiting room for what?"

Somebody tapped Darrak on his shoulder, and he turned to see the two male fairies from the bar standing there.

"What are you doing here?" the taller fairy asked. The edge of his razor-sharp teeth could be seen under his upper lip. "What are you looking for?"

Good question. He wished he knew.

"Who wants to know?"

"We do."

Darrak snorted. "And who exactly are you?"

"We're the neighborhood watch for this area making sure dumb demons don't wander off and get themselves hurt." The fairy jutted his thumb in the direction he'd been headed. "Go down there and you're in big trouble. You won't be coming back."

Okay, this was turning out to be a bit amusing. "Down

there?" He nodded at the street where he thought the red-head's apparition had disappeared.

"Yeah."

"See, you saying that I can't go down there makes me want to go for a nice long walk. Down there."

The fairies exchanged a glance. "Then you're even stupider than you look."

Darrak clenched his jaw. "I'm not stupid."

One of the fairies gave him a head to toe assessment. "Incubus, right? I can tell by the brainless, shiny surface."

"Archdemon, actually," he growled.

"Former incubus, though, right?" They both laughed knowingly.

Assholes. "You two should walk away. No reason for this to turn into something."

"First we need to know why you're here."

"He's here because there's nowhere else he can be now," Theo said. "He's on the list."

Darrak frowned. "The list for what?"

"So what's the delay?" the shorter fairy asked.

"All good things come to those who wait, boys," Theo said. "Patience is one of my seven favorite virtues."

"You said you're neighborhood watch?" Darrak asked.

"We are. Nothing happens around here without our knowledge."

"Then you should probably know there are a couple of wraiths standing right behind you. They'll probably bring down the property values around here."

He'd never seen fairies roll their eyes before. It wasn't pretty. "Don't be ridiculous. Wraiths never come this close to the hole."

The hole? The area wasn't upscale, but it was an odd nickname for it.

Darrak shrugged. "Could have fooled me. Because they're here anyway."

They began to look uneasy. It seemed as if they didn't want to move their attention away from Theo and Darrak, but they still swiveled, as if in unison, to see the two dark forms lurking behind them.

The wraiths were cloaked, their faces unseen, swathed in shadow and something that turned the hot night around them much colder. Darrak knew that they revealed their faces to you just before they sucked you dry, and that they were the most beautiful women in the entire universe—a sight which helped to freeze a victim in place, shocked that something so alluring could be so dangerous. By then it was too late.

He didn't see any beauty at the moment. All he saw were two gloved hands with pale, slender fingers dart out from each of the wraiths, fastening around the fairies' throats, drawing them closer for the kiss.

The fairies didn't even have a chance to scream before the cloaks surrounded them and their entire forms were consumed by the wraiths.

That was all Darrak really needed to see. Self-preservation was a powerful motivator. He wouldn't say he ran away, but he moved quickly, very quickly, along the path the redhead had taken before she'd disappeared.

"Theo," he growled. "You either tell me what the hell is going on here or I'm going to beat it out of you."

"You think so, huh?" Theo strolled next to Darrak, his hands casually clasped behind his back.

"I know so."

"Think back, Darrak. When was the last time you saw me? If you can answer that, then maybe you actually have a chance. Let's see how strong your survival instinct is."

Darrak normally had a joke or a quip for every situation, but this wasn't the time or the place. Something was horribly wrong here, and he couldn't figure out what it all meant. He'd woken up in a bar with no idea how he'd gotten there. He couldn't remember anything recently, apart from a fuzzy recollection of being summoned to the human world by a power-hungry witch. When was that? What had become of her?

He remembered talking to Theo, agreeing to be his business partner in overthrowing Lucifer and taking over Hell. But that felt like such a long time ago—centuries, even.

No, wait. He remembered something else. Something much more recent.

Another bar. Another meeting with his demonic best friend. Looking at him as a threat, rather than an ally. Having differing opinions of how to deal with an important situation.

There was another demon lord—Asmodeus. Theo worked for him now. It was all a part of Theo's ultimate plan to defeat Lucifer and take over his throne, to take over Hell itself. Asmodeus—he needed a body. He had set his sights on Theo's, a powerful archdemon that had the desirable appearance necessary to contain the essence of the Lord of Lust.

Darrak's voice was quiet when he spoke. "He destroyed you. Asmodeus, he burned you away and stole your body. Then I destroyed him." Darrak raised his wide gaze to look at his friend. Yes, it was true. Theo was gone. Despite their disagreements, he'd been a true friend, trying to save Darrak from a huge mess he'd gotten himself into, right till the end. And Darrak had felt grief for the first time in his long existence. "You shouldn't be here. You shouldn't be anywhere."

Theo shrugged. "Looks like you still have some brain juice left over after all."

"What is this? Why am I able to talk to you right now?"

"Thought this would be a face that would set your mind at ease."

"So you're saying you're not really . . ." A flash of anger and confusion rushed through Darrak. "Who the hell are you?"

"A friend."

"Liar."

He stormed forward to grab hold of Theo, to throttle the truth out of him, but instead he went straight through Theo's body and hit the brick wall behind him.

Darrak spun around, but Theo was no longer there. Darrak was alone.

"Okay," he said aloud. "This is even worse than I thought."

Theo was gone and something had been using his face to lead Darrak here—wherever the hell this was. He couldn't phase for some unknown reason and there were energy-sucking wraiths wandering around.

Maybe he shouldn't have said no to that last drink after all.

⇥ SEVENTEEN ⇤

Ben tried to keep hold of the shapeshifter, but she put up a struggle once they reached the exterior of the Malleus headquarters. He'd taken a shortcut to a hidden exit a guard had shown him for emergencies. In his opinion, this qualified. They had to get as far away from this place as possible.

The woman, however, wasn't making things easy for him.

A block away she finally managed to wrench herself out of his grip.

"Are you crazy or something?" she snarled.

"Possibly."

"What do you think you're doing?"

"I believe I just saved your life."

She stared at him for a long moment before thrusting her wrist out to him. "Take this thing off me."

He eyed the cuff. "You want me to remove it so you can shift form and run away?"

"That's basically what I'm thinking."

Despite himself, amusement began creeping in at the edges. Or maybe he was just losing it. With one decision he'd ruined his entire life, and there was no turning back now. "What's your name?"

"Bertha."

He snorted. "You're lying."

"You're smart."

"I already told you my name. Ben Hanson."

"Yeah, golden-boy."

"What?"

She swept her gaze over him. They were behind a corner and could hear the busy downtown traffic close by. "That was Darrak's nickname for you. He thought you were a real threat to his and Eden's happily never after."

So funny he forgot to laugh. "Yeah, some threat."

She studied him for a long, heavy moment. "The name's Kathleen Harris. But people I like call me Leena."

"Leena."

"I said people I *like* call me that." Her amber eyes slid down the front of him again. "The jury's still out on you."

He didn't have time for witty repartee. "We need to get away from here. It won't be long before they figure out what I did and this"—he brushed his fingers over the brand on his arm, currently covered by the sleeve of his leather jacket—"is going to lead them right to me. By then I need to make sure you're safe. So are you coming with me or not?"

She stood with her hands on her hips, still studying him as if he was a curious creature she'd found at a museum. "Why did you rescue me? Why would you put yourself at risk like that unless this is some sort of stupid trick?"

He didn't have time for this. "You don't trust easily, do you?"

"As little as I can, actually."

"I rescued you because . . ." His jaw clenched. "Because I'm not that person, the one they think I am. I have no interest in forcibly extracting information from women and I don't particularly care what that information is or who wants it. And if that's what they want me for then they can look elsewhere."

Leena frowned at him. "You're right about one thing."

"And what's that?"

"You did put a nice target on your back, Ken doll."

He sighed. "Thought I asked you to stop calling me that?"

"Why? You're gorgeous, blond, and way too perfect to be anything but plastic underneath it all."

He almost laughed at that. "Yeah, so perfect. I'm about as far from that as you can get."

Leena stopped arguing and followed him to the van that he'd parked two blocks away. He'd known from the moment he arrived what he was going to do and what it would mean.

"So you don't want to be the Malleus's pet anymore even though you went through the ritual and got the brand," she said. "Not the smartest move, but pretty damn brave to defy a direct order like that."

He glanced at her as he shifted the van into drive. "You sound like you know the ropes."

"I've been around a few dangerous men in my life. Some of them were mixed up with Malleus business. They always got me in deep trouble. You, I'm thinking, aren't much different, even if you're all knight in shining armor right now. I just want to know what changed. It couldn't have just been me that prompted this crazy decision. You don't even know me."

His hands tightened on the steering wheel as he pulled onto the road. "You want to know what changed?"

"Yeah. Lay it on me."

"Darrak's gone and it's my fault. But only now I realize it was the wrong thing to do."

Leena gasped out loud. "He's gone?"

"One-way nosedive into the Void." Ben never in a million years would have guessed he'd feel guilty about that, but he did.

"Holy shit." Leena pressed back in her seat and raised a hand to her mouth. "How's Eden taking it?"

"Badly." He blinked hard. "I was stupid to come between them, but I honestly had no idea how much she loved him. It was a mistake. I see that now, but there's nothing I can do about it. I can just fix other things that need fixing."

She went quiet for a moment before nodding firmly. "Fine. So now what's the plan?"

"The plan is to get you to a motel as soon as possible."

She raised an eyebrow. "That sounds interesting."

That she was able to make him blush surprised even him. "So you'll be safe."

"That's usually the reason dangerous men want to take me to motels."

A nervous laugh threatened to burst free from his throat. "Trust me, I'm not some romantic hero who's planning on ravishing you."

"Mm-hmm. Okay."

He tried to focus on the road. "The last thing I need in my life right now is a shapeshifter. This supernatural crap is all new to me, and I'm not liking it a bit. If I survive this I want to get my life back to normal as much as I can. Get it?"

"Got it."

He amused her, she wasn't exactly hiding this fact. "Once I know you're safe I have to come back and take care of some other business."

This shifted her expression from amusement to concern. "Are you stupid or something? They'll kill you!"

"There's an angel in a cell near yours. I need to rescue him, too."

Her eyes widened. "An angel? How do you know that?"

Ben came to a stop at a light and eyed their surroundings cautiously. "He had wings. They were plucked daily. Didn't you notice anything?"

"No, I . . . I mean I heard them talking to another prisoner near me. I think the guy's name was Daniel, but I didn't hear anything else that might help."

Daniel. The name sounded familiar, but he couldn't put his finger on why.

"Why would they want his feathers?" he mused.

Leena casually propped her left leg up on the dashboard. "An angel's feathers aren't really feathers. That's just what they look like in the human world. They're more like, uh, celestial Wheaties, if you get my meaning. An angel gets his power from his wings."

Ben frowned. "How do you know that?"

"I'm a veritable encyclopedia of supernatural facts, handsome. Can't help it. I retain everything I've ever seen or heard." She tapped her temple. "Werepanthers are known to have photogenic memories."

Werepanther. Terrific.

He rubbed a hand over his forehead. His head had started to throb. "Why would they pluck his feathers?"

"It would keep an angel weak and unable to fight back, which might be why they've succeeded in locking him up. Also, if their feathers are ingested by a mortal, it gives them a whole lot of power."

Ben was silent for a moment. "They eat the feathers?"

"So the rumor goes."

"It's happened before?"

She nodded. "Legend has it that Hitler had an angel trapped so he could grind the wings up into his breakfast every day. Thought it would make him invincible."

That was a disturbing image. "Didn't work though, did it?"

"No, but I'm thinking he didn't have enough time to make it work. Anyone so determined to trap an angel and suck up some of that celestial energy is up to something big. Something epic. The only question is who and what?"

Ben thought he knew who, although he wasn't sure what Oliver Gale could possibly want that would require a huge influx of celestial energy.

Hitler wanted to rule the world.

So what exactly was the leader of the Malleus after?

⇒ EIGHTEEN ⇐

The moment Eden slid the bracelet over her wrist, the floor dropped out beneath her feet. Alternating darkness and light flooded her vision, and she clung to Andy's furry neck as they fell.

A few moments later, they hit the ground, hard enough to knock the breath out of her. Sprawled on her back, she looked up at a dark, starless sky.

Noise assaulted her ears. Traffic, shouting, the bustle of a crowd.

"Eden, watch out!" Andy called.

She rolled out of the way just in time to avoid a cart with large wheels that would have gone right through the middle of her forehead. She scooted to the side of the road and realized she was in the middle of a mass of people—or, rather, *not* people. Some of these creatures were in human form, but others were in . . . other forms. Tall or short, big or small, horned, unhorned. All sorts of colors and shapes. It was like something out of *Sesame Street* if the children's show had been set in the middle of Hell itself and the

Muppets had sharp teeth and scales, or slimy skin and octopus-like appendages.

"What is this?" she whispered.

"Some sort of a market."

A demon market in the Netherworld. And she'd forgotten her camera.

"We need to find Darrak," she said.

A demon walked past, pushing a smaller cart full of some kind of product. It seemed to be a cross between a lemon and a multicolored sea anemone, its tentacles waving in the air. Other demons approached and sifted through the lemon things, shoving them into bags while the lemons made high-pitched squealing noises.

"You're not moving."

"I'm currently frozen with fear."

"Some scary black witch you are. You don't want these things sniffing around you. Call me crazy, but I'm thinking humans—or mostly humans—aren't too common around here."

Eden got to her feet and moved behind a tall stack of boxes to escape the searching gaze of the eight-foot-tall puce-colored vendor.

She turned to look into Andy's glowing red eyes. "Why do you sound so calm, anyway? You do realize where we are, right?"

His forehead wrinkled. *"Don't know. I just am. It's eerie, really."*

"This isn't a dream."

"When that guy from before—"

"Lucifer."

"Thanks for the reminder. Anyway, when he changed me, it gave me some sort of serenity that just kicked in down here. I guess that's why I get to be your guide. I'm sure I'm going to have a complete meltdown when this is all over. I mean, I was still getting used to the werewolf thing. This—well, this is in a whole different ballpark."

He was right about that.

Funny, this place reminded her ever so slightly of the Kensington Market in downtown Toronto. Food and crowds and entertainment, an energetic mix of pedestrians and vendors.

Only . . . *not*.

There were hundreds of demons here, but the storefronts weren't emblazoned with colorful signs for local businesses. They were blank. And it was night—she glanced up again. Not a star in that sky. Or a moon. Just blank, black velvet. The only light came from streetlamps that only served to cast a spooky glow over the street.

But this wasn't the same sky she was accustomed to looking at. Funny, she hadn't even expected the Netherworld to have a sky.

Was this where Darrak spent time before he was cursed? Had he ever attended this market before?

And what exactly were those lemon things for?

A large burst of fire erupted from one of the carts down the street, followed by a scream of pain and a rousing cheer of appreciation.

"What the hell was that?" she managed.

"Looks like a pet dragon," Andy said. *"It's for sale. Interested?"*

"I'll pass, thanks." She scanned the crowd one more time. "What direction do we need to go in to get to the Void? Do you know?"

"I'm supposed to know?"

"You're the guide, remember?" Her stomach sank. "How can we even go to the Void? It's a place of nothing, according to Darrak. How do we travel to nothing?"

"Maybe you're being too literal. We'll ask for directions."

"Damn it," she mumbled. "Lucas didn't make this even slightly easy for us, did he?"

"Why do you keep calling him Lucas?"

Good question. Denial was powerful, but not all that practical. "Because it helps me to pretend that he isn't really the Prince of Hell."

Saying his title out loud earned her a few gasps, and a couple cleared throats, and any demon within hearing distance moved away from her.

Well, at least now she knew what to say to get some privacy.

"Let's go," she said firmly and started walking away from the crowd. If there was a Void around here it wouldn't be close to a busy street market like this. Both she and Andy owned a private investigation company. If they couldn't figure out where they were going they weren't worth that much.

"Are you and Darrak still connected somehow?" Andy asked. *"That would be helpful."*

She exhaled shakily. "I can't feel anything. For a month he's been such a huge part of my life, but . . . I—I can't believe this has happened. All I wanted in the beginning was to get rid of him, to have my freedom again, and now . . . Andy, we have to find him."

He looked up at her with concern and his pointed ears folded back flat against his head. *"What if we're too late?"*

She couldn't even think about that. Not now. "We have to hurry."

Eden picked up her pace as she weaved her way out of the thick crowd. She would find him. She had to. There was no other way this could turn out.

Her mother used to call her a "stubborn little thing" when she'd been growing up. Caroline had been exaggerating then, feeling that any kind of disagreement constituted stubbornness. She'd been wrong then.

But she'd be right now.

"I'll find you, Darrak," she whispered. "No matter what."

⇒ NINETEEN ⇐

There was no redhead. No matter how far Darrak went down the seemingly endless street, no redhead magically appeared.

Which was fine. He'd never really had a thing for redheads before. Especially not enough to follow one of them into dark, uncharted territory. So why was he doing just that?

No damn idea.

He stopped walking and scrubbed a hand through his hair.

"Okay, enough," he said out loud. "Talk to me. What do you want from me?"

Some entity was using Theo's appearance to get close to him, but why? He refused to think about the fact that his friend was really gone. It made something in his chest ache. It was a pain that was spreading outward the longer he walked down this street, and it wasn't just from some strange sense of grief. It felt very wrong.

All of this felt very wrong.

Somebody was messing with him. It had to be Lucifer.

Yes, of course it was Lucifer. He could change his appearance at will. Lucifer had the power to play with Darrak's mind, make him forget or make him remember things that had never happened. It was like Darrak was a lump of play dough and Lucifer was the enthusiastic child smashing the colors together and making a complete mess.

"Okay." Darrak turned in a circle, ignoring the pain now swirling in his gut. "You had your fun, Lucifer. What do you want from me today? What game are you playing?"

Lucifer didn't appear. What did appear, however, were the dark forms of the wraiths, moving toward him swiftly and smoothly, as if their long black cloaks glided just an inch above the ground.

"Ladies," he said, forcing himself to hold his ground and not turn tail and run in the opposite direction. They had to already be full from the substantial fairy meal they'd just consumed. "Maybe you can help me."

"Demon," one hissed in a cold feminine voice.

"Angel," the other snarled.

"Huh?" Darrak replied. "I think you're a little off there, sweetheart."

"Demon-angel," they said in unison, moving around him like piranha circling nervous prey. "So unusual. How does it exist? How does it walk with such contrary forces at work within it?"

"Are you referring to me as an 'it'?" Darrak asked. "Because that's kind of rude, if you ask me."

"It has the sweetest smell," one said.

"Thanks. That's not a cologne, FYI, that's all me." His words were flippant, but he felt anything but.

"No wonder it couldn't maintain its life force anywhere else. No wonder it was sent here. It is not meant to exist."

"We must taste it. Such a waste to simply let it continue on to its fate."

Those pale fingers reached for him, but just before the wraith touched his throat, he turned and started walking, not looking back, not saying anything else to provoke their interest.

He wasn't scared, he was mad. Mad that Lucifer would put him somewhere like this, allow these common wraiths to think they could attempt a taste test of his archdemon energy.

One of the wraiths darted in front of him and peeled back her hood.

"Try to look away, demon-angel," she whispered. Her voice had grown more sultry, more sirenlike. Her hair was long and blonde and silky and flowed as if moved by a nonexistent wind. Her face was a supermodel's. One of those Victoria's Secret babes.

For some reason, a blonde supermodel didn't do it for him today, not even for a moment.

"No thanks," he said. "No offense, but I don't think you're my type. You haven't seen a redhead wandering around here, have you?"

She hissed, which ruined the shiny look when it revealed her sharp teeth.

Wraiths. No better than the Netherworld's answer to vampires, really.

"Go play with your girlfriend," Darrak suggested. "I'm not interested in a make-out session with either of you. Sorry to disappoint."

Both of them flew at him then, and he tried with all his strength to throw them off. He'd been fooling himself to think that he had a chance here. They were petite, but they were supernaturally strong once they attached themselves, like humanoid leeches. It was impossible to shake them off.

An image of long, beautiful auburn hair flashed across his vision as they kissed him, one on his mouth, one on his throat and he felt the edge of those sharp teeth.

A word flitted through his mind—a garden of paradise, somewhere warm and safe and beautiful where he wanted to live forever.

Eden.

Great. One mention of angels and he was getting all Adam and Eve.

Although, still, for last thoughts there could be worse ones, he supposed.

The wraiths suddenly detached themselves and recoiled from him. It wasn't something he'd expected. He'd figured that was it, he was a goner. They both had their hoods pushed back from their lovely but sour faces.

"What?" he asked. "Not as delicious as you thought I'd be?"

Their eyes grew larger, now focused on something right behind Darrak. Anything that would get a reaction like that from the walking death duo didn't make him want to turn around. He waited until the wraiths swept themselves away as if they'd just seen oblivion itself.

Darrak put his hands on his hips. "So I'm guessing that this isn't going to be my night no matter what direction I go, is it?"

"That's up to you, demon."

He finally glanced over his shoulder. It wasn't Theo again, he already knew that thanks to the woman's voice. But this face was also familiar. A woman, in her twenties, with long dark hair and a beautiful face.

"Selina," he said.

She put a hand on her hip and smiled. Her lips were red and glossy. "Sort of."

"Not Selina." Not the witch who'd summoned him hundreds of years ago. Along with the pain that had begun to infuse his core he was getting a little well-needed clarity. "Am I on an episode of *This Is Your Life*?"

Her smile held. "No."

"How about *Candid Camera*?"

"Strike two."

Darrak's eyes narrowed. "You're Lucifer, aren't you?"

She shook her head. "Wrong again."

He didn't speak for a moment. He'd been certain he was right, that Lucifer had brought him here, wherever *here* was, and messed with his memories, just to play one of his stupid reindeer games. "Then who the hell are you?"

"I told you before. A friend."

"A friend who was going to let two wraiths make a tasty meal of me."

"They didn't."

"What do you want?"

"You're clinging to the sides of existence, digging in with your fingernails so hard that I thought I'd come and perhaps give you a bit of a hand."

Darrak blinked. "Thanks?"

She continued to study him with that cool detached look of amusement. "Why don't you follow me?"

"Do I have a choice?"

"Not really."

Selina turned and started walking. She wore four-inch heels and a flowing black dress that was low cut in the front and laced up in the back.

The Love Witch, that's what she liked to be called. She'd written books—self-help books for women who had a difficult time with the men in their lives.

Darrak had made her a black witch back during the Salem witch trials—she'd cast a spell that siphoned dark power from him. She'd wanted the black magic in order to get vengeance on the men who'd put her sister to death.

Selina had tried but failed to destroy Darrak shortly after she'd gotten what she wanted from him, and he'd only recently found her again. He wanted her to break the curse she put on him. It had destroyed his ability to maintain his corporeal form. To break that curse he would have had to tear out her heart.

But he hadn't.

She glanced over her shoulder at him. "Thinking about the good old days?"

"Hardly."

"You didn't kill me when you had the chance," she said.

"You know what I'm thinking?"

"I know lots of things, demon."

He raked a hand through his hair and looked back in the direction he'd come from, but all he could see was darkness now. "Do you know why those wraiths were calling me demon-angel?"

"Yes."

"Want to share?"

"Actually, it doesn't take a genius to figure that riddle out."

"I think I hate you." He glowered at her. "No . . . wait. I do. I definitely hate you."

She cocked her head. "Would you have killed me if you'd been given another chance? Would you have done what it took to return to your normal existence even if it meant destroying someone who had sought redemption for centuries?"

"Sure," he replied immediately. It only made her smile wider.

"Think first, demon. You've always spoken before you thought first. It's one of your many flaws."

"Gee, you're all kinds of charming, aren't you?"

"Come on, it's not much farther."

The farther he walked, the more pain he felt. It was a normal sensation for one who punched a time clock in Hell itself, but it was still something that was best to be avoided. Pain, even for demons, was an indication that something was wrong.

A large black building shielded the view of what lay ahead. Darrak slowed. The pain had shifted to a burning sensation—flames blossoming outward from his chest.

Fire was his element to call, and it never hurt. Fire was such a part of him that he was shielded against this sort of pain. And yet . . . this wasn't pleasant at all.

"I have a proposition for you, demon," Selina said.

"Really. And what's that?"

"You've come to a fork in the road. It's up to you which path you choose."

Darrak came to a halt next to Selina at the edge of the building.

"Talk," he said. "I don't have all night here. Patience isn't one of *my* virtues."

She leaned back against the black wall behind her. "Do you know where we are?"

"No. I believe that's why I've been asking you that very question since I came to earlier in the bar."

"Do you know how you got here?"

"What is this, twenty questions?" He fought against the frustration that rose in his chest. "No, I don't know how I got here. I don't know what part of the Netherworld this is, only that I've never been here before and I'm not too interested in coming back."

"Do you know what you've lost?"

He gritted his teeth and tried to remain calm, cool, and collected, despite wanting to grab whatever or whoever this trickster in front of him was and shake it very hard.

"Do you even know you've lost something?" Selina persisted.

"Yes," Darrak said. "I've lost something very important, but I don't know what it is. Why don't you go ahead and tell me?"

"Can't do that." Selina's smile changed as her form shifted back to Theo's again.

"Who are you?" Darrak asked again.

"Someone who has taken a mild interest in you, demon. A *very* mild interest. Look around the corner and see what is waiting for you. It's time we move this along."

This was ridiculous. Darrak moved past the trickster and went around the corner. He took three more steps before he froze in place. Something cold slithered through him. It felt a bit like clarity.

"The Void." It was the word he couldn't think of earlier, but it now came back to him.

The street before him, pavement surrounded by cement curbs and brick buildings just . . . disappeared. There was a drop-off, like the sheer side of a cliff into nothingness. He didn't have to look. He knew it didn't have a bottom to it.

The bottom didn't exist.

He scanned the area to see that the street picked up a hundred yards up ahead and the jagged drop-off formed a wide, gaping circle. An open, bottomless mouth whose deep black hunger could never be satisfied since it had no stomach to fill.

Welcome to the Void.

"So those fairies—" Darrak began.

"Gatekeepers. Sentries. Administrators. Take your pick. They were on a break when they spotted us. It's their job to make sure no one strays too close to the Void and to double-check those who do. Don't worry, they'll be swiftly replaced. It's a bit lonely in this area, but the pay is excellent."

Darrak covered his abdomen with his hand. The burning sensation had increased, and now he felt a strange pull toward the hole in the ground. "So let me guess, I'm next up on the list to take a dive?"

"You are."

It was as if he'd known this from the moment he woke up in the bar, but had been trying to repress it. After all, this wasn't exactly good news. There was no news he could think of worse than this.

"Well, shit," he said. "This sure hasn't been my lucky day, has it?"

Then he remembered something and glanced away from the abyss to look at Theo. "You said you have a proposition for me. Does that include an option of not heading down there?"

"That's up to you."

The cryptic statements were grating, but currently his only chance. He knew that strength or smarts weren't enough to get out of this particular pickle. He'd never heard of anyone who'd survived a trip to the Void. Then again, his memories were currently shaky at best. Maybe he was forgetting something.

"Tell me," he said.

"Do you want another chance?" Theo asked.

"Of course." A demon's first defense was self-preservation. It was also his second and third. Whatever happened, he would put himself first. This was the perfect example of that. At this very moment, Darrak was willing to promise anything in order to walk away from this in one solid piece.

"There is a job opportunity that's just opened up. It would

be a demotion from archdemon, I'm afraid, but these things happen."

Darrak resisted the urge to protest. "Keep talking."

"It would involve you going to the human world and doing some reaping of human souls."

"You mean I'd be an incubus again." The thought did not appeal, but it was better than the Void.

"No, not quite as pleasant as that. In order for an incubus to take a soul, that soul needs to be willing to be taken. This job requires a bit more stealth work. You would target specific humans, kill them, and tear the souls from their bodies. As you can see things are a bit on the downtrodden side around here, especially in outlying areas like this. With a fresh influx of positive energy we'd be able to do a nice upgrade."

"Positive energy," Darrak repeated. "So they would have to be clean souls. Not evil, not corrupt, not dark at all."

"The cleaner the better."

"And I'd have to kill them."

"How else do you suggest reaping a soul?" Theo grinned. "It'll be fun, I'll even help you out for a bit like the good old days."

If this was actually Theo and not some trickster demon, Darrak might find that amusing. "So what's my first assignment?"

"A private school in England. A bunch of adorable schoolboys. Think *Harry Potter* without the magic and flying broomsticks. If it makes you feel better, a great many of them regularly break curfew to visit a nearby girl's school. Very naughty."

An image flitted through Darrak's head. A school in London consumed by a fire that he'd set with his own power. Kids screaming, trying to run, but he was blocking the door, snatching them, trapping them. Them begging for his help, pleading, crying, but he wouldn't help. They had something he needed. Souls, white, shiny, almost silvery souls filled with energy and power. Mothers and fathers consumed with grief when they found out they'd lost their children in such a horrible tragedy . . .

Definitely not Hufflepuff in any way, shape, or form.

The pain in Darrak's gut grew more intense and his throat suddenly felt tight. "Sounds . . . interesting. So what's behind door number two?"

Theo nodded at the Void. "That."

Darrak laughed, and it sounded sharp and unpleasant, even to himself. What was wrong with him? Why was he even giving this a second thought? He was a demon. They weren't your friendly neighborhood superheroes that saved kids from fires and certain death. They *caused* fires. They killed. They maimed. And then they danced merrily among the carnage.

He definitely had memories of merry carnage dancing from his many years of existence.

So why wasn't he dancing right now?

"Problem?" Theo asked.

"No. Of course not."

"You should know this is a limited time offer."

"How long do I have?"

"Ten minutes. No, actually make that nine minutes and six seconds."

"So let me get this straight. I either agree to be a murderer and reaper of innocent human kids with shiny souls or I forfeit my entire existence and get sucked into that Void right there. Is that right?"

"You're paying attention. I appreciate that. Makes things much simpler."

"Awesome."

Damn it. What was his problem? Anything was better than his own destruction. He felt the clock ticking down his remaining minutes. The fire in his gut was getting more intense. And the Void had some sort of strong pull on him—like a hellish vacuum cleaner—which was drawing him ever closer to his ultimate fate. He couldn't seem to move away from the edge.

Unless he said the word, accepted this deal, then he was minutes away from being cast into the Void.

Kill kids for a living or allow himself to be destroyed forever.

He really wished there was a door number three.

⇒ TWENTY ⇐

This wasn't good.

Eden had the best of intentions at marching out of the demon market and searching the surrounding area for Darrak, but she'd started going in circles. Just when she thought she'd found the end of the market, it was as if it folded back onto itself.

She could tell because they kept passing that dragon for sale, a thin, sickly-looking little green thing that coughed up a fireball every thirty seconds as if it had hiccups from Hell.

"It's like some sort of a trap," she said. "I don't know what to do. And we're running out of time."

"Ask somebody."

"Damn it, why did Lucas do this? Why didn't he help me? I promised him my angel side. You'd think that might earn me a little help here."

Andy kept pace with her, his large paws padding on the pavement as they continued to work their way through the thick crowd. Eden tried her best not to touch anyone directly.

"You know you're talking about Lucifer like he's just

somebody who's doing you a favor. But he's not some guy who's trying to help out, Eden. He's . . . well, he's him." He sighed. *"And I'm still convinced I'm dreaming."*

He was right, of course. Not about the dreaming, unfortunately, but about how she looked at Lucas. It showed in her continuing insistence to call him something other than what he was. She needed to face reality and clue in to the fact that he wasn't trying to help anybody but himself. And she'd already agreed to give him what he wanted whether or not she found Darrak.

Lucas wasn't a nice guy she could count on in her time of need. He was a self-involved fallen angel who wanted to go back to Heaven at any cost.

And that just made her mad.

He'd given her as little help as possible, without getting his hands dirty. And here she was. She had to stop being so damned uncertain and go after what she wanted.

"You're right."

"About what?"

"We need to ask for directions." She pushed her fears away and approached the next demon she spotted who was in human form. He was tall and handsome with broad shoulders and dark hair.

For a split second, from behind, she could have sworn it was Darrak, and her breath caught.

But it wasn't.

"Excuse me." She caught his arm to slow him down and he looked at her curiously.

He cocked his head. "Let me guess. Succubus, right?"

"Me?" She swallowed. "You guessed it."

"I can spot them a mile away. You're too beautiful to be anything else."

Andy groaned.

Great. Just what she needed right now. A pickup line from Hell.

The demon glanced at Andy. "Nice hellhound."

"Thank you," Eden said.

He reached his hand out to her. "The name's Stefano."

After a slight hesitation she shook his hand. He felt warm and human, even though she was sure he was anything but. "Eden."

"What an adorably ironic name. Tell me, Eden, are you bearing delicious forbidden fruit?"

She cringed. "And this is Andy."

Stefano released her hand after one more squeeze and glanced at the hellhound. "Are you protecting your mistress from any unwanted attention at the market today? Are you a good hellhound? Yes, you are!"

Andy growled, low in his throat. A line of drool slid off his jowls and dribbled to the ground.

"Not so friendly, is he?"

"You're an incubus, aren't you?" Eden said.

"How did you know?"

Good-looking and not too smart. Dead giveaway. "You remind me a little of somebody—somebody I'm looking for."

"Name?"

She hesitated. "Darrak."

He pursed his lips. "Never heard of him. If he doesn't show up, I have a little bit of downtime. I'd love to get to know you better, Eden. You and your hound."

"Is this loser for real?" Andy asked.

Luckily Eden was the only one who could hear him.

Stefano looked down at Andy with surprise. "Your hellhound talks?"

Okay, maybe Eden wasn't the only one who could hear him.

"He's, uh . . . special. Look, Stefano, I'm hoping you can help me with something very important—"

"A talking hellhound. That's incredible!" He crouched down and braced his hands on his thighs. "Say something else, boy. Speak!"

Andy blinked. *"I really don't need this right now. But, woof."*

Eden had to take control of this situation again. "Do you know how to get to the Void from here?"

Stefano froze and slowly looked at her before rising back up to his six feet plus of height. "The Void."

"Yes, it's a place of endless nothing where demons go when they're destroyed."

"Oh, I'm well aware of what the Void is. I'm just wondering what a beautiful succubus like yourself and her talking hellhound would want with a place like that."

Her stomach churned. "Forget it. Obviously you don't know."

"I don't know precisely. But as soon as one leaves the safety of the market you'd be able to feel its pull. It's not far from here."

She felt the first pinprick of hope since she'd arrived. "How do I leave the market?"

"Wait a minute . . ." He was silent for a moment, studying her. "You're not a succubus at all, are you? I was wrong."

She didn't like the look on his face. It was suspicious, searching, and the flirtatious friendliness from a minute ago was fading quickly.

"I need to get out of this market," she said firmly. "Tell me how to do that."

"There's a mild spell on the entire area to keep the customers shopping for as long as possible. You have to really want to leave before you can break away from it."

"Trust me, I really want to leave."

"So you can go to the Void."

She kept her mouth closed. Andy began to growl again.

Stefano drew closer, inhaling. "I smell something sweet." His eyes narrowed. "Something that shouldn't be here. What are you really, Eden?"

"A visitor."

"Whose visitor?"

"Lucifer's."

Stefano flinched at the name, but he didn't look as if he believed her. "I smell angel. An angel in the Netherworld. Not a very good idea. Much too dangerous a place for a sweet little thing like you."

Before her very eyes, he shifted his form until he grew taller, broader. His skin became leathery and the red of bricks, his horns long and curved and shiny black. His lips peeled back from sharp yellow teeth. "Maybe I should have a taste of that sweetness. I hear angels are delicious."

He grabbed hold of her arm. Andy clamped his teeth into the demon's shin.

And Eden summoned magic into her hands and blasted the incubus back from her. He landed on his back ten feet away, looking up at her, dazed.

She looked down at the demon. "I'm not that sweet anymore."

"What the—?" He tried to get up.

Eden held out her hand to stop him. "Follow me and you're going headfirst into the Void. Hear me?"

He stayed on the ground. "Yes, ma'am."

"That's more like it."

She touched the cold surface of her amulet, but didn't risk looking at it. A little black magic was worth it sometimes when she could avoid being a demon's snack.

"We're out of here, Andy. Come on."

"You got it."

Stefano said she had to really want to leave the market. This time she walked out with purpose, with no hesitation, and with every ounce of determination she could summon. There was a slight pulling sensation as she reached the outer breaches of the crowd and noise, but then with a small pop, she broke through.

Out here there was darkness, silence, and a look over her shoulder now showed the market far in the distance even though she'd only taken a few steps away from it.

"I hate this place," she whispered.

"Me too. But I have good news."

"Yeah? I could use some of that right about now."

"He said that once we were out of the market we could feel the pull of the Void."

She shook her head. "I can't feel anything."

"Well, I can. I bet Lucifer made me into a hellhound for that reason. I can guide you there."

Eden let out the breath she hadn't even realized she'd been holding and nodded. "Then lead the way."

"Well?" Theo asked. "Not to hurry you along, but I do have stuff to do."

Darrak glared at him, feeling the pull of the Void behind him. "And you're trying to convince me that you're not Lucifer."

"I'm not Lucifer."

"How do I know that for sure?"

Theo inspected his fingernails for a moment. "Because if I was Lucifer I would have already gone Sparta on your ass and kicked you into the Void just to see the look of shock on your face."

He had an excellent point.

"Does everyone get a deal like this before they're gone forever?"

"No," Theo said. "Most are introduced to the Void like a balled-up piece of garbage tossed into a garbage can before they have any idea what's going on, rather than moseying up to the edge like this all subtle-like."

"Then why me?"

"Because I think you could still be useful to me."

Darrak wracked his mind, trying to find the answers he needed. "Are you one of the other demon lords? You want me to work exclusively for you if I agree to this? Keep the soul energy away from Lucifer?"

"I'm not a demon lord. And your time is ticking away. Just over two minutes left."

The draw of the gaping chasm of darkness behind him was growing stronger, he felt it like long fingers sliding underneath his skin, like branches growing up over the jagged cement sides and wrapping around his ankles. It would be pointless to try to fight it. It already had him in its clutches, but now it was waiting before yanking him that last bit backward.

But something kept Darrak fighting, hoping for a solution. A demon who hoped. Sure, that made sense.

What was down there? Would he land somewhere eventually? Is that where the rumor of the torturous pain came from before you were finally gone forever? Who started that rumor if no one had ever survived the plunge? He was in pain right now, but it was still manageable. He'd experienced much worse in his long existence.

"What do you care about, demon?" Theo asked.

Strange question. "Care about?"

"Is it only yourself? In these last minutes, are you only concerned about yourself and your own well-being?"

"It is top of mind."

"But not completely. If it was, then you'd already have given me your answer. I need you to speak the words, demon. Say you're willing to devote your future to killing innocent humans in order to save your own skin. Come on, it'll be totally fun. Any normal demon would have already jumped on this opportunity, and you know it."

"Can't it be evil humans?" Darrak hated the catch in his voice as he said it. "Criminals, serial killers, blackhearted assholes with no chance at redemption?"

Theo laughed. "You're hilarious. Of course not. What value does a black soul have down here? Zero. Just more cannon fodder. The true value in a place of ultimate darkness comes from the smallest infusion of light."

He wanted to say yes. He did. But something stopped him, something apart from the invisible ropes that now tied him to the Void. Something else wrapped around his chest and squeezed tight.

"Thirty seconds, demon." Theo crossed his arms.

Thirty seconds to decide his ultimate fate.

That redhead . . . had he really seen her? Was she just a figment of his imagination? Why did he think of her now when he was so close to the end? This was it. If he wasn't able to wrap his mouth around the word *yes*—such a simple word considering how much it would mean—then it was all over.

His mind went again to the kids—his first assignment after saving his own sorry neck. It was a deal he once would have taken in a second and not given it another moment's thought.

But he wasn't that demon anymore. And he never would be again.

Oh, hell.

"That deal of yours?" Darrak said.

"Yes?"

"Why don't you go ahead and shove it right up your ass?"

Theo's lips curved. "Is that your answer? Are you saying no to me?"

A small part of him was screaming, wanting to change his mind while there was still a chance to survive, say anything to get out of this. But a larger part of him knew without any doubt that this was the right thing to do.

The right thing. A demon choosing to do something because it was the right thing to do. Hilarious.

"I'd tell you to go to Hell," he said firmly. "But that would be a bit moot. My answer is no. Capital N, capital O. And that *is* my final answer, asshole."

For emphasis, he gave the grinning entity the finger.

Theo cocked his head. "So it's true, you have changed."

Darrak just glowered at him. Then he staggered back a step as the Void's hold on him tightened another notch.

"One final chance, demon."

Darrak's fists clenched. "Blow me."

"No, thanks." Theo shrugged. "Okay, I asked three times. You answered three times. It is decided. For the record, I think you should feel really good about yourself. Go you! Buh-bye now."

The Void's grip tightened like an iron fist, pulling Darrak backward. He fell to the ground and clawed at the cement. The very edge of the cliff face pushed against his shoe before it broke away, and then he was hanging on to the side of the Void by only his hands, his feet dangling over endless darkness.

So this is how it ends, he thought. *Awesome.*

Was this really it? Was he willing to give up?

Something kept him holding on. Something with as much of a grip on him as the damn Void had. He couldn't let go. Not yet.

"Theo! Get back here!" he yelled, calling the name of the friend he'd already lost. The entity using Theo's face didn't reappear. He was gone, his job was done, and Darrak was alone to face his chosen fate.

No rewards in Hell for making the selfless decision, that was for damn sure.

This wasn't a huge surprise.

It felt as if they'd been walking forever when a voice echoed off the dark brick buildings surrounding them.

"Theo! Get back here!"

Eden gasped. "That's Darrak! It's him!"

"I think you're right!"

Andy started running then, although it wasn't without effort. Whatever was in the air around here was starting to cause him some pain.

"Are you okay?" she asked.

"Watch out!"

A hand clamped down on her shoulder. She spun to see who it was and was shocked to see the face of Theo, Darrak's demonic BFF who'd been destroyed two weeks ago.

He didn't exist. Not anymore. And yet here he was.

"You shouldn't be here," Theo said.

"Let go of me." She tried to summon her magic, but it fizzled in her hand before she could get even a spark going.

"It's too late, Eden. Let him go."

She glared at him. "Never!"

She turned and ran, racing around the corner up ahead and then skidded to a halt, shocked at what she saw stretching out before her. There was a huge crater in the ground that reminded her of the Grand Canyon. She'd been there once as a kid; her mom had taken the day away from the tables to take Eden on a helicopter ride above the canyon. It seemed so big and vast and expansive. A world wonder. At the time it had filled her with awe.

This, on the other hand, filled her with fear because she knew what it was.

The Void.

And Darrak was nowhere to be seen.

Theo was right. It was too late.

No, damn it, it wasn't! She'd just heard him. She couldn't have missed him by mere seconds. Life wasn't that unfair.

"Darrak!" she yelled. "Where are you? Answer me!"

⇉ TWENTY-ONE ⇇

The sound of her voice brought Darrak's memories back so forcefully it almost made him lose his already shaky grip on the side of the cliff.

The redhead.

Eden.

Terrific. Now he was hallucinating. In his last moments of existence, he thought of her. Not a huge surprise, really. After all, she was the only thing in the universe he cared about.

She'd be proud he'd made the right decision about the kids. So selfless. So unlike him. It almost made him smile.

Demon-angel, the wraiths called him.

This, too, came back to him now at the end of everything. He'd thought there was some hidden meaning, but it was exactly as they'd said. The wraiths sensed both demon and angel in him because that was exactly what he was.

It was his angel side, the annoyingly do-gooder side, that had shifted his morals enough to make his final decision—sacrifice himself rather than take a job that would force him to hurt others.

He didn't want to hurt anyone. Now he wanted to help them.

The demon side of him thought this was all kinds of lame.

Darrak was the ultimate teeter-totter of good and evil. Black and white. He'd fought it from the beginning. He refused to accept that he'd been tainted with humanity, let alone celestial energy. The two sides of himself had remained apart like oil and water. It was what had caused him the tearing pain when Eden had shifted those parts of him a bit too close together. They hadn't wanted that.

He hadn't wanted that.

It was clear to him now: The decision had always been in his hands. The pain resulted from his failure to accept that he'd changed.

But he had. And that the change had come because of Eden—well, that made it a good change as far as he was concerned. He could accept this now at the end of his existence. He was a demon-angel, filled with equal parts light and dark.

So be it.

He felt something fill him then, easing his tense muscles and relaxing his mind. The peace of accepting who he was, once and for all. Even if it was just for a moment before he ceased to exist.

Embrace your inner freak, Darrak thought. *For better or for worse.*

At the moment, it looked like it was for the worse. The Void wasn't going anywhere but down. And down.

He'd thought Eden had destroyed him by giving him her celestial energy, but she hadn't destroyed him. Instead she had made him better than he was before.

If only he'd realized this sooner.

"There you go, Eden," he whispered. "You did make me a better man after all. Thank you for that."

An animal howled in the distance. Great.

Well, any hellbeast sniffing around for scraps would be out of luck very soon. Nothing to see here. Move along.

"Where are you?" Eden's apparition yelled again. "Darrak! Say something! Say anything!"

He already missed her so much. "Good-bye, Eden."

Some of the cement fell away as his grip loosened. Only seconds now.

But then a hand reached down and grabbed tightly onto his wrist. With surprise, he looked up into the most beautiful face he'd ever seen.

Her green eyes were filled with tears and she smiled down at him. "There you are, you jerk!"

He guessed he'd memorized her face perfectly because this apparition was as real as they came. Or maybe it was her angel side coming to visit him in his last moments. He almost expected to see white fluffy wings stretch out behind her.

Sharp nails dug into his skin. "Darrak! Snap out of it!"

He blinked. "Wait a minute, you—you're not an angelic apparition?"

"Not the last time I checked. What the hell do you think you're doing right now?"

"Oh, you know." He glanced at the bottomless drop below him. "Just hanging around."

Determination filled her gaze. "I won't let you fall."

He snorted. "You're going to pull me out of the mouth of the Void."

"That was my general plan, yes."

This earned a full laugh. "I'm imagining you right now. Or maybe that damn entity is using your face to mess with me some more."

Eden's fingers dug hard into his arm as she grappled for a tighter hold on him, but he slipped a few inches farther down. "Darrak, I'm really here. I came to the Netherworld to find you before it was too late. What you see is what you get."

This was impossible. "Tell me something to make this real. It can't be real."

She hissed out a breath of frustration, but then locked gazes with him. "I'm here because losing you made me realize I don't want to live without you. Ever. I love you more than anything, Darrak, and I want to be with you forever, no matter what the future brings. Now pull your ass out of that goddamned Void right now!"

It hit him like a monster-sized fist. This was real. He didn't know how, but Eden was here.

And she loved him.

Hope flooded through him, and it gave him enough strength to grab hold of her. Enough strength to fight against the pull the Void had on him.

He spoke through gritted teeth. "Just for the record, you're crazy for doing this."

"Less talking, demon. More climbing. Come on!"

He braced his feet against the side of the cliff, and began dragging himself upward, fighting with every ounce of his strength against the Void's tight grip on him. Finally, he breached the edge of the cliff, gasping from the effort.

He looked back at where he'd come from. That was close. That was so unbelievably close.

"Darrak . . . we did it!" Her voice was filled with pure joy and relief.

A smile spread over his face and he turned to look at her, to take her in his arms and never let her go. They made it. He survived and it was all thanks to her.

But then Eden shrieked and suddenly she was being dragged backward from him. He scrambled to grab hold of her but she was pulled out of his reach.

He leapt to his feet. "Eden, no!"

The wraiths had returned, and they surrounded Eden in shadows.

"My magic . . ." Eden managed. "I can't use it . . ."

Wraiths leeched any sort of power from their victim. Made it easier for them to ensnare their prey.

Out of the corner of his eye, Darrak noticed an unconscious black hellhound lying off to the right. That must have been the source of the howl he'd heard earlier.

He'd been willing to let himself go, to be swept into the Void in order to not hurt anyone now or in the future. But seeing Eden in the grip of the wraiths was enough to bring forth the side of him that enjoyed a bit of destruction. And then some.

He wouldn't lose her only a moment after they'd found each other again.

Not like this.

Darrak wrenched himself farther away from the edge of the Void, and it was like pulling himself slowly out of quicksand. But he did it. He ignored the pain, got to his feet, and moved closer to the wraiths now twenty feet away from him.

"Demon-angel," one snarled. "We have something it loves."

"Let go of her," he warned.

"She doesn't belong here, but we're happy she has traveled so far."

The other wraith drew her pasty-white fingers over Eden's stomach. "Two lives, twice as sweet. A taste we've never experienced before. So delicious."

"Two lives?" he growled. "What the hell are you talking about?"

"Small life, it is. Created from two places, two worlds, two beings of opposite means." Wraiths were known to be cryptic double-talkers. It just made them more annoying. "And the demon-angel had no idea, its senses dulled from its curse, no true idea of what the small life created from two worlds—"

"Oh, for the love of—" Eden fought against the choke hold the wraiths had her in. She looked at Darrak. "This wasn't how I wanted to tell you."

"Tell me what?" he asked tightly.

Her gaze locked with his. "I'm . . . pregnant."

"What?" He gaped at her. It felt as if he'd just been shoved back into the Void and was holding on by his fingernails.

Eden watched him uncertainly before her eyes narrowed. "You heard me. Now do something, will you?"

Pregnant. Eden was pregnant.

This unexpected piece of news changed pretty much everything in his entire universe in one split second.

His hands tightened into fists. "Let go of her or you're going to be very sorry."

"A strongly worded warning. That should work perfectly," Eden said dryly. "Thanks."

The wraiths circled Eden, their hands brushing against her enough to keep her from moving, keep her from protecting herself with her magic. "All will be sorry soon. The shadows are restless. Their master stays away looking to take a trip to a place with no shadows."

"Shadows," Darrak repeated, glancing around. He knew what the wraith spoke about. The Netherworld was filled with the shadows. It was what made it eternally night here. No light could broach darkness like this. The darkness was what fueled Hell—evil without form.

Lucifer controlled those shadows, the darkness, keeping it from spreading, growing, branching out past the Netherworld. It was what gave him his vast power, but also what kept him chained here even while able to take mortal form in the human world.

But he'd been neglecting his duties in Hell lately, whining about wanting to go back to Heaven. What a total crybaby.

"Are you afraid?" he asked the wraiths. "Is that what this is? Afraid of the shadows? I can help you."

"It can't help. It's tainted. It's part angel now."

"Sweetheart, that only makes me more powerful. I'm an archdemon with a shiny gold star."

That was a nice way to think of it, actually. Less "freak of nature," more "awesome upgrade."

"This woman and her unborn child are too delicious to give up at any price. They are ours now." They tightened their hold on Eden and she let out a shriek of fear.

Darrak finally had had enough.

He phased from where he stood near the edge of the Void to reappear right in front of the wraiths in a flash of fire. Grabbing each by their throat, he squeezed until they released their grip on Eden.

"Did you say she's yours?" he asked.

"Yesss."

"Pardon the expression, bitches, but possession is nine-tenths of the law."

He launched the pair of them backward. They made a lovely arc through the dark sky as they flew, screaming, into the gaping mouth of the Void.

A couple less wraiths in the Netherworld was like stomping on a couple of cockroaches in a seedy motel. It didn't make much of a difference, but it was still extremely satisfying.

Darrak quickly moved toward Eden and checked her throat. Luckily, the wraiths hadn't done any damage. She stared at him with wide, shiny eyes.

"Are you okay?" he demanded.

Eden grabbed hold of him, and he crushed her against his chest. She felt so good, better than anything. How could he have forgotten her for even a moment? He'd been forced to forget, by someone, something, but he'd remembered anyway. First with the vision of her and now with the real thing.

He pulled back and took her face between his hands. "Is it true? Are you really pregnant?"

She studied his face and nodded. "Yes."

"Is—is it mine?"

Her warm gaze turned into an icy glare very fast. "Are you kidding me?"

Darrak cleared his throat. "Uh, well, it's an honest question. Demons created from hellfire aren't usually able to—"

"Unbelievable. No, it's not yours. It's Ben's. Or Lucas's. Or maybe it's Stanley's. Not sure, I'm such a tramp."

She went to pull away from him, her cheeks flushed red with anger, but he caught her hand to draw her back. "Okay, okay, I'm sorry. I get it. It's mine. But just so you know . . . that's impossible."

"There's a lot of things that are impossible. And yet here we are."

"Touché."

He pulled her closer, swept her soft hair off her face, and kissed her very hard on her lips. It didn't take long at all for her to kiss him back just as passionately. If he'd had any remaining doubts that she was real then they'd now be gone. That fire, that stubbornness, that taste of her mouth against his . . . all Eden. His Eden. The only woman he'd ever loved. Would ever love.

She'd saved him.

Eden had found a way to come to the Void because she loved him as much as he loved her—she was his princess in shining armor.

And she was pregnant with *his* baby.

It was too much to process. All too much.

But the kiss was a very good start.

Then she pulled away from him and glanced to the right. "Oh no!"

She ran toward the hellhound, falling to her knees next to it.

"Eden, be careful," he warned. "Hellhounds are dangerous."

"No . . . this is Andy." Her voice caught. "Those monsters must have attacked him when I was trying to pull you up."

That was Andy? But he was a werewolf the last time Darrak had seen him.

This . . . this definitely wasn't a werewolf.

Darrak went to the hellhound's side. "Is he . . . ?"

"Christ on a cracker . . . what happened?"

His eyebrows went up. "That's definitely Andy."

The hellhound raised his head and blinked at them through glowing red eyes. *"Those two were hot as hell but not very nice girls, were they?"*

"What happened?" Eden asked.

"I think they . . . they kissed me."

Darrak made a face. "No offense, but gross. Wraiths are nasty. And hellhounds aren't traditionally great kissers."

"Wasn't bad for a few seconds." The hellhound cocked his head. *"You're alive!"*

"I am." He looked at Eden. "Thanks to both of you."

"Thank Eden," Andy said. *"She's the one who made the deal to get us here in the first place and that also shifted my, uh, shift."*

Darrak's surge of happiness began to drain away leaving him feeling very cold. "What deal?" When Eden didn't say anything he took her by her shoulders. "What kind of deal did you make? And with who?"

"With *whom*," she said, grimacing, and not simply because of his bad grammar.

"Whatever. Eden, talk to me. Please don't tell me you made another deal with Lucifer."

She looked away. "Then I guess I won't tell you that."

"Are you looking for the buy-ten-get-one-free card?" He swore under his breath. "What did you promise him?"

Her expression wasn't fierce anymore—it was worried. But she didn't look away from him. "It was worth it. He made it so I could come here and find you without it killing me. He made Andy a werehellhound so he could be my guide."

Her intentions were in all the right places, but he'd known this was too good to be true. "I know you think that Lucas is a friendly, good-looking guy with a dark past, but you have no idea what he's truly capable of."

"I know exactly what he is."

"Do you? Are you sure about that? So you're saying that you made a deal with the Prince of Hell himself in order for a fleeting chance to pull my ass out of the Void before it was too late."

Eden held his gaze. "Well . . . yeah. That's pretty much it."

He wanted to be furious, but he couldn't be. This was the bravest thing anyone had ever done for him. He would have done the same thing for her, so he supposed that made them even in their mutual insanity. "What did you promise him?"

She hesitated, which made him more nervous than he was to begin with. "Lucas wants to go back to Heaven, but he's bound to Hell, like a chain around his ankle. I still don't understand why."

That wasn't exactly an answer to his question.

He didn't let go of her. "The darkness here needs to be controlled and that's Lucifer's job. That's what the wraith meant when she talked about the shadows. When he gets upset or loses his composure, that darkness takes him over. They make him into Satan, a being of malevolent energy that likes to destroy and wreak havoc over everything. No one else has control over the darkness. He can't leave." An unwanted piece of empathy slid through him for his unpleasant boss. Being the Prince of Hell and dealing with all of that uncontrollable darkness wouldn't be a fun job for an ex-angel, even if it had plenty of perks.

"He says he has a replacement lined up to take over for him," Andy said.

"A replacement." Darrak frowned. "So he's found a way to leave the Netherworld permanently?"

When Eden didn't reply his grip on her shoulders grew tight enough to make her flinch. He released her immediately.

"Talk to me, Eden. Tell me exactly what you promised him."

She finally met his eyes. "I agreed to give him my angel side for the chance to come here and find you. Freely give every last bit of my celestial energy to him. It will be enough to break his chains down here once and for all."

He just stared at her for what felt like a very long time. "Please tell me you're just messing with me right now."

She just shook her head, her expression pale.

"We need to leave, and we need to leave right now." He didn't say another word, he just put his arm around Eden and his other on Andy's furry back and concentrated on phasing all three of them out of there. He'd been able to channel his phasing ability when he took care of the wraiths, but it wasn't working anymore.

"Oh come on," he growled. "Don't fail me now."

"Will this help? It got us here." Eden showed him her wrist that bore the silver chain she was to use on Ms. Brenda N. Franks, potential Antichrist.

"That won't work both ways." He snorted. "So Lucifer told you to use that, did he? Did he happen to mention how you were supposed to get out of here when you were finished?"

"He didn't cover that."

"No, of course not. He doesn't care if you were able to

leave without his assistance. He'd prefer you remain at his mercy at all times."

Darrak rubbed a hand over his face, trying to think this through.

Eden looked at the hound. "If Andy's still here at sunrise, then there's a problem. He'll shift back to human form."

"Hate to break it to you but minutes and hours sometimes work differently here, like a broken clock. Sometimes it's equal, other times it's not. Time has moved fast since I got here. I already sense sunrise approaching in the human world." He looked at Andy. "Do you feel it?"

Andy looked up at him somberly. *"Afraid so."*

"You can't shift back to human," Darrak said. "Not here. Fight it."

"I'll try."

"Try very hard." The only way they were getting out of there was to either find a gateway or for him to figure out what was stopping him from phasing. And he knew for certain that there weren't any gateways to the human world anywhere close to the Void.

Then he saw something out of the corner of his eye. Someone was watching them carefully.

Theo. Or, rather, the entity currently using his face.

Darrak looked into Eden's eyes. "Wait here."

"But—"

"I'm serious, Eden. Please wait here. I need to talk to him for a second."

She didn't argue, which was a relief. Her green eyes were filled with worry, but determination also battled within them. She knew what she'd done was extreme, but she didn't regret it. She'd agreed to give up half of herself—she didn't even know how serious a decision it was—in order to save his paltry life.

Darrak would love her forever for that, but he couldn't let this deal stand. If Eden lost her angelic energy, the darkness from her black magic would grow inside of her at an even faster rate than it already did. Even Selina's magic hadn't been so powerful, so dark as this. Her soul would have taken centuries more to rot. Eden's was turning black at an accelerated rate and it scared him like nothing he'd ever known before.

For as long as she had that magic at her disposal she needed to stay a nephilim, otherwise she didn't have a chance against that darkness. She'd become an entity whose only desire would be to spread evil throughout the human world until she was killed and sent to Hell.

Eden's future then, unless she was tagged to become a demon, would be to become a wraith. Black-souled human females starved for energy had few other options here.

Darrak wouldn't let that happen. Even though Eden didn't realize it, she was hanging off the edge as much as he had been. Just because she couldn't see the drop didn't mean it wasn't still there.

He'd save her. No matter what.

In fact, he'd already come up with a plan to end this once and for all.

It might get a little tricky, though. Throwing Lucifer into the Void wasn't exactly going to be easy.

⇉ TWENTY-TWO ⇇

"Looks like everything worked out," Theo said.

"I can't phase right now."

"No, you can't. I wanted to talk first."

"You can control my ability to phase?" Darrak's eyes narrowed. "Andy's going to shift back to human any minute. It'll kill him if he's still here."

"Then we should probably talk fast."

Darrak got a sinking feeling. Well, *more* of one. "What do you want?"

Theo smiled. "World peace. Happy children smiling and dancing together. Love and harmony for all."

"I'm still demon enough for that adorable image to make me gag a little. Cut the shit, whoever you are. What do you want from me *specifically*?"

"You're a nobody, you know that, Darrak?" Theo's expression didn't change. "How do you feel about that?"

"Is this a trick question designed to make me slam my fist into your stomach really hard? Because that can be arranged."

"It wasn't meant to be an insult, believe it or not. More

like an observation. You were created from nothing but hell-fire and now you stand before me as a new creation—demon and angel combined. How does that feel?"

"It's a bit itchy around the collar, but I'm sure after a couple washes it'll soften up."

Theo's smile held. "You cover your fear and uncertainty with humor. It's as charming as it is annoying."

"Everybody's a critic."

"Answer me truthfully, Darrak. How does it feel to be what you are now, having come from your very specific beginnings?"

He was about to say something snarky, some quip to amuse himself, but after everything that had happened he wasn't feeling much like joking around. This thing in front of him wanted answers and he was somehow in control of Darrak's phasing ability, which was the only way they could get out of here in one piece.

If they stayed much longer Andy would succumb to his shift, and a human couldn't survive here. It might look like an urban landscape, but it was far from it. Andy would burn up in about two seconds flat.

Andy had helped Eden on her journey. Darrak would be forever in his debt for that. If Eden hadn't arrived when she did, he had no doubt that he'd be long gone by now.

He'd faced the Void and lived to tell the tale.

So instead of a joke, he chose to answer Theo with the truth.

"What does it feel like to be changed from what I've always been? It scares the hell out of me." He snorted. "*Literally* scares the Hell out of me. I'm changed inside and out, but if I had the chance to go back to what I was before . . . I wouldn't take it. I am exactly who I was meant to be, and it's all thanks to Eden. I love her with every fiber of my being, and if you make a move to hurt her I promise you I'm still demon enough to turn you inside out. And trust me, that can get very messy."

Theo leaned against the wall behind him. "Yeah, that's basically what I thought."

"Great. Now are we done with this little tête-à-tête? Have you gotten what you wanted out of me? Can we go now? I have something I need to deal with as soon as possible."

Destroying Lucifer. He'd always enjoyed a challenge and this was as challenging as it got.

"Attempting to throw Lucifer in the Void sounds a bit risky," Theo said.

Darrak froze. "Excuse me?"

"Mind reading." Theo shrugged and tapped his temple with his index finger. "It helps me in oh so many ways."

Even Lucifer couldn't read minds. "Who the hell are you?"

"You keep asking that question. It's really cute." Theo smiled. "Just so you know, Lucifer won't be easily beaten. You should know exactly what he's capable of. But even he will succumb to the Void if you're successful. He's not invincible. And he's not half as smart as he thinks he is. His mind can be manipulated just like anyone else's."

He was taken aback by Theo knowing his very dangerous plans. "If he takes Eden's angel side, am I right? Will she be lost to me?"

"Not all at once. But soon and forever."

Darrak's jaw tightened and he cast a glance toward the gaping mouth of the Void. "Then Lucifer has to be destroyed. There's no other choice."

"You certainly seem as if you have the drive to do exactly what you're saying. There have been attempts to destroy him before, but no one has yet succeeded. He doesn't let many get close to him lately. But you're an exception. He likes you."

Darrak laughed. "Yeah, right. We're best pals."

"You're different from the others, and he respects that. You're something he created out of nothing, but you've taken on a life of your own and a strong, individual personality has evolved. You're a being of passion and conviction. You were always meant for this, Darrak. It just took you a long time to get here."

It sounded like a compliment on the surface, but it didn't

sit well with him. This entity using Theo's face knew him too well, could even read his mind. He didn't like that at all.

"What do you want me to say?" Darrak asked.

"If Lucifer is destroyed, Hell will be without its prince."

"Don't worry. He already has someone lined up."

"Pretenders to the crown. There are many who would love to take his place—they'd line up for the chance at that kind of power. But none are worthy. There's a reason a former angel rules Hell, you see. Yes, Lucifer was prideful and not fond of humans, but he was a shining star from the very beginning." Theo smiled. "That's his name, you know. The bringer of light. That was why he was needed; why he was created. But he's forgotten this and now wallows down here in the muck feeling sorry for himself."

"That sounds like him." Darrak thought about his many unpleasant dealings with the prince. "Crybaby. Muck-wallower."

"It's not an easy job—quite possibly, the most difficult job in the universe for a being of pure light. I don't entirely blame him for seeking a way out."

Darrak glanced at Eden. The thought that she'd have to hand over her angel side to Lucifer was too much for him to bear.

"She can't hear us right now," Theo said.

Darrak's attention returned to him. "Why not?"

"Because what I need to ask you, what I need you to agree to, is not something she can know. Not right now." He was quiet for a moment. "Do you know who I am now, Darrak?"

Darrak studied the face of the demon he'd known for his entire existence. But this wasn't really Theo. Not even close. "Yes, I do."

Even to him, he sounded a bit breathless.

"When Lucifer is destroyed, I need you to agree to take his place."

Darrak's throat tightened and he couldn't speak for a moment. Very unlike him. "You want *me* to be the Prince of Hell."

"You have proven to me that you've changed. You have enough darkness in you still to not let this place or the shadows here drive you insane. But you now have enough light to make you the perfect, levelheaded choice to maintain and control the balance down here."

Darrak couldn't remember anyone ever calling him levelheaded before. "I can't do that."

"But it was what you and Theo once planned, wasn't it? To rule Hell together. To take over each demon lord's throne until you managed to seize control of them all. It would have been quite the coup if you'd succeeded."

"We never would have succeeded. Lucifer knew too much."

"You're right. But he doesn't know this. His head is full of plans for the future once he takes Eden's angelic energy."

"Is it enough to get him back to Heaven? To break his ties here to the shadows?"

"It is. And as an angel he will be accepted again in Heaven if he succeeds in sloughing off his darkness. It's everything he wants."

Darrak thought it through. "But nobody would be here, despite him lining up a candidate. Whether he succeeds or I succeed in destroying him."

"Correct. He doesn't have the final say on who would take his place. I do."

"The Prince of Hell." Saying it out loud didn't help it sound any more logical than it did in his head. Darrak the incubus turned archdemon, turned cursed and bodiless possessor of humans, turned part angel—although still ridiculously good-looking . . .

The Prince of Hell.

There was a time when this would have been the best offer ever.

Those days were long gone.

Darrak shook his head. "I don't want this. I want to be with Eden."

"I know. Which is all the more reason for you to agree to this. Knowing what you'll be giving up will make your oath to follow through that much stronger."

Darrak laughed hollowly. "You and your sacrifices. I've never really bought into that line of thinking much."

"Of course not. You've been only a demon until recently. Not the most self-sacrificing of creatures."

Darrak crossed his arms and cast a look around the area once again, his attention resting on Eden, who'd sat down on the ground next to Andy while she waited for him to return. "What will happen if I say no?"

For the first time, a trace of doubt crossed Theo's dark eyes. "You know very well what will happen."

He did. He wished he didn't, but he did. The shadows of Hell would not be kept under control and they would spread—much like Eden's darkness, but much bigger, much broader. The Void would grow larger than it already was and begin to consume everything in its path, like a black hole sucking in matter from everywhere in the Netherworld. It would consume the human world then, and go on to devour the heavens as well.

Lucifer was more than just a hellish dickwad. He, just by his very existence and position, held those shadows back. He was the vessel for them, just as Eden had been the vessel for Darrak when he'd been cursed.

Because of this trip to the Netherworld, which was supposed to be one-way only, Darrak was free from that curse for the first time in over three centuries. Free to go where he wanted, do what he wanted. Be who he wanted.

And be with who he wanted.

Or *whom*. Whatever. Proper grammar could bite it.

"Eden's black magic," Darrak whispered after a full minute had gone by in silence—a minute Andy really didn't have. "When I take Lucifer's place, I want you to make sure it never hurts her again. So she and the baby will be safe."

"Is that all you want? To ensure the safety of the woman you love and your unborn child?"

He swallowed hard and nodded with a firm jerk of his head. "Yes."

"Then it shall be done. Do you want her to forget that you ever existed? I can do that. She will fondly remember the father of her child, but his absence will not weigh heavily on her mind. She doesn't need to know what happened to you. You know she would want to be with you if she does. And you know that she can't be here—even the short pass Lucifer has given her, it will not last, especially if she loses the darkness inside of her. She's still essentially human."

"Yes." Darrak could barely hear his own voice. "Make her forget me. But not yet. Not until it's time."

"Fair enough." Theo nodded and extended his hand. "So do we have a deal? Once Lucifer has abandoned his throne, you will take it of your own free will. You will become the new Prince of Hell."

He nodded tightly and shook Theo's hand. "We have a deal."

"Thank you, Darrak."

Seemed like a deal that should have a more solid agreement than a firm handshake. But it was what it was.

As he shook Theo's hand, he got an image of Lucifer doing the exact same thing. Agreeing to become the Prince of Hell of his own free will. He'd been given the choice a very long time ago just like this.

Darrak had never known that. He'd always thought Lucifer had no choice and been cast out of Heaven, which was why he'd always had such a huge chip on his shoulder about it.

Theo said he'd forgotten this.

But why? And how?

He released Theo's hand and glanced at Eden. Just the sight of her made his chest tighten. Soon she'd forget him.

It was for the best since there was no other way this could work, but it was the hardest thing he'd ever had to face before.

When he turned to look at Theo again, the entity had disappeared.

"What, no good-bye and good luck?" Darrak murmured. "God, what a jerk."

He turned and walked directly to Eden's side.

"Are we good?" Andy asked. *"Because I'm not really feeling so hot right now."*

"Believe me, if we stay here much longer, you're going to be feeling much hotter . . . by about two thousand degrees. So let's skedaddle."

Eden grabbed his arm and looked up at him with concern. "Is everything all right? Why was Theo here? How did he manage to survive what Asmodeus did to him?"

"That's a lot of questions," Darrak said. "We'll deal with them later, okay? But everything's fine. Everything is exactly how it's supposed to be. I see that now."

He leaned over and brushed his lips against hers. She touched his face as she kissed him back and then smiled at him.

"So you're talking cryptically now?"

"It's my new thing. Now hold on tight."

Eden did as he asked, sliding her arms around his waist. It felt good to be close to her again. To know how she really felt about him.

Darrak loved her more than anything in the universe and he always would.

He wasn't doing this for the universe. He was doing it for Eden. He'd anchor himself to this rotting hellhole in order to ensure her safety. She just never had to know the truth.

So be it.

He was finally able to phase the three of them out of Hell without any issues this time and back to the comfortingly bland interior of Triple-A.

Okay, he thought with grim resolve. *Time to go kill Lucifer.*

Dawn wasn't far off.

Ben paced outside the motel where he'd taken Leena, his cell phone pressed to his ear.

"What is it?" Caroline asked when she answered on the third ring. It didn't sound as if he'd woken her up.

"I need your help."

"Haven't we already made a mess of everything? My daughter hates me. And she hates you, too."

"Why quit when you're ahead?"

She sighed. "What can I do?"

"I need you to take over the body of a guard at the Malleus so I can break out someone they're holding prisoner."

There was a long silence. "You've got to be joking."

"Afraid not."

"Who are you trying to break out?"

Ben wondered how much he should share with her and decided not to hold anything back. "An angel named Daniel."

Another stretch of silence. "Daniel."

"Makes you wonder why he's their prisoner, doesn't it? He's got something they want, which is all the more reason to free him."

"What does this Daniel look like?"

"I only saw him once. He's . . ." Ben's grip on the phone tightened. "Tall, pale, red hair . . . green eyes."

"Where should I meet you?"

She hadn't taken much convincing. That was good. In fact, she'd agreed much quicker than he thought she would. This wasn't going to be safe or easy.

Ben told her where to meet him and when—fifteen minutes. Then he headed for his rented van.

Leena was already sitting on the passenger side, inspecting the cuff he hadn't removed from her wrist yet. He knew the moment he did she'd take off on him. She must have been watching him, waiting for him to leave. It was only a little after seven o'clock.

"No way," he said. "You're staying here."

She looked at him like he was stupid. "You obviously don't know me very well. Anything I can do to screw up the Malleus's plans is something I want to help with as much as possible. Don't argue, Ken doll. I'm coming."

Ben knew anything he said would be a waste of breath,

and he didn't have time for this. "Fine. But you're staying in the van as a lookout."

"I can do that."

He got in and put the key in the ignition. "I know the real reason you want to come along."

"Oh yeah? Do tell."

"You want to stick with me because you're afraid to be alone. You think if you stay in that motel somebody's going to come for you. But when you're with me you know I'll protect you."

She glared at him. "I don't need anyone's protection. Especially not yours."

His grip closed on the steering wheel as he backed out of the motel's parking lot. "You don't have to worry. I won't let anyone hurt you."

"Yeah, well. Maybe I'm the one who's going to protect you."

"I'll take all the help I can get, actually."

There was silence for a moment. "You used to be a cop, right?"

"Yes." He eyed her sideways. "And let me guess, you used to be a criminal."

This earned him a true smile. The woman really should smile more often—it was a good look for her. "I did what I had to do to survive."

He was quite certain she had.

Ben drove to the meeting spot to find Caroline already waiting for them. Good. He was determined in a way he'd rarely felt before. It might be the last thing he ever did, but freeing an angel seemed like a good decision after a mountain of bad ones.

Caroline wasn't the only one looking for redemption these days.

"Wait here," he told Leena. "And keep the engine running."

She saluted. "Yes, sir."

Caroline followed him to the nondescript entranceway in the side of the brick wall. She looked tense.

"Everything okay?" he asked. Stupid question to ask at

a time like this but he wanted to make sure she wasn't about to flake out on him.

"The angel," she whispered. "I think I know him."

He frowned. "You're kidding."

She shook her head, her arms crossed tightly over her chest. "His name's Daniel. Red hair, green eyes. I'm not positive, but . . . I think he might be Eden's father."

It was as if someone had just thrown a glass of ice-cold clarity in his face.

He was such an idiot. Oliver told him that Eden's angel father would inevitably learn that his daughter had been possessed by a demon. Oliver said the angel would be sure to arrive and set things right.

But that never happened and Ben had forgotten about it. How could he forget?

The angel's eyes . . . they were just like Eden's.

He was Eden's father. And Oliver had him locked away in the basement and was ingesting his wings for some nefarious plan of his.

What the hell was going on?

"We'll get him," Ben promised, taking Caroline's arm as he pushed open the door and they slipped inside. It led to a stairwell and they went down three flights before they emerged on the prisoner level.

An alarm was blaring.

"What's going on?" Caroline asked, covering her ears to block out the jarring sound.

"I don't know."

This couldn't be because of breaking out Leena. That had been hours ago.

A guard Ben recognized stormed toward them, and he braced himself.

"Ben! Thank God you're here! Where have you been? We've been trying to contact you!"

Ben chose his words carefully. "Sorry, I've been busy. Came in early to check on things. What's going on?"

"A prisoner broke loose."

"What prisoner?"

"I don't know. Guy had red hair and . . . and wings. Got out of his cell and disappeared. But that's not the worst of it. It's—it's Oliver."

Shit. "What about him?"

"He's dead."

Ben gasped and Caroline clutched his arm tighter, although she didn't say a word. "What do you mean, he's dead?"

"He was murdered in his office less than an hour ago. We think the angel stabbed him in the heart with some ceremonial dagger. I saw the body myself."

Oliver was dead and the angel killed him? "No, this is—it's impossible."

"The shifter broke out last night, too. I don't know what's going on, Ben, but it's bad. I have to go. I'll touch base with you later, okay?"

Ben forced himself to nod. "Yeah, okay."

The guard was gone. The one Caroline could have possessed to help them break Eden's father out of his cell.

But he'd already been broken out.

"This is wrong," Caroline said. "All wrong. Daniel wouldn't have killed anyone. He's an angel."

It didn't make sense. None of this made sense. Why would Oliver lock up an angel like Daniel and ingest his feathers for weeks now? He'd been so interested in Eden and Darrak's strange relationship, almost too interested, but then that faded. It was as if something new had taken his attention. He still wanted to know how Eden's celestial energy had affected Darrak, enough to lock up Leena and grill her for information. But why?

He'd wanted Sandy to make Ben fall in love with her so he would be more of a help than a hindrance. So he wouldn't get in the way.

And now Oliver was dead. Murdered.

"I don't know what's going on," Ben said. "But we need to get out of here."

"Good idea."

They raced back up the stairs. Whatever they decided to do next, staying clear of the Malleus headquarters would be a good start. The news that Ben was the one to break Leena out hadn't gotten around yet. He had to count his blessings for that, at least. This could have turned out much worse.

Ben knew he had to call Eden and explain everything to her. Tell her she was in danger. *If* Daniel was the one who murdered Oliver . . .

No, it just didn't make sense, but he wasn't willing to take the chance there was a murderous angel on the loose in the city right now.

He pushed open the door to the alleyway and he and Caroline ran to the van that was still idling. Ben opened the driver's side door and looked in at Leena.

She was sprawled unconscious across the seats.

"Hey, lover," a voice called from behind him.

He slowly turned to see Sandy standing there with her arms crossed over her chest.

"So," she continued, eyeing the pair of them. "You haven't returned my calls. I have a funny feeling, between these two"—she nodded at Caroline and the unconscious Leena—"you might want to start seeing other people."

He held his hands up in front of him as she drew closer. "Sandy, what are you doing?"

"You should have had the soup, Ben. Trust me, it was delicious."

"We need to talk about this."

"Nah, let's not and say we did."

Ben's gaze moved to her throat. The necklace she wore with the light gray stone had changed. The stone was now black.

Something about that made his blood run cold.

"You're a witch," Caroline said, her voice trembling. "My daughter has an amulet like that."

Sandy touched it lightly. "Yes, pretty isn't it?"

"You killed Oliver," Ben said, the realization sinking in with dark certainty. "You killed him with black magic."

"Smart guy."

"I don't understand. I—I thought you were a gray witch."

"Baby . . ." A chilling smile stretched across her face. "I've been upgraded."

There was a crackling of energy, like lightning circling her hands as she raised them in Ben and Caroline's direction.

"Run!" Ben yelled.

But before they had a chance to take even a single step away from her, Ben heard Caroline scream, and then everything went black.

⇒ TWENTY-THREE ⇐

With a last howl, Andy shifted back to human form.

It wasn't pretty.

Luckily, a shifter's clothing went along for the ride, so he was curled up in the fetal position on the floor of Triple-A fully dressed. Eden crouched down beside him and put her hand on his shoulder.

"How are you feeling, Andy?" she asked.

He just eyed her. "Take a wild guess."

"You need a drink?"

"Oh, yes. Very much so."

Darrak entered the office. He'd taken a stroll around the block to test his and Eden's previous hundred-foot tether. It seemed to be gone.

His trip to the Void, and surprise return, had worked to break his curse.

Smashed it, was more like it.

"Look," Darrak said standing at the glass door and looking out. "The sun's up."

It was the first time they'd ever seen a sunrise together.

She grinned. "Pretty."

"I'll say."

Darrak had every chance to go away now, but she had a feeling he wouldn't. They were together now by choice rather than circumstance.

She loved him. He drove her crazy half the time, and she was sure the feeling was more than mutual, but she loved him so much it hurt. She'd made a deal with the Prince of Hell to save the life of the man she loved and, no matter what, she knew she'd do it again in a heartbeat.

And, quite frankly, she didn't really give a crap what her mother or anyone else thought about that.

Darrak looked down at Andy recovering on the floor. "You're looking good."

Andy studied the ceiling. "I need a vacation."

Eden helped him to his feet. "Go home and recover."

He nodded. "Is shifting always this difficult?"

Darrak shrugged. "I don't think so. As they say about many things, it only hurts the first time. You'll get used to it."

"Hooray." He grabbed his coat. "So what are you going to do about . . . you know who?"

"Don't worry about that," Darrak said. "I have it under control."

Eden eyed him. Under control? This was news.

"Worry? Who me?" Andy gingerly slid his coat on. "Deals with Lucifer, trips to Hell, growing fur out of places fur should never grow. Totally a normal day for me, nothing to worry about at all."

That he was able to be sarcastic after everything he'd been through was reassuring.

Darrak put a hand on Andy's shoulder. "Thank you. Really. I owe you big-time for what you did for me. I won't forget it."

Andy patted his hand. "No thanks required. Just be good to Eden. Promise me you'll do that, okay?"

"I promise everything I do from this day forward will be in Eden's best interests."

"That's the spirit, Romeo." Andy finally grinned as Eden gave him a tight hug, her throat thick with gratitude toward her brave guide to the Netherworld. She knew she never would have succeeded without him. "I'm heading home. But if you need me for any reason, call."

Eden watched as he slowly headed out to his car and drove out of the parking lot. Then she made a beeline toward Darrak, threw her arms around his neck, and kissed him.

"So happy to see you."

"As happy as I am?" He grinned before brushing his lips over hers. "That's not brimstone in my pocket, you know."

Despite the joke, there was something sad in his ice blue eyes. He hated that she'd agreed to give up her celestial energy to Lucas, but it had been the right decision. It gave her the chance to find him.

"I love you," she whispered.

"I love you, too." A smile played at his lips.

"What's so funny?"

"We sound like something out of a romance novel. Which I'm thinking about writing, by the way. Maybe I'll start with our story."

She laughed. "A romance novel about a demonic possession. Sure, that makes sense."

Darrak kissed her again, holding her face gently between his hands. She wanted to enjoy this, enjoy him, but something felt off.

She pulled back from him. "Talk to me. What's wrong?"

He scrubbed a hand through his hair, his expression darkening immediately. "Wrong? What could possibly be wrong? Other than that little deal you made with our buddy Lucifer, of course."

She cringed. "My angel side never served any purpose. Just a little unreliable psychic insight. As far as I'm concerned, he's welcome to it."

Darrak's jaw tightened. "Yeah, that's all it is. May as well give it away to the first person who asks for it."

She had no argument. She knew he was angry that she'd

give anything at all to Lucifer, let alone something he felt was this important. But she didn't need her angel side anymore. Darrak didn't possess her. He didn't require that celestial energy in order to take form any longer.

Besides, backing out on another promise to the prince would be completely impossible given her history with him.

"Tell me what the problem is," she said.

He stepped away from her and paced the office. "That deal you made is going to take away the only thing holding your black magic back. Your soul will be completely consumed in a matter of months. And when you die—in a year, a decade, a century—you'll be signing up to be one of those charming wraith chicks you met earlier. That's your future thanks to saying yes to Lucy."

She shook her head, but anxiety now churned in her gut. Or maybe it was just morning sickness. "You're overreacting."

"No I'm not."

"Lucas told me I'd be safe, that the baby would be safe, no matter what. He promised that before I agreed to anything. Maybe you're wrong."

"That's not a chance I'm willing to take."

"What if I promise never to use black magic again?"

He snatched a piece of paper off the floor where it had fallen off her desk. It was the card with the clues to find Brenda on it and he pointed at her with it. "The moment you need it, you'll use it. You have no self-control at all."

She wanted to argue, but he was right. She'd made this promise before and when she needed her magic, to save herself, to save someone else, it was as though she didn't even have a choice but to tap into it.

She shook her head. "Then I don't know what to tell you."

He was staring at the card, his brows drawn together.

"What is it?" she asked.

"This is giving me ideas."

"Brenda's faulty information is giving you ideas?"

He tucked the card into his pocket. "No, the fact that it's cloaked to Lucifer is giving me ideas. That *she's* cloaked to him. That's what we need to do. It'll give me enough time to put my plan into motion."

"Darrak, what are you talking about?" She felt hopelessly confused, as if Darrak was now operating on a different frequency from her.

He grasped her chin and kissed her quickly. "It's going to be okay. I promise you."

"Darrak . . ."

He went to the phone on her desk, picked it up, and dialed a number. "He better damn well be there this morning or I'm going to . . . There you are. You're lucky." A pause. "Yes, things are bad. Nothing really worked out the way you told us it would . . . Yeah, I know you didn't make any promises."

He was talking to Maksim. Looked like he'd returned from his impromptu trip bright and early this morning.

"We need your help and we need it now. I want you to do a strong cloaking spell. It's outside of my abilities or I'd do it myself . . . Yes, now. This can't wait."

He hung up.

Eden crossed her arms. "Maksim is going to cloak me."

"If he knows what's good for him he will."

He was taking this so seriously, which made her realize how serious it was. She was in trouble. Darrak loved her and he wanted her to be okay.

"We'll take your car," he said. "Phasing is usually a one-person mode of transportation in the human world since it takes so much energy. Too bad, since it's so convenient."

"So this is the plan? You're going to cloak me from him for the rest of my life?"

"No. I get the feeling he'll be more determined to find you than Brenda. I need a day or two at the most."

"To do what?"

He looked at her with steely determination. "I have an important date with a prince coming up. And trust me, Eden, only one of us is getting lucky."

* * *

He'd drugged and detained Eden in the past. Now it was his turn.

When Ben woke his entire body felt as if it had taken a leisurely stroll through a wood chipper. Since he was breathing and his heart was still beating, plus he didn't see any puddles of blood, he hoped that he was wrong about that.

He was tied to a chair, his legs to the legs, his arms behind him. A quick sweep of the bare and dimly lit room showed that Leena and Caroline were in the same position as he was, against opposite walls. Leena was looking at him with wide eyes. Caroline was still unconscious.

"Now what?" Leena asked quietly. "You're the one with all the bright ideas."

"Not feeling all that bright at the moment."

"If you'd taken my cuff off I could shift and get us out of here. But *no*. Of course not."

"What can I say? Hindsight's a bitch."

Leena's gaze moved to the door as Sandy walked in.

"How are we all doing in here?" she asked sweetly.

"Untie us right now," Ben snarled. He knew it was pointless and almost humorous that he was making demands in his current position, but it was better than saying nothing at all.

She patted the top of his head. "You're so cute, Ben. Never change."

"Why are you doing this, Sandy?"

"Sorry it had to go down like this, lover." She now stroked his thigh. "You've probably got questions for me, don't you?"

"Let them go." He thrust his chin at the women. "Your problem's with me."

She ignored him. "You're thinking—I thought she was such a nice girl. So young and sweet and helpful. And you'd be right. I was. But you know what they say about power." She shrugged. "Who knew how corruptible I was?"

His heart sank. "I'm sorry this happened to you."

"I'm not." Sandy straddled his lap and slid her fingers

through his hair. Any other time this might be hot. Men paid a lot of money at strip clubs to get this sort of treatment, but he couldn't be less aroused if he tried. "You really should have eaten that soup. Right now you'd be by my side doing whatever I say instead of in here waiting for death."

"Don't do this. You can make a different choice. It's not too late."

She leaned closer so her lips brushed his ear. "You were great in bed, by the way. I definitely would have kept you around for a while longer as my own personal sex slave."

"Why did you kill Oliver?" he growled. He refused to rise to any of her other bait.

"Oh, silly boy." She patted his head again like one might do to a favorite pet. "Such an upstanding citizen, you are. So good and noble. Too bad it never turns out right and everyone ends up thinking you're an asshole. The good-in-the-sack thing would have taken you far, though. Trust me on that." She glanced over at Leena. "He's not a male slut, in case you were wondering. He's a damn Boy Scout, this one. But he's got some moves that'll make your toes curl. Eden really missed out, didn't she?"

"It's funny," Leena growled. "You don't look like a skanky ho. And yet, the proof is skanking out right in front of me."

"Watch it, kitty cat," Sandy snarled back. "No catnip for you. I believe you're at my mercy right now. And it's not exactly something I have much left of."

"Sandy, you need to—" Ben began.

She covered his mouth with her hand. "Are you going to say you want to save my soul like you wanted to do for Eden? Are you going to tell me everything I've done will get me hurt and that I'm headed down a very dark path without your help and guidance? That you'll forgive me if only I let you and the others go?"

He wrenched his face away from her. "No, I think it's too late for any of that. Actually, I was going to tell you that there's an angel standing right behind you and he's going to kick your ass, but I guess you'll figure that out when you wake up in Hell."

Sandy grinned, which wasn't the reaction he'd expected. She slithered off his lap and went to stand next to Daniel. The angel had seemed frail when imprisoned in that locked cell, but now Ben could see he was tall and broad and looked like he could do serious damage if he wanted to.

"Who, *this* angel?" Sandy said, sliding her hand up the angel's muscled arm. "Let's just say, we have a bit of an arrangement already worked out. So I'm not too worried."

Ben's gaze darted between them. It didn't make any damn sense to him. He wanted to follow the clues, piece them together. He'd been a good cop—if a bit of a hothead, according to his superiors—so he should be able to understand what was going on here.

"I know you're Eden's father," he said, his throat feeling sore. "That you came here to help. I'm sorry you were locked up and that I didn't act before this. I came back tonight to break you out, but you were already gone. Sandy— she killed the man responsible for your imprisonment. Oliver Gale was consuming your feathers . . . your celestial energy."

"Yes," the angel said. "That's exactly what happened. Well done, Ben."

"Then why are you standing by? Why aren't you doing something to stop this? Sandy killed a man tonight with black magic. She's evil."

"That's not Daniel," Caroline spoke up, her voice creaky as if she'd just woken.

Ben craned his neck. "What?"

"It looks exactly like him. It looks. . . . like he did thirty years ago, not a single day older."

"But he's an angel. They don't age, do they?"

She shook her head. "It's still not him. Not really."

A bark of a laugh from Leena. "I think I get it. Is that why you locked me up in your dungeon? Well, I guess you

found your answers without torturing me for the truth, huh?
I wouldn't have been able to help you, anyway, now that I
know what you wanted, you sick bastard."

Ben didn't understand what she meant for a moment, but
then the truth finally hit him.

His widening gaze moved to Daniel again and swept the
length of the red-headed angel. So tall, so powerful. His
wings were tucked behind him, but they were unmistakably
real wings that glowed a little in the half light of the room,
as full and beautiful as if they'd never been plucked of a
solitary feather.

Oliver had been consuming those feathers because he
needed to fill himself with celestial energy. He'd been in-
vestigating what the affects of possessing a nephilim would
do to a demon like Darrak.

It had all been one big experiment with a single purpose.

"Oliver," Ben said in no more than a whisper. "It's you,
isn't it? You're inside of Daniel. You're using his form and
you had to destroy your own body in order to do that. That's
why you had Sandy kill you—a black magic ritual, right?
All so you could possess the body of an angel."

The angel drew closer and cocked his head. "You could
have been such an asset to me, Ben. To us all. I'm truly
sorry it had to turn out this way."

"This is why you had power over me since I became a
member of the Malleus, isn't it? I thought you had some
ability to tap into witchcraft, but it was the celestial energy
you've been consuming that was giving you special abilities." It all began to click into a horrific jigsaw puzzle. "But
I don't understand. Why are you doing this?"

"Why?" Oliver's new smile grew to show off straight,
perfect teeth in his handsome stolen face. "Because I've recently made a very important deal with a very important
being."

"With who?"

"Lucifer." Oliver said it reverently.

An icy chill rushed through Ben's body at the familiar

name—one that represented true evil like nothing else in the universe. "Lucifer . . . but—but why? What for?"

Oliver stood up very straight and that cold self-satisfied smile of his grew larger still. "I'm about to become the new Prince of Hell."

⇒ TWENTY-FOUR ⇐

Maksim waited for them by the front door. None of his maids or butlers seemed to be around this time of the morning. He escorted Eden and Darrak into his parlor immediately.

Darrak hurriedly explained the situation, while leaving some of the more incriminating details out. Bottom line, they needed a strong cloaking spell put on Eden to hide her here in the human world from a very powerful supernatural being.

Simple.

Okay, not simple at all considering who that powerful supernatural being was, but it had to work anyway.

Eden shook her head. "This is Lucifer we're talking about, not just some guy on the street."

"He's not omnipotent," Darrak explained. "He doesn't see all, know all. He can't read minds. Thankfully. He is a very powerful fallen angel who has a lousy day job, that's all. If it could work on that Brenda chick it will work on you. It isn't perfect. I figure it'll buy me a day, maybe two at the most before he figures out something's wrong. And you can't go back to the apartment since that'll be the first place he'll check. You'll have to stay at a hotel. Preferably on the other side of the world. What is that, Australia? Perfect. You'll love Australia. Forget chocolate donuts. I have two words that will make this all better: Tim Tams."

The auctioneer-like speed of his speech didn't seem to help her relax in the slightest. "You really think this can work?"

He glanced at Maksim. "It will, right? You're powerful enough to do this."

"Of course I am," Maksim replied confidently. "I just need a moment to prepare."

"Right. You do that." Darrak was just glad he wasn't arguing. Not everyone would work magic against Lucifer. It was a job that could come back to bite the wizard on his magical butt, even if it was for all the right reasons.

Maksim moved toward the floor-to-ceiling bookshelves that he scanned. He didn't seem the least stressed about the prospect of doing this spell.

No emotion, this guy. It was a bit creepy, considering he was about to help them screw Lucifer out of a tasty piece of angel food cake.

Eden had her arms crossed tightly over her chest. "I'm not saying I'm sorry for what I did. I'd do it again if I had to."

"You shouldn't trust Lucifer so much."

"I just—I don't know. I feel like I've gotten to know him a little and he's . . . he's in pain. He hates his existence. I guess I can't help but feel sorry for him."

His jaw clenched. "You go ahead and believe in his good side. I'll stay focused on the side that's ruled Hell for the last few millennia."

She grimaced. "That long, huh?"

"Don't worry about Lucifer, Eden. It's not all sour lemons for him. He's had his fun, too. I have to say, though, I'm glad you let Brenda go. One less victory for that guy." He pulled the card from his pocket to glance down at Brenda's name and blinked hard at what he saw.

Nothing.

The card was blank.

This was not good. Not good at all.

Eden frowned. "Darrak, what's wrong?"

He slipped the card back into his pocket and glanced across the room at the wizard scanning his extensive collection of books.

Stalling for time was more like it.

Tricky, Lucy, he thought. *Very tricky.*

Darrak should have seen this coming from a mile away, but he hadn't. He'd wondered why Maksim had known so much about them during their last visit here. Too much. He'd given Eden advice about her powers. He'd known she and Selina had twin magic. He'd given advice, which helped to break the sex magic spell perfectly, but then nearly destroyed Darrak when Eden tried to do the same to break his curse.

He should have known that spells and curses couldn't be approached in the same manner without doing serious damage.

Darrak had never met Maksim before. All he had was Stanley's word and gut instinct that this was the guy. Stanley said the wizard had called him just before Darrak called looking to see if he'd returned to town.

Talk about coincidental.

Darrak's gut had failed him this time. They'd been set up from the very beginning. Their every move had been monitored, and it had all brought them here. And now.

He just wondered how much still remained a secret, other than Ms. Franks and her magically disappearing location card.

Darrak went to Eden's side and slid his arm around her waist, pulling her back a few feet from the wizard.

The jig was up, but Darrak knew he wasn't the one leading the band.

He could play along and pretend that he still believed that they were speaking with the wizard master, but Darrak wasn't that good of an actor. Not when it came to the boss.

"Before you do that spell, Maksim, maybe you and me can have a little talk first."

Maksim raised an eyebrow and glanced over his shoulder. "A talk about what?"

"Stuff."

The curve of Maksim's lips made Darrak know that maybe Lucifer wasn't a mind reader or omnipotent, but he was a hell of a good judge of character.

Maksim's smile grew. "Have you managed to discover my secret?"

"Maybe."

"May I ask how?"

Darrak flashed him the blank card. "Surprise."

He nodded. "You don't really think you have a chance here, do you?"

"Uh-huh. Sure I do."

"I've always admired your tenacity, Darrak."

"And I've always admired your . . ." He frowned. "Well, I can't really think of a thing. Sorry."

"What are you two talking about?" Eden asked.

Maksim exhaled and went to sit casually in an armchair close by. Darrak didn't relax even a little bit. The prince was like a lion. Just because he was taking a break from the hunt didn't mean he still couldn't rip the leg off a gazelle with one crunch of his powerful jaws.

The wizard templed his fingers in front of him. "I'm actually surprised she managed to rescue you in time. Not completely surprised, but a little. No one's ever escaped the Void before, you know."

"Can't get rid of me that easily."

"The odds were against you."

He couldn't help but be curious. "Oh yeah? What were they?"

"I'd say ninety-ten. At best."

Darrak nodded. "I should head to the casino. I think I'm on a lucky streak."

"This is going to happen, you know."

Darrak's lips thinned. "No, actually it isn't."

The wizard only looked amused by this challenge. "We seem to have a bit of a problem then, don't we?"

"Looks like."

Eden clutched at Darrak's hand. The look on her face told him that she'd been following along and had managed to catch up. He always thought she should take her job at a private investigation company more seriously. She could be a fully fledged investigator if only she'd give herself a chance.

She'd figured out this mystery fairly quickly, all things considered.

"Lucas?" she asked. "Why—why are you playing this game?"

He brushed his hand absently along the unwrinkled, designer jacket sleeve he wore. "Is that a trick question?"

"Stop this." Her grip on Darrak's hand tightened. "Just show me who you really are."

"Eden, darling, you couldn't handle who I really am. But I'd be happy to humor you." In a shimmer of light, Maksim was no longer sitting in the chair. It was Lucifer, with his rumpled suit. Nothing too noticeable. Handsome, but not as hot as an incubus had to be. Brown hair, brown eyes. Warm smile. Hands folded on his lap. At first glance he appeared to be harmless and approachable.

Despite his nonchalant appearance, Lucifer regarded each of them with a look of certainty in his eyes like a cat who'd cornered a couple of mice but wasn't quite hungry enough yet to kill them.

"You made the deal, Eden. You can't take it back. And yet, here you are attempting to do just that."

Her hand had grown cold and clammy. Darrak wanted to storm forward, grab Lucifer, and phase to the Void, but he couldn't. Not yet. He had to bide his time just a while longer. When that happened, when there was no other choice, he knew he'd never see Eden again. Not like this, anyway. Sure, he could *see* her. In time, he might even be able to take day trips to the human world. But she wouldn't know who he really was.

After all, he'd made his own deal recently.

"I'm not going to resist," she said.

"Good." Lucifer stood, and she inadvertently took a step back from him. "Even now you're afraid of me when you know I've never harmed a hair on your head."

"I guess I finally clued in that you're not somebody I can trust. Takes me a while, but I get it eventually."

"This is the most wonderful day of my existence. Nothing will go wrong from this point forward. I won't let it."

Darrak felt his anger coming to a boiling point. How he despised this monster before them. Angel, his ass. Lucifer was a self-serving creature of darkness. He might at one time have meant that as a compliment. But, no more.

He willed himself to sound relaxed. "Don't suppose I can say anything to change your mind, can I? I can help you find another nephilim. They've got to be all over the place if you keep looking. Kind of like Waldo."

Lucifer's gaze swept over him. "I honestly had you out for the count, Darrak. And yet, here you are again."

"Just like a bad penny."

"That sums it up nicely." He shook his head. "I want you both to meet someone. Come with me." In one smooth motion he stood up from the chair and breezed past them toward the hallway.

Darrak found himself compelled to follow after him. It was a subtle reminder that the prince held great power over him. It was going to be tricky to get the upper hand.

He leaned closer to Eden as they walked. "When I tell you to run, you run. Understand?"

She looked at him sideways as if warning him not to say anything else.

He tugged on her hand. "Understand?"

Her expression turned bleak, but she finally nodded.

Eden had no idea what Darrak planned to do but she still trusted him. He'd lost that trust by doing some stupid things behind her back, such as borrowing her body when she was asleep and heading out in the middle of the night to take care of a few chores.

It had been a necessary evil, so to speak, although he supposed he could have gone about it in a less deceptive manner.

He'd earned that trust back, and he wouldn't jeopardize it again. No matter what.

Eden had come close to promising Darrak she'd never use her black magic again, but here they were in jeopardy and her magic automatically slid down her arms and into her hands ready to destroy something. To cause a distraction. To make something explode.

A flaming BlackBerry might come in handy right about now.

She despised Lucas for lying to her, for making them believe he was Maksim.

And she'd been fooled so easily.

In the end, she couldn't even blame him for their current situation. She'd made the deal of her own free will. She'd promised him her celestial energy.

And now he wanted her to pay up.

They were the ones trying to break the rules, not him.

She wasn't giving up hope. There was still a chance for her and Darrak to come out of this unscathed, but maybe she was fooling herself. She'd made the deal, and Darrak had just tried to screw Lucas out of it.

They were in deep trouble.

Lucas wasn't a nice guy who sometimes kissed a bit of her darkness away. He *was* darkness. That's why he needed her in the first place.

"Here we are." Lucas had stopped at the end of the flight of stairs to the basement. A man emerged from a room at the end of the hall. He was tall and handsome with broad shoulders. His hair was red, very red, the color Eden might expect a Viking to have. Erik the Red, or something. It was the color her hair would be if she didn't make regular trips to the salon.

And just like hers, his face wasn't covered in freckles as she'd seen a lot of redheads have. No, his face was pale, perfect skin. Straight nose, full lips . . . green eyes.

Just like hers.

"Oh shit," she whispered.

"What?" Darrak asked.

Eden had seen this man before. He'd visited when she'd been just a little girl playing in a sandbox a long, long time ago. She'd liked him, she remembered that much. And then he was gone as quickly as he'd arrived.

She never knew why he never returned.

"That's my father," she whispered, stunned.

"He's your . . . What is he doing *here*?"

"I have no idea."

"It's rude to talk behind my back," Lucas noted. "I'm assuming that you know who this is."

"Yes." Eden forced herself to sound strong. The spark of power in her hands faded away. "What is this, Lucas?"

"A reunion of sorts. Daniel and I go way back."

"I'm sure you do." Darrak cocked his head and crossed his arms, walking closer to the angel.

What was he doing? It was as if he had no concern for his own safety. This was Eden's father, she had no doubt about that, but she was wary. He didn't look at her as if he recognized her, that he cared that she was in trouble. He seemed utterly clueless, actually.

That worried her more than she already was.

"Nice to meet you," Darrak said to the angel and held his hand out.

The angel eyed him before shaking his hand. "The pleasure's all mine, demon. I've wanted to meet you for some time, but it never really worked out."

Lucas grinned. "Are you going to ask for his daughter's hand in marriage? How retro, Darrak."

"I like to do things *Little House on the Prairie* style

whenever possible. Great show, by the way. I think I developed half my humanity just from watching the Ingalls." Darrak turned to Lucas. "I know what's going on here."

"Do you?" Lucas said.

"Somehow you've convinced Daniel here to take over your throne. Which I find a bit hard to believe considering your plan requires you to suck all the angel juice out of his daughter first."

Eden was holding her magic in reserve, not ready to use it yet. This had all begun by her and Darrak going to Maksim to seek his help only a couple of days ago. Her magic had been uncontrollable, or it seemed that way, anyhow. But the more she used it, the better it got. The stronger it got. If it didn't destroy her soul it would be the perfect tool.

Or weapon.

She'd find a way to get herself and Darrak out of this tight situation. She just wished she knew exactly how to do that.

"I suppose I'm lucky that angel juice, as you say, is a naturally renewable resource considering how much you've absorbed over the last month." Lucas walked a slow circle around Darrak. "I wonder what it would have done to you if you'd been bound to her longer—another month, another year. Would you have turned completely angel then? Grown a pair of wings? And if so, would that have been enough to break your curse, considering that it had first been cast upon an archdemon?"

"You could do your college thesis on me. I smell an A+. Possibly a movie deal. Exciting stuff."

"Quite. The demon who became good."

Darrak's smile stretched unpleasantly. "I'm sorry, but I'm not sure you've been following along. I might be part angel now, but I'm not all that good. For example, right now I'm feeling a whole hell of a lot of malevolence, and it's all directed at you, Lucy."

Lucas's eyes narrowed. "I think you know what it's like to feel my wrath. Shall we go down that road again?"

Eden clenched her fists. Her heart felt as if it was going a thousand beats a minute.

Stay calm, just for a bit longer, she told herself. *Darrak has this under control.*

"Smite me," Darrak snapped. "Go ahead, you limp-dicked angel. Because that's what it's going to take before I let you lay a finger on Eden."

Well, perhaps "under control" was a bit of an overstatement.

⇉ TWENTY-FIVE ⇇

Thankfully, no immediate smiting occurred.

"A deal is a deal," Lucas said simply.

"You can kiss that deal good-bye. Go find your own nephilim and leave mine alone."

Eden felt the weight of Lucas's gaze on her.

"How do you feel about his taking ownership of you? You're an independent woman. Must feel a bit uncomfortable."

She shook her head. "Feels fine. I am his. And he's mine. It's an equal opportunity relationship."

"Isn't that special?" Lucas smiled. "So you're denying me what we agreed to."

She knew she should be afraid of him, but everything that had happened had just succeeded in pissing her off. She hated games. And he'd been playing with her life, with her emotions, for too long now.

Screw that.

He couldn't help her, but she still had questions that needed answers, that might help her put the pieces of her life together after all this time.

Eden turned to the angel. "Is that really why you're here? To take over Lucas's throne?"

"Lucas?" Daniel repeated with a flick of his gaze to the prince.

Lucas shrugged. "I have many names. That's one of them. Although, I do prefer it to Lucy, I must say."

"You didn't answer me," Eden said to Daniel. "Why would you do this? Why don't you help me? You're my father."

"Biology works in mysterious ways."

The flippant answer only worked to enrage her more. This might be her only chance to find out the truth. "Why would you leave my mother pregnant and alone? You didn't even tell her what you were. I should have known I was half-angel. It might have made a difference."

Daniel shrugged. "Sorry."

She gaped at him. "*Sorry?* That's all you have to say to me?"

"I'm probably not exactly the one you should be having this conversation with anyway."

"No? Well, that's convenient, isn't it? Why did you visit me that one time when I was a kid? Were you feeling guilty about leaving us? I'm not saying we could have been a family, but I don't understand. It was one thing when I could have convinced myself you were some one-night stand or a traveling salesman, or whatever, but you're an angel? And you just turned your back on us for all that time?"

Daniel shrugged. "Angels rarely procreate. It's fascinating to me, really, that this could have even happened."

Yeah, that was such a good answer. It solved so many mysteries of Eden's life. No, actually it just made her angrier. His green-eyed gaze moved to her hands where the black magic had been triggered by her roller coaster of emotions. Darrak put his hand on her back. The warmth of his touch was enough to calm her for the time being, but only slightly.

She turned to meet his eyes and felt the sting of tears. "He didn't want me."

"His loss."

Daniel laughed then, a sharp crack of sound that made chills run down Eden's spine. "This is rather awkward, Lucifer. Shall we get on with it?"

"What?" Darrak snarled. "You're going to do it right here, right now? Drain Eden's angelic energy and then attempt to swap places like this is some sort of relay race?"

"Yes, that's the plan exactly," Daniel said.

"This doesn't have to be unpleasant," Lucas soothed. He was speaking to Eden directly. "It won't hurt you. And there are ways to keep your soul from turning darker without the angelic energy to balance you. I promise no harm will come to you."

"How can you promise that?" Darrak demanded.

Lucas's jaw clenched. "I'll discuss this matter with Eden alone."

"Not going to happen."

"Don't stand in the way of this, Darrak. I've given my word that Eden and your unborn child will be protected no matter what happens." Lucas shook his head. "I still don't understand how something like you could have created a new life."

Darrak glared at him. "It's kind of sad, if I gave a moment's thought to feel sorry for your hellish ass. You've never felt true love, not a moment in your entire existence. It's all been about serving your own interests. Your own worldview. Oh, you have a shitty job. Boohoo. I had the worst job ever for hundreds of years and did you ever hear me complain?"

"Yes," Lucas replied. "Constantly."

"Yeah, well, I like to air my grievances. It's healthy."

"Are we finished here?" Daniel asked. "I've sacrificed much and am not in the mood for a pissing contest."

"You think that's what this is?" Lucas's tone turned sharp. "A pissing contest? Be patient or you will get nothing from me at all."

Daniel looked cowed by this. "My most sincere apologies, my prince."

Eden couldn't help but be disappointed. Her father was

a wussy peon who caved at the slightest challenge. She'd thought he might be able to help her, but she saw that was only a pipe dream now. She had to figure out how to save herself and Darrak and she needed to do it now.

If that required her giving up her celestial energy in order to get everyone out of this in one piece, then that was exactly what she'd do. But first she needed to know something.

She turned to Daniel. "Why are you willing to become the next Prince of Hell? Is this an official assignment? A changing of the guard?"

That would be enough to reassure Eden that this was the right thing to do. After all, Lucas had served in Hell for a very long time. She had to admit, even *he* deserved a break.

Daniel moved closer to her and gently cupped her face in his hands. This close to him she could feel the celestial energy radiating off his tall and strong angelic form. It felt nice and warm and safe.

"Yes, that's it," he said softly. "It is my time and I shall do what I must to help the greater good of the universe. Do you believe me, my daughter?"

She dug her fingers into his hand and wrenched herself away from him. "Nice try. But you're a very bad liar. What the hell are you?"

The warmth in his expression and from his heavenly energy had never once touched his eyes.

"Eden!" A shout came from the room down the hall. It sounded like Ben.

She didn't wait; she ran directly over and pushed the door open all the way.

Ben, Leena, and her mother's rented aspiring-actress body were tied to three wooden chairs. Standing next to Ben, her fingernails digging into his throat, was Sandy, a gray witch Eden had met before. She'd helped Eden escape once when she'd been in a bit of a bind.

She took the entire room in in a split second.

"See, Ben?" Sandy purred. "I told you I could make you scream her name if I wanted you to. Looks like I was right."

Magic sparked into Eden's hand and she focused it at

Sandy without a second thought. She didn't need a program to tell who the players were here. Despite her issues with Ben, he was in trouble, big trouble. And so were Leena and her mother.

Sandy flew backward and hit the wall hard enough to knock her out.

"Eden!" Caroline called out to her. "You need to run! This is a trap!"

Yeah, she already knew that much.

Darrak pushed past Lucas and joined Eden in the room.

"What is this, Lucifer?" he demanded. "Blackmail? That's low even for you."

Lucas shook his head. "Not blackmail. More like an insurance policy. Nothing can go wrong now. Don't you understand that?"

"I understand. And I concur. Nothing can go wrong."

"*Concur.* That's a big word for a little boy like you."

Darrak glowered at him. "I really hate you."

Lucas grinned. "That temper of yours is going to get you in trouble someday."

"I'm going to destroy you."

"How?" Lucas asked. "By phasing me to the Void and attempting to throw me in?"

Eden had never seen Darrak go pale so quickly, but he did. By the look on Darrak's face, that was exactly what he'd planned to do.

Panic swelled inside of her. What the hell was he thinking? He was going to get himself destroyed. *Again.*

"I'm going to tear you apart the moment I—" Darrak began fiercely.

"Darrakayiis," Lucas cut him off, using his full name. "Shut up."

Darrak went silent. He had no choice. Using his full name gave Lucas full and complete power over him.

"Leave him alone," Eden growled.

"You need to behave yourself, too." Lucas's eyes narrowed. "My patience wears thin with both of you, Eden. I've given you much more than I have ever given anyone else in recent memory. And now you try to take away what is rightfully mine."

"It's not worth it. He"—she nodded at Daniel—"doesn't deserve your power. He will not do the same job you've done."

"I don't care. I'm finished. They've locked me out of my home for long enough and it's time for me to finally go back."

"But my father—"

"That's not your father," Ben spoke up. His throat was bleeding from where Sandy had clawed him. "It's Oliver Gale. He did a black magic ritual to be able to possess your father's body. It's the only way he could go to Hell and become the prince."

Eden's mouth fell open with shock. Oliver Gale had somehow possessed her father's body all so he could take over for Lucas. "This is impossible."

"I'll destroy Darrak," Lucas warned. "You know I can. I've been playing up till now, but the game is losing its entertainment factor for me. I'm tired. I'm so tired you could never understand."

She shook her head. "Then stop this. This is wrong, Lucas. *You're* the Prince of Hell. You can't believe that the leader of the Malleus is going to keep the balance you've maintained. If he was this corrupt as a human just imagine what he's capable of doing with your power at his fingertips."

But her words weren't sinking in. Nothing she said would ever change his mind.

Lucas looked at Darrak. "You believe she loves you, but I'm still not entirely convinced. This form of yours, what if you no longer had it? Would that make a difference to you, Eden? If he wasn't this tall, dark, and handsome man you've fallen for. You've seen his true form, right? A little less presentable in everyday society." Lucas raised an eyebrow. "Show us, Darrakayiis. Show us your demon visage."

When a witch or human used his true name, there was sometimes a short delay as he fought against their power over him, but with Lucas—his maker—there was no fight.

Lucas had absolute power over his creation, even now that he wasn't fully demon.

As a half-angel now, Eden wasn't sure what to expect him to look like. But amber flames flowed over his now leathery flesh, his form grew another foot taller and much broader, horns curved outward from his temples. It was still Darrak, but this was truly a demon—one from a horror movie or a nightmare.

He didn't look even a little bit angelic.

Darrak's lips curved back from sharp teeth as he glared at Lucas, still unable to speak.

"Not so pretty now, is he?" Lucas said. "Not the man of any girl's dreams."

Her eyes narrowed. "I guess I have different dreams than other girls."

She went directly to this demonic version of Darrak and slid her arms around his thick waist. His skin was hot and very dry, like sand beneath her fingertips. The fire didn't burn her.

Eden looked up at him. "I love you, Darrak. No matter what."

His eyes were filled with uncertainty until she said those words, but then clarity filled them. He couldn't speak while under Lucas's control, but she didn't have to be a mind reader to know what he was thinking. He finally believed her. And that made anything that happened today bearable for him.

Even the really bad stuff.

"Disgusting," Daniel, or rather Oliver said.

"Oh?" Lucas replied. "You don't approve?"

"Can't say that I do."

Eden knew she could say Darrak's true name and free him from Lucas's influence and turn him over to her own, but she didn't. She wasn't playing tag with another witch here. Lucas had power over Darrak with or without the use of his name.

It wasn't only Eden's fate at stake here. It was Darrak's, her mother's, Ben's, and Leena's. It was even Daniel's, a father she'd never known, who had no control right now because that control had been stolen from him by an evil human with a big agenda.

Whatever Daniel's reason for not being around when she grew up, he didn't deserve this. What had they done to him for a human to take over his body?

That was truly black magic.

She eyed Sandy, currently unconscious. Despite her dark power she was still human, still as fragile as any other. This was her doing. Something had changed Sandy, made her choose the darker path. All Eden knew for sure was that she'd chosen wrong.

But Eden also had magic at her disposal, and she wasn't going to let anyone she loved be hurt here today. No matter the cost.

Darrak stared down at her as if trying to get her to do something other than stay by his side. He didn't want to be at Lucas's mercy. But what had he been thinking to even consider making an attempt on Lucas's life?

"Do you have something to say?" Lucas approached, his arms crossed. "That's too bad, because I don't want to hear it."

"Tough shit," Darrak growled.

"Wait." Lucas frowned. "I didn't give you permission to speak."

Darrak pushed Eden out of the way, launched himself forward, and grabbed Lucas by his throat. A split second later, they both vanished in a flash of fire.

⇒ TWENTY-SIX ⇐

Eden stared with stunned realization at the empty space in front of her.

He'd fooled her. He'd fooled all of them.

Darrak might have retained his demonic visage, but the control his true name had over him was a thing of the past. He'd been playing along, lulling Lucas into believing he still had power over him.

Sneaky, very sneaky.

Normally she'd approve, but not this time. She knew his plan. He was going to get himself destroyed if he tried to defeat Lucas.

Oliver approached. "I'll need to restrain you until the prince returns."

"Restrain this." Eden flicked a finger at him and he cringed as if she'd slapped him. She'd meant to throw him like she'd done with Sandy, but an angel—even a fake one—wasn't quite so easy to throw around.

Her attention turned to Leena, Ben, and her mother. They were her priority right now. Everything else would have to wait.

"Be careful, Eden!" Caroline yelled at her while Ben and Leena struggled with their bindings. "He's dangerous!"

Leave it to her mother to point out the blatantly obvious. The time for careful had passed.

The angel's eyes began to glow—this must be how an angel powered up. He was about to do something very, very bad.

"You need to behave yourself, little witch," Oliver snarled. "Or I'll *make* you behave yourself."

"So you got in that body thanks to black magic, did you? Does it work the other way around?" She thrust her hand out toward him, freezing him in place.

He gasped and sweat broke out on his forehead as he fought against her hold on him. "You're incredibly powerful, even more than Sandy is. You could serve at my side. When I become the Prince of Hell I could make you a very powerful demon."

Eden raised an eyebrow. "Bargaining so soon, Oliver? Makes me think that you're a little bit scared now. Maybe that hold you have on my father's body isn't as strong as you thought it was. I chose to let Darrak share my body, but Daniel's fighting you, isn't he?"

"This is everything I've worked for. Everything I want. I've given up everything for this chance."

"Why?" Ben demanded. "Why would you do this?"

Oliver's gaze shot toward the ex-cop. "Because I was always meant for something like this—something bigger than any human could ever achieve before."

Ben shook his head. "You were the leader of an organization that could have done good things for the world."

"It was only a fraction of the power I'll have when Lucifer returns. I will rule the Netherworld. I was born for greatness."

Eden watched the madness slide behind Oliver's stolen green eyes. "You know, seeing things only in black and white is a good way to get bad vision. You had it all, and you didn't even realize it. Greatness? You know what's really great?"

He turned to her as if she might have an answer to help him. "What?"

"Not you."

She twisted her hand, drawing out Oliver's soul through Daniel's mouth in a long gray stream. Daniel collapsed to the ground and the smoke hung in the air. She held it still with a focused thought.

"Don't worry, Oliver," she whispered. "You wanted to go to Hell. It's still your final destination. Have a nice trip."

Another twist of her magic and the smoke vanished in a flash of fire.

Powerful magic. Powerful *black* magic. She'd reversed Sandy's spell as if it was nothing more than rewinding a videotape.

Eden fell to her knees as if a chair had been pulled out from under her, gasping for breath. She had no idea she could even do that, but it had taken a lot of her strength.

And a heavy price as well. A glance at her darker amulet confirmed that she'd delved deeply into her bag of tricks this time.

"Eden!" Leena shouted. "Behind you!"

Sandy had finally come to and was rising to her feet. The other witch's amulet, Eden noted with a sinking feeling, was already as dark as it could get.

She'd killed Oliver's mortal form with black magic. She'd crossed the line. Her soul was black. The formerly gray witch had nothing left to lose.

Sandy smiled coldly. "I'm going to kill you."

"Let's get the party started," Eden said, and more magic coursed through her.

Darrak had been aiming for the Void.

Close, but no cigar. They'd landed just to the edge of it. Darrak's self-preservation had unconsciously kicked in. After all, if he'd sent them directly into the Void upon their arrival it would have been a trip for two.

He stayed in his demonic form since it gave him more strength.

Plus, he'd always been fond of the horns.

Lucifer brushed off his suit, looking annoyed. "So this is how it ends for you, Darrakayiis. Kind of anticlimactic with no other witnesses, isn't it? I thought you liked an audience."

Darrak glanced around the dark and deserted area. "There were a couple wraiths here earlier. They would have made an excellent cheering section."

Lucifer shook his head. "Eden went to great measures to save you, and now you turn around and destroy yourself yet again. Seems a bit ungrateful if you ask me."

He shrugged his hulking shoulders. "I guess I'm a slow learner."

"That much is obvious. What's funny to me is that none of this is my fault. She agreed to my deal."

"She didn't know what the deal meant."

"Not my problem."

Darrak couldn't help but snort humorlessly. "You know, you almost convinced me you'd grown to care about her. Forgiving her the screwups. Her own personal summoning crystal. The whole French kiss, darkness-sucking action from time to time. Thought I had some romantic competition for a moment there."

Lucifer's expression didn't change aside from a small smile. "We can share her. After all, I only want half."

"I don't share. I'm greedy like that."

"One last chance, Darrak. Don't get in my way. You still get the girl and walk away from this."

Darrak flexed his fists and his talons bit into his skin. "You were right about one thing, Lucy. Your time is up."

The prince's smile faded and his eyes narrowed. "Call me Lucy one more time and this ends now."

Darrak grinned. "Finally getting to you, am I?"

"Congratulations, you succeeded."

"Thanks. I feel . . . strangely accomplished."

"My previous pick was unworthy. I should have realized

the solution was too simple, too eager. He was overly motivated by his own greed."

"It's a deadly sin. Total bonus."

"Not helpful in a situation like this, I'm afraid. He was a bad pick, I'll admit it. Which leaves us with a large problem. If you want to destroy me, there is no one to rule Hell and keep all the demon lords from losing control of the shadows."

Darrak shook his head. "Wrong. There is someone already lined up."

"Who?"

"You're looking at him."

Lucifer stared at him for a long moment and then burst into laughter. "Oh Darrak, you do amuse me."

Darrak knew he'd have the last laugh today. "You know, I think I'll go all out with a crown, scepter, the works. Maybe I'll sign up a couple of jesters to keep *me* amused for the next millennium or two. We all know the job will suck the personality out of anyone with a tendency to feel sorry for themselves."

Lucifer sobered. "So you've just appointed yourself to the position, have you?"

"No, I didn't. I accepted an offer presented to me."

"By whom? There's only one being who could . . ." Clarity went through his brown eyes. "Is that so? And you're the one who's been chosen, have you?"

"Uh-huh. The one and only."

Lucifer swept his gaze over Darrak's expansive and fiery form. "They must have been grading on a curve."

"Bite me."

"I knew you wanted the power once, but now—I would have thought . . ." Lucifer's brows drew together. "Wait. You're not doing this for the power, are you? You're doing this for true love. Oh, how romantic, Darrak. I see little butterflies and kittens and rainbows right now."

Darrak crossed his thickly muscled arms. "You're way cooler when you're not trying to be sarcastic. It really doesn't suit you."

"All for her." He shook his head. "You would take on this heavy burden all for Eden. To save her from mean old Lucifer."

"That was the general idea. Also, again, bite me."

"You're ridiculous."

"*You're* ridiculous."

"And this is the comeback of the next Prince of Hell." Lucifer shook his head. "Pathetic."

"*You're* pathetic." Darrak sighed. "My snappy comebacks do need a bit of work, I'll admit it. It's been a rough week."

"I will find someone else for the job, but that changes nothing today. I would rather see Asmodeus on my throne than you."

"Too bad I destroyed him then, huh?" Darrak frowned. "Wait. Does that make me the Lord of Lust now? Because my new business cards never arrived if I am."

"If you were residing in Hell instead of playing house in the human world, then yes, his power would have shifted to you. As it is, his throne had to be manually reassigned. You know, maybe I'll get that nice human Ben Hanson to take over for me. I'll kill him, take his soul, make him into a demon—bingo. I'll have myself a nice upstanding prospect to take on the shadows for the next eternity."

"Not the first time me and Ben have competed for something we both wanted," Darrak said. "Keep in mind, I won last time, too."

Lucifer came toward Darrak and grabbed hold of him. Lucifer had no true power over him anymore, but Darrak realized with a strong sinking feeling that the prince's brute strength was much greater than his own.

Lucas pushed Darrak backward toward the Void. "I don't give second chances."

"We're a lot alike that way."

"Eden will be fine without you if I shove you in, I promise."

"How about I promise to hang on tight and take you with me?"

"Either way, you're gone forever."

Darrak's eyes narrowed as he felt the edge of the cliff at his heel. "Have I asked you recently to bite me? It's on the very tip of my tongue."

Any remaining humor left Lucifer's expression. "You would really give everything up to rule this dark, cold, unforgiving place for the rest of eternity? No one would choose this of their own free will, Darrak."

Darrak clutched on to the prince, knowing he wouldn't loosen his talons until they were both in midfall. This could only end one way now. Both of them would have to be destroyed.

He hoped there was another plan in place in the universe because Hell would soon be without its prince.

"No one would choose this of their own free will."

An image of Eden went through his mind then, holding a baby in her arms. *His* baby.

He didn't want to give her up, so it looked as if Lucifer was right. He'd chosen this path, but it wasn't because he felt he had any other option.

The thought was enough to make him lose both his concentration and his footing. Suddenly there was nothing behind him. He clawed at the ground, at Lucifer, at anything, but it all crumbled away.

And then he was hanging on to the side of the Void just as he'd done earlier.

Rinse and repeat.

"Good-bye, Darrak." Lucifer straightened up, brushed himself off, and turned away.

"Who'd give up everything to rule this place?" Darrak snarled up at him, only raw anger now giving him the strength to continue holding on. "You would, that's who. Why don't you remember that? You gave everything up—you gave up Heaven—in order to help keep the balance down here because you knew it was the right thing to do."

Lucifer froze and looked over his shoulder at the demon swinging above the gaping black hole of the Void. "No. I was cast out of Heaven for having a different opinion of how the world should be. Because I despised humans."

"Bzzz. Wrong. You did it to keep the darkness from expanding and destroying those humans you claim to hate, along with everything else. You agreed to this, and now *you're* the one who's going back on a promise."

Lucifer's expression darkened. "You lie."

"You're experiencing memory loss. Maybe one of those other lords poisoned your mind with something in an attempt to take over your throne. Maybe your memories were damaged through years of being stuck down here in the pit as you controlled the shadows and maintained the balance. I don't know. But you agreed to do this and now you forget. Now you're looking for an out. Well, I'm your out, Lucifer. I'm willing to do it, just as you once were. But you can't have Eden's energy, too. I won't let you destroy her."

"*You* destroyed her, not me," Lucifer spat back. "You're the worst thing to ever come into that woman's life."

Darrak struggled to hold on. "I thought that once, but now I don't believe it. This was all meant to be—and it's all led to this moment. Right here and now."

"You're in no position to argue right now, incubus."

"I'm not an incubus. I'm a demon. *And* I'm an angel. I'm the very first of my kind. And I'm willing to be the next Prince of Hell because it's obvious that you're too selfish and cowardly to keep doing the job you originally agreed to."

Lucifer crouched down in front of Darrak and stared into his face. Darrak couldn't read his expression—it was cold and dead.

"Thank you for your opinion."

Lucifer pried Darrak's talons away from the rock until he had nothing left to hang on to. Scrambling for a handhold that he no longer had, Darrak began to fall backward into the hungry mouth of the Void.

"Watch out!" Ben shouted. "Sandy's dangerous now."

Eden flicked a look at him. "No kidding."

Sandy's gaze moved to her amulet. "Maybe I won't kill you, after all. We're almost in the same boat, Eden. You and me, black witches. We could cause a lot of damage together."

"What, you want to start a girl band or something?"

"Something like that." She glanced over at the unconscious body of Eden's father. "He'll wake up soon. He's not going to be happy."

"Your point?"

"An angel like him will destroy you. He won't care if you're his daughter, all he'll see is evil. You're dangerous. Can't you feel it? Your soul is nearly as black as mine. Trust me, when that happened, the world opened up like nothing I ever could have imagined. All of that power at my fingertips."

Eden hated to admit it, but she did feel it. That darkness, that power, so much of it, like a bottomless ocean. So addictive, so perfect. It felt right, and that, by far, was the scariest thing of all.

"Don't listen to her," Ben growled. "She's evil."

Eden narrowed her gaze at him. "Not sure I should listen to you, Ben. You and my mother sent Darrak to Hell."

"He survived," Caroline spoke up.

"No thanks to you."

Ben had the decency to look guilty. "We were wrong, I see that now. But I tried to change things, I tried to make things better."

"He did," Leena insisted. "I was being held prisoner by the Malleus and he freed me. Took him long enough, but he did it."

Eden looked over at her ex-roommate. She had wondered where she'd gone after being chased away by Darrak. "I still have the key you left behind. Never had a chance to check that locker."

Leena nodded. "Uh, remind me to get that back from you. You know, if we all live through this morning."

Sandy laughed. "Listen to them, Eden. They've all betrayed you in some way. Abandoned you, too, when you needed them the most. You should kill them for what they've done to you and Darrak. That's all it would take for you to give in fully to your magic. You could have whatever you wanted, then."

All it would take to turn her soul black was to murder any one of the people in this room. But murder wasn't in Eden's true nature. Had it been in Sandy's? Or had Oliver forced her into this?

"Don't listen to her, Eden," Caroline said, her voice tight. "You're better than this. Don't give in to the darkness. You can fight it."

Eden's gaze snapped to the young brunette tied to the chair to her left. "Can I, Mom? Really? Having you on my side is such a nice change from the first thirty years of my life when you treated me like a burden."

"Oh, get over it, will you?" Caroline snapped. "I made my share of mistakes. So what? You've turned into a great woman anyway. So pull your head out of your ass and do something to prove that."

Eden really hadn't been expecting an apology so she wasn't disappointed.

Sandy rolled her eyes. "Let me get started, Eden. You'll see it isn't that difficult at all. Let me kill Ben for you."

Sandy grabbed Ben and energy flowed down her arms. "Good-bye, lover."

A muffled yell escaped Ben's throat as he thrashed around in the chair. Whatever Sandy was doing was hurting him badly.

"No!" Eden grabbed hold of the witch, digging her fingers in hard enough to make the witch flinch as she pulled her away from Ben to face her instead.

"Maybe I will kill you after all." A second later, Sandy's hands wrapped tightly around Eden's throat and her dark magic shot through Eden's body.

Luckily, she'd already put up a shield to protect herself—a shield that was quickly slipping.

Sandy squeezed tighter. "You're either with me, Eden, or you're against me."

"I'm sorry." Eden gasped for breath. "I guess . . . I'm . . . against you."

Black magic flowed through her hands and shot like lightning directly into Sandy. Sandy screamed, raised up off the floor so she hung there for a moment, suspended in midair, then she flew backward against the wall.

Her open, glossy eyes stared up at the ceiling.

"Damn it," Eden said, her voice shaky. "I didn't mean to . . . to . . ."

"She's dead," Ben managed.

Yeah, that. She didn't mean to do *that*.

The witch had been too close and Eden's magic too strong. Not a good combination to allow Sandy to walk away in one piece.

Eden quickly moved around the room to untie all three of the prisoners. Then she moved back from them until her back hit the wall. She needed the support or she thought she might fall down to the floor.

"You did the right thing, honey," Caroline said. "She was going to kill you. Kill all of us."

"I know," she replied softly.

"Are you . . ." Ben began. "Are you okay?"

Eden shook her head. "You all need to get out of here while you still can."

"Eden . . . your necklace . . ." Leena approached her.

"No. Get out of here. Now! Run!"

After a short hesitation, the three did what she asked without saying another word.

Eden didn't have to look down at her amulet to have the truth confirmed. She'd gone over the line. She'd killed a mortal with black magic—even if it had been accidental. Even if the witch she'd killed had deserved it. Even if it had been in self-defense.

She'd killed her.

And Eden's soul was now black.

⇶ TWENTY-SEVEN ⇷

Darrak saw his life flash before his eyes. It was a short flash for such a long life, but really, the only good things had happened recently. It was more of a slide show, really.

He'd tried. But it hadn't been enough.

I'm so sorry, Eden.

His last thoughts.

Well, his last thoughts until someone grabbed hold of his wrist.

He looked up with surprise, a surprise that only grew when he saw that it was Lucifer who held him over the Void by his thick, demon wrist.

Before he had any time to truly register this, Lucifer tossed him up over the edge. It was a strong enough throw to land him about a hundred feet away. He lay on his back, looking up at the blank, black velvet sky over this part of the Netherworld.

"Not finished torturing me yet?" he asked, when Lucifer's form loomed over him.

"Why would I want the fun to ever stop?"

A flash of fire appeared before Darrak's eyes and then

suddenly they were back in Maksim's mansion. Darrak scrambled to his feet and swept his gaze over a scene that took his breath away.

"What happened here?" His demon voice boomed out loud and raspy. It was more than enough to fill most humans with deep fear and a loss of control over their bodily functions. He knew this from amusing personal experience.

The redheaded angel was unconscious on the ground to the left. That he was still here was enough to prove that he hadn't been destroyed. Angels, just like demons, vanished in the human world when they'd been decimated, leaving no body behind. He figured the heavens had their own version of the Void. Or perhaps there was only one Void where all creatures lacking souls were tossed when they were gone for good.

To the right was Sandy, and she wasn't only unconscious. Her eyes were open and glazed.

Ding dong, the witch is dead.

Ben, Leena, and Caroline were nowhere to be seen.

Eden sat in the chair where Ben had previously been tied. She looked up at him as he entered the room.

"Oh, good," she said. "You're back."

"Eden . . ." He made a move to draw closer but then froze in place. His gaze dropped to her amulet. "No."

Such a simple word for every fear and raw emotion that flowed over him in that split second. Her amulet was black.

Her soul—she must have been the one to kill the witch. Something bad happened here, something he couldn't protect her from.

"I didn't mean to," she said. "But I'm not sorry I did it."

The others—somehow she'd saved them.

But it was at the cost of her soul.

It felt as if a hand clutched his throat, making it hard to speak. "I'm so sorry, Eden."

The smile she gave him then was enough to chill him to his very core. The coating of hellfire did nothing to help warm him against that emotionless expression, so different from what he was accustomed to. It was as if she didn't care about what had just happened and what it meant.

A human *was* their soul. It was their personality, their warmth, their goodness, their joy. When it turned dark, so did everything else. The black of her soul wasn't a color, it was a force that absorbed everything good.

Even a demon understood that.

"It's okay," she said softly. "There's no other way this can be. I see that now."

Darrak took her by her shoulders. His fire wouldn't hurt her, he wouldn't let it. "You're wrong. I'm going to be the next Prince of Hell. I can fix this. You won't come to any more harm, I swear it."

Lucifer approached. "It won't matter if I take her celestial energy now, will it?"

"Take it," Eden said firmly. "We had a deal. It's yours."

Darrak had failed. He'd started out with such good intentions—destroy Lucifer, save Eden. Instead, Lucifer had pulled him out of the Void so he could return to see this. See that everything he'd done had led to losing Eden even if she was standing right in front of him.

Eden's angel half wouldn't save her now. It was too late.

"Take it," Darrak growled. "Before I change my mind. Take it and I take your throne. Go back to Heaven. Find a fluffy cloud and learn to play the harp and leave us the hell alone for the rest of eternity."

Lucifer looked at him. "For the record, I think you were right."

"About what?"

"A very long time ago I'd agreed to do a job, one that never had an end date. No yearly assessment. No pay increase. Somebody made me forget about that. Or maybe it was no one's fault but my own. My memories"—he held his hands to his temples—"they're cloudy when the years grow long and there's no one who truly understands how lonely it can be."

Darrak rolled his eyes. "Maybe *I'll* learn how to play a

harp. Anything to block out the self-pitying whining. Seriously. Just do it, Lucifer, and get out of my face once and for all."

Lucifer smiled. "So you, my lowly creation, no more than hellfire with a personality, are going to take over my throne, my responsibilities. You will control the shadows. You really think you're worthy enough for that?"

"I guess we'll find out, won't we?" Darrak's patience was at an end. The sooner he took over Hell, the sooner he could do something, anything, to help restore Eden's soul. She was standing right here in front of him. She wasn't lost to him. Not yet.

"Not yet," he remembered the entity using Theo's face saying. *"But soon and forever."*

"Do it," Darrak growled. "Now before I change my mind."

Lucifer approached Eden, who stood up from the chair to face him.

"Ready?" he asked.

She nodded. "Take it all, Lucas, and then go away. I never want to see you again."

"As you wish." Lucifer pulled Eden against him and crushed his mouth against hers. Darrak fisted his hands at his sides, only sheer determination keeping him from pulling the prince away from her and pounding him into the ground.

This wasn't jealousy, not anymore. This wasn't a kiss of passion. It was one of a thief. He was stealing her angel half so he could use it for himself.

Greedy bastard.

Darrak had never felt so much hate for anyone in his entire existence. But that hate made him stronger. It would have to. He needed to be strong, stay strong, for Eden. For what was to come.

When the kiss ended, Lucifer staggered back from Eden and inhaled raggedly. Eden collapsed but Darrak was able to grab her before she hit the ground.

And then something caught his eye. Her amulet.

It had turned white. Completely white.

His gaze snapped to Lucifer.

Dark veins appeared around his mouth. His eyes were not brown anymore, but black. Completely black, even the whites.

Darrak's eyes widened. "You didn't take her celestial energy. You—you took her black magic."

Lucifer grinned, but it was shaky. "Not delicious, let me tell you. It was a bit on the bitter side, actually."

Confusion crashed over him. "Why would you do this?"

Lucifer swallowed hard. "Look after her. Look after both of them. They need you more than I do."

Eden stirred, her chest hitching as she gained consciousness.

None of this made any sense to Darrak. "But I said I would do your job. I would be the Prince of Hell."

Lucifer smiled then, an eerie look on his haunted face. "Oh Darrak, I don't hate you that much."

The next moment he gasped and hunched over as pain wrenched his body. Flames poured out of him, covering his form in an instant. He grew taller and broader as if taking on a new visage—one Darrak recognized immediately. Nine feet tall, four hundred pounds. His skin turned black as coal. His upper lip peeled back from his teeth to show they'd grown sharp and long as knives.

Eden trembled in Darrak's arms. "Wh-what's going on?"

"The darkness he consumed . . . it's turning him into Satan."

Large, batlike wings spread out on either side of Lucifer.

No, not Lucifer. Not anymore. This was a true monster from the fiery depths of Hell. The shadowy beast that controlled everything, that wanted to break free and destroy anything it touched.

It was pure evil made flesh.

"You can't be here," Darrak snarled, holding Eden closer to him as if he would be able to protect her from something this horrific. "It's not allowed! Go back where you came from!"

Satan couldn't take form in the human world. It was a safety precaution. The only reason Lucifer could be here at all was because he took mortal form. He had some power, but not enough to truly harm anyone, apart from one of his own creations like Darrak.

And yet, here he was. Satan was making his first personal appearance on human soil.

Black eyes tracked to Darrak, and a cold smile snaked across the creature's face.

Satan snarled at him. "You wanted this for yourself. All this magnificent power. And you would give it up for a mere woman?"

Darrak shielded Eden as the monster drew closer to them.

"Hey, Satan," he said evenly. "Go to Hell."

Satan's smile disappeared.

Lucifer was still in there somewhere, and he knew exactly what he was doing. He was the one chosen for the job in the first place, after all. He'd wrangled this beast many times before.

With a last, soulless, black-eyed glare, Satan wrapped the huge, leathery wings around himself, and disappeared in a violent flash of fire.

He was gone.

That had been too damn close. Pun fully intended.

Darrak pulled Eden closer. The room was lit up by his own fire, the same hellfire from which he'd been created once upon a time. He controlled this fire, it was a part of him in this form, and it would do no damage unless he wanted it to.

He grabbed hold of Eden's face, checking to make sure she was okay.

"Eden," he rasped. "It is you? Is it really you?"

She nodded and threw her arms around him. "It's me."

"I thought I lost you."

"I'm not going anywhere."

"That makes two of us. Only . . ." He swallowed. "There's a problem."

She pulled back. "What?"

"My form . . . I—I think this might be it. I might be stuck with this demonic visage for a while."

Her gaze moved over Darrak's fearsome face, along the curved horns. She touched his sharp cheekbones, ridged jaw, and down his heavily muscled arm until she entwined her fingers with his that were tipped in sharp talons.

"I can get used to it," she said very seriously.

Darrak couldn't help but grin, hoping she wouldn't be too afraid of his razor-sharp teeth. "I'm just messing with you."

He shifted back to human form.

She punched him in his arm. "Don't do that."

"Sorry."

She kissed him then, very hard on his much more kissable mouth. Considering that he thought he'd never be able to touch her again, it was quite possibly the best kiss they'd ever shared. He took the time to fully explore her mouth, before he kissed every inch of her face. Finally he felt her push against his chest.

He moved back a bit. "Let me guess. Your father is currently standing behind me about ready to unleash heavenly fury on me for defiling his beautiful daughter."

"Pretty much."

He turned to look at Daniel, who stood there, his white wings stretching out behind him.

Maybe he hadn't escaped decimation after all.

This time Eden blocked Darrak. After everything they'd survived today, meeting her father was not going to be the end of everything. She wouldn't let it.

Angels were powerful creatures.

Well, so was she. Even if she wasn't a black witch anymore.

"Don't even think about hurting him," she growled.

Daniel shook his head. "Wasn't planning on it."

"Well . . . good." She still wasn't quite ready to breathe yet.

"You're yourself again?" Darrak asked.

"I am." Daniel nodded and cast a glance down at himself. "When Oliver Gale took over my body, I could still see and hear everything. I know you were willing to sacrifice yourself for Eden, and that you tried to save her from Lucifer."

"I tried," Darrak said. "Wasn't all that successful."

"You love her."

Darrak looked at Eden. "Yes."

Her heart swelled. "And I love him. I don't care what anyone thinks. Including you."

"Good," Daniel said. "That will help you a great deal."

Well, it was nice to have a vote of confidence for once.

Darrak slid his hand down her back. "Lucifer consumed the darkness in her. All of it. It sent him directly back to Hell, do not pass go."

Daniel took in this information. "Are you sorry not to be the next Prince of Hell?"

Eden watched Darrak carefully for his response. It was a lot of power to give up, even if it meant dealing with that monster she'd just seen. It would have made Darrak one of the most powerful beings in the universe.

"Am I sorry?" Darrak repeated. "Nope. I might have wanted that once, but I've changed. A lot. I'm exactly where I want to be."

"Good answer." Daniel then looked at Eden. "And as for you, daughter—"

"Daughter, huh?" she said tightly. "I still don't understand what happened with my mother and why you never acknowledged me."

His handsome face grew serious. "I know it's difficult to understand. And I wish I had a meaningful story for you, but you may be disappointed. When I met your mother, I was at the end of my job as a gatekeeper to one of the Netherworld entrances. Seven years of living in the human world. I was weak, and your mother was beautiful. That's all it was. I'm sorry you felt abandoned, Eden, but I had no choice. My place was in Heaven from that point forward."

He was right. That was a bit disappointing. She'd hoped for something a bit more magical than that even though she knew it hadn't been more than a one-night stand for her mother. Why should it be anything else for her father? "So why did you visit me when I was just a little girl?"

"Because I'd just learned of your existence and had to check on your safety. There are those who'd like to use a nephilim for her power—just as Lucifer wanted to do."

She laughed. "I've never had any power. A bit of psychic insight, but nothing very reliable."

Daniel nodded. "There's a very good reason for that. When I came here I was able to cloak that magic—from others and from you as well."

Eden inhaled sharply, remembering what Lucas had told her about nephilim being cloaked to him. How only her black magic counterbalanced that and made him see what she was underneath. "So that's why."

"You're ready now, Eden," Daniel continued. "I can finally remove the cloaking from you once and for all."

She hooked her arm through Darrak's. He hadn't said a word this whole time, letting her father speak uninterrupted. "What will happen to me then?"

"Your psychic insight will be more acute, more controllable. I think it will come in handy in your line of work—private investigator, right?" He smiled. "Also, when you were a black witch, you had the capacity for immortality. A nephilim isn't truly immortal, but she is very long-lived and will retain her youth for as long as she breathes."

A breath caught in her chest. "How long-lived?"

"Very. Consider it a pleasant bonus to being half-angel. Even if you never learned you were nephilim it wouldn't have been much longer before you realized you were no longer aging."

She'd lost her black magic that had given her so much power, given her the chance to live for a long time with Darrak. While she'd been glad to have it removed, she'd known it meant she was mortal again—helpless, fragile, and short-lived.

This . . . well, this was a wonderful gift her father had given her.

Then again, he did have nearly thirty birthdays to make up for.

Eden nodded, bracing herself for more pain. "Then go ahead and take away the cloaking. I'm ready."

Daniel shrugged. "Sorry to disappoint, but I already did that the moment I woke up. You didn't even feel it, did you?"

She didn't. She felt no different at all. There was no pain, no discomfort, not even any sensation of morning sickness from before.

Eden put her hand over her stomach. "But the baby . . ."

"Don't worry. She's fine."

Her heart pounded as she looked at Darrak.

He nodded and gave her a big grin as he hugged her against him. *"She."*

A girl. They were going to have a daughter.

Darrak tensed against her, his gaze fixed on the angel. He watched Daniel as if waiting for her father to pull them apart.

But he didn't. Instead Daniel reached his hand out. Darrak eyed it for a moment as though he was uncertain of what to do. Then he grasped hold of the angel's hand and shook it.

"Be good to my daughter," Daniel said. "Or else."

Darrak couldn't help but grin. "Yes sir."

Eden felt a lump form in her throat. "Will I ever see you again?"

Daniel leaned forward to kiss her cheek. "You can count on it."

Then, within the blink of an eye, Daniel disappeared in a flash of light.

He was gone. She'd met her father for about the same amount of time as he'd been in her presence before. And now he'd gone back to Heaven.

"So," Darrak said after a quiet moment. "Your father didn't destroy me."

She nodded. "I think you've been destroyed enough lately."

"Agreed. And he didn't beat me up or get out a shotgun when he realized you were pregnant."

"He handled it like a champ. No shotgun required." She swallowed hard then, remembering all that had happened. "Will Lucas be okay?"

"He just swallowed enough black magic to choke a hundred hellhounds. I think even somebody like him will need a while to recover from that."

She looked down at the spot Darrak had stood when she'd thought he was frozen, before he phased both himself and Lucas out of there. "You didn't kill him."

"No, and he didn't kill me. In fact, he saved me."

"Looks like he saved me, too." Her eyes widened with surprise as it all sank in. Gratitude flowed through her for the prince who'd deceived her, demanded things from her, and nearly destroyed her. "I knew he wasn't all bad."

"He's my hero," Darrak said dryly. "However, I'll still kick his ass if he ever comes anywhere near you again."

"And that is why I love you so much." Eden took his face between her hands and kissed him before hugging him tightly against her. "You're my guardian angel."

He snorted. "Come on, now, let's not end this with an insult."

She smiled. "You don't have to possess me anymore."

"We'll look on those as the good old days. Although, I have to admit I was getting kind of used to living in Eden, my own personal garden of paradise. This is better, though. We can be together because we want to, not because we have to."

"You're sure about that?"

"Positive." He frowned. "Aren't you?"

She pulled away from him and walked to the doorway leading to the hall, her arms crossed. Then she turned to face him. "I—I have a question for you first, Darrak. An important one."

The certainty in his eyes slipped a little. "What is it?"

Eden studied him carefully. "You promise to answer me honestly?"

He nodded solemnly. "I promise."

"Okay, now I understand based on how things have gone down before if you need to think about it, but . . ."

His dark brows drew together. "Eden, what is it? Tell me. What's the question?"

"I just need to know . . . will you marry me?"

He stared at her for a long moment before a grin stretched across his handsome face. "Finally a question I know I'm smart enough to answer."

Ben watched with relief as Eden and Darrak left the house. He and the others had waited outside, pacing, not knowing what to do next.

Sandy was dead. He wished he felt even a bit of sadness over that. He supposed he did. It wasn't fair. She'd been nice, he knew that hadn't all been an act from day one. But power had corrupted her swiftly and completely. He wasn't able to save her. He hadn't even realized she needed saving until it was too late.

He wanted to talk to Eden, to explain everything. To apologize.

There'd be time for that later. After all he'd been responsible for, maybe it was best if he just faded away into the distance.

Ben turned to leave and found Darrak standing behind him with his arms crossed.

"Did I have a chance to thank you so much for locking me in the office at sunset?" Darrak asked dryly. "Nearly destroyed me, but I'm thinking that might have been your goal."

"I know you'll never believe this," Ben replied tightly, "but it made me realize I was wrong. About everything. I've changed. And I'm sorry."

Darrak studied him carefully. "Seriously?"

"Yeah."

"You're not just being funny right now."

Ben shook his head. "I don't think I could be funny if I tried."

"I think you're right about that." Darrak blinked. "You're still a member of the Malleus. You have the brand."

He touched his arm. "I've decided to quit. I don't care if that's against the rules."

"Smartest decision you've ever made."

"I'm trying to make more of those."

"Ditto. Back to the police force?"

"I don't know yet." He didn't. He had no idea where his future would take him. All he knew was that he still had a future.

Darrak nodded. "So was this enough small talk between us to clear the air?"

"More than enough."

Leena came to Ben's side. He'd finally removed her cuff while they waited to find out how it all turned out, but she hadn't left yet or shifted to her werepanther form.

She eyed the demon. "I can't believe you knocked Eden up, gruesome."

Darrak eyed her warily and crossed his arms. "Somehow I'm thinking today isn't going to end up with us all in a big group hug."

Leena grinned a little. "And here I didn't think you were that smart."

"I've missed you since you moved out, Leena."

"Yeah?"

"Yeah, the apartment doesn't have that pungent odor of kitty litter to it. And the furniture doesn't get clawed up anymore."

Ben expected her to snap back with another insult, but instead she laughed out loud. "I hear you're half-angel now. Guess you keep that side hidden."

"As much as inhumanly possible."

"Take care of Eden," she said very seriously. "I swear, if I hear you're being a hellbeast, I'm going to kick your ass."

"This seems to be a common refrain." Darrak smiled. "But I honestly wouldn't put it past you to follow through."

"Some chaperone I was, anyway. You still got her pregnant."

"Consider yourself fired. Now, if you'll excuse me. Both of you." He left them alone to join Eden, who was talking with her mother by Maksim's bay window.

"So," Leena said.

"So."

"I'm sorry about Sandy."

Ben shook his head. "Don't be."

"Do all your girlfriends end up dead?"

He looked at her sharply. "Nice."

"It's not a joke. It's an important question I need the answer to."

Ben shook his head. "You and me, it's not going to happen."

Leena glared at him. "As if. You're not my type, Ken doll. I prefer men with more of an edge to them."

He frowned at her. "I have edge. Lots of edge."

"Besides . . ." She waved a hand. "I'm not sticking around this city. I hate the winter. I have big plans."

"Like what?"

"Traveling. Seeing the country. Going overseas. A werepanther likes to roam, you know. She doesn't like getting tied down to any one place."

He couldn't help but smile at her certainty. "Okay. Then what are you still doing here, werepanther?"

She ran a hand absently through her long black hair. "Well . . . I just wanted to check something first."

"What's that?"

Leena grabbed his shirt, pulled him closer, and kissed him hard on his mouth. It only took him a second before he was returning the kiss with an equal amount of passion as his body, heart, and soul all reacted to her. He was breathless when she finally broke off the kiss.

She bit her bottom lip. "Well, that's unfortunate."

Ben found his voice enough to say, "What is?"

She shrugged before giving him a slow, sexy smile. "Looks like you *are* my type after all. Who knew?"

"I have edge." He grinned before it started to fade. "However, I have no job, no money, and no prospects."

She laughed and slid her arms around his waist. "*Now

you're more like the kind of guy I usually date. See? That's much better than Mr. Shiny-Perfect. Besides, I don't need your money."

"No?"

Leena shook her head. "That locker key Eden's holding on to for me? I have a little bit of sparkle locked up in there. Enough to keep us very comfortable for a few years at the least. You interested?"

He eyed her skeptically. "Is this a treasure obtained through legal means?"

She cocked her head. "Sorry, no. But trust me, nobody will miss it and nobody got hurt."

He scratched his chin as a smile spread across his face. "Then I think I just might be okay with that."

Leena smiled and grabbed his shirt to pull him closer for another kiss.

She was a werepanther as well as a beautiful but dangerous woman with a shady past. This was a bit different for an ex-cop and ex-Malleus member. But, as he gave himself completely to her kiss, Ben realized that different was more than okay with him.

⇾ TWENTY-EIGHT ⇽

Eight months later

"She's absolutely adorable. And I don't see any horns at all!"

Andy had shut down the office for the day so he could come to the hospital. He gazed down at his goddaughter.

"No horns," Eden agreed. Her daughter felt right in her arms. Perfect, actually. And she'd already checked several times. No horns. Or talons. Just ten fingers, ten toes—a beautiful, healthy baby girl.

"Have you decided on a name yet?" Andy asked, glancing at Darrak, who stood by Eden's bedside amidst a colorful backdrop of bouquets of flowers sent by well-wishers.

"We're having a bit of trouble agreeing on something," he admitted. "So we're open to suggestion."

Andy was thoughtful for a moment. "Rhonda's what I call my Porsche. You're welcome to use that. It's a very strong name."

"We'll add it to the list. Eden wanted Destiny or Hope or Faith, but . . ." He cringed. "I'm just not feeling it."

That their biggest problem at the moment was what to name their daughter was a very good thing. The last eight months had been virtually without incident other than the chance to get to know each other better.

They got married a couple of months ago in a small ceremony at city hall. Andy attended as their witness and best man. Stanley and Nancy had tied the knot right before them, choosing not to wait for a larger, more complicated and costly ceremony. They were each other's guests of honor.

After everything they'd been through, Eden couldn't believe it had all worked out so well.

Not that their lives were full of bliss 24/7. She and Darrak were opposites in so many ways and always would be. They argued and debated over practically everything from where to live, what to eat, and of course, what to name the baby.

But it didn't matter. Their love for each other still seemed to get bigger with every day that passed. Darrak didn't have to literally possess her for their bond to be stronger than ever before.

Half-demon and half-angel—the man she loved. The father of her beautiful daughter, which he still insisted was impossible.

But just because something was impossible, didn't mean it still couldn't happen. Eden had seen more than enough to know that was the absolute truth.

She'd been a black witch on the very cusp of losing her soul to the darkness forever, but she'd recovered. Being an uncloaked nephilim helped when it came to doing private investigation. She could channel her psychic ability better than before. She wasn't all-knowing and all-seeing, but it was an edge that worked to her benefit.

Every little bit helped.

Andy left ten minutes later, leaving an armful of flowers behind that they put next to the bouquet sent by Leena and Ben—with a card that said they were currently exploring Italy as part of their world travels.

"I still can't get over how beautiful she is," Eden said.

"Of course she's beautiful. She looks just like her mom." She grinned. "She has your eyes."

"And your hair."

The baby had ice blue eyes and bright red hair—more like bright red fuzz, anyway.

"Your mother called when you were talking with Andy earlier," Darrak told her.

"Yeah? And what did she have to say?"

"She's coming to visit next week to see her grand-daughter."

Eden nodded. She'd made her peace with her mother. Caroline was still a bit neglectful, a bit selfish, but she was still her mother. Even when she'd done stupid things, Eden knew they were to try to help her. For Caroline to try to be a good person. To redeem herself and one day get the chance to go to Heaven.

They'd never be super close and that was okay, but she was going to be a hell of a great and generous grandmother. Even though the new body she was currently "renting" was yet another lingerie model/aspiring actress.

At least she was consistent.

Eden and Darrak had moved out of the apartment and into a house not too far away from the office. She'd sensed that the neighborhood was right for them. It was a neigh-borhood full of Others—including a few fairies living in the human world, a couple of werewolves (who liked their pri-vacy), and a white witch who enjoyed gardening at midnight under the stars.

They made the perfect neighbors for a nephilim and her angel-demon husband.

Speaking of werewolves, Andy didn't turn into a hell-hound after that first full moon. Lucas hadn't changed him permanently. It was one thing to deal with a very large friendly dog one night every month, and another thing alto-gether to deal with a very large hellhound with an urge to explore the Netherworld.

Darrak shook his head. "So many names to choose from,

I'm sure we can find something we both like. How about Bella?"

"Definitely not."

"Buffy."

"No."

"Um . . . how about Crimson? That's kind of cool. It's the color of her hair. Or blood."

"Darrak. No."

"Elvira?"

"Now you're just trying to be funny."

"Well, it's better than Hope. I mean, *gag*."

She grinned and slid her right hand up his arm. "You can take the demon out of Hell . . ."

Darrak waved her off. "Mocking me isn't nice, you know. I could go back if I wanted to. The whole 'You'll be destroyed the moment you enter the Netherworld with all that shiny goodness inside of you' was probably just to try to scare me off."

"You're looking for a vacation spot down there?"

"It would be nice to have the option."

"What about the other place?" She thrust her thumb heavenward.

Darrak glanced up at the ceiling. "The fifth floor?"

"You could jump sides completely, you know. Be a guardian ang—"

He covered her mouth. "Do not finish that sentence."

Eden pulled his hand away. "Fine, be that way. Just know that my father has plans for me up there someday. That someday will probably be a very long time from now, but it will happen eventually. And I can solemnly promise you one very important thing, Darrak . . ."

He raised an eyebrow. "And what's that?"

"I'm taking you with me."

He cringed. "Are you sure that's a promise? Sounds more like a threat."

She laughed. "I think you'd kick ass at playing the harp. It's just a hunch."

"I've always been musically inclined." He slid his fingers

through her hair. She'd let it go back to its original color—
bright red. It was beautiful, actually. She wasn't really sure
why she'd always insisted on covering it under the darker
auburn color.

No, that wasn't exactly true. She knew. She'd been hiding what she really was. Now she didn't hide. She was
proud of what she was, who she was with, what she'd accomplished. And for the first time in her life, the future
stretched before her, and she was excited at what was yet to
come.

That was definitely progress.

"If there's one person in the universe I'd be willing to sit
on a fluffy cloud for, Eden, it's definitely you." Darrak
stroked his daughter's head. "Actually, make that two of
you now."

She shook her head. "Just look at us. We're . . . a family."

"I know. I'm looking forward to telling her how her mom
and dad met."

"We'll take out the scary bits."

"Nah. I think she'll enjoy those parts best of all."

Eden looked at him skeptically. "You don't really want
to name her Elvira, do you?"

His brows drew together, his expression turning pensive.
"I'm not sold on it. What about Morticia like from the *Ad-
dams Family*? No, wait . . . Maleficent! That's perfect. She
was the evil queen in *Snow White*."

She sighed. "Not in a million years."

"Mal for short. I'm loving this."

There was a knock at the door and a nurse entered car-
rying a large bouquet of pink roses. "Mr. and Mrs. Riley?
Where should I put these?"

The room was already full of flowers and balloons and
stuffed animals, but Darrak cleared a spot on the table next
to Eden's hospital bed. "Right here's perfect."

The nurse left them, and Darrak grabbed the small card
attached and read it.

"Who are they from?" Eden asked.

He looked at her bleakly. "Take a wild guess."

They could be from anyone, but the expression on his face told her all she needed to know. She nodded slowly. "So . . . how is he?"

"He doesn't go into detail about his health and happiness. All he says is 'Congratulations.'"

Lucas hadn't been seen or heard from since he absorbed her black magic and disappeared. Eden knew she was supposed to be afraid of him—he was Lucifer, the Prince of Hell, after all. He was the being responsible for controlling the darkness that threatened the human world. Threatened everything.

He'd wanted to leave, to go back to Heaven, and he'd come so close to doing just that. Instead, he chose to stay and keep doing exactly what he'd signed up for in the first place.

He'd lied, manipulated, and deceived them shamelessly, using them as part of his master plan.

And he'd also saved her soul and Darrak's life.

"I think I know what her name should be," Eden said after a moment.

Darrak held up a hand. "Don't say it."

"Lucy."

He sighed. "I just *knew* you were going to say that."

"What do you think?"

Darrak put the card down and came to Eden's side, climbing in the bed next to her and putting his arm around her shoulders. He looked down into the face of his tiny daughter and nodded. "Yeah, that works for me."

She smiled. "Don't pout."

"I'm not pouting," he pouted.

"You're going to make a great father," she whispered to him.

"Going to try like hell."

They both looked down at Lucy, who seemed to smile up at them a moment before a faint glimmer of fire appeared behind her pale blue eyes.

"She didn't . . ." Eden began.

A wide smile stretched across Darrak's face. "You said she had my eyes. And she does! That's my little girl!"

Eden started to laugh. "Well, hell. I guess it's fate."

"Would you look at that?" Darrak said before leaning over to brush his lips against hers again. "You took the words right out of my mouth."

Keep reading for a preview of the first book
in a new paranormal series by Michelle Rowen

BLOOD BATH & BEYOND

Coming summer 2012 from Obsidian!

The fangs don't get nearly as much attention as you'd think.

Your average, everyday person doesn't notice that they're sharper than normal human canines. If they did, they'd have to deal with the possibility that vampires really existed. It's a survival instinct on their part, culminating from centuries of living side by side with something they'd prefer to think of as a fictional predatory monster. Or, more recently, as an eternally sparkling teenager.

Real vampires make up approximately 0.001% of the population—that's one in a thousand. So, worldwide, there are about six million vampires.

Humans just don't see us. It does help that, despite what you might have heard, we can go outside into the sunshine without turning into a pile of ashes. We blend in with regular human society just fine and dandy.

It's kind of like we're invisible.

Someone bashed into me when I glanced down at the screen of my phone as I walked down the busy sidewalk.

"Hey!" the woman snarled. "Watch where you're going, you dumb bitch!"

"Bite me," I replied sweetly, then added under my breath, "or I might bite you."

She gave me the finger, stabbing it violently in my direction as if it was a tiny, flesh-colored sword.

Okay, maybe we're not *totally* invisible.

I couldn't help that I had a natural-born talent to rub people the wrong way. It had very little to do with me being a vampire and more to do with me just being . . . me. I liked to think it was part of my charm.

I looked bleakly at the phone again. No messages. No calls. It felt like everyone I knew had recently deserted me. It wasn't far from the truth, actually. Last month, my parents had moved to Florida to a retirement community. Two weeks ago, my best male friend, George, had left for Hawaii to open a surf shop after he won a small fortune in a local lottery. And now, my best girlfriend and her husband were in the process of moving to British Columbia so she could take a job in cosmetics management out there.

"We'll totally stay in touch," Amy said to me at the airport before she got on her flight an hour ago. I'd met her there to say a last good-bye.

I swallowed back my tears and hugged her fiercely. "Of course we will."

Her husband stood nearby, giving me the evil eye like he usually did. We'd never really gotten along all that well. You win some, you lose some. "Are you finished yet? We're going to miss our flight."

I forced a smile. "I'm even going to miss *you*, Barry."

He just looked at his wristwatch.

Amy smiled brightly. "This is a new beginning, Sarah. For both of us. We have to embrace change."

I hated change.

I did hope to see her again soon, not too far into the future.

The future was something I thought about a lot these days. After all, as a fledgling vampire, sired only seven months ago, I had a lot of future to look forward to. I just hoped it wouldn't suck too much.

Yes, that was me. Sarah Dearly, immortal pessimist. I had to turn my frown upside down. Right now, I was so far down in the dumps that the raccoons had arrived and were starting to sniff around. Metaphorically speaking, of course. The only real raccoons were the ones around my eyes as my mascara smeared from my pathetic sob-fest after leaving the airport.

It seemed as if new opportunities and new adventures had been presented to everyone but me, like they'd won the lottery—literally in one case—and I'd mistakenly put my ticket in the wash and now couldn't even read the numbers.

"You look sad," someone said.

I glanced over my shoulder, surprised to see a clown standing at the side of the street holding a bunch of balloons.

White makeup, poufy costume covered in colorful polka dots. Red hair. A hat with a fake flower springing out of it. Big red nose. The works.

It was like a bad omen. Clowns scared the crap out of me.

"Sad? Who me?" I said warily, slipping my phone back in my shoulder bag. "Nah, I'm just melancholy today. There's a difference, you know. Please don't murder me."

"Somebody needs a happy happy balloon to make her happy happy." He handed me a yellow ribbon tied to a shiny red balloon. I looked up at it.

"Yes," I said. "This will make all the difference in the world. Thank you so much. Now life is happy happy for me again."

The clown glared at me. "No reason to be sarcastic, lady."

"I don't need a reason."

"The balloon's five bucks."

"Three."

"Four."

"Sold." I grinned, then fished into my purse and pulled out the money. "Thanks so much, Bozo."

"It's Mr. Chuckles."

"Whatever."

The balloon did cheer me up more than I would have guessed. It reminded me of going to the National Exhibition with my mother every fall when I was a kid. Popcorn, cotton candy, hot dogs, and balloons. High calorie memories with a little bit of helium and latex thrown in for good measure. Those were good times.

I'd needed the walk to clear my head. My head was officially cleared, so I returned to the huge townhome I shared with my fiancé and let myself in.

Immediately, I sensed there was something different there. A big clue to this was the large black suitcase placed at the front door.

I heard Thierry on the phone, speaking French to someone. I didn't speak the language, despite taking it all the way through high school. Thierry was fluent since he was originally from France centuries ago.

Yes, my fiancé was significantly older than me—by about six hundred years or so.

Some of the words I understood:

"*Aujourd'hui*," which I knew meant *today*.

"*Seul*," which meant *alone*.

"*D'accord*," which meant *alrighty*.

"*Importante*" . . . well, that one didn't really need a translator.

Thierry entered the front foyer with his phone pressed to his left ear. He stopped when he saw me standing there gaping at him.

"*A bientôt*, Bernard." He slipped the phone into the inside pocket of his black suit jacket. "Sarah, I was about to call you. I'm glad you've returned."

He didn't have an accent. His English was flawless, since he'd spoken it for at least five hundred years.

Thierry de Bennicoeur appeared to be in his midthirties. He was six feet tall, had black hair that was usually brushed back from his handsome face, and piercing gray eyes that felt like they could see right through you clear to the other side. He always dressed in black Hugo Boss suits, which wasn't the most imaginative wardrobe choice but looked consistently perfect on him anyway. He was, in a word, a total fox. Even after all the time we'd spent together, there was no doubt in my mind about that.

Some people perceived him to be cold and unemotional, but I knew the truth. That façade was for protection only. Down deep, Thierry was fire and passion. Only . . . it was *really* down deep. Most people would never see that side of him, and I was okay with that. I had the rock on my finger that proved I *had* seen the fire and hadn't been burned yet.

However, I had to admit, that suitcase was causing a few painful sparks to fly up in my general direction.

"What's going on?" I asked cautiously. "What's with the luggage?"

"I have to go somewhere."

"Where? And . . . when?"

The line of his jaw tightened. "I've been called upon to meet with someone about some important Ring business in Las Vegas."

The Ring was the vampire council. Thierry was the original founder of the organization that tracked any potential vampiric issues worldwide and did what they could to neutralize them. He'd left a century ago after dealing with some personal issues and he hadn't looked back since. The Ring had carried on without his input or influence.

"What business?" I asked.

"I've been offered a job with them. One I can't decline."

My eyes widened. "What kind of job?"

"Consultant."

"What do you mean you can't decline it?"

He hesitated. "They made me an offer I couldn't refuse."

"Who were you just talking to, Don Corleone?"

He raised a dark eyebrow. "His name is Bernard Du-Shaw. He was the most recent of several people I've spoken with over the last couple of hours. It's his position I would be taking over now that he's retiring."

I thought of my parents settling in to Florida's sand and

sunshine now that they'd reached their retirement years. "He's immortal, isn't he? He doesn't ever have to retire."

"After a contracted term with the Ring, one is permitted to leave to pursue other interests if one wishes to. He wishes to."

I tried to breathe normally. Contrary to one of many popular myths about vampires, we needed to do that regularly. "Okay. Well, the universe does work in mysterious ways. I guess this isn't a bad thing. I think you'd be a great asset for them. Keep them from making any mistakes or judging anyone too harshly without a proper assessment. So . . . you're going today to meet with Bernard about this job?"

"Yes."

"And when will you be back?"

His expression was unreadable. "Perhaps you should sit down, Sarah."

"I don't want to sit down." My anxiety spiked. "You are coming back, aren't you?"

His expression tensed. "I'm sorry, but I won't be returning to Toronto. The position calls for constant travel. I won't be able to stay in one place for very long during my term as consultant."

I tried to absorb all of this, but it was too much all at once. "How long is a term?"

He didn't speak for a moment. "Fifty years."

I just looked at him, momentarily rendered speechless by this unexpected news. Silence stretched between us.

His gaze moved to my balloon. "What's this?"

My mouth felt dry. "My happy happy balloon. I got it from a clown named Mr. Chuckles."

His lips curved at the edges. "I thought you were going to the airport."

"I did."

"You stopped by a circus on the way home?"

"Thierry," I said sharply. "What the hell is going on? How can you just leave? Fifty years? It sounds like a prison sentence, not a new job. Are you saying . . . are you saying that—" I didn't want to speak my thoughts aloud. After everyone else I loved putting thousands of miles between me and them, perhaps I should have expected this. But I hadn't. This was a complete and total shock.

Everyone was leaving me. And now Thierry was joining the list.

"Sarah—"

"I heard you on the phone. You said *seul*, which means you're going alone."

He nodded slowly. "That's what they want. This job requires focus and 24/7 availability. I assumed you wouldn't want to travel so much, never knowing where you're going next. There's a great deal of uncertainty involved with this job."

"This job that you can't say no to for some mysterious reason. A job that you're going to be doing for half of a damn century all by yourself with no prior warning." I crossed my arms tightly. Everything about this made me ill. "You know, maybe this job came at just the right time for you to change your mind about being with—"

"Please don't finish that sentence." He took me by my shoulders, gazing fiercely into my eyes. "All I want is for you to be happy, don't you know that by now?"

I swallowed hard. "The clown thought a balloon would make me happy."

"And did it?"

"For a couple of minutes."

He looked up at it. "It is a nice balloon."

"Screw the balloon." My throat felt so tight it was difficult to speak.

I knew people had their own agendas, their own destinies to chase, and most of the time those destinies were not meant to intertwine. Thierry's and my path hadn't been an easy one, not since the very first moment we met. It wasn't every day a twenty-eight-year-old fledgling hooked up with a six-hundred-year-old master vampire—we were so completely different in temperament and personality it was frequently glaring and often problematic. But we had and it felt right, but somehow I knew, down deep, that it might not last forever. Forever was a very long time when you're a vampire.

Just because I knew it didn't mean my heart didn't break into a million pieces at the thought of losing him.

I tried to compose myself as much as possible after realizing that someone else I cared about would be moving away from me. This, though . . . *this* stung even more than saying good-bye to Amy. This felt permanent. Forever.

I wanted to be cool about getting dumped for a "job he couldn't refuse," but I wasn't sure if I had it in me.

My heart ached and my words twisted with the pain I felt. "I get it, Thierry. You don't want to be distracted by someone who has a tendency to get into trouble at the drop of a hat. I can take a hint. I'm a liability. You want me to stay here."

He let out a small, humorless laugh. "What I want is irrelevant. Can you honestly say you'd come with me if I gave you that choice? Would you leave behind your life here in Toronto, everything you've ever known and most of your possessions, in order to accompany me on a job that will be frequently boring for you, never knowing where your true home is?"

I stared up at him, my eyes burning. "Are those rhetorical questions?"

"No, they're real questions." His brows drew together. "Would you come with me if I asked you to?"

I let go of the balloon, which floated up to the high ceiling of the front foyer before catching on a sharp crystal from the chandelier. It popped on contact.

I grabbed the lapels of his black jacket. "In a heartbeat."

Something I rarely saw slid behind his gray eyes then, something warm and utterly vulnerable. "Then I suggest you quickly pack a bag. Our flight leaves in three hours."

My eyes widened. "*Our* flight?"

"I wasn't sure you'd be open to this abrupt change, but I did purchase you a ticket just in case."

A smile blossomed on my face at the exact moment a

hot tear splashed to my cheek. "You're so prepared. Just like a Boy Scout."

"I try." A smile played at his lips. "I just hope that this trip doesn't make you change your mind about you and me."

"Don't be ridiculous." My smile only grew wider before faltering just a little. "But I thought they wanted you to come alone. Won't they give you a hard time about this?"

"If they want me for this job, then they will get my fiancée as well. They'll just have to deal with it." He took my face between his hands. "I love you, Sarah. Never doubt it."

He kissed me, and I couldn't think of any happy happy balloon that could make me this happy happy.

Change was good. I liked change.